Caretakers

Jamie Sheffield

2014

Published by SmartPig through CreateSpace and Amazon.com KDP. This is a work of fiction. Names, characters, places and incidents are either products of the author's imagination or are used fictitiously. While the descriptions are based on real locations in the Adirondack Park, any resemblance to actual events or persons, living or dead, is entirely coincidental.

ISBN-13: 978-1492862307
ISBN-10: 1492862304

This book is dedicated to my wife Gail;
her help, support, understanding, patience, and tolerance of my
myriad shortcomings makes life, and my writing, possible.

PROLOGUE

Camp Topsail, Upper Saranac Lake, Adirondack Park, New York — Saturday, August 22, 1958

Four minutes before she disappeared forever, Dee Crocker walked into the dark cabin without reaching for the light switch. She still had trouble finding it, having changed cabins only a few nights earlier, and was more focused on getting to the bathroom, which she needed to use; it also had a light switch that was easier to find. Had she turned on the light, she would have been taken that much earlier by the man who had been waiting patiently for her for nearly two hours in the dark; this way she got an extra three minutes.

The man waited until she closed the bathroom door to move; he could use the seam of light coming from under the door to make his way quietly through the cabin. He was cat-quiet, quite a feat considering his size and workboots, but Dee heard or felt or smelt something anyway, in that way that people do when a house they presume to be empty isn't. Nothing registered on a conscious level, but she suddenly knew that there was somebody on the other side of the door. Perhaps it was a barely creaking board, the tiny cabin shifting minutely on the four concrete piers it rested on as he moved his bulk across the room, or the latent smell of cigarettes on his hands or from his lungs; he had changed his clothes, but not washed, before coming here tonight.

Dee ran through her options while running water in the sink to cover her delay, finally deciding, long seconds later, to climb out the window and run to her parents' cabin. She went so far as to slip her low-heeled shoes off, unlatch and open the bathroom window, and pop the screen-frame out and onto the bed of pine needles below, before coming to her senses and declaring herself a silly city mouse, scared of the woods at night. She closed the window, debated getting the screen right away, and then agreed, with herself, that it was only sensible to wait until morning. She scooped up her shoes, walked out into the waiting darkness, and into the strong encircling arms of the man waiting in the dark.

She had distracted herself from what she considered a groundless and silly fear of the dark by recalling drinking beers and flirting down on the dock with her handsome new boyfriend; actually, watching him drink eight beers while she sipped her way slowly through two. She had imagined being swept up in his arms. Instead, she was literally swept up in an even bigger and stronger set of arms. The man wrapped his arms around her, overwhelming her struggles and screams for help with muscled hands across her mouth and around her waist.

The man held her off the ground and whispered in her ear, "All I want is money, but if you make a sound, I'll have to kill you." This had seemed ridiculous to the man, but his partner, his mentor, had assured him that a girl from the city would understand and accept a mugging, even in the woods, at least for a minute, which was all the time that it would take. She relaxed a bit, stopping her muffled shouts and ceasing to wriggle in his arms. He walked her, awkwardly, like his attempts at dancing, back into the light from the bathroom door so that he could see better, and relaxed his hold on her slightly, still holding her by the shoulder in an iron grip.

She turned to speak to her attacker, seemed to partially recognize the man, as he spoke her name. Her eyes went wide and then clever and calculating as she started to work things out. The man cut the process short by slamming her head into the solid doorframe of the bathroom, once, twice, three times, until she stopped moving or making noises, and slumped in his arms.

The man swept Dee up, slung her over his left shoulder, listened to her breathing for a minute while he caught his own breath, and then walked out and into the dark chill of the late summer night. He could see lights from the main building, smell wood smoke from the fire pit back by the lean-to at the edge of the woods, and hear splashing and a mix of laughter as people dove or were pushed into the lake. He was surrounded by pockets of summer fun, but was free to escape into the night with his prize, which he did.

Dee Crocker disappeared that night in what would become an overnight sensation in first local, then regional and statewide, and finally, national news: gossip to some, cautionary tale to others, family tragedy to those who knew her. The story faded quickly though, with no ransom demand made or body found. It was widely assumed that she had either run away with a secret lover, drowned in the lake, or been taken and killed by a wandering tramp who had escaped from a lunatic asylum and just happened on the poor girl; unlikely though it seemed, this sort of thing was popular in the fiction of the day, and was accepted as an outside possibility.

The truth was much worse than anyone imagined.

"I lived a life
in a sunlit world,
a world with sky and light
and doors and people;
all of those things are gone…"

Stoney Creek Ponds, 7/13/2013, 2:27 a.m.

When the sound of a snapping branch and loud chuffing breathing behind and over my left shoulder woke me, I hoped it was a bear. I was gently swinging in the breeze off the northernmost lobe of Stoney Creek Ponds, a fleshy piñata for a bear to bite if it was so inclined. I had heard the bear snuffling around my campsite looking for food the last few nights (*it wouldn't find anything, I always hung my food and smellies*), and knew that I would not make its top 100 list of favorite foods. Whatever/whoever was blundering through the woods towards me was clumsier than the average bear, so I wasn't worried … I don't worry, as such … about the bear so much as other nighttime visitors. I couldn't easily picture who/what else would come for me in the middle of the night, but it wasn't likely good news.

"It's the forest-cop Tyler. He's come to roust you for squatting, ya homeless fuck!" Barry suggested, with a bite of savage glee in his voice.

Barry's suggestion was most likely correct, but it was bothersome for a number of reasons nonetheless. I had seen the DEC ranger a few times in the last two weeks, and he had doubtless seen me. They all knew that I tended to overstay the three-day limit in places ... without benefit of the required permit, but they hadn't seemed worried about it in the past (*I've been camping like this for nearly twelve years*). Saranac Lake, the small town in northern New York that I live in, is like a fishbowl ... everyone sees what everyone else is doing. If I got ticketed for squatting/overstaying/permitless-camping, it might draw attention to the fact that I am, in point of fact, homeless (*I have an office, but no home address*). None of this, potentially troublesome as these points were, was as disturbing as the fact that the man who made this suggestion, Barry, was dead ... a ghost ... and my brain was the house that he haunted.

I had met, and subsequently murdered, Barry ten months ago while investigating the disappearance of my friend Cynthia (*insofar as I'm capable of making and maintaining friendships, she was a friend*). In the days and weeks after the events of that tumultuous time, Barry started to creep back into the world ... or at least my perception of the world. I don't believe in ghosts, and know that Barry isn't real, that he is a construct my psyche supports for reasons that I don't yet understand. While he talks and looks like Barry, he thinks and notices things like I do (*which makes sense, since he is an outgrowth of my mind*), so I took his word for it that the person snap-crackling his way through the woods towards me was the forest ranger.

"Over here," I said in a voice quiet by city/daytime standards, but certainly loud enough to guide the ranger to my hammock/campsite. I provided further assistance by standing up and out of the hammock, and turning on my headlamp. He clicked on a handheld light, and walked the rest of the way over to me.

"Good evening, sir. Everything okay?" he asked.

"It is … or was, until I heard you coming, so I should probably ask you the same question?" I answered.

"Sorry to wake you (*I don't believe that he was, a friend of mine was similarly rousted by this ranger a few years ago, also in the middle of the night, about some empty beer cans left neatly piled by his fire-pit when he had gone to bed*). I wanted to be certain of the location so that I could find the site tomorrow. Your car's been parked in the lot across Route 3, by Old Dock Road, for about a week now, and you're only allowed to camp in one spot for three days."

"Do you need me to pack up now, or can it wait until morning?" I asked.

"Morning will be fine, but I'm sorry to say that I'll have to ticket you for the violation." He didn't look or sound very sorry about the ticket, but I'm notoriously bad at reading emotions from facial or tonal variations.

I read, almost literally, everything, and know from Adirondack news sources that there are only a few rangers to cover this part of the Adirondack Park, and that they mostly do backcountry patrol … and mostly during daylight hours; so this visit was unusual, to say the least. I have some difficulty with the concept of grudges (*lacking the emotional software to hold one myself*); but this particular ranger would likely need to have some reason to seek me out in the middle of the night to ticket me for staying too long in this small chunk of wilderness. I was struggling to connect a series of dots that I couldn't understand or relate to when Barry cut in with the answer.

"This muttonhead must be friends with Mike Todd

and, seeing that stupid toaster-car you drive in the same place everyday, he figured out a way to get back at you a bit." Mike Todd works for the Adirondack Park Agency (APA), which is housed over in Ray Brook, along with the DEC offices and this ranger (*when he isn't ticketing people in the middle of the night for camping too long in one spot*). I had recently sent a letter-to-the-editor into the Adirondack Daily Enterprise with some valid, but apparently embarrassing (*and compelling*), reasons why Mike Todd would not be a good candidate for the school-board. (*I don't care about his candidacy, or the school board, or his indiscretions, but my friend Meg, a counselor in the Saranac Lake Central School District, cared very much, so I had looked into things for her a bit*). Barry had made the logical leap that must have been knocking around in the back of my brain, but I still had trouble with his pseudo-presence ... especially since nobody else could see or hear him. It's not surprising that I hadn't made the connection instantly, as I was still 43% asleep; what was surprising was that "Barry" had made it (*and a number of other useful ones in the 98 seconds since the snap had awoken us*).

"Okay," I offered, "then I'll be going back to bed now," and I shuffled back towards the trees I'd hung my hammock from.

"Please be sure not to stay in any one place for more than 3 days unless you have a permit, and to get in touch with me or the DEC offices in Raybrook if you have any questions," the ranger said to my back, and then feet, as I climbed back up and into the Hennessy hammock through its velcroed hatch.

I grunted in the affirmative, and as an afterthought, said, "Please put the ticket in one of my boots, and I'll make sure to pay it first thing in the morning."

He started to say something else about the severity of

the violation, and monetary penalty attached to the ticket, but I wasn't interested, and as I do with things that don't interest me, I shut him out, and focused on getting back to sleep; it took me 71 seconds.

As I was drifting off to sleep, I could hear Barry whispering from underneath my hammock (*living—Barry was a mountain of a man, who moved ponderously and likely couldn't have fit between the ground and the underside of my hammock, but hallucination—Barry moved without a sound and often appeared in unlikely spots*). "Living in the Tri-Lakes is like livin' in a small pond, Tyler; if you make waves, you better know that they'll come back and splash you eventually. There's no such thing as privacy, and no secrets either. You pissed locals off messing with Mike Todd; his people have been here for almost 100 years. Smart as you are, you still don't get how this place works. Sleep tight, I'll keep an eye out for the bear, and make sure the forest-cop doesn't mess with any of your silly camping crap."

Dead he might be, but Barry had a point. I had found out at numerous points in my life that my keen intelligence doesn't help much when it comes to interacting with people. I don't understand emotions, how they affect the decision-making process in normal humans, and why history and tradition seem to trump logic and fact in people's thinking ... but it certainly does, and when I make mistakes, it is most often because of these factors. It had happened last year, in my dealings with George and Barry and Justin (*and it nearly resulted in my death*). Now, with Mike Todd, this ranger's vendetta might possibly endanger my wilderness camping lifestyle. It would continue to prove to be embarrassingly troublesome over the next few weeks in my exploration of Adirondack socio-cultural rules and norms and taboos surrounding summer-people and year-rounders.

With the words of a dead man echoing in my thoughts as I fell asleep, I resolved to try to be more careful/aware/circumspect when dealing with complex (*and sometimes even simple*) human interactions and customs. For someone wired differently than other humans, this sort of minor miss was likely inevitable. My fervent hope is for the more dangerous type of misunderstandings/ underestimations (*like what had occurred last summer*) to become entirely evitable.

SmartPig Office, 7/13/2013, 7:43 a.m.

I woke up again as the light level came up enough to bring a gentle glow to the tarp over my Hennessy hammock. I dropped down out of the opening underneath the hammock, wasted a microsecond of worry on Barry as I hit ground, but then saw him trudging uphill from the direction of the water's edge. He was silent as I stuffed the ticket into my pack and broke down my camp; he seldom talks much in the mornings. I wonder if he's not (*wasn't?*) a morning person, or if I'm slightly less crazy immediately after waking. In any case, he outpaced me and was waiting in my Honda Element when I got to the trailhead. I crossed Route 3 to get to the parking lot.

I drove into town and shot past the turn that would take me to the SmartPig office, in favor of a quick run out to the Saranac Lake Dunkin Donuts for a breakfast dozen (*four each of jelly, chocolate glazed, and regular glazed ... I like crullers, but they're almost always stale in the SLDD*). I reached behind me to put the box on the floor in the back. I drove back through town, and around to the parking space behind Main Street, and I carried my gear and the donuts up to SmartPig. I was looking forward to a long and productive day of SmartPigging (*or thneeding, depending on how you/I/they look at it*).

I set up the SmartPig Thneedery above the swanky part of Main Street soon after arriving in Saranac Lake. Shortly thereafter, I discovered year-round camping, decided that I didn't want to keep renting both an apartment and an office, so I ditched the apartment. I fill my days with a transplant's (*what locals refer to people who find their way here and decide to stay*) zeal: creating charcoal sketches and watercolor renditions of the local wilderness, making leashes and other dog equipment for the area's animal shelter, evaluating/creating various types of camping gear, splitting and stacking wood, making fishing lures and flies, and so on (*we transplants often string together a half-dozen or more jobs/callings to help us stay in the area, I call it thneeding*). Being a consulting detective was probably the weirdest of my jobs, and hardest to explain (*to myself, to the police, and to the very few people I consider to be within my family/friend circle*). It came about as an outgrowth of my obsessive reading/analysis of dozens of mystery writers, starting at the age of four, and continuing through today.

My brain works differently than other people's, and I can often find a solution that more traditional investigations miss or overlook. I was surprised the first few times it happened (*as the path from problem to solution generally seems so obvious to me, that I have trouble believing that they, whoever they happen to be, cannot see it*). I quickly realized that not only was it satisfying to think and act and investigate and solve like the characters from my favorite books (*Travis, Bernie, Matt, Mike, Parker, Nero, Lucas, Spenser, Lincoln, Philip, Sam, and so on*), but that people were grateful enough to give me gifts. Not money, generally, (*I have enough money from my parents' deaths to last me several lifetimes at my current rate of consumption*), but people almost always have something that I would like to have or borrow, such as: a gorgeous pinhole camera, or a vacation home for a week in Bermuda, or a monthly slab of bacon for life. So I have added consulting detective to my list of odd jobs.

As I climbed the stairs I could feel myself growing bored with my run-of-the-mill thneeding and was considering various ideas to occupy my mind, maybe taking a trip somewhere diverting (*Moab?*). These thoughts were pushed out of the way, as I neared the top of the stairs leading to my office, by the sound of excited scrabbling of toenails behind the door. My officemate and life partner was anxiously awaiting my arrival, having spent last night at the office, while I was hanging in the woods.

Hope, my rescue dog, was excited to see both me and the donuts. After I grabbed a trio of Cokes from the Coke-fridge (*a high-tech fridge devoted solely to keeping my supply of real-sugar Canadian Coca-Cola at the optimal temperature of a few degrees below the freezing temperature of pure water*), she joined me on the couch, sitting nearly in my lap waiting for her donut. I took out a jelly for me and a glazed for her, gave Hope her breakfast, cracked a Coke, and settled down to refueling. I was into the third Coke and the eighth donut (*Hope stopped at two, turned three tight circles on the couch, dropped down into a tight hockey-puck of brown dog, warm against my leg, and promptly began snoring and occasionally farting*) when I heard a key in the lock.

My troubles of last year began with unwanted visitors, so I now, whenever I am in SmartPig I am always careful to lock my door (*and secure it with a bar that runs from just below the knob to a hole in the floor*). This safety measure would keep out anyone short of a rhino, and it was keeping Dorothy out quite effectively now.

"Tyler, open up!" she said when the door refused to push inwards. "I came by to take Hope for a walk in case you weren't home yet, but I also have something that I'd like to talk with you about."

Dorothy runs the Tri-Lakes Animal Shelter (TLAS). She is as close to me as anyone in the Adirondacks, knows everything about what happened last summer, and ... if I had friends, would be my best friend. She knew that I was going to bring Hope home to live with me even before I did. She got more involved in the insanity that ran roughshod over my unusual but relatively boring life for those two weeks in September than was safe or prudent, and she has been involved in others of my adventures ... both before and since. She enjoys the role of sidekick (*possibly too much sometimes*), has fun exploring the grey zone where legality and morality get fuzzy, and may be one of the few people on Earth who actually understands what I am and accepts me. The feeling I got when I removed the door-bar, opened the door, and saw her smiling at Hope and me made me imagine that I know what 'happy' feels like to regular people.

"Gimme a leash, grab a new Coke, and ... look!" She pointed out the window behind me, and took the remaining jelly donut when I half-turned. I threw the leash at her, took the last donut, grabbed a Coke from the Coke-fridge, and followed her and Hope out and down for a walk. Hope knew we were headed out at the first jingle of the leash. She was ready for a walk, since I had left her behind last night ... the bear out at Stoney Creek Ponds had freaked Hope out a bit. She had spent much of the previous few nights growling/crying/shivering, and I had been worried that she might either have a heart attack, run away, or foolishly jump down and try to tangle with the bear.

Hope is an elderly beagle mix who came to live with me after my big case last summer. We found each other at the TLAS, and even though we both had concerns about relationships formed under great stress, it had worked out well for us so far. She doesn't like camping quite as much as I do, but is perfectly willing to guard the SmartPig office in my absences, with the understanding that she'll be paid later in treats and snuggling and long walks in town. She hated most people, having had what I can only guess was a hard and abusive life before we met, but one of the few other people she tolerates is Dorothy; so she was about as happy as she gets with the two of us taking her for a walk down by the river.

I didn't relay the news of being visited by the ranger during the night, as Dot sometimes treats me like a little brother and might actually complain to someone, or confront the ranger. I had seen a folded sheet of paper in her hand as she walked in, and I knew from past experience that she only wrote her thoughts down in extreme situations when she felt that she had to say whatever it was perfectly. It has been my experience that asking people what they are thinking/worrying about only serves to derail or confuse them ... so I tend to wait quietly for them to initiate, assuming that they will eventually, and if not, then I can read or eat or take a nap.

"Tyler ..." she began hesitantly, a few silent minutes later, "I have a favor to ask. It may be a total waste of your time. It might not be interesting enough for you to enjoy (*Dot knows that I don't take cases for the money, but because, and only when, some aspect interests me*). It may be an impossible job. She may not like you or vice versa, when you meet, assuming that you meet. I think that she can pay, but we didn't talk about ..." I cut her off.

"Dorothy. You're talking too fast, and worrying too much. I have time right now ... even time to waste. If it's something that you want me to do, I'll do it ... period. It doesn't matter if it's fun/neat/interesting or pays well; or if 'she' is unpleasant or boring or mean. You're my friend and I owe you my life ... either of those is reason enough." Then I suggested we loop up and around Moody Pond, it's a nice long walk, and should give us plenty of time to talk through whatever she had in mind ... provided Hope could make it (*on occasion, Hope has gone on strike mid-walk, once I had to carry her over my shoulder when she stopped walking in the middle of a loop hike off of the Floodwood road*).

"Sounds good, Tyler ... and thanks!" Dorothy looked, according to my admittedly poor read on human emotions, both relieved and a bit nervous at the same time. She looked up and to the left, took out the folded paper to consult her notes (*or letter to me ... I don't know which it was*), and started talking. She spoke rapidly and in a low voice for about fifteen minutes, before I told her ... again ... that I would do it, and that she should arrange a meeting between the old woman and me.

When we finally got back to the backside of the building that houses SmartPig, she gave me a hug (*knowing full well that I don't like that sort of physical contact, but that I would tolerate it because of her need for the feeling of closeness/closure*). She then peeled off to her own car, and drove off to start her work day at the TLAS.

Camp Topsail, Upper Saranac Lake, 7/14/2013, 10:47 a.m.

Dorothy and I pulled into the Crocker camp on Upper Saranac Lake at a bit after ten in the morning. She had come along to make introductions (*beginnings with new people are something I am horrific at, due to shortcomings/ differences in my personality and social software*), and as we climbed out of the Element (*leaving the third passenger quietly asleep in the back, with windows cracked*), we both paused to take a look around. I hadn't seen or heard Barry's ghost yet this morning, and I was glad; he sometimes leaves me for days at a time, but so far has always come back. The Crocker camp was big and old and comprised of many buildings, all done in dark brown shingled siding and green roofing ... from the water it might look like a series of short/fat pine trees in amongst the taller ones. I noticed that some of the white pines on the property were taller than any I'd seen anywhere else in the Adirondacks. These had been growing unmolested for more than a hundred years, while everything else in the park had been cut at least once in that time. Something about the camp looked and smelled and sounded different/older/monied in a way that the McMansions of Lake Placid couldn't compete with … never even had a chance.

"A dozen miles away, and it's like we've gone back a hundred years, right?" Dorothy asked, reading my mind.

"13.8 miles … sorry (*she hates when I insist on exactitude*) … but yes, you're right. I'd love to try and hang my single-point-suspension hammock from that tree. You just don't see horizontal branches that big on a white pine in the wild," I said, pointing to a tree with carefully random branches growing out from it at various heights standing alone, near a huge central building/lodge.

"A person should dream Tyler, and I'm glad to see that you can still appreciate the finer things in life." Dorothy elbowed me, and started walking towards the large building.

Before we had crossed half the distance from the gravel parking area to the main building, a man about my age (*29*) came out and started towards us … he must have been watching for us to arrive. I took him in from head to toe as he stepped gingerly off the porch, then turned my head in response to a noise from one of the cavernous garage bays that adjoined the space where I had parked.

"Check out the suit," Dorothy whispered to me out of the side of her mouth. "That 'Mad Men' escapee looks like he's afraid he's gonna get some nature on those fine Italian shoes."

"The shoes, and the suit, are London, not Milan," I said. "He is wearing a banker look rather than the ad-executive. Milan is flashy and trendy and implies sexy … London is intentionally stodgy, promising respectability and trustworthiness. He's a minion dressing for the job he wants, not the job he has." Dorothy looked at me like

I suddenly started speaking in Mandarin. "Remember, Dorothy," I replied, "I grew up in that world."

It was easy for people to overlook or forget that I was born and raised in New York City; it never really took hold of me, and I fled the city in 2001 after it taught me an ultimate lesson on the second Tuesday in September. I had learned, and eschewed, the rules of NYC protocol early on in life, but still remember Lars Thorsen walking me through the basics of 'Suits 101' during one of his teaching sessions. I had grown up one of a few dozen children (*the kids varied from year to year, as parents, and their children, came and went from the cooperative/collective*) who were homeschooled by a group of friends/parents frustrated with a broken public school system. I remember every word that every one of them said in every session, even the boring/stupid/inaccurate ones, which Lars' had not been.

The smarmy smile and stiff handshake that I could see the young man preparing to deliver took me back to a nested subset of things that I didn't/don't like about NYC. He reached us, and extended a hand in my direction, "Anthony Kistler, thanks for coming today." It was delivered with a careful single up and down pump of the hand, and a smile that never reached his eyes; he was assuming the role of gatekeeper for the old lady, and was obviously (*it had to be if I had noticed it*) not excited about us/me being there ... we were out of profile, he didn't know which slot to file us in, and it made him uncomfortable. I had spent too much of my youth on the wrong side of various/numerous doors, forced to wait (*and waste time, which I hate*), thanks to people like Anthony, for the people with whom the buck stopped.

Although his shake was firm, the hand delivering it was slack and soft; mine is covered in callouses and worn down by work and winters to bone and knots of muscle … we were both aware of the differences, it made him adjust his tie. I had endured many such handshakes in the days and weeks after my parents were killed … suits trying to manage or control the newly acquired assets of a kid whom they didn't/couldn't understand. It offended them on some level … my life and lack of ambition (*in any traditional sense*), and the choices I made with what they deemed a sum of money somewhere between 'comfortable' and 'sizable.' He had done nothing wrong or offensive in the seconds that I had known him, but I took an immediate and irrational dislike to him (*which I imagined would interest Barry and Meg, who both enjoy analyzing me, albeit for different reasons, and certainly from different perspectives*).

"Hi, Anthony," Dorothy finally said, after I failed to say anything in a socially acceptable amount of time. "We're here to see Kitty. She should be expecting us." Dorothy and Anthony, and most people, don't like silence in social situations, and often fill them with useful additions/admissions or gestures, which is why I often wait to see what happens.

"Yes," Anthony pivoted quickly, and shook Dot's hand, "come inside. Everyone else is off at church." Anthony turned and led us up and into the building, out of the bright morning and into the perpetual half-light of the camp's great room. We walked past a Stickley dining table that could have seated 40 (*but was set for a measly seven, plus a high-chair, all clustered at one end*), and followed him through a swinging door, into the kitchen and pantry area (*I passed a restaurant-sized fridge/oven/stove and stacks of twenty different sizes of plates and bowls*). Anthony pushed open a door and took us back into a surprisingly modern bedroom suite, which looked as though a 21st century hospital had been grafted onto this 19th century camp.

"It used to be Cook's room, back when I was a girl; that and some storage space." The tiny voice came from a tiny wrinkled face, white against a sea of white linens and blankets in a huge bed; my eye had very nearly skipped over her when we entered. "My grandmother would be shocked at my use of this space. Back in her day, no person of note or bearing would be housed this close to the main lodge, or so far from the lake; if I were further though, I wouldn't see my children, or grandchildren, or my first great-granddaughter, Deirdre, who I met for the first time yesterday." This last piece of information was delivered with a sad hiccuping sound, and either the sound or the sharing itself elicited a minute look of disapproval from Anthony (*and in the same instant, a look of understanding and pity from Dorothy, which got the clever bits in the back of my head working on things*).

"Anthony, please fetch the cooler you'll find in the pantry for Mr. Cunningham, and then leave us. Dorothy, my dear, it is splendid to see you again, and I so appreciate you arranging this meeting, as well as the next. Were you able to take care of the other thing we had talked about?" She spoke to Anthony and Dorothy as valued underlings, a not unfriendly tone that she seemed well-accustomed to.

Dorothy nodded, and gave her a quiet, "Yes Ma'am." and seemed to give a slight curtsy, which is very un-Dorothy, but seemed in keeping with my summoner.

"Then if you would be so kind as to do me the favor of taking our other guest down to the lake for a swim and a walk, I would very much like to receive you both in twenty-five minutes. The smell of a wet dog, and the feel of a cold nose will do me some good, and twenty-five minutes should still be well before my family and nurse return; they would be shocked at the thought of a dog in this 'ward' in which I find myself." Dorothy nodded and smiled as the old woman spoke, then turned and left, to get Cheeko, I assumed. Cheeko is the star pupil of a new program that Dorothy has been working on at the TLAS, therapy and hospice dog training for the homeless cats and dogs living in the shelter that she runs. Her hope is to help people in the Tri-Lakes, raise awareness and support for non-purebreds (*and non-dogs*) as therapy and hospice animals. As a sideline/hobby, it's better work than most people do their entire lives (*certainly better than what I'm doing with my time*).

Dorothy gave my hand a squeeze on the way out, and Anthony came back in with an elderly metal cooler, which turned out to be stuffed with salted ice and Cokes (*I wondered briefly if the old woman was psychic, before settling on Dorothy as a more likely medium of information transfer*). He bent down to whisper in the old woman's ear, and the briefest storm crossed her face before she shook her head and told him that she was fine, and that he could go. He did.

"My name is Catherine Crocker, Mr. Cunningham, and my friends, as I count dear Dorothy, and hope to soon count you as well, call me Kitty. A silly nickname, but I've worn it almost one hundred years, and will wear it around the final turn." She didn't offer to shake hands, and I didn't move forward; the wasted claws on her lap looked as though they might snap or crumble if washed with strong soap.

"Please call me Tyler, Kitty. Dorothy said that you had a problem, and that I might be able to help you with it." I stopped there, having nothing more, at the moment, to say.

"Straight to the point, I like that. Everyone in my

world is careful and circumspect when speaking with me, and I simply haven't the time for it any longer; a simple and direct conversation is to my liking. But before we get to that, Dorothy mentioned, when we spoke the other day, that you are partial to very cold Coca-Cola, from Canada; I had my Anthony run up and get some the other day, and it's been cooling as she directed since Gwen, the cook, got going this morning on the day's food. Why not have one while we talk, and I'll see if I can explain my 'problem' as succinctly as you offered to help me with it a minute ago."

I bent down, opened the cooler, and grabbed a can. I could tell by the label that Anthony had, in fact, driven all the way up to Canada (*probably 3 hours in a round trip, if there was no wait at the border*). I could tell by the way the can felt to my fingertips that it would be chilled nearly to the point of ice-crystals forming, so I opened it gently to avoid nucleation of the supercooled soda until it was in my mouth; the first sip was a delight. This method of cooling Coke also adds a savory element to the experience, in that the rim tasted lightly of what I assumed was the finest sea-salt that rich people could buy. I drank most of the first can before it could warm in my hand, and then looked over at Mrs. Crocker (*who I would call 'Kitty' because she had asked, but would likely always think of, and mentally file under, Mrs. Crocker*) and said, "Thank you, that's perfect."

She smiled, cocked her small head a bit, and replied, "When you take another, would you be so good as to pour me a small glass? I haven't enjoyed anything as much as you appeared to enjoy that cola in a long time, and would like to try it. One advantage of dying is that you needn't be afraid anymore, of anything." This had the sound/feeling of a set phrase, and I wondered if this was an entree into her description of her problem; I prodded a bit (*as is my way*).

"What are you dying of, and what needn't you be afraid of anymore, Kitty?" I thought briefly of offering to share my current Coke, but got sidetracked/derailed with concerns about the social niceties of sharing my germs with Mrs. Crocker, her refusal, or worse … her grudging approval. (*It occurred to me that this sort of concern was a step along a short path to Dorothy 'yes Ma'am-ing' her, and wondered at how some people seem to have the ability to manipulate people just by your expecting them to be manipulators*).

"It has been a tightly run, if dreadfully slow, race; and will likely be a photo finish. The front runners are thyroid cancer, congestive heart failure, and kidney failure; I am rooting for the heart condition to take me, in my sleep, before the summer ends and I have to leave this heavenly place." She didn't seem sad/upset/concerned about this prospect, so I didn't shape my face into my ersatz version of one of those emotions. She also didn't seem finished, so I didn't say anything, in the hope that she would.

"I'm no longer afraid of a great many things. My imminent demise has shaken me free of a lifetime of, not to put too fine a point on it, bullshit. Excuse my language, Tyler (*I made a gesture I've seen other people use, shooing away her concern*). For too long, I've been worried about what the people in my family, or in the camp, or around this lake, would think of my focus, my obsession, my dwelling on the past. Being able to see, to feel the end, Tyler, has given me the courage to throw all of that to the side and indulge myself, to wallow, in the problem that has brought you and I together on this glorious day."

I didn't point out that she seemed to have planned it so that I would be here when most of the camp was at church (*I would bet they were at The Church of the Ascension, a pretty little rough-hewn log church at the northern end of Upper Saranac Lake built a few years before the turn of the century, if I was the type of person given to wagers*), but couldn't see any upside to distracting/angering her at this point, when she was just getting to the point.

"My daughter was taken from me nearly 55 years ago, on a Saturday. I had dinner with her. She had brought a new beau to camp that she was quite taken with, some of the children and my husband went for a ride in our inboard runabout, she stayed with her beau on the dock, and I was up in the boathouse, part chaperone, part cheering section; I liked that one, he was a much better choice than the others she'd brought around before."

"No, don't interrupt me, Mr. Cunningham. I can see questions on your face, but wait until you've heard the whole thing. She went up to her cabin a few hours later, and the boy, no I simply cannot remember his name, stayed behind to swim. I can remember him swimming out to, and sometimes all the way around, Green Island, quite an athlete, but his name refuses to surface. At any rate, she went up to her cabin, took off her shoes, turned on the bathroom light, and disappeared."

I looked at her, waiting for her to continue, but she was done ... for the moment.

"Did the police find her body?" I asked, with a bluntness that would earn me a slap on the back of my head later from Dorothy, when I shared the details of my meeting with her.

"The police found nothing, did nothing, helped not at all," Mrs. Crocker stated in an angry tone that suggested (*even to me*) that she had more to say on the matter. "They were reluctant even to come until we, my husband and I, insisted quite strenuously. By then, it had rained, wiping out any traces or clues that might have been around her cabin or the woods. Worse, they missed a small spot of blood and some strands of what must have been her hair on a doorframe in the cabin she was using during that visit. A detective we subsequently hired was able to find it. This man, Pinchot, his name was, funny that I remember that, seemed aggressive and assertive in his investigations, but yielded, sadly, no results. He focused intensively on Deirdre's, that was her name, the same as my great-granddaughter, Deirdre's boyfriend, but finally was convinced that her beau was not involved at all." She paused, slightly out of breath, a bit of color had crept onto her face and neck. Her eyes were shining with tears.

I took advantage of the temporary interruption in her story to grab another Coke from the cooler, carefully pouring out two ounces into a water glass on a table by the door. I passed the glass to her while her wet/rattling breath sounds subsided, steadying the glass in her shaking hand for a few seconds until I was certain that she had it securely enough to raise it to her mouth. Two fingers and the thumb of her right hand had touched me in the exchange, and the skin was dry and hot and brittle/crinkly feeling, like the parchment paper envelopes that I sometimes cooked fish in. When I was close to her, I could smell age and sickness and menthol and medicines, and behind all of that, corruption; parts of her, inside, were dead … kept from the grave by machines that go bing and IV bags of medicine with long names and a final wish/dream/hope.

"I'm going to ask you thirteen questions, Kitty. Don't think or worry or plan too much about the answers to any of them, nobody will hear your answers besides me. Okay?" I asked, preparing the first few as she took a few tentative sips of her (*my*) Coke, and nodded her assent.

"What was the date of your daughter's

disappearance?"

"Late in the evening of Saturday, August 22nd, 1958 was the last time that I saw her, heading up from the dock to her cabin. I suppose that she might have disappeared early in the morning on the 23rd, but I can't say."

"Who, besides you, was here that night, someone who could give a me a walk-around tour of the camp, to get a feel for the space?"

"Dee's brother, my son, Mike. He'll be back from church soon, and was here that summer, but he doesn't talk about Dee, Mr. Cunningham. He'd be upset knowing I spoke with you about it, now, after so long."

"Why did you want to talk with me about it, and what do you imagine that I could do after almost 55 years (*I had it worked out to approximately 54.85 years, but didn't want my love of precision to throw Mrs. Crocker off, when I had her relaxing into these first few easy questions so nicely*)?"

"I want to know. I made my own peace with her being gone after a year, and sometime after that felt her shift from being my daughter who was missing to being my daughter who had died. I never buried her though, Tyler. Never really mourned her." A silvery tear, huge and perfect on that tiny/ravaged face, rolled down a pale cheek, fell into a deep wrinkle, and was trapped ... like she was ... like I was. I waited for her brain and heart and mouth to start up again; I drank more Coke, trying to minimize my slurping in the quiet room.

"People talk about the loss of a child. They generally mean to a childhood illness or accident. They can see the child, dead. They can touch the body and weep over a corpse and put it in the ground. I was denied that by the thing (*she said this word with such venom and hate and bleak sadness, that I took an involuntary step back, awed a bit by her depth of feeling*) that took her from all of us, from me, her mother." She paused again, no tears this time, just her breath sawing in and out, wet and smelling slightly of ruined tissue.

"I want to know. Where she went, who took her, how she died, why her?" The last words came out a whisper.

I don't have feelings in the way that other people do; it's a blessing and a curse, at times, in turns. I have watched people my whole life, and can make most of the expected facial expressions, guess at the right things to say, or noise/gesture to make, but lack the empathy most humans share. This old woman, this mother, had had a piece ripped off her body/soul most of a lifetime ago, and I was making her relive it; and now had to turn the volume to eleven.

"Her abduction was planned and carried out by someone that hated her, had reason to hate her ... who was it? Don't think! Answer."

"Nobody hated Dee. Everyone loved her. Maybe a jealous boy ...." She trailed off, hopefully (*although why that might be better than some other alternative was beyond me, but many things are*).

"No. Ex-lovers, jealous boyfriends, and spurned suitors leave bloody bodies behind, not an empty pair of shoes." I was not being pointlessly cruel, I told myself as she bent under my harsh and hurtful words, I needed to push her beyond her regular patterns of thinking about this ... past 54.85 years of myth and wishes and tears.

Mrs. Crocker drew herself up, as much as was possible for her in her state, and glared at me before answering. "She was a girl. Pretty and clever and funny and nice. She moved through the world making friends, not enemies. If she had a fault, it was that she liked to drink. It might have gotten her into trouble in the long run, but she didn't have a long run; she got a few tickets, and her picture in the papers a time or two in the year before her ... before she disappeared, but nothing serious. Nobody could have hated her enough to ... that much." She finished with a tone and a look that signaled an end to that particular subject, and after a few moments of thought, I nodded.

"I'll do it," I said

"What? That was only four questions. What about the other nine?" She seemed genuinely curious, and maybe even a little disappointed.

"I only needed to ask you a few questions, but I wanted you to be thinking/worrying about more, so that I might get honest, unprepared answers from you. I know enough to begin looking, and will, in point of fact, get better information from almost any source besides you."

She finished the last sip of Coke that I'd given her, and waggled the cup at me. I finished the can in my hand, and took a new one from the cooler, giving her the first two ounces, and then starting to work on the rest myself.

"It is quite good. Better than I remember," she said, working herself up to speak on a painful subject. "How will you proceed, Mr. Cunningham (*her switching back and forth from first to surname basis had confused me at first, but now I think it had to do with business and personal address and issues*)?" she asked.

"I'll take a walk around the camp with your son to start. Next, I'll talk to people who might have been around that summer. I know some people down at the Adirondack Museum, and may be able to ransack their archives a bit ... I'm a good researcher."

"That all sounds rather nebulous, Tyler."

"Well, yes, it is. A lot of what I practice is what I think of as 'Informational Echolocation.' Are you familiar with the term?"

"Not the information part, but there was a wonderful Richard Attenborough (*David, I assumed, but did not correct her*) special on bats, and their use of echolocation. Is that what you mean?"

"Somewhat. My experience has been that the act of looking for information sends out signals of various sorts, and when the signal interacts with a person or research resource of some sort, it echoes back at me, like the bat's squeak bouncing back off a moth. The bat and I adjust our flight/research pattern, and sometimes get lucky."

Mrs. Crocker looked at me through a veil of confusion, with just a hint of understanding growing after a few seconds.

"It's not necessary that I understand your methods, is it young man?"

"No, Ma'am (*my first Ma'am … ever, I think*). I don't always understand what I'm doing, I just trust that my subconscious does, and that things will work out. I can't promise you that I'll be able to tell you what you want to know about your daughter, but if the information is out there, I will find it."

"This man, Pinchot, the detective we hired when Dee went missing, charged us so much per day plus expenses; can I assume that you operate in much the same way, Mr. Cunningham?"

"You cannot, because I do not. I am not a licensed private investigator, as he likely was. I do favors for friends, and in return they do favors for me."

"Ah yes, this was the point at which that dear girl Dorothy got flustered and stammered her way out of the conversation in which she first mentioned you. Niceties of New York licensure aside, I would like to fairly compensate you for your time and effort. What favor could I possibly do for you? Dorothy mentioned something about vacations; we have houses in California, Florida, New Mexico, and Maine, if any of those would be of interest."

"Whose Porsche is that in the garage?" I asked.

"My son's," Mrs. Crocker replied, with a hint of hesitancy creeping into her voice.

I thought back to Niko, a boy that I'd been schooled with briefly as a child. He had loved, obsessively, cars, in particular Porsches, and even more particularly the model owned by his father, the 993, a variant of the 911 sold in the 1980s and 1990s. Niko and his father had taken me on a series of rides in lower Manhattan one October and November, and I could still remember the sounds and feel of the car running flat out, nimble and powerful, like a cheetah dashing among cows. I hadn't had time to inspect the machine being worked on in the garage, but I was reasonably certain that it was a 993.

"I would feel more than fairly compensated if I could borrow the Porsche during the course of my research ... investigation," I said, and then looked at her, waiting. I live a life with few wants, having, in general, everything that I need/want. Caught up in her nostalgia though, and seemingly indulging some of my own, I found myself wanting this, very much; it did not sit well with me, and I tried to bury the feeling, so that it would not spill out of my eyes or face, onto this old woman sitting in front of me.

She leaned back and looked at the ceiling and seemed to weigh things for a long 17 seconds before smiling a bit, and responding. "Yes, by God, I like it. Mike will be upset, no, angry, with both of us, but he can do this for me; I gave him the car for his fiftieth birthday anyway. You must promise not to put the slightest scratch on his car, Tyler. He warehouses the thing up here, and only drives it a few weeks each year; he told me it has less than 10,000 miles on it, and is more than 20 years old. This will be difficult, but we've lived without thinking about her for too long, and he can give me this one thing before I go."

"We've kept Dorothy and the dog waiting long enough now. When you go out and send her in, tell Anthony that you'll be staying for lunch, and to have a place for me at the table as well." She looked past me, and through the door, towards Dorothy and the wet dog waiting to mess up this neat and tidy hospital-feeling room, in much the same way that I would likely be messing up this camp, her family, and the quietly buried past ... all for an old woman's satisfaction.

I smiled at Dot on my way out, gestured her in, and nodded, in answer to her raised eyebrows and look at the bed and occupant beyond and behind me. She and Cheeko, a sweet and mellow dog, went in to let the old woman smell wet dog, receive loving dog kisses, hear the thwacking of a glad tail, and rub happy ears and belly. There are worse ways to spend a Sunday mid-morning, especially if it may be among your last. We were all basking in Cheeko's love and kisses when the rest of the Crocker clan (*at least those up visiting Topsail, and previously off at church*) crunched down the gravel drive, and Kitty shooed us out to go and say hello while she got ready for lunch.

Camp Topsail, Upper Saranac Lake, 7/14/2013,
1:26 p.m.

It was awkward/difficult/tense at first, and only their
deep-seated WASPiness kept my entry into their regular
Sunday schedule from causing an angry mob, albeit a
small one, from raising my head on a pike outside the
ornamental gate that separated Camp Topsail from the
road (*and the rest of the world … and the present day*). When all
was said and done, however, Kitty was the queen of
Camp Topsail, and what she said was law. The family
arrived home from church in two cars, a Saab and a
Subaru. From out of the Saab climbed the older
generation: a fit and hard looking man, possibly in his
sixties or seventies, and a soft and smiling woman,
looking 15 or more years his junior. A toddler in a pretty
church dress boiled out of the Subaru and ran over to
Dorothy and Cheeko, with an au pair in tow, followed
less quickly by the girl's tired looking parents. Thinking
back to the table settings, I guessed that Anthony must be
taking his meals with the Crockers (*I didn't know if it was*

open-minded or practical to have the lawyer eating with the family, and decided probably a bit of both), which left one person/place-setting unaccounted for ... I spend time on things like this.

Cheeko was a big hit with the toddler, and it was obvious that the adults were all familiar with Dorothy (*she had told me on our way over with Cheeko this morning that the Crockers were large and long term supporters of the TLAS, and had held a benefit at Camp Topsail a few years previously, which raised a few thousand dollars to support TLAS programs*). I was, as I generally am, content to smile and nod in the background (*with a friendly dog and happy 2.5 year-old, it's a pretty easy thing to do*). Everyone talked and milled around for a few minutes, until Dorothy started edging towards my Element, and the Crocker tribe started drifting towards the main lodge for drinks and to check in with Kitty and possibly lunch for the kid; I was left stranded in the middle, and was forced to define my role.

"Hello, folks, I'm Tyler Cunningham, a friend of Kitty's, and she's asked me to stay for lunch." Dead silence ... except from little Deirdre, who wandered over, and held out her hand, possibly hoping for more treats for Cheeko, who she obviously wanted to become her big brother (*I handed her a few treats, which made both her and Cheeko happy*). I could tell that while the Crockers appreciated Cheeko for his calm demeanor, they were more of an AKC registered purebred kind of family, so little Deirdre was destined to be disappointed in the long run (*but aren't we all*).

I wished that I could have scripted this portion of the day (*I am scared of nothing so much as new or unexpected or unscripted social situations, as I'm horrible at handling/managing them*), so that we could have avoided the awkward stretch that came next ... Dorothy looked at me goggle-eyed, and said, "But Cheeko and I have to go Tyler. How will you get home?"

I have been watching/studying people since I realized that I was fundamentally different (*at age four*), and noted that the smile is an ubiquitous facet of humanity that largely eluded (*and still eludes*) me. I have been practicing for years, and have nearly two dozen smiles in my repertoire (*of varying levels of functionality/believability*) but in this instance I fell back on Smile #3, friendly/sincere/helpful.

"Kitty and I were talking about it, and I'm reasonably sure that we'll work something out." I did not want to talk about 'borrowing' Mike's Porsche, or even allude to it, before he had given me a walking tour of Topsail, and a memory tour of the night that his sister went missing. I'm sure that he already had some idea of why I was here, but I didn't need to throw gas on the fire of his suspicions just yet, if I could help it.

"If you get a chance, could you park, and leave, the Element, at the Ampersand Bay end of Lower Saranac Lake?" I asked, knowing that the ranger would find my car in short order, and waste days paddling to all of the official and unofficial campsites on Lower and Middle Saranac Lakes, hoping to catch me squatting for longer than allowed, or without a permit at one of the pay-sites.

Dot must have seen some level of the desperation in my eyes beneath my attempt to distract her with a chance to harass the ranger, or heard it in my voice (*she knows me better than anyone else on Earth, except possibly for Mickey Schwarz, and could read the tiny signs I give that most people miss altogether*), because she let Cheeko swoop down on baby Deirdre for one more round of kisses, and then peeled out of the gravel parking area and driveway nearly fast enough to shower us in pea-sized indignities and gravel.

I got an awkward round of introductions, with the highlight being a leg-hug from the short, but enthusiastic Deirdre; I perhaps got some kid-cred for being a member of Team Dorothy and Cheeko. Mike walked us all inside, was surprised to note two extra settings for lunch, and arranged drinks for everyone (*and a snack for Deirdre*) and then led a discussion about the service, and paddle trip-planning for the afternoon and/or tomorrow as everyone settled into the overstuffed furniture around the room engaged in pre-lunch conversation, talking as if I wasn't there.

"Back from church, time to begin drinking," said a woman who had walked up from the direction of the boathouse to join us. I nodded, taking in her different-ness … outside tan and wrinkles and fancy earth/sky tone clothes and lots of turquoise and silver (*Santa Fe, I guessed internally, to be checked against the facts, should they come to light*).

She made a quick scan of the room and then headed right for me, looping her arm in mine and ushering me over to the large bay window and its views of the lake. "Elyse Portner, I'm a friend of Peggy's, Mike's second wife, the current one," she said. "I'm up visiting for a week or so. Peg's helping me put together a show in 'The City' (*emphasis hers*) this fall, and we're hashing out some details before I talk with her people at the gallery." She talked with an assurance of (*or lack of caring about*) my knowledge of her and her relations with the Crockers, which I found interesting … I nodded, and waited to see what else she would say; it worked.

"I was hiding down by the water in the upstairs of that magnificent boathouse while they were all off being churched up. I saw your girlfriend and the dog, but just kept painting those two lovely islands off to the left of the tiny one (*Tommy's Rock and Dry Island, I thought, but didn't say. I also didn't say anything about Dot not being my girlfriend, a type of relationship I couldn't/can't imagine for myself, with Dot or anyone else ... not from a desire to keep secrets/truth from this woman, but from a lifelong habit of not volunteering information that might be used to further unwanted social interactions).* What is that tiny one, Loon Island I believe Mike called it (*Goose Island, actually, but again, I just smiled and nodded politely*), and the big one in front of us—what's it called?" She ran down, hoping perhaps for me to supply the name for her, which after a somewhat long pause, I did.

"Green," I said, pointing out at the island, so that she wouldn't think that I was just telling her my favorite color (*which is, in point of fact, green*).

"Yes. At any rate, I was starting to get hungry—and thirsty," she said this last with a wink, the meaning of which was lost on me, "when I heard the cars and commotion that heralded the arrival of the churchgoing Crockers, old and small." She spun me around to gesture at the room full of Crockers who were busying themselves with post church/pre-lunch activities.

"Peg is so glad to have Daniel and Kristen up, with little Dee. They haven't seen them hardly at all since Dee was born. It was so sweet of Kitty to arrange for Tessa," she said gesturing towards the au pair who had just re-entered the room with Deirdre in tow, freshly changed out of her church fancies and ready for an afternoon of camp play. "Although," Elyse went on without missing a beat, "I think perhaps 'Tessa from Odessa' is almost too attractive to be spending all that time within reach of Daniel, or possibly even Mike, don't you think?" she asked. I couldn't have commented, even if I wanted to; I'm generally not aware of beauty or the lack thereof in humans, beyond symmetricality and obvious disfigurements (*Tessa had, and did not have any, in turns, if you*

41

were wondering). I was getting tired, absorbing all of this information, and wondered if there would be a quiz later; Kitty could have talked for a week without letting slip this much personal data.

"You're the secret, the surprise, the mystery that everyone knows about, but they're all much too polite to talk about, right?" She said/asked/guessed. I smiled vaguely, my #2—friendly/gentle/clueless-ish, and re-directed.

"How do you know Peggy?" I asked.

"We met at Bennington, both of us in the process of trying to escape that glorious green state. After school, the two of us opened a gallery in Girlington, grinding painfully along for a few years until she met Mike, and I fled the winters for Santa Fe (*I credited myself with a win*).

"That was a nice try, Tyler, but I'm going to spill my Bloody Mary on you if you don't tell me your secret," she said, smiling in a way that would let most people know if she was kidding or not; I took a half-step back and saw her eyes widen with what might have been pleasure.

"Mike will know after lunch, and I assume you can get it from Peg shortly thereafter. I've had worse on these clothes, and still worn them for a couple of days. Can you say the same?" I said.

She looked for me to be kidding, saw that I wasn't (*can't*), tried to decide whether to land on angry or shocked, and eventually settled on a loud and comfortable laugh. Everyone else in the room turned to look at us, in much the same way that Frank and Meg look at my dog Hope when she farts loudly during a visit. I took advantage of the interruption to orbit away from Elyse, and study a trio of Blagden watercolors on the wall ... they looked to have been done at this end of Upper Saranac: Dry and Goose islands from a point just to the northwest of Green Island, Spider Creek coming from Follensby Clear Pond, and Buck Island from the mouth of Saginaw Bay, unless I was wrong (*which I mostly add for politeness' sake, because I'm not, except in very rare cases*).

As I slid around the rim of the Great Room, taking in the details of artwork and taxidermy, I was enjoying the sights and smells and sounds of an old great camp, while all of my sensory recording equipment kept running; I didn't mind being isolated from the majority of the conversation. Mike's wife and children (*Peg and Daniel and Kristen, as I now knew*) made a few attempts to either steer the conversation in my direction and/or to loft a conversational slow-pitch my way, but I am horrible at polite conversation, and was able/destined to avoid getting caught up in whatever they were talking about. I took in the old and dark wood all around me, the fancy but well used silver at the table (*and in Deirdre's hands and mouth*), the birchbark placemats around the table decoratively stitched with porcupine quills, the smells of old wood and dust and moth balls and pitch and Murphy's Oil Soap and coffee and lake and pine needles, the sound of a loon out on the lake yelling at a jetskier and the help rattling around in the kitchen while 'the wealthy Spanish landowners' (*a phrase my father had always used to describe America's old money, a Zorro reference I believe*) debated the merits of various pastors in their log-built summer church and canoe trips they had all done dozens of times over the years. I took it all in, taking advantage of the chance to be a fly on the wall.

The mood, and my reverent study of the great camp environment, was broken when Anthony came into the room, followed, noisily, by Kitty Crocker. She rattled through the door, propelled and held aloft by an incongruent (*both in this setting, and apparently, by design*) aluminum walker with bright/new/glowing tennis balls on its feet. The walker seemed to bang into everything, establishing its territory like an aggressive dog, and fit into the calm (*and calming*) room like poop in a punchbowl (*a saying that popped unbidden into my head, my mother's, from my childhood ... this place seemed to evoke memories of long ago times*). Kitty scowled at attempts to help her, at her walker, at Anthony for suggesting that they should pull up the old Persian carpet to allow her easier access to the room, at Mike's too-large/too-early bourbon, and to a lesser degree, at my presence (*I know that she wanted me to do what I do, but I had complicated her day in a number of ways, and so had certainly earned the scowl*); little Deirdre was our saviour.

As if scripted, she reached for the walker as Kitty hunched and shuffled past her, grabbing one of the brightly colored balls, and nearly making the old woman fall. Everyone drew breath at the same moment, anticipating disaster/anger/shouting/crying (*except me, I like to watch crises not of my creation unfold, to log/ learn about human emotions under stress*), then Kitty turned to me, and said, "Tyler, get one of these balls for her so she doesn't kill me."

It broke the ice, made the kid happy, let the family know where I stood (*somewhere between acquaintance and hired help*), and helped Kitty get past her awkwardness about being old and cranky and dying and difficult. I pulled a ball off the walker, gave it to Deirdre, and helped Kitty negotiate her way into the seat at the head of the table. Anthony hustled in with a drink for her, which smelled like rum and tonic (*which seemed horrific to me, but I find alcohol nasty and stupid stuff to consume in the best case, so I should not be trusted to judge other people's drink choices*).

As soon as Kitty was settled comfortably, the food started coming in, and the au pair (*too attractive Tessa from*

Odessa', who did, it was only fair to say, get watched more closely than seemed warranted by three of the four male humans in the room) got Deirdre into a strikingly modern-looking highchair. Talk shifted to news, and eager anticipation of reading 'The Times' (*which isn't available in the Adirondacks until after church on Sundays, apparently a hardship on par with plague or famine*), with opinions sought and offered about current events among the adults, as food was being passed and served and eaten. Sunday lunch was cold and casual and yummy, although surprisingly it came with both salad and dessert.

I resumed my imitation of a fly on the wall, interrupted only once by Deirdre's au pair, who was seated to my left, when she asked what I did. Everyone but Kitty (*and I*) looked at Tessa as though she had beaten the child (*although Mike's and Anthony's and Daniel's looks seemed tempered by some mitigating forgiveness*), and Kitty shut the conversation down with a simple shut-ended reply.

"Tyler is helping me with some loose ends, and needs a tour of the camp after lunch … Mike." Mike looked genteel daggers at me, and continued eating his way through a stack of avocado, tomato, and fresh mozzarella, dressed with basil and balsamic vinegar, while the rest of the table restarted a discussion of the newest Middle-East peace efforts, and why they were destined to fail.

Anthony was mostly quiet, but would occasionally offer an opinion on financial or legal matters. His role and station seemed similar to mine: minor functionary in the service of Kitty, not a minion, but also not family or guest. I would later find out that he had been travelling with Kitty for weeks, helping her work through the final disposition of her will, and family asset/property allocation after her passing.

When the meal was finished, and had been cleared by

the cook (*and her assistant*), Kitty asked if I would help the younger generation load boats on cartops for the afternoon paddle while she spoke briefly with Mike. Mike's wife, Peggy, announced that she would be reading her book up on top of the boathouse (*which the knowing and significant nods and winks from the younger Crockers led me to believe that that was code for a nap in the sun, which seemed to me a perfectly acceptable activity for a well-fed Sunday afternoon, code or no*). I went out of the cool quiet of the great room, into the bright light and mild heat of the Adirondack afternoon to help the younger Crockers tie boats up onto the roof of their Subaru, and talk about the merits of various canoe trips (*they were heading out to paddle around Follensby Clear Pond, a nearby and pretty little pond, filled with pleasant islands for Deirdre to play on and explore*). I mentioned Floodwood Pond to Fish Creek, which was met with groaning and knowing nods, so followed up with Jones Pond to Osgood Pond to Church Pond ... a fun little trip through a series of gorgeous ponds and canals and beaver-choked streams; they said they hadn't tried it, and might give it a shot tomorrow.

We finished, and they were just crunching out of the driveway, when Mike came up behind me, tapped me on the shoulder, and pointed down towards the boathouse, "Come on then, Tyler. The tour has to start down at the boathouse." He paused before continuing, grinding his teeth a bit, trying to plan his way through this unpleasant conversation and chore. "I understand Mother's desire to know about Dee before she dies, but have no patience for anyone taking advantage of our pain for their profit. Also, if you so much as scratch my car, I'll get the roofing contractors working here this summer (*he pointed to a number of buildings with signs of roof work in various stages of need or preparation or completion*) to grind you into gazpacho."

As Mike delivered his tasteful threat, I could see the ghost of Barry walk around the back of one of the long garage buildings, and turn towards us. He seems to appear when I am feeling threatened, when the subject of violence is raised in general, or in the presence of loud noises. He was a nearly constant companion during hunting season last fall, made a number of visits during various firework displays that Saranac Lake hosts during the year (*Winter Carnival, and July Fourth come to mind*). Sometimes he speaks, sometimes we carry on a conversation, other times he is a quiet guest; this appeared to be one of the latter visitations.

Knowing that he exists only in my imagination was no help at first. He would speak to me in the presence of other people and I initially answered by turning to face him. Active listening and responsive conversations are hard habits to break, especially as they had been so hard for me to learn (*my response to a dizzyingly stimulating world as a baby was to focus only on what had my attention at that instant, and tune everything else out … something most people do not do*). I knew that I had to take some control of my relationship with Barry when Hope started turning to face him during our conversations too (*taking her cues, I assume, from the direction of my eyes/face/hands*). In this case, it was easy to tune him out as he wasn't (*yet*) speaking to me, and had likely been drawn by Mike's threat if I damaged his car.

The three of us walked down to the water, with me sucking in every detail I could hold in eye and ear and nose … some of it might even be useful in finding Mike's sister, although I doubted it.

Camp Topsail, Upper Saranac Lake, 7/14/2013,
1:52 p.m.

"Mother told me to give you the VIP tour of the camp, as well as my memories of the night she ...." Mike broke off and shook his head like a wet dog, or in his case like an aging polo pony, before starting up again on a new tack that brought Barry in closer to us.

"What the fuck are you doing here? Do you actually think that you can find anything after all this time, when the others over the years have failed? Or are you just taking advantage of a sick old woman's pathetic hope?" he asked, punctuating his questions with a finger poking into my chest, five inches south of my Adam's apple ... it hurt ... I flinched and winced with each poke.

"I'd twist that finger right off, and shove it up his ass, Tyler. You can't let a guy like that get up on top of you." Barry was right behind me, speaking down into my right ear from his towering height, close enough that I should have felt his breath on my ear (*but of course, I couldn't*).

"Not helping," I said, under my breath, hoping that Mike wouldn't hear me. Barry refuses to respect or respond to my wishes or thoughts if not spoken aloud, which is both tricky and annoying behavior for a symptom.

"Mr. Crocker, I'm here because your mother asked me to come and apply my investigative talents to your sister's disappearance. I do believe that I may be able to find something that others missed because I take a different approach to problem-solving than others generally do; if I did not think that there was a chance, I wouldn't be wasting my time. If I were taking advantage of your mother's hope, I would have a fat check in my pocket right now, instead of the promise to borrow a car nearly as old as I am."

"What's the deal with borrowing my car anyway? Do you have some beef against me personally, or a chip against rich people with fancy cars? The Porsche was a gift, and is, as you say, probably as old as you, and likely worth more."

"The father of a friend of mine (*not really a 'friend', but I didn't want to confuse Mike*) had a 993. Niko, my friend, was obsessed with the car, as a way to try and get close to his father … it failed. I joined in with his obsession as a way to try and get close to Niko … that also failed. But we both learned a lot about the 993 variant of the 911, and I remember all of it to this day, along with that throaty roar the last air-cooled model that Porsche makes when you unleash it, from my drives in it with Niko and his dad. I have nothing against you personally, or against rich people, with or without fancy cars. I grew up in and amongst rich people, and until your mother dies, I would bet that I both have more money in the bank than you, and care about it less than anyone you know. Are we good? Can we look around Topsail, and talk about your sister now?" Mike glared at me a bit, turning my words over in his head; as per Barry's advice, I wanted to back him off of me, and get on top of him a bit.

"Also, I like the 993 because the number has 2 factors, both awesome prime numbers: three and 331. Pythagoras thought three the noblest of all digits, it is the first prime in both Fermat's and Mersenne's sequences ... and the only number in both. 331 is even better ... it's the 7th cuban prime, and is both a centered pentagonal and centered hexagonal number." When I finished this statement, Mike actually took a step back, and away from me ... I have trouble reading fear versus awe, but my nerdery had done the trick in either case. Barry gave a nod and orbited out and away from the two of us as we walked down and out onto the dock running out into the water beside the large boathouse.

"Um ... Dee and her boyfriend, the Miller boy, Tommy, came down here after dinner, and watched the moon come up while the rest of us, Father and I and my cousins Mindy and Robyn, went out in the Chris Craft to cruise the lake and watch for stars. No, correction, Mother stayed behind, and noodled around on the upper porch of the boathouse." Mike pointed back behind us, and upwards, to the upstairs of the boathouse, and more specifically to a weather-grey rocker behind a low rail of rustic twig construction. "She worried Tommy was pressuring Dee, and wanted to be nearby for 'moral support.' Funny how things turn out, he loved her, beyond all reason, and the way she ... was gone, all of a sudden, hurt him, maybe more than us ... than me. He kept driving up and put those damn posters up on every signboard, gas station, and police station within 100 miles. He literally died looking for her; went off the damn road driving out to a hospital in Watertown that November in a storm." He shook his head again, to bring himself back on track, this time looking more like a dog than a polo pony.

"Tell me about what happened when you came back from your boat ride," I prompted.

"We stopped off at the Deane's camp, 'Cayuga,' for drinks and dessert. We were gone for pretty close to two hours, maybe a bit more. When we got back, we could see Tommy about 200 yards out from the end of this dock, wearing a white swim-cap that caught the moonlight nicely. Father 'waked' him with the boat, and then we shadowed him in, as there were other boats motoring up and down the lakeshore that night, and Father didn't want him to get run over. Tommy pulled himself out of the water and helped to walk the boat in and get her tied up for the night. I waited for him to finish up while Father went up with the others. I noticed Mother asleep with her needlepoint in that chair there, and went in to wake her while Tommy went up to his own cabin for the night. I remember pausing at the top of the boathouse stairs, to see if he was going to stop off at Dee's cabin, but he didn't. Things were different then. Not better or worse, just different." He stopped and looked up at the boathouse and squinted his eyes, maybe trying to see back through the years to that night, wondering if he could have changed things.

"When did you know that she was … missing?" I asked, to get him rolling again, and because it seemed that standing on the dock talking with me had freshened the memories of the events 54.85 years ago.

"It's a bit embarrassing and makes us all sound stupid, and rather like one of those English farces, where people are going in and out of different doors, just missing each other, and jumping to the wrong conclusions about the state of affairs; although of course, it wasn't funny, just sad." He drifted away again, and I was about to cough or something when he started up on his own.

"She wasn't at breakfast, but we assumed that she had gone fishing with Da, my father. Then, a number of us, Tommy and myself included, went on a canoe trip, to Middle Saranac, I think, while others went to another camp, 'Three Pines' I believe, to play in a tennis round-robin. In this way, we got through most of the day, everyone thinking that she must be with one of the others. It wasn't until five, when we always came together for cocktails and to talk about the events of the day, that it came out that nobody had seen her since the previous evening. I got a horrible feeling in the pit of my stomach, and ran with Tommy down the line to her cabin, way at the end. Nothing there, just those stupid white shoes she liked so much. We both called out for her, like morons. I'll show you, you'll see; her cabin is too small to miss a person. I could smell her on the air, but it was probably just her things smelling of her. I never did see that blood and hair that day, not for weeks. We didn't see any of it until the detective Father brought up started looking around. He found it all in the first thirty seconds and showed all of us, local constabulary included, to be asses." He paused in the story here for a moment, took off his glasses, which I could see by the distortion when he held them up to inspect for dust were progressives (*Barry had waited outside, but would know/remember everything that Mike said, when we talked about it later, in my hammock*). We walked up the path Deirdre Crocker must have walked, all those years ago, and he brought me up creaking stairs and into her musty cabin (*it looked as though it hadn't had much, if any use in the intervening years*).

"I spent the twenty years after that night mad at the local police for not finding the blood, finding clues, finding her. I would leave a room or cross the street to avoid Bender, the cop who first came out to 'investigate' that first night," Mike said. I am horrid with tonal expression and expressiveness, and even I could hear the finger-quotes in Mike's use of the word 'investigate.' He put his glasses back on and picked up where he had left off.

"There was nothing though, not for us, not for Bender, not for the detective ... nothing beyond a tiny knot of blood and hair and those silly shoes in the middle of the floor like dead rabbits. There wasn't anything that night, or the next morning, or in the weeks and months and years since then. It's like she was swallowed up by an angry God. Like she had never existed, except for her things; Mother and Da left them here, waiting, as though she'd return from some unannounced trip at any moment. I cleaned the cabin out, took all of her stuff to the dump in Lake Clear, on the day of what would have been her 25th birthday. I woke up and couldn't stand the thought of it all in here; so even though it was mud-season, I drove up here from New York (*New York City, or Manhattan, I corrected him, but silently ... nearly everyone from my birthplace is guilty of this*), and threw it all away. When she found out, Mother wouldn't speak to me for weeks."

He sat down on her bed, exhausted by the story, or by the unexpected flood of memories, or from church and then bourbon with lunch, rubbed his face with his hands, looked up at me, and asked, "What else?"

Camp Topsail, Upper Saranac Lake, 7/14/2013,
2:23 p.m.

Mike Crocker and I walked north from Deirdre's cabin
along the front/lake facing cabins and buildings. Mike
named the cabins and buildings as we walked by, and
then through, them. Some were named for family
members, 'Da and Mother's lodge,' which was bigger
than most and had a small kitchen and attached living
room and spare bedroom, some for generic occupant/use
types, 'kids cabin' or 'guest cabin' or 'playroom,' and
some with names that I couldn't guess at, and Mike only
shrugged, 'Mouse House' and 'Skunkville.' He was lost in
thoughts about a sister he had buried a lifetime ago, who
I was digging up to no good end (*that he could see*). He
explained that the front line of buildings of a camp,
relative to the waterfront, were for the owners and their
guests. The housing nearest the main building/lodge was
for children and less important guests. It appeared that
rank and status were measured by distance and a lack of
connectedness, via a covered walkway, to the main body
of buildings. (*This seemed odd to me, as it seemed that if I built a*

big camp like this, I would want my room next to the kitchen, and with a covered walkway, so that I could walk over during a rainstorm in my socks ... maybe it was a privacy thing). The second row of decidedly smaller, and less fancy, cabins was originally built to house staff, but as their numbers had decreased over the years, some of these had been repurposed for children or guests wanting/needing to be a bit off the main strip of great camp life. We walked through a few of the cabins, at my request, mostly so I could get a feeling for the history. I didn't see how this exploration could help me find out what had happened to Deirdre Crocker all of those years ago, but it couldn't hurt. In all honesty, my involvement in this case was entirely based on owing Dorothy a favor (*any favor she cared to ask, so this one was easy*) and my interest in the history of the Adirondacks and Adirondack great camps.

Most of the cabins still had tiny wood-burning stoves in each room, and when I wandered over to look more closely at the intricate ironwork on one of them Mike came back to life a bit, and showed it to me. "If you look inside this one, you can see that it couldn't hold full-sized logs. They had to be cut shorter than for standard woodstoves or fireplaces, and were also split into smaller pieces than for use in regular stoves. I remember when I was twelve, feeling like such a big boy when I heated my room with a fire that I had made." He grinned at me, perhaps forgetting who I was, and why we were here for a moment, wrapped up in the happy memory. "They're pretty little stoves, but they burn hot and fast, so the room is either roasting or freezing. I remember one Thanksgiving when we came up, Da came through all of our cabins to feed them in the middle of each night; he slept through his Westclox alarm clock on our last night, and my room was like ice the next morning."

Mixed in with cabins for the help were buildings for storage and maintenance, along with other, more arcane, rich-person support infrastructure that no longer exists; Mike walked with me, explaining what each building had been used for in his childhood, and what it was used for now. At a huge building with numerous small rooms, tubs, tables, and laundry lines inside and out he remarked, "This was the laundry. I remember playing tennis in the morning, changing for lunch, and having my clothes cleaned and pressed in my cabin for the afternoon."

A small building with no windows and heavily secured door intrigued me. When he opened it, and gestured me inside, he explained the metal walls, ceiling, and floors with delight, "We just called it the 'Tin Room,' for obvious reasons. It was used to store bedding and some dry goods in here between periods of occupancy, to keep mice and porcupines from them; before my time, mostly. I remember it smelling like mothballs, and being very dark with the door closed. Playing 'Murder in the Dark' in here as a kid scared the hell out of me." I could see from his eyes that he meant it, and could momentarily remember the fright of someone hunting him in the pitch black.

I knew the next one, from my explorations into Adirondack history in the Saranac Lake Free Public Library, but let it go by when Mike looked questioningly at me as we walked up to the long and low building with a door that looked as though it belonged on a restaurant's walk-in refrigerator. I had read about them, and even been inside the ruins of one while trespassing the ruins of long-abandoned 'Frontier Town' in North Hudson (*'Frontier Town' was an amusement park that closed before I was born, but some of the buildings are still standing, and it makes for a fun trip*). "It's an ice-house. Back in the day, the caretaker and a hired crew would wait until the ice on the lake out front got nice and thick, then cut out blocks, bring them up here, and cover them with sawdust for insulation. The walls have a gap of almost two feet between inner and outer wall, also filled with sawdust (*I remember standing between the walls of the ruined ice-house in 'Frontier Town' knee deep in rotted sawdust*), and when you're inside, you can't hear a sound. I put the first fish I ever caught in here for Cook to prepare for my supper after my Da helped me clean it. Dee snuck in here with a boyfriend of hers the summer before ... to hide from the heat and the prying eyes of Mother; she would have gotten away with it entirely, except that my grandmother found a small cache of empty beer bottles and nobody could lie to my grandmother's face."

"Was your grandmother here the summer, the night, that Deirdre disappeared?" I asked, not knowing exactly why I was forcing myself back on the clock.

"What? Yes, she was, but she and my grandfather went to their cabin, at the far end of the camp from the boathouse and Dee's cabin. She was actually the one who finally noticed that nobody had seen Deirdre all day, and she was the one who bullied that useless Bender into coming out that evening—much good it did. She was quite a terror, a powerful figure in the family, scared me weak-kneed back then. She told my Da the following spring, when we opened Topsail, that Tommy had been a fool to keep looking for her, to get himself killed for a dead girl who had never loved him. Da slapped her face, once, and I would swear to this day that time stopped while the noise of it echoed around the room where you ate lunch today. Da grabbed a bottle of bourbon off the rolling bar on his way out of the room, and stomped down to the boathouse in the dark. My mother nodded at me to go find him ten minutes later, and eventually I did, out on the lake in a crappy Grumman canoe that I bet we still have hanging in the rafters down in the boathouse. I never would have found him but for the pipe smoke; I could smell it, and then once I knew what to look for, I found an intermittent glow out on the water. I sat on the wet moss, watching my Da drink and load pipe after pipe, for hours, afraid that if I went to bed, I'd lose him too, drunk or drowned or just gone. Every son reaches a day when they can see the end of their Da, not weakness or death necessarily, but the reality of the man's limits; you're never the same after. I wasn't. My dad had hated Tommy sniffing around Dee, was positive that he wasn't good enough for her, but after his death, Da loved that boy more than a little." He looked up from his reverie, and seemed a bit embarrassed to have shared so much with a stranger (*I wondered briefly if he would feel better if he knew that I didn't care as much about the story as about looking at the rolling bar or the Grumman canoe he had mentioned before I left ... I decided that he wouldn't ... people never did, they just got angry with me for reasons that neither they nor I could explain or understand*).

"Your mother mentioned that Deirdre had gotten a few tickets, and had some minor issues with drinking in the year before her disappearance," I said, hoping to roll the ball in another direction.

"Well, it was a bit more than that actually—nothing to do with her going missing, mind you, but she did drink a bit much the previous summer. She straightened out after a crash sent her and a friend to the hospital." Before he had finished, I was on point, feeling the beginnings of a handhold.

"Tell me about it," I asked, modulating my voice, trying to aim for a tone that was interested, but not over-eager. I did not want to scare him away, or make him cautious; people tend to filter information about the dead, so as to cast them in the best possible light, and I wanted the truth, without filtration.

"Coming home from the Woodmen's Days in Tupper Lake, she wrecked her car near the turn-off from Route 3, by the Wawbeek (*where the Wawbeek used to be, I thought but didn't say, not wanting to interrupt his flow*). She said that she swerved to miss a deer, but the trooper who brought the girls to the hospital said that they were both drunk as skunks. No seatbelts in those days, and they both had some bruising and bashing and black eyes and the girl in the passenger seat had a broken arm. Da got a call as soon as they got to the hospital in Saranac Lake, and rushed over to take care of things."

"What?" I asked, hoping to prod without provoking.

"He made sure that they got the right doctors, paid for everything, talked the trooper into Dee's version, with the deer. They were both essentially fine, and went home that night; stayed friends, I think. Anyway, after that, Dee drank much less, and was a nut about safety."

"Do you remember the other girl's name by any chance?" I asked, not hopefully.

"Ach – nnnnnno, maybe Bonnie? Pretty girl, local. Summer friend, that sort of thing. Why do you ask? It was nothing, really." But my question had gotten his brain moving in directions he had avoided for decades, and been happier that way, so I jumped in with a conversational jump-starter (*partly because of the stricken look that had been growing in his eyes and threatening to spread down through his features, but more out of a keen desire to keep him or anyone else from muddying the waters I would be swimming through in the coming days and weeks*).

"What's the deal with the huge garage? Do you guys

have a plane that you hangar at Topsail for the winter?"

"No, although I know a guy on Rainbow Lake with a seaplane hangar for a boathouse. He flies his floatplane out to remote lakes and ponds for trout fishing from time to time. The long garage is a great camp feature from way back. We keep a few cars and trucks here in the off-seasons, my Porsche among them. We'll also haul the Chris Craft and a few of the other boats up to have some work done on them, and keep everything climate-controlled. We used to have a caretaker on site year round, and he would fuss with all sorts of projects for the family, using the big heated garages as a home-base for his work. Most camps have given that up now, but there are a few holdouts."

We walked over to the garage, and entered the gigantic room just as a mechanic was sliding out from under the 'Forest Green, Metallic' Porsche that I'd seen briefly on my way down to talk with Mrs. Crocker not quite four hours ago. I knew him slightly from some research I'd done fifteen months previously, and he smiled at me (*unseen by Mike*) before addressing his employer, "The car is in great shape, Sir. I changed all of the fluids, switched out the spark plugs, charged the battery, checked the tires, and filled them to five pounds overpressure, as you specified. She's ready to roll for a test-drive if you want, before I leave."

"Thanks Bill, but Mr. Cunningham's going to be taking the car for a few days," Mike Crocker said, with a lustful fire dying in his eyes before it had fully burst into flame. He wanted to drive his baby down to Tupper, or Long Lake, or Old Forge, but didn't want to embarrass himself asking a favor of me; I caught the keys when Bill tossed them our way, ignoring/avoiding the questioning look he flashed my way when he was certain that Mike

Crocker wasn't looking.

I had more to discuss with Mike and Kitty, but now was not the time; Mike's look said that clearly enough for even me to understand. I climbed down into the seat, enjoying the sense and muscle memory of the cockpit of the Porsche. The smell of the leather, along with the gentle creaking sound of it yielding to my weight, brought back a flood of memories. The partly reclined couch (*and the car in general*) fit/cradled my body better than it had Niko's father; he'd been six inches taller than my 5'8" and likely double my 144 pounds. Leaning back (*so much further in the Porsche than in my Honda Element*) almost made me feel as though I were laying down. With my eyes closed, I could feel where the pedals were (*much closer than in the Element*); and when I opened them again, I noted how much better the optical quality of the windscreen was than in my Honda. Mike and Bill shuffled and coughed a bit, perhaps thinking that I was scared of the car (*now that I was behind the wheel*) or couldn't find the right gear (*given the unusual shifter and gearbox*), so I slid the stick smoothly around the horn and into reverse, peeled backwards in a tight U, and dropped down through second gear and into first (*a trick that Niko's father had taught us*) and re-engaged the engine before the car had finished rolling backwards. I kept the car in first gear until I hit the main road, executing a tighter/crisper turn than was absolutely necessary (*and which kicked the rear end out a foot before the giant patches of soft rubber caught the road again*), encased in a nearly perfect carapace of steel and glass. I impulsively turned left out of the fieldstone gate with ironwork letters spelling out 'TOPSAIL,' away from Saranac Lake and home, planning to put the spectacular car of my memories through its paces, and see how it withstood the test of time (*and a young boy's dreams*).

SmartPig Office, Saranac Lake, 7/14/2013, 5:18 p.m.

As I drove Mike Crocker's 993, (*too fast for the taste of any troopers that I might pass*), along the road from the north end of Upper Saranac Lake towards the southern end (*with me thinking 'top' and 'bottom,' based on the map I had running in my head*) and beyond that Tupper Lake, I worked at transporting my brain back into the time, and world, of Deirdre Crocker and Camp Topsail. From talking with the Crockers, mother and son (*still struggling with 'Kitty'*), I had a feeling for the environment and the incident. The motive was likely the key to the entire event, but it would certainly be hard to get at after all of this time; both Mrs. Crocker and Mike had told me different inaccurate stories about Deirdre's drinking (*and related consequences*) for example. I don't think that they intentionally lied to me, but it has been my experience that humans polish and reshape their memories of the dead/past, especially where family is concerned. I would much rather read a primary document produced at the time of any given event; even if it is slanted in one direction or another, it won't suffer the wholesale alterations that history held in the human heart tends to fall victim to over time.

As Route 30 made a 90 degree turn to the right at Panther Mountain Road, I could picture Deirdre and the 'local' girl to be named at a later date missing the same turn and ending up in the ditch or trees beyond the shoulder. That car crash felt important to me (*it had happened up here, after all, and was a reasonably big event in an otherwise reasonably small life*), maybe important enough to be a fulcrum point for the events that were to follow. I had no way of knowing of course, unless I was able to find a police report of the incident, but as I felt gravity and inertia trying to pull the Porsche and I off the road, Deirdre Crocker seemed not have lived an important enough life to warrant the sort of hate/pain/planning/focus that went into her disappearance, unless it had something to do with the crash. Lots of people go missing, but most are found very quickly, living or otherwise. The fact that her body was not found floating in the lake, by the side of the road, in a motel room, or by hunters five years later likely means that she was taken and killed by a planner, by someone who wanted her erased from the Earth.

This was both bad and good news ... bad because it meant that finding her would be a hard task, (*made harder by 54.85 years of accumulated and lost information*); good because there wouldn't be many people in my search pool capable of that sort of behavior, or planning, or follow-through. (*It's easy to snatch someone, anyone ... much harder to get away with it for decades and not leave a body for others to find somewhere/sometime*). My brain yelled at me, the clever bits in the back of my head insisting that they had made those intuitive leaps that make what I do fun (*at times*). Unfortunately, it came at exactly the wrong moment for me to lose focus, and my attention to the road in front of me greyed out a bit just as I arrived at the intersection of Routes 30 and 3. I stepped hard on the fat brake pedal, and felt the wheels all lock (*pre-ABS*) as the wide harness bit into my left shoulder, causing me to wince as this was sensitive scar tissue and still-jumbled nerves from the injury that I had received last summer in the course of an investigation. We, the Porsche and I, skidded off the road and into the grass to the right of the 'STOP' sign; Barry stepped out from behind the sign to wait for the car to stop scraping its way through grass and small bushes and saplings that the road crews had neglected to trim. He waited in exactly the right spot to bend over and speak to me as I shut off the engine and bounced out of the car, willing the adrenaline to finish burning through my extremities. (*A calm and rational part of my mind posited that Barry could have only judged the correct spot to wait in with my understanding of physics and this particular car's abilities, further proving that he was nothing more than a creation of some odd corner of my consciousness, and must serve some purpose*).

"Smooth move, Ex-Lax! Hah!" he snapped in my face, in that deep voice of his, and leaned back. I nodded.

"That thing ain't your Honda, Tyler. The toaster may be a silly car, but it's got safety features out the wazoo. Anti-lock brakes, airbags everywhere, reinforced cabin frame, less than half the horsepower of this thing (*I was going to interrupt and give him the exact numbers, but remembered just in time that if I knew them, he knew them, so I just sat, and waited*)."

"Your shoulder hurts right? Where Justin shot you. You don't know how lucky you got, Tyler, with that, with us, with me." He looked me in the eye (*not having to say 'when you killed me'*). "This thing you signed on for, for the dog lady, it could bigger than the stuff with Cynthia and

George and me and Justin last summer, much bigger; and we, I, nearly killed you last time out."

I should have felt silly, parked in the grass off to one side of the street, at the end of a serious set of skid marks on the road and in the grass, being lectured to by a dead giant, but I didn't. (*My lack of the social software, that virtually all of humanity comes pre-loaded with, has marked up and down aspects, at various times, and in different situations*).

"So what are you saying, Barry, that rich/powerful/fancy people are more dangerous than you and Justin and George? Remember, I grew up with rich and fancy people ... I didn't grow up in the Adirondacks. I was born and raised in Manhattan. I know these people," I finished, already knowing where he was likely going with his rebuttal (*I should, given that both sides of this discussion originated in my head*).

"You are the dumbest smart guy I ever met, you know that Tyler? You know money, may even have money, but that doesn't mean that you understand the way it works, the way it can be used, the way it affects those with, and around it over time." The sentence structure seemed more complex than living Barry would have been able to use, but my sub-conscious had something to say, and it was using what it had, so I let it go rather than point it out to ... myself, essentially.

"These people, people like the Crockers—fuckin' Kitty and Skip and Pip and who knows what else—they may be like regular people back in New York (*City, I added, smiling at how crazy it was to be correcting my 'imaginary friend'*) or Boston or wherever, but up here, the ones with old money and old camps, they're like royalty. Less now than the way it was when my dad was a kid, but their money, taxes and what they spend, make this place work. Without it we'd all be living off of poached deer and government cheese, and anyone who tells you different never went to bed hungry."

"So what you're saying is …? I should skip this one, because I don't understand money and power, and there might be some/plenty of both mixed up in this thing," I prompted.

"Don't be an asshole. You said yes before dog-girl finished asking. I get that … friends. And I think you like the idea of maybe figuring out something that nobody else could, prove you're the biggest swinging brain on the block. Hah!" he laughed at his own joke, which saved my trying to fake a laugh (*with which I'm horrible*).

"Nah, what I'm saying, Tyler, is that you need that high-speed, low-drag melon of yours for something other than a place to pour those tasty Cokes of yours. What I guess I'm saying, is that you need to do your 'rain man' thing, but also try to think like the bad guy a bit more; also, pay attention to what's going on around you more, no good being the smartest guy in the woods if you die in a dumb car-wreck. Right?"

It was hard to argue with him, even if I wouldn't have felt silly arguing with a figment of my imagination. I climbed back in Mike Crocker's car, walking around it first to give it a quick visual inspection (*everything seemed fine*), and then pulled back out onto Route 3, back towards Saranac Lake, leaving Barry shambling into the woods in my rearview. I turned the radio on, Radio Bob of NCPR was hyping Bob Marley as Adirondack summer music, and I flashed on a line from Dickens', 'A Christmas Carol': 'You may be an undigested bit of beef, a blot of mustard, a crumb of cheese, a fragment of an underdone potato. There's more of gravy than of grave about you, whatever you are!' (*segueing from Barry to the radio in an odd shift of my thinking bits*). I drove off, thinking about things perhaps a bit more than Barry would have liked me to, but still paying adequate attention to the road, even taking the time to enjoy the car as I put it through its paces leaping up and down and around the stretch of road that slalomed between the ponds and lakes and mountains between Tupper Lake and Saranac Lake.

I zoomed into the parking lot for the Tri-Lakes Animal Shelter (TLAS), cutting off a van full of kids in a green Paul Smith's College van. My Element was parked in the first slot, and the only other cars belonged to people who worked there, as the TLAS is closed on Sundays and Mondays. The front door would be locked, to discourage well-meaning animal lovers who couldn't be bothered to check the hours of operation, so I went around to the side door, and let myself in. The people who work at the shelter know me, at least partly as 'the kook who walks the difficult dogs.' I also make, and bring, treats for the people and dogs (*and even the cats, although cats and I don't interface well*), a deliberate (*and effective*) ploy to ingratiate myself with everyone living and working within their walls.

"Hi, Tyler, we got a new pit-mix that's seen the vet, and is ready for a walk, if you're lookin'," Sandy said, as we passed in the hallway, her loaded down with a cubic yard of clean bedding in her arms. I nodded noncommittally, and walked the rest of the way to the front office, dodging cats, while they did the same to me (*dogs like me because on the surface, I'm a belly-rubber, treat-giver, and long walk-taker … cats don't like me because they look past the surface, and either don't like what they see, or worse, don't see anything; Dorothy and I spend a fair amount of time talking about this*). I pushed through the throng of people and smells and cats on my way to the desk, and Dorothy.

"So, I guess it went okay, but how come Cheeko and I

weren't invited to lunch?" Dorothy didn't care about lunch, but this was her way of telling me to give some details about my new and (*she surmised*) exciting case as a consulting detective, while keeping it semi-private in the offices of the TLAS.

"Kitty explained her need to me, Mike (*these were the names that Dorothy would use herself, she expected me to use them, so I did … it made things easier*) showed me around the camp, and gave me more details and background, and eventually, at his mother's request/command, his car … for the duration of my investigation. That being the case, do you mind my leaving the Element here for the next week or two? You can use it for shelter stuff as needed."

She squealed and reached out to punch me, "GET OUT! That pretty green thing is yours?"

"Not to keep, just as my fee. Want to see it?" I asked, anticipating a drawn out and rambling story of new dogs/cats and paperwork; instead, she grabbed her backpack, ducked under the counter-gate, and raced out the door before I was really aware of it.

"I'm heading out, see ya'll tomorrow," I heard as the front door closed behind her rapidly diminishing form. I raced out to catch up with her, but by the time I got to the car, she was already settled in the driver's seat, holding out her left hand, and grinning up at me. I detoured briefly to grab my go-bag from the Element and drop it into the tiny backseat-ish space of the Porsche, placed the keys for the 993 in her hand, and hurried around to the passenger side, so that I wouldn't get left behind.

"You have to drop me back off at my car behind SmartPig anyway," she argued, as we rocketed past the turnoff that would bring us to the backstreet parking lot where we had left her car this morning before heading out to Camp Topsail.

"I'm just going to take us out to Kiwassa and back, to stretch her out a bit," she said when I looked questioningly at her, after she had missed the second viable turn to get us to her car. Last summer must have been on her mind as well, despite the fun, because she was taking turns, knowingly or not, that would take us past the house where George Roebuck (*the man who had Cynthia killed, and very nearly been responsible for my death*) had lived.

Either because it had happened to someone else, or because she viewed it as self-defense or a fun adventure, Dot had not been bothered/scared/scarred/changed by the violence that we had been involved with in dealing with George and his crew at the end of last summer. It was only because of her help that I had lived through that period, but it had left more marks on me than her, as was quickly evident.

"You have to promise me that you'll bring me along for the fun this time, Tyler."

"Dot! What are you talking about? The fun when two guys beat me up … or the fun when they tried to shoot me and dump me in the lake … or the fun when they tried to finish me off once they found out that I was still alive … or wait, what about the fun when their fellow meth-cooking friends almost killed me and my dog?" My words didn't get any louder, but she must have heard the tension in my voice because she pulled over to talk with me. She looked at me curiously, I tend not to get emotional, but had been showing frayed nerves more easily and frequently since the events of last summer.

"Lighten up, Francis. None of that stuff. I was talking about the planning and maps and racing around the Park and beating them at their own game, that stuff. I wanna help, Tyler, and I hope that none of the other things are on the agenda this time around."

"None of them were planned the first time around, Dot ... they just happened. Things don't go according to plan when you're dealing with crazy people or criminals; they don't follow any logical patterns of behavior, and things get messy. If I thought this might be like last September with George, I'd pack up Hope (*my dog*) for a vacation in Iceland."

"Right, right, I get it. You know what I mean, Tyler. I want to help you with this; Kitty is a nice old lady, and a good friend of the shelter. I can't imagine how that must feel for her, not knowing for so long. Besides, it'll mostly be research, you said." She sounded like she understood what I meant, but I could still see the fun in her eyes, and worried about ... trouble.

"Probably," I admitted, "but there's no way to know for sure until something goes wrong, and I'm not comfortable with that, with you, ... I was just talking with ...." I had been about to say Barry, and clacked my jaws shut quickly, hoping she hadn't guessed where I was going. I had told her after the first time I had seen Barry's ghost, before he ever spoke to me, and it freaked her out. She had asked a number of times since then if I'd seen him again, and I'd been evasive.

"Let's get back, okay? I need to release the hound for a pee, and make some plans for my research. I promise to bring you in as much as I can, once I know it's safe." She put the car in gear and drove us back to the parking lot behind the building that houses SmartPig, but she was quiet, and looked at me suspiciously the whole time, and gave me an intense stare when I walked her over to her car. She knew that I hadn't spoken to anyone about what had actually happened with Cynthia and George and Barry and Justin and Hope and I last September; I had related a PG-13 version of the events to Mickey Schwarz in February, when he came up for the tail-end of the Winter Carnival in Saranac Lake. (*I had helped to bail him out of some trouble in January, and as a consequence, he needed to be told something about what it is that I do*). Dorothy and I made a dinner date for Wednesday at the better of the two Chinese places in town (*with the caveat that I might miss it if things got busy that quickly*), and went our separate ways, me to Hope, and she to Lisa, her wife.

I went upstairs to fetch Hope for a brief walk, and then put together an abbreviated camping kit for an overnight with Hope. I wanted a night outside to think about what I had learned and guessed during the course of the day, along with what gaps there were, and how I planned to fill them in the coming days and weeks. The very end of Floodwood Road has some nice wooded campsites for car-camping, and is civilized enough for the 993, without having many people head out that way (*most stop at the put in for the paddle trips on either Floodwood or Long Ponds, so Hope and I would likely have the peace and quiet we both enjoyed*). I brought my hammock and sleeping bag, choosing not to bring a tarp (*it looked to be rain-free for the next few days*), and a fleece blanket in case Hope chose to sleep on the ground (*she normally likes to sleep on top of me in the hammock, which I like too, since I worry less about her wandering off or being dragged off by coyotes when she's up with me*). A 2.5 gallon jug of water from Kinney's meant that I could skip lugging and filtering water from a nearby pond, and I brought along some no-cook food for both of us (*'Taste of the Wild' kibble for Hope, and what Dot called 'Tyler Kibble' for me: my proprietary mix of almonds, tiny hunks of venison jerky, dark chocolate M&Ms, dried blueberries and mango pieces*); I bought a vacuum-sealer this spring, and had a ready supply of 1-cup servings of both kinds of kibble, so

I threw three of each into a duffel. My Kobo e-reader (*it was new and light and cheap, and I was trying it out, comparing it to the Kindle Fire*), and a small stuffsack filled with other essentials (*TP, lighter, knife, headlamp, SPOT beacon, tiny first-aid kit, and a fews lengths of paracord and amsteel*) rounded out the kit.

I didn't know how Mike Crocker would feel about me taking his Porsche camping with my shelter-dog as co-pilot, but I assumed, as always, that it is better to ask forgiveness than for permission (*although in point of fact, I planned to do neither*).

The base of Floodwood Mountain, 7/15/2013, 12:49 a.m.

Hope loved our new car. Something about the sound or smell or being closer to the road invigorated her, and she kept her head on a swivel throughout the whole drive. I stopped at Donnelly's for a pair of cones (*Chocolate/Vanilla twist, which people insist will do horrible things to my dog, but I trust Hope's judgment and we ignore those people*). The car felt sleek and light after years of driving the Honda Element, which, to be fair, is like a toaster on wheels, and I made the drive out to the gate at the publicly accessible end of Floodwood Road in one third less time than it normally takes. The Porsche felt low and wide and nimble; four-wheel drive and grabby tires and Adirondack roads topped with pea-gravel instead of smooth blacktop made for a noisy ride, but the trade-off was that it felt as though the 993 was rolling along a set of invisible rails designed by my mind and hands moment by moment. We pulled off the side of the road eventually, up near Floodwood Mountain. I grabbed the overnight kit (*I bought Hope a dog pack last year, after she came to live with me, but she refused to walk when I put it on, so I carry her camping gear as well as my own*), and headed in a mostly southerly direction towards the mountain.

Hope was happy to get out of SmartPig and Saranac Lake, and spent the first ten minutes of the walk ranging far ahead and behind and to both sides in search of squirrels/birds/monsters/food, coming back to check on me every minute or two before running off again … tongue hanging out, tail wagging, eyes bright. I was glad to see her so happy and … doggy; the winter had been tough and long for her. She didn't like camping in the cold (*as I do*), and her joints all bothered her, so she spent most of the winter on the couch, on a heated dog-bed that I bought for her, going for sleepovers with Dorothy whenever I went out for more than one night. She deserved to be happy, after having endured a tough life before we met.

I'd spent the spring and early part of the summer exploring new sections of the Adirondack Park with Hope, modifying my trip parameters/goals to fit an aging beagle mix. There are a huge number of places to get lost for a while with a dog who hates people and leashes and steep rocky trails, and this chunk of perfection at the end of the Floodwood road was one of them. I was happy to be walking with Hope and a backpack and not to feel/hear/smell another human within miles. This might be an indoor kind of project, and I wanted to enjoy the time with Hope in the woods, since it might be a week or two before we could do it again.

We set up camp literally in the shadow of Floodwood Mountain, next to a babbling brook that would provide more background noise than water for us. Hope loves to camp, but feels that it is her duty to investigate and report every sound in the nighttime forest (*which is a lot of sounds*); the brook, in combination with her failing ears, would allow both of us to get some sleep. I hung my hammock, laid out her blanket underneath it, got out our bags of kibble and my Kobo, and settled down on the ground, leaning against a tree, to read for a few hours. Hope explored the area, drank from the brook, found a perfect stick, and spun the proper number of times before laying down, snugged next to my right thigh.

I had been re-reading my way through some of my favorite authors' early works; enjoying the beginnings of Travis McGee, Matt Scudder, Lucas Davenport, Parker, Nero Wolfe, Jack Reacher, along with some others. I remembered the books from having read them earlier, of course, but the pictures the authors painted of the characters and storylines were wonderful and comforting to sink into. The patterns of words/actions/interactions provided a suitable framework for my forebrain while I let the less conscious bits in the back of my head pore over the events of, and information gleaned during the day, in the hope that by morning I would find/see the way to advance with my research and investigation. I could feel the beginnings of thoughts about how I would proceed, the shapes, but not specific details, which was good enough for a start, so I went to bed at 8:32. Hope jumped up to join me seven minutes later, and we were both asleep by a quarter to nine.

"It's nothing, Tyler. A branch broke off a tree about 100 yards up the hill from us, and crashed into stuff on its way down," Ghost-Barry said, from a spot about 30 feet to my left. Although it was pitch black, my recall of the area, and a triangulation of his voice placed him sitting on the big boulder by the little creek.

Hope was growling at the woods from the safety of my sleeping bag; she had pulled the bag open and climbed down into it when the evening cooled off a bit beyond her comfort zone. She was invisible, except as an odd lump in my bag that had settled into/onto my lap/groin/stomach. I reached a hand into the bag, and rubbed her ears for a minute, until she went back to sleep.

The wind must have picked up after we went to bed, because I could hear it racing through the treetops, banging branches together. After a minute of feeling the trees and branches above Hope and me, I unzipped my bag all the way, slipped out from beneath her, and found my pack at the foot of the tree the head-end of my hammock was fixed to. I got out the amsteel, basically a strong and lightweight synthetic cordage that I used as a ridgeline when hanging a tarp or hammock sock while camping, and strung it a few feet over the hammock that we had been sleeping in. The amsteel would likely be strong enough to catch and hold a falling branch, if one happened to fall straight down towards us (*not a foolproof plan, but better than nothing*). Hope was in full-on boneless mode when I tried to shift her to climb back into the hammock, so I decided to read for a bit before trying to sleep until morning.

Barry was sitting there, in the dark, watching me read. He wasn't, really, but I believed that he was, and since I only had my sensorium to go on, I had to move forward as if he was. I don't fully understand why my brain is inserting the ghost of Barry into my life, but I have some idea that it is a witch's brew of PTSD from the series of traumatic events last September and my subconscious' inability to play nicely with emotions such as fear and anger. His pattern is to appear during, or just after, periods of noise, surprise, stress, and physical contact.

After the first time, I chose to assume that his presence served me (*and my brain*) some useful purpose; the alternative was that I was simply crazy and/or that he really was/is a ghost (*which is, oddly perhaps, a less appealing possibility to me*). Since I had the time (*and Hope was asleep and wouldn't be freaked out by my talking to a person that she couldn't see or smell*), I decided to try speaking with Barry for a few minutes.

"Barry, you know that you're not really here, don't you?"

"It feels like I'm here, Tyler."

"Do you remember me killing you?"

"Yah, with Justin down near Newcomb. Lights and noise and a long fall down that cold hole in the woods." I shivered a bit here, remembering the long wait I had had, lying on the stone floor of the mine near Tahawus.

"Why are you here, Barry?" I asked, not really hopeful that I'd get a different answer this time (*Einstein had once suggested that this was the definition of insanity, which was not heartening*).

"There must be a reason, but I don't know it, Tyler. If I have to be a ghost, why do I have to haunt you, and not some hottie or a person who lives in a cool place like Hawaii or Disney, instead of a mostly-homeless geek who lives in the woods near where I grew up. How about when we're done doing whatever we're doing, I could go haunt a hottie living in Hawaii?"

"Sounds good to me, Barry, when do you go?" His last response had actually been a bit different from previous ones, but still close enough that I wasn't too/more nervous.

"I dunno, when we're done, I guess." This response seemed promising, but we'd been here before; he didn't know what we needed to finish. He (*or really I, I suppose*) just knew that we had 'stuff' to do before he could/would go. At this point I decided to take off on a new, and hopefully useful, tack.

"I have some ideas about how to proceed with the Crocker investigation ... what do you think?"

"The old Tyler standby of research in the library and online won't help yet. You need the door open a crack first. Remember the 'Informal excoriation' that you talked with the old lady about? You should try some of that?"

"Informational Echolocation?" I find it slightly off-putting that my brain chooses for Barry to occasionally stumble on big words (*as the original/actual Barry did*).

"Yah, that. It worked well with George, almost too well. You got in touch, and his reaction (*over-reaction, really*) let you know that you were right about him. You could try the same thing here."

"What you're suggesting is that I make some waves/noise/fuss about finding Dee Crocker, or finding out about her disappearance, and that if people get back in touch, regardless of what they have for me, it could help direct my further research."

"I guess. How would you do it?" Since he lived inside my head when I wasn't hallucinating him in the real world, and he didn't know, I must not know, so I thought about it for a bit.

"There is an Upper Saranac Lake Association (USLA); I could get in touch with them online and otherwise, and ask for pictures or for interviews with people who were around during the summer season of 1958. It would probably be better not to mention Dee Crocker at first, unless I have to, to improve the quality of signal return."

"Huh?"

"Nevermind, Barry. While that's cooking though, I need to do something else, something more ... got it. The

Adirondack Museum in Blue Mountain Lake (*I say it this way these days to avoid people confusing it with the Wild Center, another museum in the Adirondacks, but a natural history museum, and as such less likely to be useful with research into a girl missing for 54.85 years*). I got an email 13 months ago talking about their new program to digitize their massive collection of photos."

"I remember going down there with my dad when I was a kid, and looking at those conveyor-belts of black and white pictures and postcards, it was like looking back in time; like a time machine." Sometimes, the Barry construct surprised me, especially when its use of language or figurative language differed from mine. My assumption is that, based on our few conversations, my brain took a snapshot of his speech-patterns, and tried to mimic them for me ... it seemed like a lot of effort for my PTSD to go to, but who knows.

"I'll need a picture of Dee Crocker; I can't believe that I left without one yesterday."

"You couldn't wait to beat feet with that old guy's sweet ride," Barry pointed out.

I was starting to feel tired again, so climbed back up into the hammock, lifting Hope up and out and then back into the bag, on top of me; she pretended not to wake up, but snaked a tongue out with unerring accuracy when my nose went by hers. I was satisfied with the progress that we (*me really, but from two slightly different perspectives*) had made. I had things to do tomorrow, and once they were in motion, I anticipated some returns from the noise that I was making.

"Remember," Barry said, from deeper in the woods, as I settled down into the warm bag, "it was when things started moving last year that you almost died, and ended up having to kill me; so by all means push, Tyler, but be ready for when someone pushes back." Lots of people might have had trouble getting to sleep after a ghost told them that in the dark woods ... but I'm not lots of people.

"… For your crimes, you have been judged."

Camp Topsail, Upper Saranac Lake, 7/15/2013,
11:27 a.m.

I'd slept for a few more hours, until a loon in (*I was reasonably certain, based on my mental triangulation*) West Pine Pond starting making enough noise to rouse Hope. We got up and took care of morning business, ate and drank a quick meal, and quickly climbed the rest of the way up Floodwood Mountain to catch the sunrise over the ponds and lakes and woods to the east of us; I thought it was lovely … Hope was less impressed. We ran back down the hill, picked up our gear from where I'd hidden it off the trail and walked back out to the car. The drive back into Saranac Lake was quiet and quick and fun; I took Forest Home Road for the curves and wildness, although nobody would argue that it was faster.

I shot through the still-sleeping town of Saranac Lake, on the road to Lake Placid to load up on Dunkin Donuts for my morning's work back at SmartPig. By the time I had finished a cruller, two jellies, a maple frosted, and a chocolate glazed, I had a small pile of eye-catching fliers including tearoffs with the number of my newest burner phone and an email address that would bounce to my permanent email account. I had sent similar messages to all of the emails that I could glean from the Upper Saranac Lake Association (USLA) website links/contacts/about/blogs/Facebook branching, asking for information and/or pictures from the summer of 1958 on/around Upper Saranac Lake for a book that I was (*not actually*) working on. I was certain enough that I had sent out enough informational 'squeaks' that I would start getting returns quite quickly (*even though I hadn't used Dee Crocker's name*). I also put out feelers to a contact at the Adirondack Museum (*in Blue Mountain Lake*), asking for a good time to drive down and put in some serious time in their archives.

I fed the beasties in my saltwater tank, took a washcloth-bath in the sink and changed into some clean/presentable clothes. I tossed a few cookies at Hope (*who had gone to sleep on the couch within moments of our walking in*), and headed downstairs to see about car-topping my canoe on the Porsche (*it seemed like a bad idea, with the only possible arguments in its favor being that the canoe was carbon fiber and tough as nails, and the car wasn't mine*).

Hornbeck boats are built in the Adirondacks by Peter Hornbeck, and mine was a Blackjack 12', made entirely from carbon fiber, and weighing a few grams under thirteen pounds. I loved it because it was light and fast and tough, and because I didn't have to treat it gently. I have carried mine for miles along trails in the woods to explore ponds that may never have been paddled before, and also bashed it mercilessly on stretches of the Hudson and Moose rivers. I was anticipating a need that would call on a number of its strengths at some point in the next week or so, when I gently put a foam sleeping pad on the roof of the Porsche, balanced the boat on the roof, ran one strap through both doors, and tied the bow/stern to attachment points under the front and rear bumpers. It was relatively secure, and I was certain it would be fine as long as I kept my speed under control. I also put a lightweight 2-piece paddle into the car.

I drove back out to Upper Saranac Lake, via routes 86 and 186 and 30 this time, to minimize twists and turns, although I felt strangely exposed on this busy series of summer-busy roads. My first stop was at the boat launch at the north end of the lake, to stick up some of my fliers in various places where locals and summer people would likely see them. There were some fishermen running huge and shiny boats into the water who didn't pay any attention to my activities; a number of people walking their dogs along what must be an accustomed route swerved over to look at the fliers I'd stuck up on the board, and followed me with their eyes when I drove down the lake towards my next stop ... something cool and unfriendly/unhappy in their eyes and stances (*except for the golden retrievers, who are always friendly and happy*).

Next, I went past the turn-off for the Crockers, cruising by the wooden sign that Dorothy had classified as 'slightly precious' when we had pulled in the day before (*a hand-painted illustration of a sailboat with a gang of barefoot children rigging a topsail*). I gently followed the curves and hills and dips along the road that followed the contours of the lake, mindful of the canoe on the roof of my borrowed Porsche. The public campground at Fish Creek had a steady flow of people passing in and out of the gates in their Winnebagoes (*a number of bumps down the scale from a great camp, but still a nice way/place to spend the summer*), which slowed the traffic enough that I didn't need to brake to turn left and into Donaldson's once I crossed the bridge.

Donaldson's is a general store and gas station and ice-cream parlor and coffee-shop that serves as an anchor point for much of what goes on midway down the length of Upper Saranac Lake, between the fancy camps at the north end and the fancy camps at the southern end. They own a sizable chunk of waterfront parcels that can be leased for terms ranging from seasonal to 100 years (*another couple of points along the continuum between great camps and my style of Adirondack living, homeless and hanging from a pair of trees most nights*). The feeling was different here than at the north end of the lake. The Porsche and Hornbeck got more notice ... from year-rounders who resented moneyed 'summer people' and from other summer people who weren't driving Porsches and paddling carbon fiber canoes (*nothing new in the Adirondacks, but since I was on the clock, I tried to pay more attention to how people paid attention to me*).

"Lost yer dog, young man?" I heard a voice behind me ask; to get to the bulletin-board, I'd waded through a sea of working locals, not working at the moment (*single-color outfits in blue or green, stained with grease and paint and dirt, drinking coffee and/or smoking away a small chunk of morning with other workmen or handymen or caretakers or contractors before getting back to work, likely at a camp like Topsail*). The tone and phrasing sounded deferential and polite, but Barry's appearance from around the corner of the building led me to suspect otherwise.

"Nope, I'm doing some research, hoping to write a book." I hoped that would be enough to let me walk away, allowing the signs to speak for me (*as I'd always prefer to do ... I dislike initiating conversations about potentially stressful topics with people that I know, much less those I don't know*). Barry shook his head and chuckled ruefully at me.

"Photographs and stories wanted about summer life on Upper Saranac Lake during the late 1950s." The guy who had asked about my dog read off of my flyer, tearing the whole thing down and walking back towards the group he had been with before, picking up his coffee for a swig before continuing.

"Shit. You wanna know about Dee Crocker." Seven words. He said only seven words, but the effect was startling. All of the men in his circle sat up a bit straighter and took a look at me. A few of the younger ones looked back to him with questions in their eyes.

"The girl that disappeared summer of '58. Tough for the family. Tough for everyone working on the lake, too," he said, by way of explanation. There was some aggression or anger underlying the words that seemed to interest Barry and he began to circle closer.

"Yes, I'm interested in Deirdre Crocker. Why? Do you know something that could help me?" I asked.

"Help you what? Upset things between summer and winter people again? Not like you're gonna find the girl. Not after all this time," he replied.

"I'm trying to find out what happened. Why is that a problem for you?" I asked, at which Barry grinned and limbered up his shoulders, as if anticipating a fight or something similar.

"Tyler, you are a dumb ass. The old man was ten seconds from just sitting down and grumbling about you after you left. Now that you challenged him in front of his boys, he's gotta take you on, or he loses," Barry said.

"Lose what?" I asked before remembering that I was facing a group of grumpy handymen, none of whom could see or hear Barry; it actually worked in my favor a bit … the old guy facing me paused a moment, trying to squeeze some relevant meaning out of what I had just said, apparently to him.

"Wha? Huh? Yah, it's a problem for me. Lots of things changed around the time the girl vanished. The way things worked around the lake, at the camps, it all changed. Took years, more, to get right again. Last thing we need is someone fucking around with things now. She's dead. Been dead almost my whole life I reckon. Leave it alone. It's a nice day, go take a ride in your fancy car."

My whole life I've been too emotionally flat for most people, it creeps them out when I don't react to provocation; today though, I could feel something bubbling inside me, and then spilling out of my mouth before I could assess it. "I'm looking for information and photos from the summers at the end of the 1950s, and I'll find them with or without the help of the green chino brigade. Once I get what I need, I'm going to find out what happened to Deirdre Crocker, and I'll post a sign about that up here as well. Problems, old-timer?" I could feel a shake in my voice, as well as in my arms and legs, so I started moving, direction not important. I found myself in front of the bulletin-board again, so I avoided a silly about face by tacking up another of my fliers, a replacement for the one the old man had crumpled in his fist and dropped to the ground by his chair by the time I started back to the 993.

"If anyone's gonna do anything, it'll be in the next three, two, one, you're clear, Tyler," Barry said, when I had passed through the cloud of men sitting quietly/awkwardly in the silent bubble of anger and resentment that we, the old man and I, had created in the circle of tree-stump stools by the bulletin-board at Donaldson's.

I felt stupid and hot and shaky as I drove away, back

northwards and away from the parking lot. I don't get
mad or lose my temper or act stupidly/impulsively in the
heat of the moment ... my moments are generally very
cool. That being said, I had done exactly that back at
Donaldson's, and it upset me. I don't like change or the
unknown in my world, and here was change and
unknown within my person. Feeling a stranger's reactions
to stress was off-putting and scary, it made me question
all of the stuff that I was happy to take for granted about
myself.

I felt the canoe rumble and shake a bit on the roof of
the 993, and noted that I was cruising at 72 miles per
hour; I dropped the speed to a more reasonable (*and
numerologically pleasing*) 47 and continued until the right
hand turnoff for Moss Rock Road. Moss Rock Road is a
looping road that exists only to bring summer people out
to their camps on Upper Saranac Lake, but to get them
there, it must cross about 500 yards of State Forest
Preserve; it was this land in which I was interested.

I pulled the 993 over to the left hand side of the road,
flashers on, and shut it down 100 yards from the first
driveway on that side. Quickly untying the front and back
lines, then the strap securing my Hornbeck canoe to the
Porsche, I lifted the boat up and off the roof and jogged
into the woods with it. I put the canoe down and then
went back for the paddle and other gear I'd stowed in the
car, hiding it all behind a fallen white pine about 30 feet
into the woods (*further than people were likely to look/wander*).
I ran back to 'my' car, rolled the sleeping pad up, stowed
it and the straps in the backseat (*such as it is in a Porsche*)
and drove back to Moss Rock Road to Route 30 again,
turning right and driving back almost exactly a mile to the
Crocker's driveway, and down into Topsail.

The Subaru was already (*still?*) gone from the parking

lot (*the trip that I had mentioned from Jones to Osgood ponds, I wondered?*), and there were no other signs of life as I stepped out of Mike Crocker's beloved car, and soaked in the peace and quiet, a welcome change after my busy morning. I made my way to the main lodge, certain of finding someone there, not caring too much who it was, as my needs were simple in this case. There was a bell hanging at the top of the stairs, outside of the great room, and I rang it to no discernible effect. After ringing again, then knocking on the doorframe, and finally calling out a decent 'hello,' I waited another minute before I walked into the room with the huge dining table, empty; there were a number of juice and hot beverage carafes on the table, glasses and mugs, along with a wood-handled silver bell. I poured myself a glass of cranberry juice, rang the bell, and waited.

A young woman that Mrs. Crocker had referred to as 'Sarah,' who had been helping shuttle food and drinks and plates and bowls in and out during lunch yesterday, came out through the swinging door that led back to the kitchen and pantry and, eventually, to Mrs. Crocker's suite. If she was surprised to see me sitting alone at the table, she didn't show it; I'm pretty sure that no cook's assistant or serving girl ever got a Christmas bonus for exhibiting surprise at what they saw while working for their wealthy employers.

"Yes, Mr. Cunningham? Can I get you something from the kitchen?" she asked.

"Thank you for offering, Sarah." I was somewhat impressed that she remembered my name, but didn't show it (*I generally don't show any emotions, except for those I'm trying to show, and I'm pretty bad at that*). "I've already had breakfast. I was hoping to speak with Anthony, or Mr. Crocker, or Mrs. Crocker, if she's up and receiving visitors."

"Were they expecting you?" she asked, starting to look/sound a little nervous now, at the potentially unwelcome person in the Topsail Main Lodge.

"No, but it's related to what we were talking about yesterday. Kitty's daughter's disappearance." I had guessed that an unguarded sharing of Crocker family business would send her fleeing the room, and I was correct. I had a few minutes of uninterrupted quiet in that spectacular room, sharing it with nobody except for a slightly dusty moosehead whose left glass eye was canted a few degrees upwards. I admired the cool and solid and heavy feeling Stickley table briefly, standing up to get a feel for its heft (*a useless exercise, I have no idea how much it weighed, only that it was more than I could move in the slightest*). In a perfect world, I would have a table such as this to spread my research materials out on when working a case; but that would require expanding my offices into the next space, and Maurice, my landlord, would have to reinforce his building to support the furniture (*even assuming a way could be found to get the table up there ... maybe remove a wall?*).

"Tyler, what do you need?" Anthony strode into the room wearing a similar suit to the previous day's, but a slightly flashier tie. His tone seemed to suggest annoyance at speaking to a minion who has overstepped in some elementary manner.

"Anthony. What do you do for Mrs. Crocker ... for the Crocker family?" I countered.

He was instantly flustered, and checked/adjusted his tie and heavy sterling cufflinks for a moment before getting his tone and stare back into place. "A variety of things, none of which I can discuss with you."

"Yup, you're likely helping Kitty get her affairs in order, as she expects to die soon. You look too young to be handling all of the Crocker assets, so I would bet that you're an entry-to-mid-level cog/wonk/stepinfetchit sent up as a favor to the family and Kitty by the senior partner, who actually does know them, and might have a vacation place over in Placid. Am I close?" His silence was answer enough. I could see/feel that I was being pointlessly/needlessly antagonistic with someone who might end up being a gatekeeper for vital information/resources at some point in my investigation. I was treating Anthony poorly for no reason beyond some excess stress bleeding off from the unpleasantness at Donaldson's, combined with uncomfortable/ unpleasant feelings and associations from dealing with similar legal minions at earlier times in my life (*most particularly in the days and weeks after the death of my parents, while settling their affairs*).

"I don't need anything tricky ... or bank-y. I need a few pictures of Deirdre Crocker that were taken as close to her abduction as possible, during the summer of 1958 if they have them. I would prefer to get at least one of each of the following: a close up full frontal shot of her face, a picture of her sitting, one standing, and a group shot with her and some friends/family; I assume that in most of those pictures she would be dressed in casual clothes, but if possible, I also need one of her in a bathing suit. Do you need to write this down?" I was being mean, but it wouldn't kill him, or me (*he was, after all, a wonk*), and my assumption, based on similar interactions in the past was that he would strive to do what I wanted quickly and with precision, to show me up.

"That won't be necessary, Mr. Cunningham."

"Tyler's fine, Anthony," I said, aiming for faux-graciousness, but probably coming off as sincere ... I stink at tonal inflection and manipulation, but refuse to give up trying. "Insofar as they are able, could you have them identify people that they recognize in the photos, and include that information on a separate sheet of paper?"

"Will you be waiting, or should I have them sent, or bring them around, to your office in Saranac Lake?"

"I'll wait, if it's not too much trouble."

"Mr. Crocker is in with Mrs. Crocker just now; we've been going over some of her 'affairs,' as you say, and they may be ready to take a break and focus on other things. I believe that she has a number of albums in her rooms. Would you like to wait here?"

"All things being equal, I'd love to see the boathouse, although to be fair, I'm not sure that it will help me with what I'm doing for Kitty." He winced each time I used the familiar name, which oddly evoked a desire to keep doing it (*and I'm not normally one to play with my food … again, I blamed the old men at Donaldson's and my past associations with other 'Anthonies'*).

"Certainly … Tyler. I'll look for you there, then." He went back out through the kitchen, and I topped up my cranberry juice, and meandered down towards the boathouse, walking up the stairs that we had skipped in my previous tour.

Within five seconds of walking in, the boathouse was my favorite feature of Camp Topsail (*I momentarily wondered how long it would take them to notice my moving in, permanently*). It was a single big room, 40 feet on a side, with windows on all sides, and comfy looking couches and reading chairs arranged so as to divide the space into a couple of 'rooms'. There were bookshelves lining the walls, between each set of windows on the three sides not facing Upper Saranac Lake. The lakeside was all glass, from waist-height to the ceiling, with a set of French doors in the middle that opened on a porch with clumps of rockers and other chairs and a few low tables, with flower pots filled with flowering red geraniums along the railing. (*I could picture Kitty Crocker sitting at one end in her rocker, watching Dee and her 'beau' enjoying some quiet time together on the dock*). The door came in through the back right corner of the boathouse; there was a huge stone fireplace in the center of the back wall, and the back left corner was devoted to games; board games were on bookshelves and tables, and there was a bumper pool table. The room smelled of dust and old books and pipe smoke and caramel popcorn and old woodsmoke and fine bourbon (*which, like pipe smoke, I don't enjoy myself, but find the scents comforting and home-ifying*). There was no bathroom or running water, but such a minor shortcoming could certainly be overlooked ... at least by me.

I scanned the bookshelves on my way around the room, selected a copy of "Canoeing the Adirondacks with Nessmuk," pushed through the screen doors leading out onto the deck and dropped down into one of the rockers facing Green Island. There was a table waiting for my glass when I reached to put it down. I could hear the drone of motorboats and jet skis off to either side of me, but there was a clear view of water and mountains in front of me (*Boot Bay, Ampersand, Scarface, and MacKenzie ... with Whiteface and some others in the distance*). A pair of loons was working the shallow water in close to shore, fishing and enjoying the summer, as I was. I'd read the book before, so opened to a random spot to begin reading, enjoying the feeling of this old camp around me while I read about Nessmuk, a flatlander who fit himself into the Adirondacks, not the other way around.

A short while later, I could feel someone moving through the space behind me, trying to be quiet, but unable to avoid shifting the old building slightly with each step. I let them sneak up on me, and such was my serenity that ghost-Barry didn't appear with me on the porch, squished into one of the chairs, to lecture me about sitting with my back to an entrance. My money was either on a caretaker I'd seen earlier, or Anthony, with the pictures. A few seconds before he pushed open the door, a breeze wafted the smells of cologne and collar starch and a bit of hospital, not cigarettes and combustion byproducts and deet, so I was able to ruin his surprise just before he delivered.

"Hi, Anthony. Were they able to find what I needed?"

"Yes, they were, and they hope that you'll get these back to them after you're done."

"Let me see what you've got," I said, and dragged the table so that it would be more usefully in front of my chair, moving my now empty juice glass to the side.

He laid down a pile of pictures, which I shuffled into the four basic groups that I had asked for: close-up, sitting, standing, and group. Being a consulting detective, I was able to deduce the common element/girl in each of the pictures, and selected a few from each pile that seemed to best represent her look/pose/poise/manner. As I had suspected, most pictures were mid-to-late 1950s casual, but I made a point of including a picture in fancy dress and one of her in a modest two-piece bathing suit (*which probably seemed racy back then, and Barry's voice in the back of my head categorized as boring*). Anthony passed me a sheet of paper ripped from a yellow legal pad with description of where and when the pictures were taken (*I had noted that some of the photos had this information neatly penciled on the back, some did not*), and identifying some of the people in the pictures, by their clothing or location in the picture.

"I assume that you have an iPhone5, Anthony, or some analogous high-end phone?" I asked.

"Yes, I do. Why do you ask?"

"Can you take the highest quality pictures possible of the pictures I've selected with your phone, and send them to my email address?" I asked, laying the pictures out on the table in the order that his notes had been taken, circling the ones I'd used. Anthony saw what I was doing and took the pictures in order, pausing between each one to tell me which .jpg number went with which description; we had finished inside a minute.

"Thank you very much. I know this is not what you are paid to do, and I have no further need or wish to waste your time Anthony," I said, handing the pictures back to him, and pocketing his notes (*gleaned, I assumed from Mike and Kitty Crocker's memories*).

"I was surprised at how many names they could come up with, given how long a time has passed since those days," Anthony observed, with a friendlier tone in his voice than I'd noted before.

"They've obsessed about that day, and everything that happened directly before it for decades; I bet they remember things from that night in better detail than what they had for lunch two days ago … it's the way human brains work."

"She's been decent, him too; more than they needed to. They've stretched my stay up here to give me some paid vacation time away from Manhattan. If you get stuck on something that I can help with, just ask." He smiled, and I gave him my attempt at a mirroring shaping of facial muscles; it may have worked partially.

"You're from the city originally. They were talking about you last night a bit, that you weren't born here." It is amazing to me that I still hold membership in the club, just because I was born on the island of Manhattan (*St. Lukes Hospital, so barely*), but I do. "Why ... how did you settle up here, doing this?"

"Where were you on 9/11, Anthony?" I asked.

"Stuyvesant. It was a messed up day; I walked home, took me hours."

"Me too ... walked home, I mean. I was on my way to MOMA, when it happened. I walked home, and waited for my parents to call or email. They worked in the WTC, both of them, one in each of the towers." I said this and tried one of my newer, wry and self-deprecating smiles, to show that I was explaining, not looking for pity.

"Anyway, thank you for all of your help, Anthony. Here's my card; it's got my email address and a phone number, in case you or one of the Crockers needs to get in touch with me." I stood up and got out of the chair, knees cracking, replaced the book in the proper place, brought my glass back up to the main lodge, and headed back out again ... without ever having seen Mike or Kitty Crocker (*it occurred to me that although they wanted my services, that actually seeing me might not be desirable/comfortable for either of them, for various reasons*).

I was just pulling out of the Topsail gate when my newest burner-phone rang; it was Frank's number ... that was quick. "Hello, Frank. What can I do for you?" I knew, because he was calling the phone that I'd bought at Kinney's yesterday afternoon, instead of the one I'd been using for an unusually long three months.

"What the hell are you doing poking into the Crocker thing?" He, or someone, had made a leap, because my flier had specifically not mentioned the Crockers, so that I could gauge the signal strength of any response (*from an informational echolocation standpoint*); this therefore represented a strong return, both in terms of specificity and speed (*since I'd only sent the emails/FB stuff this morning, and posted the fliers 107 minutes ago*).

"I can tell you all about it when we meet for lunch at … Mountain Mist, say 1:15, if you can hold out that long," I suggested.

"Sounds good, Tyler. I'll see you then, and don't stick your nose in, anywhere, or piss anybody off between now and then."

"No promises, Frank. You never can tell where a favor for a friend is going to lead." This would likely get him sputtering, as he has been pushing me lately to abandon my consulting detective hobby. He had no idea how rough it had gotten in the past, but he and his wife Meg think of me as a gifted toddler who wandered into a big kids' pickup game, in which I don't entirely understand the rules. They're not entirely wrong, but I have found that I enjoy the game, regardless (*or perhaps because*) of the challenges/risks inherent in playing this sort of game.

"Dammit Tyler …." Frank began.

"I'll see you at Mountain Mist (*a soft ice cream place and hot-dog stand by the water in Saranac Lake, that is loved by locals and summer-people alike*)." I cut in, and then hung up. I made the right hand turn opposite the road leading out to Floodwood, and headed down to the Upper Saranac Lake boat launch, on a hunch. All of the fliers I had put up 109 minutes ago, had been torn down (*little white corners, flags, remained of each*); seeing that they had had such a strong response, I replaced them, and then headed into town, turning onto Forest Home Road just past the fish hatchery in Lake Clear, to take advantage of the twists and turns and car in my hands to do some driving/thinking/meditation.

Mountain Mist, Lake Flower, 7/15/2013, 1:38 p.m.

I took the stairs up to SmartPig two at a time, took a pair of Cokes out of the Coke-fridge, and rubbed Hope's belly while my computer woke up. The pictures that Anthony had taken of Deirdre Crocker were waiting in my email inbox, and, as always, I was astounded at the quality of the pictures a phone can take. I saved the email to a "Topsail" file, opened it on my iPad's gmail app, and saved each of the pictures to my photo gallery (*so that I could access them on the road, and hopefully down at the museum, if my contact got back in touch with me*). By the time I had finished my first Coke, Hope was waiting over by the door, leash in her mouth; I picked up the second Coke, and we went out for a walk.

Frank works for the Saranac Lake Police Department, and for him to have been pulled into this so fast must mean that someone knows/thinks/fears something, but also (*as the sudden appearance of Barry's cottage-sized shadow next to me would seem to indicate*) that things might begin to move in unanticipated directions. Time and again in my investigations I had been surprised that people did not act and react in logical ways to the stimuli that life, or I, threw in their paths. It was something that I struggled with, and tried to overcome through reading (*which was generally my answer to every problem, somewhat like the hammer/nail saying about problem-solving*).

"Feels like the ice might be cracking. Not going out yet, but those deep sounds that tell you something is gonna happen." Barry is normally more straightforward in his manner of speaking, not given to figurative language, so I looked over at him as we walked down the hill on Broadway, towards the river. He moved out of the way of people who couldn't see, or run into, him, probably for my sake.

"Frank Gibson looks like a cartoon cop, all fat and bald and dumb, but he ain't. He's fat and bald, all right, just not dumb. He knows things and people and this place like you never will. Using him right is important. You don't want to blow it, and piss him off. He could shut you down on this, and all your stupid games along with it." Barry considered my investigations games because I didn't normally get paid for them; he might be right, and that might be how/why I like it.

"I'm not interested in using him, Barry. He and Meg are people that I care about," I countered. I was pretending to talk to Hope, to avoid being recognized (*as opposed to being 'taken for'*) crazy, but Hope could tell by my tone that I wasn't speaking to her, and she refused to look back at me, sulking.

"Yah, whatever. You're still gonna ask him about the car accident in the summer of 1957, right? Just do it careful, subtle." If I could smile for real, now would be one of the times that I might ... being schooled on subtlety by the ghost of a dead leg-breaker and murderer, who had to turn sideways to get his shoulders through doors.

I had been planning on reaching out to Frank at some point for some background on Dee's accident, and Barry was right, this might be the perfect chance. It was likely a dead end. It was reasonable to assume that everything would be; Deirdre Crocker had likely been dead for 54.85 years, and just well-hidden, like ...

"Yeah, I was just thinking about that," said Barry. He knows everything that I do, but ordinarily doesn't read my mind during a conversation; it was slightly more unnerving than just talking with a ghost, not much, but a little. "Even money they don't find me and Justin for fifty years, or fuckin' ever. She could be down a hole somewhere, in a foundation, somethin'."

"True, Barry, but assuming/admitting that doesn't give me anything useful to do." I paused here, feeling on the edge of something massive, but it slipped away as Hope began barking.

Hope is generally not a friendly beast, hating men and women and cats and dogs equally (*her life before she showed up at the TLAS was rough, and she has the physical and psychological scarring to prove it*), but she generally keeps her hate to herself, disliking everyone but me quietly and from a distance. The exception to that rule was, strangely, Irish Setters; she hated them with a passion that was ... disturbing. She now was shrieking and pulling and snapping and jumping, trying to get at the setter across the street from us, walking up, and into, the little park in the middle of town; the worst thing was that the setter couldn't have been less interested (*much less scared*). It glanced our way once, and just kept going, completely bored by Hope's slavering animosity. By the time we'd gotten far enough away from each other for Hope to rationalize calming down (*with me assuring her that she had scared the big nasty dog off*), Barry had vanished, taking with him the intuitive leap that I had been on the verge of making a minute earlier. We walked down to the firehouse, I waved at Smokey, the Dalmatian who lives at the firehouse, sleeping on the couch that backed up to the big picture window upstairs (*Hope hated Smokey, but not enough to bark or even growl, just the generic hate that everyone not me or Dorothy evoked in her*); then we turned around and headed home via Olive, Sumner, and Dorsey streets, to mix things up a bit (*and hopefully avoid the Irish Setter on our way home*).

I took Hope back and inhaled a few more Cokes and three cans of vienna sausages, giving Hope the juice and one 'sausage' from each can. Dot would be furious if she saw me giving Hope the cans (*she worried that Hope would cut her tongue on the edges*), but Hope liked it better that way, and was always careful, almost delicate, in cleaning out the cans.

By that time, I needed to head out for my date with Frank at Mountain Mist, and Hope was exhausted. I rubbed her belly, told her that she was a brave and good dog, and that I loved her, and went to see Frank.

I got there seven minutes early, pulling in to park at Fogarty's Marina (*leaving the parking spots right in front of Mountain Mist for the summer people*) and wasn't surprised to see Frank sitting on the hood of his cruiser, waiting for my Element to pull into the lot. I climbed up and out of the Porsche and saw Frank do an actual double-take as he finally noticed me.

"Tyler, tell me you didn't steal Mike Crocker's toy," he said with a smile on his mouth, and in his voice, but missing from his eyes.

"Nope, Mrs. Crocker arranged for me to borrow it while I'm checking something out for her." Since he already knew, there was no point in pretending. He knew a bit about how I worked my consulting detective gig, and guessed a good deal more; while he didn't/couldn't approve, he thought/believed that I did more good than harm (*a belief which I tried to maintain in him, although I didn't always believe it myself*).

"It sure beats that cargo container you normally drive. Watch yourself going through Tupper. They like a Porsche," he said with a smile. Tupper Lake, the westernmost of the Tri-Lakes towns, was famous for speed traps. I had been pulled over, but not ticketed, for 37 mph in a 35 mph zone; at first I had assumed that the officer was joking, but he was totally serious, and if there had been anything in my driving history I'm certain that he would have written the ticket.

"Let's grab some lunch, and then we can talk." Meg, his wife, insists that it's a low blood-sugar thing, but Frank is universally in a better mood after eating, and my assumption was that if I could stuff a big lunch into him, he'd be easier to deal with than he might otherwise be.

I ordered four chili dogs, fries, onion rings, and two large cups of Pepsi (*blech*); he raised his eyes at the last bit, but I told him that I could suffer through inferior cola beverages if it was to support a local business. I paid, and when he raised his eyebrows, I assured him that he could pay for the ice cream we'd get after lunch. We found an empty picnic table, and sat down. We let each other eat in relative quiet, cleared our refuse, and moved to the shady bench a bit away from the water to get a little more privacy for our talk.

"So, the old lady asked you to find her daughter?" he

asked, keeping a straight-face, but just barely.

"She didn't say it, but I got the feeling that she's known Deirdre's been dead for decades, Frank. She just wants to know what happened … maybe why. What if Austin (*his and Meg's son, soon to be entering his senior year at SLHS*) vanished one day, wouldn't you do anything … everything … to find out what happened, even if you couldn't help him … just so you would know?" He nodded.

"Yup, sure. I get that, I really do. And I don't begrudge her, or you looking, but it's going to make waves. It was sort of a big deal a million years ago (*54.85, I thought, but didn't say*), I can remember my dad and granpa talking about it in a general way. A huge fuss in the papers, lots of staties, guys in suits from Albany, even someone from the FBI; it built a wall between locals and summer people, bad feelings that stuck around for years after." I started to see why someone had taken down my fliers.

"So you got a call today from …?" I prompted.

"Dougie Preston, been working as caretaker at one or another of the camps on Upper Saranac since he was fourteen. Good guy. He and my dad went to school together, and I shot my first deer up at his camp near Dexter Lake. He's got nothing against you or the Crockers, but he's worried about someone picking at an old scar."

"I'm not great with metaphors, Frank, but sometimes you need to go back in under old scars to fix an old break or repair the tissue or squeeze out some pus and a splinter. I'm going to talk with a few people, look at some pictures, do some research here and down in Blue Mountain Lake (*the museum was implied, as the rest of Blue Mountain Lake consisted of a wide spot in the road, where it splits to bring people to Raquette Lake and Indian Lake, more tiny towns by big lakes).* See if I can turn anything up. No FBI, no suits from Albany, no newspapers ... just me."

"That's what I thought, and that's what I'll tell old Dougie, but I just wanted to make sure. Take your time, have fun with the car, but try not to piss off either the locals or the summer-folk; things work better when we're all one big happy family *(with rich relatives from out of town, I added, to myself, who pay for schools and police departments)."*

"Speaking of that *(we weren't, but it was close)*, there is one thing that I could use your help on. Just the one, I promise." I looked at him. The truth was that he owed me, from the big mess of last year; it had ended with me shot, and him getting a commendation *(although the two were not directly related).* I didn't want/plan to call it in *(as I might need him on something bigger or trickier at some point in the future)*, but I could see that I wouldn't need to.

"What?" he asked.

"Deirdre Crocker was in a car accident somewhere out near the Wawbeek *(it was gone now, but that wouldn't matter to locals giving directions for another 30 years)* with another young girl at some point during the Woodsmen's Days in the summer of 1957. I'd like to get as much about the accident and the other girl as you can find without making you uncomfortable."

"Easy. Done. I can probably have it for you in a day, two if I have to dig. Now, black-raspberry and vanilla twist is yours, right? A small?"

"Large, you cheapskate, and make it a dip-top just for trying to skate on your end of the lunch."

We ate our cones down by the water, watching boats/boaters paddle and motor by, and eventually sharing bits of cone with the ducks who summered at Mountain Mist. A serious-looking mother in capris pants and fancy shoes gave us disapproving glares (*I know that it's not nutritious fare for the ducks, but they really like the cones, and I enjoy watching ducks race around after them*), even Frank in his uniform; he mumbled a low "Sorry Ma'am" and tromped back to his cruiser, waving at me over his shoulder as he climbed in.

I was feeling great about the lunch and talk and ducks until I saw Barry waiting for me over by the Porsche. The quacky distractions must have dulled my perceptions, and now I would have to figure out what was bothering Barry/me.

Green Island, Upper Saranac Lake, 7/15/2013, 7:16 p.m.

"It's not gonna work Tyler, so don't you even fucking try," Barry said, apparently reading my mind.

"What's not going to work? Finding Dee Crocker, switching Hope's dog food to the senior formula, finally getting behind the scenes at the museum in Blue Mountain Lake for some research, fitting more Cokes in the Coke-fridge using the new stacking plan I dreamt of last night ... what?"

"Driving away before we talk. If you get in this silly car, I'll have to try and get in also, and it will ruin the illusion. We both know that I could never fit in a size-two like that car. So I suggest that you lean on the hood for a minute and listen before you knock off for the day; yes, I know you're planning on bandit camping on the lake, so you can get a feel for all'a the big camps near the Crockers."

"Great camps, Barry, they call them great camps; and that's working, by the way."

"Yah. Anyway, hold your hand up by your ear so that guy behind you doesn't have you carted off to Arkham." I had wondered about this reference the first few times Barry used it in this context, and eventually decided two things: that he must have mentioned it in one of our few actual conversations, and that he was referring to the DC comic universe rather than H.P. Lovecraft's stories. I held my hand up though, mimicking a cell-phone conversation (*hopefully well enough that nobody would notice that I didn't have a phone in my hand*).

"Your date with Deputy Dawg seemed to go well, but it sounds like he's gonna blow what little cover you left yourself on those fliers when he talks with his pappy's friend about you. You're not as low profile around here as you once were, Tyler. People know who you are, and they know what you do. Not exactly, but everyone in the Tri-Lakes is related or dated (*that sounded like a rehearsed saying, but it was also mostly true*), and you've helped and pissed off enough folks that people know. Gibson will tell 'Dougie' (*said with a smirk, which is a facial expression that I haven't bothered trying to learn/mimic yet*), and he'll tell everyone he knows with thumbs inside of an hour. Those old-timers, caretakers and guides, they're the worst gossips on the planet."

"So ... at this point there's nothing productive I can do about Frank or 'Dougie,' and I'm not interested in not following through with this, so where does that leave me/us?"

"Exactly where you were a couple of minutes ago, but maybe a bit smarter and better prepared. That spiderweb camping (*Barry enjoys mocking my hammock-camping*) you like is prolly a good idea, but sleep somewhere new every night, and don't be seen going there if you can help it. You're exposed and trapped when you go to your office, or home, or whatever the fuck it is; the door-bar is good, but I coulda gotten in through that, either talking or with my boot. What you need is some portable form of weapon that can even the playing field between a puny guy like you, and any hoods that want to stop you pokin' your nose where you shouldn't; if only there was something like that so regular, decent folk could get to defend themselves from guys like me and Justin."

"No guns!" I said, too loudly for my faux cellphone conversation, and I could feel attention shift towards me for a second.

Barry smiled at me and said, "No Capes!" He had been a fan of "The Incredibles," and liked to quote it at me from time to time (*I'd been forced to watch it one night with Dot and Lisa last fall, and when the phrase came up one time, I paled ... so now he quoted it whenever possible*).

"I think you're whacked, not wanting a gun. You never would have gotten the drop on me and Justin last year without one, and we'da dropped you in that fuckin' pit in the woods, instead of the other way around; but you're the one who can touch and buy stuff, so you win. I still think you should get something to protect yourself, though; just sayin' is all."

"I hear you," I replied; and I did. I never wanted to own a gun, or shoot someone with a gun (*again*). But the truth is that my investigations often make people angry, and they're usually angry at me (*which isn't fair/just/right no matter how you look at it, because I don't start people's problems, I just happen to be good at sorting problems out*). While I didn't want to shoot/kill anyone, I also didn't want anyone to shoot/kill me, which presented a challenge: how to balance risk and protection in a manner that kept me out of the hospital/morgue and also out of jail (*for weapons charges, the state of New York has strong feelings about firearms and other lethal devices*).

"I've got a few ideas to bolster the door-bar, and help out when I'm on the road or camping also. Thanks, Barry," I said, and closed my fake cell phone, thus ending my real conversation with the ghost of a man I'd killed 10 months earlier (*the curse, 'may you live in interesting times' is attributed to the Chinese, although I've been unable to verify its origins when, over the years, my life has been 'interesting' enough to warrant giving the curse some thought*).

Barry gave me a desultory 'yah' and a wave over his shoulder as he wandered back towards the waterfront, muttering something about hot waterskiers, and I drove back into town, parking behind what I thought of as the SmartPig Building (*although it housed other people and businesses as well*), and walked up and into my own personal batcave.

Hope seemed happy to see me, but gave lots of sniffs and judging looks around my hands and face and shorts; she could smell my lunch and was jealous. Hope and I met under adverse conditions made manageable by shared donuts and jerky and canned beef stew and ice cream; her love of junk food is an integral part, possibly a cornerstone, of our relationship, and she sulks when I indulge without her. I managed to talk her out of a snit with the offer of a walk, sweetened with a slice of Velveeta cheese before we headed out; the combination was apparently irresistible, and we were friends again. I took a nearly freezing Coke from the Coke-fridge, scratched Hope's butt, and stepped lightly down the stairs after her stiff and slow thumping steps.

Walking down the (*thankfully Irish Setter free*) street, I got a few ideas for death/injury/crime/jail preventative methods of making myself a bit safer if things took a violent or angry or aggressive turn. I didn't think that they would, but neither had I thought that the previous year, until I was already neck deep in trouble; so I decided to make the small investment in time and money, and hoped that I would feel foolish about it later.

Hope pulled at my arm, intent of getting to the dead sunfish that someone had left by the water as we walked through Riverside Park towards the boat launch, drew me back, reluctantly, to her. It didn't make sense to me that someone would/could hurt my ancient and gassy beagle mix, but I tend to underestimate people's capacity to act illogically (*and violently*) in almost any given situation, especially stressful/criminal ones. It would probably be safer for her if she stayed with Dot and Lisa for a few days, but living with Hope is not always a picnic; she hates the cats in their apartment, and has been known to get between the ladies in bed and then growl at Lisa, wanting Dot all to herself. The real reason for my reticence was twofold I suspected: I didn't want things to get out of hand like they had last year, and I didn't want to be alone. Neither of those were good/logical enough reasons to warrant putting Hope in danger, so after some quality growling at geese, and a quick off-lead swim, we headed back to SmartPig, where I had decided to call Dot and ask about a sleepover for Hope (*at least for a few days*).

Dorothy said that she and Lisa would love to have Hope come and stay for a few days (*an exaggeration, I'm certain*), but hinted during our conversation that she wanted to help me out, especially if it got 'tricky.' It made me feel good that she wanted to help … less alone. It also reinforced my decision to avoid putting her in harm's way, especially before I knew which direction harm/danger/threats might come from this time around.

I packed Hope's bed and toys and bowls and a five-gallon bucket of kibble for her visit. For myself, I grabbed a Bushnell monocular that I like to bring along for scouting paddling/camping options, a gravity-feed water filter which is basically a bag that you hang on a tree and let gravity pull the water through a filter … (*pump water filters are for chumps, I either use the gravity filter or Clorox at 3-4 drops per liter*), a gallon Ziploc bag with Tyler-kibble (*which is enough for 3-4 days, more if I didn't mind going hungry, which I do, so I don't*), and shoved six ice-cold cans of Coke into the stuff-sack … they wouldn't be cold for long, but the lake would keep them cool-ish, and the worst Coke I ever drank was pretty good.

We were in Dorothy and Lisa's little house out near the TLAS, conveniently located for the shelter, but not much else (*beside "The Red Fox," a restaurant that always feels just slightly too fancy to me, but has great fresh bread that they bring out in tiny loaves, throughout your meal if you eat as much, and tip as well, as I do*). "Tyler, promise me you'll give me more to help out with than babysitting Hope. That mess last year was cool; scary, but cool. I know you're nervous about me helping with your stuff, but don't be. I want to help, especially because it's Kitty; her help over the years kept a hundred dogs like Hope alive and fed and warm."

This last made sense to me, so I acquiesced. "If something comes up that you can help with, and I'm reasonably certain that it won't put you and/or Lisa and/or Miss Hope at risk, then I'll get in touch." I bent down to give Hope a kiss, and Dot surprised me with a hug, and whispered into my left ear to be careful. I told her that I would and walked out and away from two of my favorite lifeforms on the planet.

I stopped twice on the way out of town, at Blue Line Sports (*which is the only store for sporting goods in town*) and at Aubuchon Hardware (*which isn't the only, or even the best, hardware store in town, but I'd seen the items I wanted in there a week ago, so I knew they would have them*). I opened one of the Cokes, and downed it while speeding by the hospital facing Lake Colby. I was tempted briefly to buy an ice cream cone at Donnelly's, but was able to resist the pull, knowing that their one flavor (*'you choose the size, we'll choose the flavor'*) was 'nut surprise,' my least favorite in their flavor rotation. I made the turn onto Route 186, and found myself keeping an eye on my rearview mirror. The concept of 'a tail' in the Adirondacks is almost silly, as there is generally only one way to get from anywhere to anywhere else up here; if I picked up a tail, losing it would be quite a chore. At any rate, I didn't see anyone following me, and just in case they were really good, I neglected to use my turn signal when I made the right-hand turn into the boat launch for Follensby Clear Pond (*something that would have disappointed both Mickey and Niko's father, who had taught me to drive ... a skill my father thought useless when living in Manhattan*).

There were some people struggling to get their canoe and gear from an overnight trip out of the water, and into/onto their cars; I offered to help, in the interest of helping to empty the parking lot. Once they rolled cautiously out and onto Route 30, towards Tupper Lake and points west, I crossed the street and ran into the woods before anyone came along the road from either direction. It was somewhat nasty bushwhacking through the woods: buggy and sweaty and scratchy, and the confusion and tangle of dead and down and new and growing trees did their best to pull my backpack (*containing my camping gear and supplies*) from my shoulders. Giving in to my paranoia, and feeling rightly/properly foolish about it at the same time, I stopped every few minutes to listen to the dense woods behind me for anyone following; there wasn't ... it would have been impossible for anything other than a blackfly to move through those woods without making enough noise for me to hear.

I moved west parallel to the road, but staying roughly thirty feet in, and eventually found my canoe and paddle, just where I'd left it. I debated making two trips, and decided that I had no desire to cover this ground any more than was absolutely necessary. I found that I could balance the Hornbeck canoe on my head, and make reasonably good (*not fast, but faster than I had thought*) time towards the lake. In about the same amount of scratches and bug-bites (*a better measurement than time when traversing the deep woods*) as it had taken me to find the canoe, I found the lake ... admittedly a bigger target. I stopped to breathe for a minute, and to definitively kill a deer-fly that had been harassing me inside my canoe-hat for the last few hundred yards, and then climbed into the water.

I paddled along the shore northerly for a bit, and then pulled out, so that I was fifty yards out, which seemed right to maximize my view of the camps and buildings and occupancy levels, while minimizing the notice of people on the docks and boathouses and walking around the camps. One quarter of the camps that I passed seemed occupied only by people working on the buildings in some fashion. I had learned from my conversation with Mike Crocker and with others, over the years, that the great camps always have one or more roofs in need of repair, as well as frequent plumbing and electrical needs, stemming largely from their age and the seasonal nature of their occupancy. Some great camps are jointly owned by a group of the grandchildren and great-grandchildren of the people who originally built the camp; these collectives often rent the camps for much of the summer to support the maintenance and tax costs of owning a piece of Adirondack history. Others, like Topsail, are still held by the patriarch or matriarch of the family, and are often visited by the owners only during the long-preferred month of August (*a part of my back-brain wonders if this will change as climate change continues to rampage across the globe, including this corner of the Park*). I tried to guess which camps were peopled by renters versus owners, doing repairs versus opening camp for the season, and which were some combination; it was interesting to try, but I kept finding myself back in the Topsail boathouse, living the life of people who could/would stay for a month or more, like the Crockers.

I paddled north to the top of the lake, around the bay with the boat launch and the one next to it, until I ran out of camps. At this point, I began to paddle in a southwest direction across a big open section of the lake, that would take me between Dry and Goose islands (*both private, which for no logical reason, bothers me more than landlocked private property … jealousy maybe*), and bringing me to Green Island, where I would be camping tonight.

Green Island is shaped like a piece of candy corn, laying on its side, with the pointier end facing towards the western shore (*where most of the camps are*). The DEC campsite was on the eastern end of the island, with a nice protected beach and cove for landing and launching, flat spaces for plenty of tents, and nice rocky faces for sitting and sunning (*if that's the sort of relationship that you have with the sun. I avoid it like it's trying to kill me, because it is*). I had seen upon launching from my hidden spot in the woods that this spot was occupied, which didn't matter to me as I was planning on stealth camping anyway. I paddled around the north side of the island to the pointy tip, checked to make sure that the wooden rib-bones of the old sunken rowboat were still there (*they were/are*), and made for shore. There's a nice spot to picnic at this end of the island, but that was not my goal. As soon as my feet were on rock I chucked my pack up into the woods, and then followed with my canoe and paddle. The Hornbeck Blackjack is dark grey in color and once I was fifty feet up from the shore, I was certain that nobody would see it. I went back for my pack and headed up to the high point of Green Island. The whole south side of the island has cliffs, and at some point in time, people must have snuck in and cleared a spot at the top of one of them and made a bench of logs and this was my chosen spot for the night.

Nobody knew where I was at the moment (*the parking spot of the Porsche suggested that I was on Follensby Clear Pond, which had dozens of legal campsites ... not to mention the stealth sites that I often used*); Hope and Dorothy were safe from risks that I couldn't see or even imagine (*although Barry could*); I had a couple of irons in the fire (*and was hopeful that both Frank and my contact at the Adirondack Museum, Terry, would open some informational doors for me by tomorrow or the next day*); and I was getting to camp while arguably working at the same time ... life was pretty good. From my spot up in the highlands of Green Island, I could see all of the camps along the western shore of Upper Saranac, some from my hammock through the tree with my 10X monocular, others with a short walk across the island to another rocky highpoint.

I reached into my pack and got my iPad, which (*intentionally or not*) Apple sized perfectly to fit in a gallon sized ziplock baggie (*the freezer-weight bag, in combination with a swaddling of fleece, rendered it ready for camping and rough handling*). I leaned back into the hug of my hammock, and really looked at the pictures of Deirdre Crocker for the first time. Human men and women would notice her beauty and poise and confidence; the pictures said that with my initial flip-through ... she looked symmetrical and unmarred by scars/blemishes, and healthy and happy and as though her appearance mattered to her (*she didn't evoke any response in me beyond that, which is par for the course with me*). To prep for this session, I had done some background research into clothing and jewelry in the late 1950s. My research and interpretation of the pictures on my iPad indicated that the nice clothes and jewelry, were slightly nicer and more expensive and fashion-forward than her peers in the pictures. Indeed, looking at the group pictures more closely on a third time through the 'folder,' focusing on postures and facial expressions (*admittedly not my strong suit, but I'm an eager student*) and relative proximities, she could arguably be said to be the alpha female in her group, any group that she established herself in. If I were to look at similar pictures from my past, I would have always been the one taking the picture, or off in a corner facing the wrong way, or at the extreme edge of a back row in organized pictures ... outcasts understand social structure and hierarchies, even if we don't understand the forces that shape them very well.

I had by now memorized the features of Deirdre and her contemporaries in the other pictures, and felt confident of being able to identify them in other settings/scenes, which had been my original point in acquiring them, so I now turned my attention to the camps that I could see from my hammock. One had workmen and owners/renters at it (*each party scrupulously avoiding the other*) and the other had just workmen, seemingly occupied with tasks all over the camp (*possibly getting it ready for the arrival of the owners*). The camps were similar in layout to Topsail, many buildings spread out facing the water and in orbit around a main lodge; by changing my angle of observation slightly, I could see between the front row to some of the support and infrastructure buildings beyond. It initially struck me as odd that workmen had parked their trucks in back, in the huge hangar/garage in one camp, while in the other, the trucks were all over the place. Eventually it clicked that the trucks were out of site in the camp inhabited by owners/renters, and out in plain sight in the otherwise empty camp.

I rolled out of my Grand Trunk hammock (*which is lighter/smaller than my Hennessy mostly due to the lack of insect screening ... I could get away with it as we were enjoying a shockingly light summer in terms of biting insects*), shoveled in a few mouthfuls of Tyler-Kibble, emptied and then refilled my Nalgene container from the hanging filter, and headed across the island to spy on some other camps for a bit. The other camps that I could see seemed much the same as the first two, although only one of six had trucks out and working in the camp (*I threw this back into the hopper at the back of my head, hoping that information gained further down the road would relate to it in some meaningful way*). Having put in a fun day of nearly no work, I stealthed my way back to camp, listening to the people camping less than 200 yards from me, enjoying the feeling of being hidden, found a good tree to pee against, and got ready for some quality hammock-time.

I went to sleep after loading up on more kibble and water, and reading with my iPad (*which allowed me to avoid using a headlamp, bonus stealth points!*) and didn't wake up until the first light was creeping into the sky at nearly five the next morning (*significantly longer than my lifelong habit of cat naps, but longer periods of sleep had been the norm in the last year*).

Follensby Clear Pond boat launch, Lake Clear,
7/16/2013, 9:48 a.m.

By the time I had eaten some breakfast (*which was the same as dinner in this case, kibble and water*), and broken camp, there was light slanting across the water of the lake from the east, between the mountains. I made my way back down to my canoe and the shore as quietly as possible, and slipped into the water, quiet as the wisps of fog rising from the warm lake in this cold morning. I paddled back across to the spot I'd entered the lake from the day before, unseen except by a pair of loons working the shallows in the first morning light. I pulled my boat up into the woods, far enough back into the State Forest Preserve land to be invisible from the water, and walked out to Moss Rock Road again. From there I walked down to the boat launch for Follensby Clear Pond, where I'd left Mike Crocker's car. I decided that I had been too paranoid the previous afternoon, when walking through the heavy brush and downed trees the entire way *(apparently there are shades of useful paranoia, and then a line where it is just too much)*; I was surprised to see one of the Adirondack Watershed Institute Stewardship Program interns already at work so early in the morning.

The Adirondack Watershed Institute Stewardship Program, run by Paul Smith's College, places interns at boat launches and on the top of St. Regis Mountain to track usage numbers, inform the public about invasive species, track and map loon nesting, and assist with trail maintenance. I often run into them and they're always friendly and helpful. I asked the young lady about her early start, and she seemed surprised to see me *(of course, most people arrive at her station either by canoe or car, so it made sense that my approach on foot would startle her)*. We talked about the futility and expense of divers harvesting invasive plants from one part of a lake, but not a connected pond and stream system that feeds into it, and the number of people using this launch as opposed to the old launch at Spider Creek ... this launch is easier and nicer and puts you more in the middle of the pond more quickly than the old one, but more than a decade later it's still 'the new launch.'

When I walked back to unlock and throw my stuff into the Porsche, I saw/felt her watching me walk back through the sparsely filled lot, and was a bit suspicious/surprised to see her make a call when I stopped by the 993. The Porsche was bumping its way out of the parking lot a minute later *(the low-slung car had to straddle dips in the road that I just ignored, or didn't even see when driving the Element)*. She returned my wave, but seemed to have her mind on other things, and was messing around with her clipboard and writing stuff down as I pulled out, although when I gave a last look in the rearview before turning left and towards Saranac Lake, it looked as though she was watching again, and speaking into her phone again.

I drove up past all of the great camps that I'd paddled past the day before, only much quicker, and completely unable to see any of the buildings or people, or the secrets they might hold from this side. A beauty strip of trees blocked the camps from the road (*and vice versa*), the trees and space absorbed the sounds and sights that might dispel the illusion of enjoying Adirondack great camp life of 50 or 100 years ago. As I neared the point where I knew the top of the lake was, I entered a series of turns that were both fun and challenging in the Porsche; and, channeling Niko's father as best I could, I accelerated through the turns, rather than braking as my instincts told me to do. When I got through the turns, and was slowing down a bit to cross the golf course (*I worried each time about a retiree intent on his play driving his golf cart straight into the road*), I noticed a beat up white van closing on me, jouncing and bouncing as it came out of the last of the turns that dumped it onto the relative straightaway of the golf-course crossing, and right behind me. The van began flashing, as if for me to pull over and stop.

As soon as I saw it, I pressed the gas to the floor. I reconsidered a half-second later as the 400 plus horsepower that the 993 could deliver pushed me back into my seat. I brought the speed up until I was clearly pulling away from the van, and then considered the road ahead with my built-in mental map. The turn I wanted was less than a mile away, so I tried to open up the distance between the van and I a bit by downshifting and using the gears to help me grab the road with the car's nimble power. I hit the right-turn signal only moments before turning left onto Fish Hatchery Road, then made another left onto a dirt road leading back into the woods, to a series of little ponds. I straddled the potholes and dips and mudholes in the road as best I could, but I heard the bottom scraping a few times.

A part of me had hoped that the van might miss the turn, but it was too easily visible *(as was the speeding Porsche)* and I could see it coming after me; only now I had just four choices, all of them dead ends. As I bumped across the train tracks, I could have turned either left or right down dirt paths that followed the tracks for miles, but even my Element had trouble on these paths, so I went straight. My next choice point was a fork in the road, the left led to Little Green Pond and the right would take me to Little Clear Pond. I had only a split second to think/decide, and picked right, to Little Clear Pond; it was, in my experience, marginally busier, and the road would be easier on the Porsche.

Having decided, I rocketed down the dirt road, way off on the left edge to avoid the biggest dips, but still having a jouncy and noisy ride. Barry was waiting by a pickup at the far right hand end of the parking lot when I jounced in, and I noted that there was nobody loading or unloading boats for a trip. I pulled in by Barry and grabbed a pair of the countermeasures that I'd picked up the previous afternoon; Barry sneered when he saw them.

"Tyler, what's with the junior-varsity solutions buddy? Don't you remember last year? How did your shoulder *(where Justin, Barry's partner, had shot me)* feel all last winter in the cold?"

"Shut up Barry, it's possible that I have a broken taillight or a tire going flat, or he needs directions. I don't want to hurt someone who may need my help, or be trying to help me." This noble line of reasoning died in my throat as a trickle, as the van parked sideways across the entrance to the parking lot, and the driver got out, wearing a balaclava that hid his face entirely.

"You were saying?" Barry said. "I bet you wish that you'd grabbed what was behind door number two now, don't you." As he said that I looked on the floor behind the driver's seat at another of my self-defense ideas/items, and indeed wished that I'd grabbed it.

"Well, this is what we've got, so get ready," I said, to myself really, as Barry had nothing to worry about from this guy alive or dead.

"What did you say, Mr. Cunningham?" said balaclava-guy, who was now about thirty feet from me, and must have heard part of my discussion with Barry. It was not particularly heartening that he knew my name ... it eliminated the possibility of a mistaken identity (*although that had, admittedly, been a long shot even before he opened his mouth*).

"Nothing. What do you want? What can I do for you?" I asked, in a voice that barely betrayed the adrenaline thumping through my heart and brain and lungs ... I felt that every part of me was pulsing/jumping/humming in time with my heart, which was way up over 100 bpm (*I forced myself to stop panting for a few seconds to count and extrapolate ... 132*).

"You're sticking your nose where it doesn't belong. Stirring things up. What you can do for me is leave this shit alone! Forget the Crocker bitch and leave town." I wondered briefly if he was referring to Deirdre or Kitty, but realized that it a) didn't matter much, and b) would just push an angry masked man further if I asked.

"Okay," I said.

"What?" the masked man asked me, clearly ready for some other, perhaps movie-macho answer/repartee.

"Okay. I was doing this as a favor for a friend, but I don't need this. I'm out." I shrugged and half-turned, as if to get in my car, not entirely sure if I meant it ... hoping that I didn't.

"Stop!" he shouted (*argh, I thought to myself, and out of the corner of my eye, I could see Barry smile and nod, either knowingly or approvingly, I couldn't tell*). "The time to get out painlessly was before this morning, before you started asking questions. Now you get a stomping." Barry smirked a bit at this, and pantomimed stomping and grinding something beneath his heel, then shrugged as if it were bush-league in the world of thuggery. The man started towards me, cracking knuckles and shaking out kinks in his arms and shoulders as he closed the distance between us.

I tried to peer down various probability hallways for a better way of getting home without getting hurt, couldn't see one, and so pulled both pins and yelled as loudly as I could, "You'll never take me alive ... GRENADE!!!"

I'm not proud of it, but I was reasonably certain that it would give him pause for a second while he sorted through the shouted and visual input. There were objects bouncing and rolling towards him on the uneven ground, and after years of movies where people sometimes have grenades, he might have even convinced himself that I had thrown a pair of grenades at him. He reversed his progress and stutter-stepped back a few half paces, while his brain chewed on all of the data; that was exactly what I had been waiting/hoping/praying for ... I turned and ran at full speed into the woods and away from him.

Of course they weren't grenades, I got them at Aubuchon Hardware (*not my shady underground ex-military contacts, which parenthetically, since these are parentheses, I wish that I had ... not for grenades, but because it'd be cool*). They were a pair of personal safety alarms, rated to scream in alternating tones and pitches at 130 decibels; I heard them begin to shriek before I made it into the woods. I had been expecting the noise, and it still came close to scrambling my thoughts (*which were simply 'run'*); I was betting that even if he had figured that they weren't the exploding type of grenades, he was trying to fit his brain around the new information involved with sound grenades. There were people around somewhere … at the campsites ringing Little Green Pond, at the hatchery, hiking the trails all around us … somewhere. He was a man in a mask, with his van blocking a parking lot; he had new problems besides me, and I was willing to bet that he wouldn't try to catch me, since I had to have at least a five second head start, was quick and wiry (*compared to his strong and brawny, which is awesome for stomping, but not so good for running people down in dense woods*), and wasn't doing anything wrong in the eyes of anyone who we/I happened to run into.

Just to be on the safe side, I kept running and dodging my way through the woods for a few hundred yards before I stopped. By then he had silenced the noise-grenades (*by stomping I was willing to bet*), and it was quiet enough in the woods so that I would have heard his sounds of pursuit, if there were any to hear … there weren't. I thought that I could hear the sound of glass breaking, then a car starting and eventually receding. I (*my aching lungs and wobbly legs, really*) decided to wait in hiding for a few minutes before heading back to the parking lot.

"Boy, Tyler, that was really impressive how you ran away like that. Really taught him a lesson he's not likely to forget. Back in the 'Sand Box,' we called that 'retreating with extreme prejudice.' Hah!" I doubted that Barry had served in the military, but kept it to myself, as I didn't feel like trying to score points off of my imaginary friend just then.

"Barry, shut up." He did, although he was still chuckling to himself every few seconds. "Did I get out of that shut-ended situation without getting 'stomped'? Was I able to avoid shooting anyone? Do I live to fight another day? I'm going to consider this a win, and if it will make you happier, I'll go with the heavier countermeasures next time ... if there's a next time."

"There will be. Mask-boy came ready to play. So are we going to go back and ask the lake-greeter about who she called?" I had gotten there as soon as the van came into my field of vision, so it only made sense that Barry had as well.

"Yup, but I bet either of us can think of ways that it was done that won't leave a trail back to him. Still though, better to try and fail, than to not try, and miss something easy."

I walked slowly back, as quietly as I could manage (*which honestly, was pretty quiet ... what I lack in brave and strong, I make up for in quick and quiet*). I backtracked the dirt road a bit, looking for the van or the guy, and could see neither; I snuck up on the parking lot, and sat watching it for twenty minutes ... nothing. I broke cover and made cautiously for the Porsche, ready to run again if needed (*or even if need was hinted at*); it wasn't.

The man and van were gone from the pond (*the fact that this sounded like the beginning of a nursery rhyme didn't make it any less gratifying or satisfying ... or confusing*). Playing the scene back in my head, I could now see the faded printing on the side of the van; it had been one of the junkers from Hickok's Boat Livery, roughly 1.6 miles away. His vans schlepp people renting his boats all over the area, and are 'borrowed' by locals wishing to prank Hickok, because of his well-known policy for keeping keys in the machines. They're so run down and well-known in the area, that nobody would worry too seriously if one went missing for a couple of hours during some summer day; when locals see the vans left somewhere, they simply call Hickok's and tell them where to pick it up. My assumption was that following up on the van was a non-starter, but I made a mental note to get there sometime soon, today if possible, to speak with whoever had been around.

He had busted out the Porsche's driver's side window, in anger/frustration/release, the door was unlocked, so he hadn't needed to break the glass. I swept the irregular cubes of safety glass out of the car, debated (*and nearly as quickly dismissed the idea of*) picking up all of the pieces, rationalizing that they were chemically inert and not sharp enough to hurt anyone/anything, and that it would be a pain to harvest them all from the grassy parking lot ground; it worked, I left.

I drove back to the Follensby Clear Pond boat launch, just to be thorough, and checked with the Watershed Steward; she looked stormy/nervous when I drove back in, parked, and walked over in her direction. She was just finishing a canned speech about nesting loons and respecting wildlife with a boatload of overnight paddlers who looked excited to be heading out; I waited off to one side until they had launched, and were 100 yards out, heading north, to the wild end of Follensby Clear Pond.

"Hello, again," I said, using my #2 smile (*friendly/gentle/clueless*).

"Hi. I bet you're here because the owner of the SUV who dinged your bumper caught up with you?" She asked.

"Yes, he did. Thanks for connecting us. How did he let you know?" I think that I had the shape of it now, but I wanted to see the whole thing … to see if he was smart, or just clever.

"He must have hit your car last night after I'd gone. There was an envelope waiting for me in the Watershed Stewardship information kiosk, with a description of your car, his cellphone number, a request to call if I saw you, so that he could talk to you and give you his insurance information, and a 50 dollar bill." She might have been a little more amazed if he had left her a baby unicorn instead of the 50, but just a little.

"Ah, okay," I said, just to keep her going.

"So when I saw you go to your car this morning, I called the number, he said that he was close, and would try to catch you. I'm glad it worked out." She seemed nervous/uncomfortable, maybe that she had taken the 50.

"It worked out as well as it could have," I said, truthfully ... he didn't stomp me, and I didn't kill him.

He was more than clever, he was smart ... I had some work ahead of me, because I wanted not only to figure him out, but I needed to do that while preventing him from catching up with me again. The alarm trick wouldn't work again, I didn't want to up the ante if it could be avoided, and I certainly didn't want him to stomp me (*besides which, I was reasonably certain that he had guessed that I wasn't going to just quit my investigation*). I thanked the steward again, hopped in the car, and headed towards the village of Tupper Lake to talk with Bill (*the mechanic who had gotten Mike Crocker's 993 up and running so nicely*) about replacing the driver's side window, and not telling the car's owner about it.

SmartPig, Saranac Lake, 7/16/2013, 1:27 p.m.

Bill laughed when I explained how I had clumsily punched out the driver's side window. He promised to get a new one here and installed as fast as possible, and that he wouldn't tell Mike Crocker about it. Two years ago, his one true love, a funky looking Australian cattle dog name Moe, had been poisoned; I had investigated, found the culprit and, in an unlikely (*and between you, me, and the written page, fabricated*) coincidence, the poor guy had gone inside for a long time and had many of his assets seized when it was discovered that not only did he like to hurt animals, but he had been building bombs in his basement. I was confident that Bill would be as good as his word.

I was working hard to convince myself that I preferred the wind howling at me through the 'open' driver's side window on the drive back into Saranac Lake, along Route 3, when I once again started to feel things coming together. It was as though various threads were knitting themselves into a fabric that made sense, but when I looked at them too closely, everything came apart again. My back-brain was obviously feeling something but I needed to feed more data in before anything useful would result. As soon as I was close enough to town for my cheap burner cell-phone to find a tower, I called ahead to the good Chinese restaurant (*there are three Chinese restaurants in Saranac Lake nowadays, the bad one, the good one, and the buffet ... which I enjoy, but is only for eating in, which I didn't want to do today*) for some hot/spicy/fatty brain-fuel.

"Hi, I'd like to order for pickup. An order of fried dumplings, a small order of boneless ribs, and a special order with chicken and broccoli and red peppers and garlic and chilies and ginger ... okay? Thanks!" They didn't mind special orders at the good Chinese (*which was part of the reason that they were the good Chinese place*).

I circled my building, the block, and my parking area a few times once I got into the downtown area, looking for the white van or the guy (*which was dumb ... he'd already dumped the van somewhere, and all I'd seen of the guy was someone a bit under six feet and roughly 180 pounds, which was plenty/lots/most of the men in the Adirondacks ... but I did it anyway, and felt a bit better afterwards*). I found a parking spot, hustled up to grab my food while it was still too hot to eat, and took the stairs up to my office as quick as I could. I locked/bolted the door and put the bar into its niche in the floor, and only then did I breath a sigh of relief that had previously been a held breath.

I got my computer up and running and while I did, plugged in my phones (*both burners, but one bought just for the Crocker case, and the other my regular phone, which I would keep for a few months before changing ... an old and odd habit, which just felt right to me, so I stuck with it*) to a charger. Then I hooked each phone up to a little speaker in turn, so that I could listen to my messages without holding the thing to my ear. My Crocker-phone had two messages on it, none were voices that I recognized, both sounded elderly, and each offered that they might have some information/pictures concerning the summer of 1958 on Upper Saranac Lake; one was a landline with an 891 number (*the original Saranac Lake exchange*) and the other was one of the newer cell prefixes. My other cellphone also had two messages: one from Frank Gibson with the information that I had asked for about Deirdre Crocker's car accident in summer 1957; the other was from Terry Winch, my contact at the Adirondack Museum, telling me to come down any day in the next week for my 'little research project.'

I called the first number from my 'echoes,' and it was answered almost immediately by an old man with vague recollections of the summer of 1958, and the assumption (*correct*) that I was asking to find out about Deirdre Crocker. He remembered the furor surrounding her disappearance, and was vaguely angered at his feeling (*probably also correct*) that the response and vigor with which it was investigated and covered by law enforcement and radio/newspapers was more than it would have been for a local girl. He also remembered seeing her and her friend drinking and dancing the summer before at the Woodsmen's Days in Tupper, on the day of the accident he thought (*although he allowed that it could have been another time as well*).

"A high-speed crash and driving drunk is no big deal if you're rich," he said. "I drove by the next day, lot of us did once we heard. That fancy little car was about fifty feet into the woods, had plowed through a young stand of those crappy red pines folks planted after clearing woodlots back then, might have kept going too, but she fetched up against a big boulder, and that was enough to stop her, no matter how fast she was going. Tommy Reegan, who pulled the thing out of the woods a day or so later, said she must have been going 70 miles an hour. And if there was a deer, like she said, she didn't swerve or brake, no marks on the road or grass; she went straight in like she just missed the turn."

"Interesting," I said, although since it wasn't likely related to the disappearance, I wasn't sure that it was, in fact, interesting ... but it's been my experience that people keep talking/sharing/downloading information if you seemed fascinated by what they're saying.

"Sorta, young fella, although you tell me a time when rich people didn't have different rules than the rest of us, and that I'd be interested in. Anyway, since we're talking, let me tell you the other thing I remember from the Woodsmen's Days. She and her friend had been drinking and dancing with various boys, not just fancy rich kids slumming in Tupper neither; some of the guys she danced with still had sawdust in their hair and clothes from competing that day, and some old enough to be her dad. She wasn't teasing, just loved to dance is all. She spun and twirled from one to the next, like a ball of light ... like she was the light, brightening up whatever corner of the room she was in. I never did work up my nerve to ask her, and at this end of my life, if I got any regrets, that's one of 'em. That night, in that sweaty tent, swilling beers with the rest of us, she was a god ... goddess, I guess. This'll sound crazy, coming from an old fart like me, but right at the end, before she left, she climbed up on the bar Brad Rousseau had knocked together that morning from rough-cut lumber and danced ... for all of us ... with all of us. She had a glow, and she knew it then; I think she saw me, back in the corner, and she smiled right at me, and my heart like to burst." I could hear the old man come back through the 54.85 years to the present, and take a deep breath of age and the passage of time, before continuing.

"I helped them search the lake and woods for her later ... after. Her old man musta known someone who knew someone who owed a favor, and they had jets from Plattsburgh down flying low over all the lakes and ponds, making high-speed runs up and down, day after day, hoping the sonic booms would dislodge the body; but it never did come up. We never found her in the woods either, even with dogs. I saw guys from the beer tent, besides me, helping with the hunt; maybe we all loved her a little bit." He stopped, and I thought he had run down, run out of story, but he had one more piece for me.

"What I think, the reason nobody ever found her, was she was a goddess, and her time on Earth was done. So she left, simple as that. Can't think of no other reason. We'd a found her; somebody would'a."

I thanked him awkwardly (*as I do most things involving emotions, and especially love*), and pulled the ripcord on that phone call, but not before he elicited a promise from me to get back in touch with him if my investigations turned up anything about Deirdre Crocker. I promised the old man, although I wasn't sure that I'd be doing him any favors in sharing anything that I might find.

My next call was also picked up as soon as the phone rang, and this person had an old and wheezy and tired voice, offering some pictures they'd found in a box from that year. They had a camp out on Church Pond, and would love to let me see them. I took the address, and we agreed on a meeting time for later that afternoon.

My next call was to Terry Winch, at the Adirondack

Museum, and I asked him if first thing tomorrow morning would be good for him. He allowed, cautiously (*as he always sounds ... about everything*) that that would be good for him, given the way his week was shaping up (*whatever that meant*).

My final call, as I finished off the last of the Chinese food was to Frank Gibson, which went to his voicemail, as it usually does. I tidied things up from my lunch and waited for him to call back; he did within three minutes (*I don't know if it's a control issue for him, or if he is always busy when I call, but it doesn't matter much as he always calls back*). He said that he had a bunch of things to show and talk with me about, and that Meg, his wife, had made him promise to refuse to give it to me unless I agreed to come to dinner first. (*Frank's wife Meg mothers me, which is both sweet and annoying, but unavoidable when I needed something from him/them, as I very much did in this case*). I agreed to stop by their place at six for dinner, hung up, and laid down for a nap (*which would let both the Chinese food and the information from my first call settle and be digested by the systems that functioned within me, completely divorced from my knowledge or volition*).

Church Pond, 7/16/2013, 4:28 p.m.

I slept for two hours and twenty-four (*which makes 144*) minutes, which is the thirteenth number in the Fibonacci sequence, and 13 is itself a Fibonacci number, and one of only three Wilson Primes, all of which I liked/chose to take as a positive sign about my upcoming meeting out on Church Pond.

We had agreed that I would present myself at the given address at 4:30, and I was only a few minutes early as I pulled off Hoel Pond Road and onto Church Pond Road. Church Pond is a 15 acre pond surrounded by private land with a number of private camps ringing it. It is less than a mile from the northern end of Upper Saranac Lake, so it made sense that a person might have a camp on Church Pond and still be a part of the community, when it came to some of the parties and other events that may have been hosted during that summer. I was eager for some data to input, to prod the mysterious machinery in the back of my head into action. I had felt the beginnings of, if not discovery, at least interesting ideas, for much of the time that I'd been working on this investigation, but it seemed to stay just out of my reach, or dancing away from me as I stretched out for it. I hoped that with this person's help, McGreevy it said on the mailbox at the head of the driveway as I drove past, I would be able to move forward.

I drove past Mr. McGreevy's driveway, skipped the next one as well, and pulled into the one beyond that; I was hopeful, but still planned on being cautious. Barry was sitting on the porch of the little cabin at the end of the driveway that I finally turned down, and stood up as I got out of the car. He cocked his ear, and I found myself doing the same.

"Quiet out here. No noise. Nobody doin' nothin' on Church Pond today. Better not slam the door, eh?" he advised; I agreed.

The pond was very quiet. There are no motored crafts allowed on Church Pond, and it didn't sound as though anyone was playing with a chainsaw or a log splitter in anticipation of next winter, or hammering on a new roof or hosting a kegger. After a minute of standing there with my mouth slightly open (*which I am convinced allows my ears to work better*), I could just make out what sounded like a baseball game on the radio coming from the next camp over, in the opposite direction of my travel as I retraced my steps back to the McGreevy camp.

I cut through the trees, taking my time, and watching where I placed each foot. Barry moved silently along beside me (*which would have been impossible were he real, given his size and bulk*). We both stopped every 30 seconds to listen for 30 before moving on again. I crossed the first driveway and saw a car parked down by the house, but didn't see or hear anyone (*napping, maybe, or reading down by the water, on the other side of the house*). I paused for 30 seconds on the hump in the middle of the driveway, feeling the moss give beneath my weight, and the stones under the moss poking up into the bottom of my feet through the thinning soles of my sneakers. I could smell wood smoke from one of the camps around Church Pond, and the distant clonk of a wooden paddle on the gunwale of an aluminum canoe, but nothing was registering on my senses within a hundred yards or more, even with them working overtime in the stillness and my paranoia (*or was it, since my caution had been more than justified this morning*).

I kept going, moving and stopping, creeping and listening; feeling ahead of me with all my senses (*and desperately trying to grow some new ones all the while*), but finding nothing. I came eventually to the McGreevy driveway, stopped, standing, chest heaving while I worked to breathe as quietly as my adrenaline flooded system would let me. I looked up and down the driveway and saw nothing and nobody; listened for a minute and heard nothing ... a squirrel or other tiny beast shifting behind a downed log near the head of the driveway, about twenty yards toward the next driveway along. I listened for it to move again, and heard nothing, so I turned towards the house.

The house had an attached garage, and a reflection through one of the garage windows showed a parked vehicle of some sort. I could see a short stack of cardboard boxes on a low table at the top of the stairs on the front porch, a shoebox on top of a pair of the sort of box that held a ream of paper or hanging folders, back in the days before they simply shrink-wrapped everything in plastic. There was a pair of chairs on either side of the table, and what looked like a pitcher of lemonade and glasses on the table next to the boxes, as if Mr. McGreevy had just gone inside for a minute while waiting for me to arrive. I started walking down the driveway, and was nearly to the steps when both Barry and I noticed something at the same second (*logically enough, since we're both currently living in the same brain*).

"There's no ice in the lemonade, and no sweat on the side of the carafe." I would have said condensation, but Barry was right; Admiral Ackbar would agree, it was a trap.

I turned around, hearing that I was too late even as my rotation started ... I could now hear small noises on both sides. One of them stepped out of a latticed and mossy woodshed at the end of the porch, the other from behind a huge rock with 'Welcome to Camp!' painted on it by successive generations. Both men were wearing full suits (*including masks*) in 3D hunting camo patterns (*that worked altogether too well at breaking up patterns and fooling the eye, at least to my eyes*) and they each carried baseball bats. As I took them in, they shifted a few steps towards the driveway in a way that effectively cut off my retreat in any direction except possibly up the stairs and into the house (*which didn't seem likely, or smart*). They closed to within 10 feet of me, and then paused, waiting/thinking/relishing.

"Boy, it sure would be nice if we had some grenades, don't you think?" Barry said, with perfect, if unappreciated, timing.

"Jayne is a girl's name," I said in my best River Tam voice.

"What the fuck did you say?" asked the guy on the left, clearly not a 'Firefly' or 'Serenity' fan as both Barry and I are.

"Sorry, I wasn't aware that I'd spoken aloud," I

replied, hoping to forestall the need for action by a few seconds while I tried furiously to make the correct choice. Right was the same guy I had seen the morning, I was reasonably certain, based on his height and build. Left moved and sounded younger, was both shorter and less muscled, but seemed to move almost too nimbly when he had slid from behind the big welcome rock, as though he were fresh from the factory showroom, possibly a serious athlete of some flavor ... it made my decision easier.

I had been hugging my sides since turning around, as though my chest hurt, and now I grabbed the cans inside my jacket and, before either of my potential attackers could react, (*I believe that their outnumbering me, as well as having bats, had taken an edge off of their readiness, although in hindsight it's also possible that they meant to scare, rather than beat, me ... but I doubt it*) I sprayed Left with both cans of 'RAID WASP & HORNET SPRAY: 25 Foot Range', mentally aiming for the bridge of his nose with both powerful streams.

It took me only a split second to see that I had nailed him in the eyes and nose and mouth (*even with the camo mask he was wearing, which was thin, nearly see-through stuff, and useless when called on to protect him from the wasp and hornet spray*). Left dropped the bat, bringing both hands up to his face, and inhaling a lungful of the poison as he began a scream of pain/surprise/rage, which transformed instantly into coughing and vomiting as he fell to the ground hard, as though he'd been dropped from a plane. As my eyes took this in, I turned, still spraying, and ducked, assuming that Right would be swinging for my head; I was mistaken, he was captivated, watching Left squirm and scream in the previously quiet, and perfectly planned, ambush. My aim was too low on Right, since I was ducking a blow he had never launched, and he was almost a foot taller than Left. I tracked the jets onto his broad chest and quickly raised them to his face, now taking my time, and aiming one for his eyes, and the other a few inches lower for his nose and mouth.

Right staggered towards me for a few steps, surprising and scaring me after the near-instantaneous results with Left, but fell to his knees an arm's length from me. I kept blasting the spray into his face for another ten seconds before turning to give Left another dose. By the time the cans were both emptied, my two would-be assailants were throwing up into their camo masks between screams of pain, and raking their eyes and lips with clawed hands … it wasn't pretty, and I didn't know how long it would last, so I left, running back through the woods to my car waiting two camps over.

I likely needn't have run, but there was no way for me to be certain, so my feet decided for me; it was not the kind of question that you could ask the guys roaming the aisles at Aubuchon. My thinking had been to get some sort of mace or pepper spray, but that's quite strictly controlled in New York, and I had no clear idea what could happen to me if I was stopped carrying it concealed in my car or on my person. Wasp spray, however, is freely available, and in the Adirondack summertime lots of people have it in the cars or on their person. I don't know what the long-term effects of that level of exposure to the stuff would be, but as Dorothy might have said, if she were running with me through the wood, 'if you can't hang with the big dogs, then stay on the porch.' I wasn't a big dog by any definition, except that when it came to physical violence/intimidation, I was willing to cheat and fight dirty. My belief is that fighting/playing fair is for losers, and that except for playing Monopoly/Sorry/Risk (*or something similar*), there's no reason not to take every advantage you can grab, even if it's frowned upon by proponents of 'fair-play.'

"That was fucking awesome, Tyler!" crowed Barry. "Why didn't we ever use bug-spray in the old days? You see those guys puking and crying like babies, Tyler my man; fucking awesome!"

"It was a bit more ... active ... than I had imagined it would be." I kept telling myself that if they hadn't come looking for trouble, that Left and Right wouldn't have found it, but I couldn't stop replaying my internal 'tape' of Left screaming in higher and higher pitched registers.

"You shoulda yanked off their masks, and seen who they were, or taken their pictures, or chained them to the porch or something."

"Believe me, I thought about it Barry, but in every crappy movie with masked bad guys, that's when they grab you ... and there were two of these guys, no telling when one could have worked through the pain to tackle me or something. It would have been tough to get a good picture anyway, with eyes screwed shut and vomit and blood and snot everywhere. I had some cable ties all ready to tie them up and let Frank deal with them, but they never touched me ... I'd go to jail, or at the least get arrested for that ... Frank's got a soft-spot for fair play, and he'd be pissed."

I got into the Porsche, started it up, and motored out of the driveway, continuing around Church Pond the other way (*so as to not have to pass Left and Right's driveway, if they had managed to clear their eyes and throats*), taking another route (*Wallace Wood Lane*) out and away from my unsuccessful information gathering session.

SmartPig, 7/16/2013, 5:18 p.m.

I did some quick thinking, and decided that I had time to stop at SmartPig before my dinner-date with Frank and Meg, also before Left and Right recovered sufficiently to ambush me in my own lair. I wanted to get whatever things I thought that I would need between now and the end of the investigation. I parked on Main Street, outside the front door to the SmartPig building, blinkers going, and ran up to take care of things as quickly as was possible. Once inside the office, I locked/bolted/barred the door. I made sure that the back window was locked and secure. I grabbed a duffel and filled it with the following: my laptop, phone/electronics charging kit, a 12-pack of Coke from the Coke-fridge (*it wouldn't be nearly enough, but I didn't want to weigh myself down with more at the moment*), GPS receiver, digital camera, camping tarp, a few more days' worth of clothes, an item I had ordered online a while ago after reading one of the Davenport mysteries by John Sandford (*most likely I wouldn't need it, but would feel silly if I didn't bring it along in the Porsche*), and a wad of money from my safe. The duffel, when zipped shut, could be worn on my back, which I did. I looped a 65-foot section of climbing rope around the radiator by the front window, and sat on the rope while leaning out the window to screw an eyelet into the outside of the window frame. Once that was done, I looped a 50-foot section of paracord through the eyelet, evened out both sets of ropes, looked both ways for SLPD cars, called out "Watch out below!" and dropped both ropes down to Main Street, ignoring amused/annoyed/frightened voices from below, and hoping for the police-free 30 second window of opportunity that I needed.

Holding the climbing rope in both hands and looped around my body so that the strain was largely taken by my hips and back, I lowered myself as quickly as was possible down to the street below. Once I touched down, I pulled one end of the looped climbing rope as fast as I was able, freeing it from the radiator up in my office so it pooled on the street around my feet. I then grabbed hold of the looped paracord and pulled with a slow and steady force, hoping that the eyelet would hold long enough to pull the window down and shut … it did. Then I repeated the process of pulling one end of the looped paracord up and out of the eyelet, so that it would all end up on the ground at my feet; forty seven seconds after touching down on Main Street, I was throwing both pieces of rope/line/cord into the trunk of Mike Crocker's Porsche.

I hopped into the car and drove out of town as fast as I felt that I safely could, making plenty of turns along the way. I had the better part of an hour to kill before I was due at Frank and Meg Gibson's house for dinner, and I needed to think. I needed to think about all that had happened so far today. What the two attacks/ambushes meant. What the old man's love-story/sob-story about Dee Crocker meant. What Frank might have for me. What I should look for with Terry at the Adirondack Museum. Where I could live for the duration of my investigation, given that I was driving a valuable piece of Porsche history. What I was hoping for in this investigation, beyond staying un-stomped (*which seemed an adequate goal for today, but not for the long term*).

I unzipped the duffel part way, grabbed a still freezing-cold Canadian Coke, and popped the top; it fizzed a bit, but I caught it before any spilled on the car. My immediate concern was dinner, then getting clear of dinner, then getting out of town and to a remote camping spot (*but not so remote that the Porsche would bottom out and leave me stranded for all time*) where I was not as likely to be spotted/noted/harassed by the forest ranger over the next week or so. I threw my big mental map up in front of me while still keeping an eye on the road, and thought about possibilities. I had been building this map of the Adirondacks one day at a time since the late fall of 2001, so had more than a decade of explorations to fall back on. I was, however, used to exploring the park (*my world*) with the relatively high clearance of my Honda Element, which the Porsche 993 did not have.

{{{Horseshoe Lake}}} popped into my head, so I adjusted the map to show me the area leading to, and away from Horseshoe Lake, and liked what I saw, given the particulars of my current need/want equation … it would do perfectly.

Having settled that, I drove back into town, looping and keeping an eye in my rearview all of the time, and decided to arrive a bit early before Frank got home for six, and risk surprising Meg by asking her to let me park my Porsche in her side of the garage.

Gibson Household, 7/16/2013, 8:38 p.m.

Meg had no problem with me housing the Porsche in their garage during dinner, when I filtered it through the 'borrowed car' rationalization; I breathed a sigh of relief once it was under cover, and we'd gone inside. Meg Gibson knows me first and foremost through the TLAS ... we share a love/obsession for dogs. She works as a guidance counselor in the local school system, and as she found out more about me through a combination of observation and well-meaning intrusiveness (*which might be in, or comprise most of, her job-description*), she passed quickly through nervous and scared to concerned and nurturing, and finally landed on something between a big sister and the cool aunt. She'd been nervous last year when I'd crossed briefly over (*in her mind*) from being a dog-loving trustafarian to doing some crazy and dangerous stuff for the police; as it always seems to be, the truth was somewhere in the middle.

"Tyler, I haven't seen you in months! (*It had been 17 days*) What have you been doing with yourself, and why are you driving that delicious green car?" I enjoyed that she described the car in terms of food (*as she did all good things, in my experience*), and that she clearly had no idea what kind of car it was, but would remember the color for the next ten years. "There's nothing wrong with the Element, is there? Frank's not making you..." She tailed off, having nowhere left to go. She'd been very scared last September when my Element had gotten banged up while I was helping Frank with some things (*actually, Frank was helping me with some things, but he didn't know it, or see it that way, which worked out well for all of us*).

"I'm borrowing the car from a friend for a while, that's all. There's nothing wrong with the Element, and this is important, so listen up ... your husband is not, did not, and will not, make me do anything. What happened last year was entirely my choice/fault, and Frank is helping me this time, not the other way around."

"Come out back, the dogs'll be happy to see you (*it's true, they would be*), and I've got some Cokes chilling in the cooler, along with a growler of Ubu for Frank when he gets here." She chills Cokes for me with salted ice and brings home half gallon bottles of local microbrews for her husband ... it's how she loves.

Toby and the new dog that they were fostering, Lola, were all over me the instant that we got out into their big fenced yard, and it seemed as though things would be easier if I just rolled around on the grass for a bit, so I did. I made a New Year's resolution in 2002 not to live a life that required suits and ties and dry-cleaning and ironing and dress-shoes and worrying about grass-stains or dog-prints ... so far, it's been working out pretty well; I don't miss any of those things. I opened the bag I had in my pocket containing some cookies I'd recently made for the dogs (*here, at the TLAS, and a few other spots with dogs that I visit frequently*), and put the dogs through their paces to earn some treats for a minute, while Meg raced back inside for the wine which she was surprised that she had forgotten to bring out (*I wasn't ... she always forgets to take care of herself*).

"Does Toby still miss Chester?" I asked, when the dogs had run off to play tag at the far end of the fenced run. Toby and the ancient Gibson Golden, Chester, had been great friends, and when they'd had to put Chester to sleep this spring, Toby had moped around the house looking for his friend. Frank and Meg had taken in Lola, another dog from the TLAS, to foster for a while, and it seemed to have helped, but Frank had confided in me during our lunch that he still thought Toby spent some time thinking about, and looking for Chester. (*Things like this helped me to understand the Frank/Meg dynamic, and also to tolerate Frank hassling me from time to time*).

"Maybe, a bit, but less every day. I think we'll end up keeping Lola; they get on so well together." The danger of fostering a second dog had always been that they would become a family member, instead of simply being more socialized/adoptable.

"Makes sense," I said, and left it at that, having learned not to delve too deeply into peoples' dog lives.

We talked about dogs and public education and summer and summer people and locals and things slowly drifted towards my looking into the disappearance of Deirdre Crocker.

"Frank and I talked about it a bit last night, just what we remembered our parents talking about over the years." Both Frank and Meg had been born in Saranac Lake, and would have heard a different version than the Crockers would hear, or tell. "It was, of course, a shame," she paused here, which led me to believe that I was going to hear from the anti-Crocker side of things in a moment, "but as the days and weeks went by, Fred Crocker, Deirdre's father (*and Mike's 'Da', I thought*) stepped on more and more toes, and got more and more outspoken as nothing was turned up."

"What do you mean?" I asked. I thought that I could hear the crunch of Frank's car in the driveway on the other side of the house, and wanted to get a little more out of Meg before Frank appeared. Meg understands people and emotions and relationships in ways that I don't even start to comprehend; hearing that side, the side having to do with feelings and human/social bonds, is always interesting, and often useful in informing the facts and statistics that my worldview is drawn from.

"That summer people versus locals dynamic. It's even more pronounced with great camps, especially back then; people like the Crockers had a few on-site staff year round, and even more during the season to support their visits. That's a lot of money, besides just taxes, going into local pockets. After the Crocker girl vanished, Fred was hurt and suspicious and angry. He brought in outsiders to look for her, and then to staff his camp, and eventually to do all of the work associated with opening and maintaining Topsail. It's shifted back a bit since he died, but they never went back to a local caretaker, or cook, or having a local lawyer for camp issues, like a lot of summer families used to do." Meg's father had worked his whole life as a lawyer in town, and I wondered if there were something there beyond second-hand knowledge.

"Some families make the relationships work, and others keep it to a working relationship; in the end there's a big difference. On-site caretakers have a great deal. The owner gets the peace of mind that their property has someone year round providing maintenance and security—the caretakers get to live in a beautiful place rent free. That symbiotic relationship can become quite close. I have family members, the Reinegers, who have been working for the Edelmans on Upper Saranac Lake for 80 years, maybe more. Uncle Robert is one of the few remaining year round on-site caretakers left in the Tri-Lakes, and the men in his family have gone hunting with the Edelmans for generations, working as guides, but also out west a couple of times, I think. I also know that Bobby's sister Emily went to school with lots of help from the Edelman's, and his daughter, Louise got a lot of help from the Edelmans when it was time for her to go off to school."

"At the other end of the spectrum, the Crockers pay a service to maintain their camp, based up in Plattsburgh with local sub-contractors doing the work; they bring all of their domestic help up with them from Manhattan. It may be a bit cheaper, but they've got more money than God; my guess is they like avoiding the relationships that the Reinegers and Edelmans seem to cherish. Most camps are somewhere in the middle, I guess."

"Middle of what?" Frank asked as he came out through the door, frosty mug in hand (*I suspected a note was responsible for his having the mug, Meg left lots of notes, to make things run smoothly, which they did*), and was rushed by happy dogs. Fresh from work, Frank had a couple of treats in his pocket for the dogs (*reminding me why I liked him despite our sometimes being on opposite sides of a legal issue*) and he got the dogs to sit/shake/kiss before coming over to get his beer out of the cooler.

"Middle of talking about something else, Franklin Porter Gibson." She softened this with a wet and noisy kiss which got the dogs jumping up to try and get in on the action (*and made me a bit nauseous, although it didn't show, because I don't emote ... much*). "How was your day?"

"I caught some bad guys, some got away, I'll deal with the rest tomorrow." It was a set piece with them, but routine is nice (*I'm a big fan of routine, preferring even things that I don't like to things I'm unfamiliar with ... that's why I study/read/research anything and everything, it sounds, and is, simplistic, but the more I know, the less there is to surprise me in this world*).

"So, what do you have for Tyler, stud-muffin?" Meg asked, giving Frank a sloppy kiss and then turning around to watch how/if I would react; she likes to play at studying me, but there's always a hint of genuine interest which leaves me feeling a bit like I'm in a Skinner box when she does it.

"Jesus, Meg, gimme a minute to shake the day off won't ya? I left the stuff inside, and figured I might have a drink before I started, if ya don't mind. A little foreplay before I get screwed, if you know what I mean." I didn't. Either Frank was in on Meg's ongoing experiment, or something was wrong; he seemed significantly more tense than this situation would ordinarily warrant. The dogs and I looked nervously back and forth between them, hoping someone would tell a joke or fart, to break the tension.

"Screw that, off with the clothes!" Meg shouted, and jumped him, taking both of them (*along with a pair of pouncing dogs*) to the ground. They all rolled around for a few seconds, and then I could hear Frank laughing, followed by him going on the offensive and tickling Meg, while the dogs jumped and barked and wagged and kissed. A minute later, they both got up, Meg grabbed Frank's mug and poured him a dark beer from the growler, and brought it over to him with a kiss.

"All better now?" she asked.

"Yup," Frank said, wiping some foam off of his mustache on his sleeve, "that'll about take care of it. Thanks honey!"

Now he turned to me, "Tyler, can you tell me why the hell you were rappelling out of your office and down onto Main Street at a bit after five this afternoon, one of two times every day when anything anyone does on Main Street will be seen, and if the slightest bit hinky, reported." He looked at me with honestly curious eyes, and held me with his stare until Meg started giggling. Ten seconds later a chuckle bubbled out, despite his best efforts to stifle it.

"Meg, it's not funny." He gave her his serious face, which she tried, and failed, to return. "Well, it's a little funny, but dammit Tyler, I can't help thinking that this is related to the Crocker thing, which you promised you'd keep low-profile. I've seen low profile, and son, this ain't it. Honest to Christ, Meg, Tilly Auer said he came down the rope like a ninja, or some special forces guy." He was smiling too, now.

"We must have gotten fifteen calls, Tyler. What the hell were you thinking?" he asked, shaking his head and chuckling into his mug, as he took the beer down another inch and a half.

"I wanted to lock up SmartPig with that lock, you know, the bar that goes from the door to a hole in the floor. But you can't lock it from the outside, or lock it and leave, so..." I trailed off at this point.

"Tyler, how are you gonna get back in?" he asked, smiling at me like he'd trapped/outsmarted me, but I was ready, had thought about this ahead of time.

"I'll rappel down from the roof to the same window and open it," I answered plainly; it was the only sensible answer.

"Like a frickin' ninja!" Meg blurted out, and started to giggle again.

"Tell you what, Tyler me boy," Frank said, after finishing his first mug of Ubu, "How about you try not to do that during what passes for 'rush-hour' in Saranac Lake. Okay?"

"Deal," I answered, although it was hard to know when/why I might need to get into SmartPig, so I couldn't really guarantee to do what he asked.

"So, do I want to know why you felt the best thing for all involved was for you to rope down from your offices like Seal Team Six during drive-time, or should we talk about dogs?" He looked at me, and waited.

I thought about his question, what it meant in a surface interpretation and implied beneath the top layer (*I'm not very good with nuanced language and rhetorical questions, but I'm trying*), took five seconds, and then answered, "Meg tells me that she thinks Toby is getting over the loss of Chester, now that Lola's here on a permanent basis." Frank got a stormy/angry/frustrated look on his face for a second, and then it seemed to bleed out, when he took in the blue sky, loving wife, sweet dogs, cold beer, and ... me. We sat out in the fading day for most of an hour, until the beer and Coke and wine ran out, and then we headed in for dinner. Meg had made pulled pork in the slow-cooker, and told me all about it; I don't have a kitchen in SmartPig, so food that's easy to make without actually cooking is right up my alley.

As we settled down at the table to eat, and the dogs worked out the right spots to lay down (*apparently my presence threw off established norms of behavior and begging and food recovery, and the geometry of food/family/room matrix changed enough to stress out the dogs a bit, and they spent five to seven minutes at each visit redrawing the lines of sight and supper-supplication*), Frank patted a thick manila folder meaningfully. He was about to say something so I cut in before he could.

"The name manila folder comes from the fiber originally used to make the folders, manila hemp. Manila hemp is actually derived from the Abaca, or Musa Textilis, plant, a relative of the banana, not at all related to cannabis, and the name Manila refers to the fact that the Philippines was, and still is, the country which produces the most abaca fiber. The fiber is harvested from the trunk or pseudostem, and now-a-days it is most commonly used in the production of teabags, not manila folders." I smiled at him (*a #8, sucking up and obsequious*), and he looked up at Meg helplessly as she came in with the huge bowl of salad.

"How?" he said to the room.

"You try to stump me with something every time I come to your house; I could see you thinking about the folder, and wanted to preempt with one that I knew, rather than wait for you to pick something I've never read up on."

Meg beamed at me with an angelic smile, and asked, "Tyler, how and why is a second date different from a fifth date; and how would the answer differ for a 15 year old versus a 21 year old?" Frank stood up to get the wine bottle, refill her glass, pausing for a casual high-five before returning to his seat ... I was speechless. Frank basked in the glory of my embarrassment and humiliation (*such as it was ... I just didn't/couldn't know the answer to that question, so I sat and waited for someone else to talk*) for 17 seconds before reading from some notes that he pulled from the folder.

"July 13, 1957, Deirdre Crocker, 17, and Kimberly

Stanton, 18, were in a one car accident on Route 30, roughly a mile from where it connects with Route 3. It was called in by Trooper Neil King, who drove by the scene a few minutes after 11 p.m.. When he arrived, Trooper King saw one still functioning headlight in the woods. He opened the driver's side door and his initial notes (*Frank held up photocopies of notes from a steno pad*) mention a smell of alcohol, although the report (*Frank waved a copy of a more official-looking filled out form*) was written up as an accident resulting from swerving to miss a deer in the road. Both Crocker and Stanton were lucid, and able to identify themselves and emergency contact information. King's notes reflect that the driver, Crocker, had broken her nose on the steering wheel, but was otherwise not visibly injured. Stanton, the passenger, had shattered the windscreen with her head, and slammed her midsection into the console. She had multiple lacerations on her face and scalp, complained of some difficulty breathing, and had obviously vomited numerous times, some of it suggestive of internal bleeding or injury." He paused and breathed and ate some pulled pork. We were having it wrapped in warm tortillas, with a little shredded cheese, some sliced dill pickles, and a ribbon of barbeque sauce ... it was better than all of Shakespeare's sonnets, and I was thankful for my exquisite listening-memory, without which I would have been too focused on the food to take in what Frank was saying.

"Upon calling the hospital, Trooper King was told that there wouldn't be an ambulance available for an hour—a multi-car accident in Raybrook tied everyone else up for hours—so he made the decision to transfer them to AMC in his vehicle, to facilitate quicker treatment of Stanton. Both women arrived at the hospital at 11:34 p.m., were checked over, received medical attention, and were released in the morning with their doctors' blessings and a relatively clean bill of health. Bruises and broken nose and fingers and some cuts and such, but having gotten as lucky as a car-crash victim can be."

He patted the folder, and continued, more informally, "I scanned through this stuff, as I assume will you, Tyler, and King's notes clearly tell a different story than the final report did. The hospital lost the records in a fire, or reorganization, nobody is sure, but they're gone. The doctors attending to the girls both died, and the one living nurse that I was able to track down was convincing about having no recollection of the event. I think that there was no deer in the road, that Deirdre Crocker was driving drunk; that being the case though, so what?"

"Were you able to talk with Kimberly Stanton?" I asked.

"Nope," Frank said, licking some sauce from his fingers, "dead."

"When did she die?" I asked, ignoring the brief look that Meg gave me, which suggested that I was ghoulish.

"Not until the year after the Crocker girl went missing; so, sad, but probably not related."

Meg's head snapped up, and she smiled at both of us. "Back in a minute. Wait right here. Have another pulled pork roll." We did, the dogs followed Meg into the kitchen, where she made a call. She came back in 13 minutes (*which worked out to 2.3 more pulled pork rolls ... I split my leftovers between Toby and Lola ... What?*) with a satisfied, but sober, look on her face.

"I did it Tyler. I solved your case. You have to split your fee with me," she said.

"Fine, you can drive the car tomorrow, I'll come by in the morning, and we can swap. Now tell me what you solved and how," I answered.

"There's a ton of Stantons up here, especially in Tupper; I'm even related to some of them. I called my great-aunt Betty, she's like a hundred. I asked her about Kimberly's accident, and, of course she remembered."

"Why 'of course'?" Frank asked.

"Because it was one of those family tragedies that people carry with them forever. She was the bright and pretty one, 'Kimmy', the one who was going to college with her friend, Dee. But the accident changed everything. Apparently they didn't have ultrasounds in every doctor's office, much less ER back then, but if they had, they would have seen that she had slightly perforated her bowel. 'Kimmy' went home the next morning all right, but was back in the hospital the next week with a raging infection, 'Sepsis' Aunt Betty said, that pretty much ate her alive. She survived that round of infection, but there were others, and either the car accident or that first infection essentially destroyed her liver and kidneys. Aunt Betty said that the family's sweetheart was poisoned from the inside very slowly, and painfully, over the next year and half, until she died, 'a mercy' Betty said, in the middle of January of 1959. The Crockers were helpful and responsive the whole time, Betty helped Kim's parents keep track of the bills and expenses, and everything went to a law-firm in Manhattan, and was paid instantly, and without question. But the girl died as a result of the car accident, just in slow-motion."

"And ... " I still didn't have it all. " What does that mean? Who took/killed Dee Crocker? Why would they do it anyway, when the Crockers had helped with Kim's medical expenses?"

Meg looked over at Frank, who shrugged and rolled his eyes.

"Jesus, Tyler, you are capital 'S' stupid. It means that

Dee Crocker extinguished the light, the hope, of the Stantons, or that particular line of Stantons. Something you probably can't appreciate about life up here is that everyone is related, except you and other recent transplants to the 'dacks; so knowing who kidnapped the Crocker girl would be almost impossible, 'cause there'd be hundreds of people who felt wronged by her loss. Up here, especially after the war, families saw their kids' futures tied to escaping the Adirondacks and going to college. It sounds like this girl, Kim, was the one that a whole bunch of people in the Stanton clan pinned their hopes and dreams on."

"And ... I'm still not there with you."

"And ... Dee Crocker took Kim, and their dream away from them. Investigators might have gotten there after Dee vanished if Kim Stanton had already died, but she hung on for another couple of months (*five, I thought, not two, as the phrase 'a couple' implies*), which was enough time for the investigation into Dee Crocker to all but end before the motive was made fully clear."

"Okay, I'm there now," I said, as we cleared the table and I helped Meg with dessert, ice-cream sandwiches, "so why no body?"

While we were still in the kitchen, I peeled and halved a sandwich, and gave the pieces to Toby and Lola; Meg looked horrified, but didn't say anything. Frank would have rushed in and chastised all four of us at length for feeding them non-dog food (*which seems a fuzzy line to me, Toby and Lola agree*).

Frank was waiting, and smiled at me when I handed him two of the frosty treats. "Yeah, if you're pissed enough at her to kill her, I can see that, but where's the body. You shoot or stab her, either at Topsail or somewhere else, somebody's eventually gonna find the body, unless you entirely destroy or perfectly hide it; neither of which are easy to do."

Meg gave us both funny looks as Frank and I warmed to the subject, and each also broke into our second sandwich.

"In an 'eye for an eye' kind of justice, poison might make sense, but she was healthy until the day she vanished," I offered.

As this thought sunk in, Meg and Frank (*possibly inevitably, although I can't be sure, I don't think much about death or poison as they could be applied to me … it's a waste of time*) paused, and took a look down at the ice-cream sandwiches in their hand; then Lola farted and scared herself with the noise, and we all moved past the moment.

"Okay, Tyler, but looking past the good news of my wife and I doing your job for you, I have a concern, which I imagine that you share. Based on your ninja-ing down to street level from out of SmartPig this afternoon, I would bet the rest of this sammich that somebody has taken exception in one form or another to you looking into Dee Crocker's disappearance," Frank observed.

Meg thought about this for a second, and then shifted from fun to scared mode remarkably quickly. "Tyler is that true?" I looked into her eyes, long and hard, thinking about the masked men wanting to beat me with bats this afternoon before answering.

"Yes, a bit. I put out a number of feelers hoping for some feedback to help guide my next steps, and besides the stuff that you and Frank have helped with, there's been some other contact. Some of it (*thinking of the old man who remembered Dee, and probably Kim, at the Woodsmen's Days beer hall*) pointed me in other directions, towards other research/study. Other feedback suggests that there are people who would prefer me not to mess around with this; the speed and vehemence with which their 'feedback' has occurred would seem to support Meg's great-aunt's story, and point to someone not wanting old crimes uncovered." I was glad that my lack of emotions made it easier to lie to those I care about, and who care about me.

"I'm worried about you and Hope, Tyler. Maybe you two should come and stay here for a while," Meg blurted, and before Frank could raise his many objections to this idea (*which says more about my speed than Frank's thoughtful deliberation*), I spoke up.

"Hope's already staying with Dot, and I'll be moving around too much for them to find me. I just didn't want to leave it easy for them to break into SmartPig." Frank breathed an audible sigh of relief, and Meg glared at him, unconvinced by my explanation and grumpy with Frank's reticence at having me stay with them.

"I've picked out a spot to camp for the next little while that's nearly at the ends of the Earth. Nobody will find me there."

"Not even Timmy Gillis? I heard that he found you the other night; found you and ticketed you." He ended this with a small laugh; Frank doesn't care about my overstaying the DEC 3-day limit in a spot, but he takes a bit of pleasure from it whenever I get busted. I thought of the Element parked at Ampersand Bay, and wondered how much paddling the ranger would be doing in the coming days looking for me … if I was a rueful or wry smiler, this would have been a good time for it.

"It was after two in the morning when he woke me up to give me the ticket. Scared me and … it took me a while to get back to sleep (*I had almost mentioned Barry, and I think that Meg picked up on my detour, but I kept going anyway*).

Anyway, yes, even he couldn't find me way out past Horseshoe Lake, and even if he/they did, I'm reasonably sure that I'm currently driving the fastest vehicle in the Adirondack Park, including floatplanes and helicopters."

That led to questions about the car, many of which I think Frank asked just hoping to stump me, but my weeks of trying to be Niko's friend by studying endless facts about the 993 had paid off. We all went out to look at the thing, and to listen to the roar of Porsche's last air-cooled engine. I put the leftover-containing Tupperware in the back, and waved goodbye to Meg and Frank, circling their neighborhood twice to see if any lights pulled into my rearview.

West of Little Pine Pond — near Horseshoe Lake, 7/16/2013, 10:26 p.m.

I made a nice fast run from Saranac Lake through Tupper Lake on Route 3 most of the way (*just taking advantage of the cut off by the Wild Center to avoid downtown Tupper Lake*) then switching to Route 30 heading south for a bit. I was missing the driver's side window in the cold night air, but actually enjoyed the wind more than I would have thought. I pulled in by the causeway over Rock Island Bay, a few miles outside of Tupper, and waited for ten minutes for pursuit before continuing for just short of three additional miles before turning right onto Route 421, which took me out to Horseshoe Lake and beyond.

I pulled the 993 down an increasingly unlikely series of dirt roads and paths until I had trouble projecting my location on my internal map, and then parked and set up my camp. Before going to sleep, I strung three loops of fishing line going out from my campsite in concentric circles (*at five, ten, and 15 feet, roughly, from my belly button when I was laying down in my hammock*); to these, I attached empty Coke cans with two pennies in each. I felt as though it was likely overkill, but nobody ever regretted being too safe (*especially when stomp-y members of the Stanton*

Clan were on your trail). I went to sleep thinking about what I'd learned and seen and heard in the last few days, and how I could bring it to bear in my research in the Adirondack Museum's archives to help further my investigation.

Somewhere West of Little Pine Pond — near Horseshoe
Lake, 7/17/2013, 3:18 a.m.

I woke to one of the cans comprising my crude alarm
system jiggling at 2:54 a.m..

"Fuckin' deer! Go back to sleep," Barry yelled from
the direction of the thumps and crashes as the scared
animal bounded away.

My mind raced, partly from unspent adrenal products
racing through my system, but also in searching for
significance, not my own, but in the time. I've always
invented my own games (*even when I wasn't picked last, I
didn't like/understand or excel at games that other children played*),
and one of my longtime favorites has been numbers. I
love numbers: their precision, their power, their span
across fields of thought and endeavor. I love sequences of
numbers also; I love the patterns and rules and seeing
them pop and glow on the number lines in my head. 254
was tough for me to place for a minute though; I could
feel neurons snapping and popping all through my head

until it suddenly came to me ... Lazy Caterers!

254 is the 23rd number in the lazy caterer's sequence, which is an informal way to refer to the central polygonal numbers. It measures the maximum number of pieces that a circle (*think reindeer, goat-cheese pizza*) can be cut into with a given number of straight cuts/lines (*for example, a reindeer, goat-cheese pizza could be cut into a maximum of 254 pieces with 23 cuts by a lazy/imprecise caterer, a neat one would make 46 similarly sized pieces with those same 23 cuts*). I wracked my brain for a minute trying to think of the corresponding cake number (*which is the same proposition, using a three dimensional cake, instead of a flat pizza or pancake, and allowing cuts in those three dimensions*), and eventually came up with 1794 pieces ... by the time I had worked it out, and decided to try it when the investigation for the Crockers was all settled, I was ready to go back to sleep.

"About time, you dick. That shit hurts my head, and, now I'm hungry, and we're on the other side of the fuckin' planet from the nearest pizza or cake. Go to sleep Tyler, you drive me nuts, but we're safe way the hell out here," Barry said as I was falling into sleep once again.

Adirondack Museum, Blue Mountain Lake, 7/17/2013, 10:47 a.m.

I slept until it was light without further alarm, and had a breakfast of Tyler-Kibble and warmish Coke; I'd had better, but I'd also had worse (*corned beef hash came to mind, as it always does at times like that, as an example of how food could be worse ... it tastes to me exactly like cat food smells*). I had slept last night with a clear view of the sky, but wanted to add a tarp to my hammock setup for a couple of reasons: it was supposed to cloud over today and possibly rain a bit over the next few days; and my tarp was camouflage colored, rather than the straight black (*and slightly more visible*) hammock alone. When I eventually puttered off for the day, I stopped a hundred yards away from my campsite to drag a heavy log across the access-road I'd camped at the end of, and felt more safe/comfortable, knowing that even I couldn't see my hammock/tarp setup.

Zipping quietly through the morning fog that still covered the hamlet of Long Lake, I noted that Hoss's Country Corner wasn't open yet, but Stewart's was, so I pulled in to fill the car with gas, and load myself down with junk food for a day of research. The smell of their egg and sausage sandwich seduced me while I was in line, and I got two of those in addition to the Coke, and egg-salad, and cheese, and candy that I picked up to fuel my body and brain. I left my bag of stuff with the woman behind the counter, and ran into their bathroom for some morning splashing and brushing that couldn't be taken care of in the woods earlier; smelling and looking clean(*er*) couldn't hurt my chances of getting access to the premiere collection of Adirondack artifacts and the help of those who kept/ordered/loved it.

Going back through the three-way intersection at Hoss's, this time I went south and west out of town, towards Blue Mountain Lake, picking up speed once I left the main cluster of buildings centered around Hoss's. The drive was pleasant and deserted, so I opened the Porsche up a bit, remembering Niko's father, a tall man with wild white hair that blew out behind us like a cape as he sped through the lower west side of Manhattan's quiet mornings with his son and me. He had always insisted on 'warming the rubber' with a series of gentle arcs across the painted lines on the road (*'those lines and lanes and limits are there for the lowest common denominator behind the wheel, Tyler, cabbies and tourists'* he had said, time and again), then pushing the gas pedal to the floor, and spilling out gales of maniacal laughter as the power pushed me/us back into the seat and headrest like a gentle but bossy God.

Coming around the last big turn before getting to the museum, I was nearly startled (*which at 84 mph means killed*) by a rafter of wild turkeys coming out of the town dump (*really a transfer station, as no towns actually dump/bury garbage inside the Blue Line anymore*). They were headed downhill, and back the way I had come, and besides one gigantic tom, there were at least a dozen other turkeys spread out across and down the road for 100 yards. In the Element, I would have lost traction and ended up in the woods, but the rubber was warm, and I kept my foot on the gas (*possibly even increased the pressure a bit*) and let the car grab the road and slalom through and around the extended family of birds. I could hear the Cokes and food jumping around in back, and made a mental note to let the soda sit for a while before opening it, but found myself enjoying the thrill. Most of the time, driving is a bit boring, mostly composed of waiting and braking and stopping; in comparison, this morning's drive was all happening at the outer edge of what my eyes and brain and hands and feet could handle. I hadn't touched the brakes, and wouldn't dream of stopping. The last turkey, an immature thing not fully feathered out yet, kept walking across the road despite the noise and spectacle that the 993 and I must have presented, and we missed it by less than a foot (*I saw it spin delicately around, as though it had been dancing with us, in the rearview as I pulled onto the last steep grade towards the museum*).

I pulled into the museum parking lot, and drove up and around to the top of the raised parking structure ... both for the spectacular view, and so I could keep an eye on the comings and goings of any people potentially interested in stomping me. Once the Porsche rolled to a stop, I stretched, unbuckled, and grabbed some food/drink and my Kindle to pass the time until my appointment with Terry Winch, Collections Manager. The Porsche kept running at a low idle, to keep the chill off, and to charge up my iPad and phone (*I had a charger for both in my backpack, but wanted to start the day with them topped up*). A few cars started coming by 7:30, and by almost 9 a.m., the lot around the side of the building was more than half full. Organizing/checking/loading the contents of my backpack one more time, I pulled down and out of the raised parking, and around/behind the sprawl of main building that housed boats and artwork, parked, and went in to find Terry.

The first time that I met Terry Winch, it occurred to me that he must have been vat-grown or cloned to match some idealized image of an Adirondack researcher, literally from the ground up. He wears old and creased, but clean, work boots to work every day. Dark green wool pants washed smooth and soft, with suspenders arching over a medicine ball belly that stretches the front of his worn chamois shirts. I've never seen him without two pairs of glasses on librarian leashes: one his regular bifocals for walking around and reading, the other a pair of extreme magnifiers for fine-detail work/examination. His eyes are bright green and alert, and never stop measuring and moving and cataloging and comparing. His hair's an unusual salt and pepper mix, and combed straight back with something that smells like woods and bug dope to me, but must be some kind of hair tonic (*Terry once told me that it's the pine tar that makes me think of the woods, and also why he uses the stuff in his hair*). He reached out to shake my hand in a slightly too-firm grip, that felt more calloused than a sixty year old office worker's hands should be, and clapped me on my bad shoulder (*although since he didn't know about my getting shot last year, he couldn't be blamed for this*).

"Tyler! Good to see you. I hope you're going to give our new systems and people a good stress test. We've been improving the cataloging system and archives organization and the staff and interns know our collections better than at any time in our history. I told them you were doing some research for a book, and could have access to anything we've got. I implied that you were a billionaire, and that if you were impressed with our system, you might fund a position in the back of the building (*an archivist or curator, as opposed to a displays-geek or guide or educator*), permanently. They'll be looking to make a good impression on both of us, and I'll be looking for you to run them, and the systems we've set up, ragged. Find the holes or weaknesses in the systems, write them up for me to deliver to the board, and you can have whatever you want."

What I wanted was Cynthia Windmere, the woman who used to help me with my research projects at the Saranac Lake Free Public Library (SLFPL); she had died, been murdered, last year though, so I couldn't have her. Dorothy and I had ended up leaving her body where it was dumped in Lower Saranac Lake, deciding that the potential difficulties and dangers of retrieving and moving her would outweigh all possible benefits (*she wouldn't be less dead, after all, and I didn't/don't believe that we're anything but rotting meat after our heart and brain stop working*); we had walked out to an abandoned cemetery near Olmstedville, and held a two-person service for her this spring, once the snow had gone. I had tried to adjust my old patterns of using the SLFPL without her, and it just didn't work; I still used their collections and access to networks and databases and the inter-library loan system, but had adjusted my expectations and work-habits in the library to accommodate her absence in the world.

"Okay, Terry, how does this work? How do I know what's there?" I asked, pointing to/through/beyond the wall of the entry hall, in which we still stood.

"Let me give you the short version of the VIP tour, and you're smart enough to ask me questions along the way. Once you get the lay of the land, I'll introduce you to the intern that'll be helping connect your brain with our collections. Sound good?" I nodded, and gestured for him to go. I was eager to see what they had 'in back.'

I'd helped Terry a few years back with a problem, and he'd seen something of my gift for research. We'd spent days poring over old maps and letters from people dead for a generation, and at the end of the time, my brain had somehow digested/processed the mass of information and excreted an answer letting me know the who and where in that particular challenge. It occurred to me that he might want to watch me work in his environment, to see either: how/why it worked, or if it was luck the last time around. I turned the concept around in my head, looking at it from all sides, and decided that he probably wasn't ... but that even if he was, I didn't care, as I was getting what I wanted.

We had been walking down a fairly ordinary workplace hall ... coffee-makers, desks, Dilbert, Far Side, elderly desktop computers, acoustic tile ceilings, smiling people taking a break from their work to look up as we passed by ... and then we passed through a sturdy metal door with rubber gasketing all the way around and into the first of the collections. The air-handling system buried the office sounds entirely, completing the feeling of isolation/separation. Sealed concrete made up all sides of the container that I was in, and it felt cold to me. I walked over to the machines literally conditioning the air to optimize preservation of the museum's collections, and saw the temperature was set for 55 degrees and 40% humidity.

"I hope you brought a sweater along, Tyler. We keep it

this cold in all of the collection rooms, and the room you'll be working in is set to the same environmental conditions to avoid condensation and such."

"I'll be fine, thanks. What about the lights?" It wasn't that I actually needed to know, but I was curious.

"They're specially formulated, carefully modulated wavelengths. Some people get headaches or feel funny after working under them for too long; shouldn't be too bad for you though, you're a short timer, and you spend a lot of time outside, getting the right kind of light."

He grabbed the handle of what looked like a wheel on the side of a floor to ceiling bookcase, and cranked it over to one side, the bookcase rolled across the floor on tracks. "We can fit more shelving in each room this way. The museum has in excess of 70,000 photos, and thousands of diaries and letters and journals and ledgers, and that's just the documents. We have rooms and rooms of artifacts: furniture, furs, guns, fishing rods, skis, clothes, tools, machines, and we get more all the time."

"How?" I asked.

"People give it to us or loan it to us mostly, although we do buy pieces from time to time, mostly art or singular pieces of historical value." Terry was starting to talk museum at me, so I pushed forward.

"I anticipate sticking to documents. Photos and letters and diaries/journals probably, but I might see what comes up through looking at a few of the ledgers. You never can tell."

"Indeed not," Terry said, warming to the subject, "shopping lists, menus, guest lists, construction materials, trips the owners completed during the course of a summer ... some of the ledgers offer one a rare look into the life and times of the people who lived and worked and played in the great camps." I might have felt guilty or creepy about invading the privacy of these people if: a) I had those sorts of feelings, and b) that wasn't exactly the sort of thing I was down here looking for ... Terry nodded his appreciation for the understanding of the power of these documents he could see (*or thought he could see*) in my eyes.

"Photographs are cataloged when we receive them with dates and subject matter and location and people when possible; we're in the process of going through our entire collection to digitize them into a searchable database, but are only a bit better than 20% through the process. The best way to find what you're looking for is still a brute-force attack; look at hundreds of pictures to find the one that you need" he said.

He talked more about the organization and searching, but in those areas, I would be a hostage to the people helping me, so I tuned it out, and just looked at the collections. We walked from one room to another to another to another to another, some needed keys, other touchpad codes; I remembered which keys Terry used, and the codes that he had entered for certain rooms, not through any desire or plan to make ill-use of the information, but simply because it passed in front of my eyes and into the stronghold of my brain. My excitement and anticipation at the upcoming massive research project had my entire sensorium highly tuned, I could feel the differences in the air in the hallways and stairways between collections rooms, and felt my brain plotting a map of the spaces that I visited with Terry, adding them to my pre-existing map of the public sections of the museum (*I was surprised to see staff passing through tiny doors out and into the public display areas in places where I had never noticed entrances before*). We went through seventeen different storage spaces in all, seeing even more things than Terry had promised; I could have spent a lifetime studying them (*and felt a rare twang of jealousy at Terry's being able to do exactly that*). The tour ended in a climate and light controlled room next to the first photo-vault that we had seen.

"Okay, my guy will be here in a bit," he said, checking his watch (*and holding it to his ear as if it were stopped, although I'd heard it in the quiet depths of some of the collections rooms*). "He'll tell you all of this, I hope, but here are the biggies. Anything you touch, you touch with gloves." He pointed with his elbow to a big box of cotton gloves on the table. "No food or drink is open or out in this room; there's a picnic table out back, and you'll need the air and sun after a few hours in here. You can't take, or keep, anything. No flash photographs, this one is tough for some people ... okay?" he asked.

"Yessir, no problem, I brought my iPad, and it has a camera built-in, and I've got some document scanner apps ... is that okay?" I knew the answer, but wanted to show my willingness to be compliant.

"Yup, it is; your iPad is passive, lightwise, so it can't damage the documents," he paused, finding his place before continuing. "If you need something copied, we have a special machine; it's pricey per page, so don't go nuts with it; but, you know, do what you need to do." I always do.

A young man walked in, and waited by the door until Terry invited him to come over and join us with a summoning wave of his hand.

"Tyler Cunningham, this is Tom Bailey. Tom, Tyler. Tom's brain may be a bit like yours Tyler, which I mean as a compliment to both of you. Tom has learned his way around the collections faster than anyone I've seen since I got here (*which was just after the 1980 Olympics, up in Lake*

Placid). Tom, he knows the rules, but keep an eye on him; my friend Tyler has been known to cut a corner or two in his day. Everything should be back into storage in the same shape it was before his visit ... better, because I want you to check the cataloging on everything you pull, and put it in line to get it scanned before you reshelve it. Questions?" Terry asked, looking at both of us; we both shook our heads side to side, and watched him leave before we were done.

"Well, Mr. Cunningham, where would you like to start?"

"Tom, I'm Tyler, not Mr. Cunningham. Let's start there. Next, we should go to the room where Terry said it's okay to eat, because I need to fuel up before I get started, and I want you to do the same. Grab your lunch or snack and a pen and paper, and we can talk while we eat."

Adirondack Museum, Blue Mountain Lake, 7/17/2013,
5:53 p.m.

We sat down at the table in a break room that smelled like
… break room: burnt coffee at the bottom of the carafe,
repeatedly-cooked tomato-based splatter on the inside of
an unclean microwave, questionable leftovers in a
communal and unpoliced fridge, lingering cigarette smoke
from the last lungfull taken outside before coming back
to work, paper, human sweat and oils. I ate three egg-
salad sandwiches, five sticks of mozzarella, two bit-o-
honey bars (*I don't see them often in stores, but whenever I do, I
buy a stack for later consumption*), four Cokes, and a liter of
water (*I considered rewriting this sentence to get the items in
ascending numerical order, but decided that I liked having them
listed in order of fuel efficiency better*). Tom ate two PB&Js, and
drank a Mountain Dew. While he watched me eat, I
explained a bit about what I was looking for, and how I
wanted to go about doing it.

"To start off, I'll be looking for pictures of one person

in particular, and a group of her associates," I looked to ascertain that he was taking the word in its definitional sense, not as business jargon, he nodded that he was, "at parties/events/gathering on or around Upper Saranac Lake during the summer of 1958. I would like to establish, and then expand, a social circle of the target individual. I'm hoping to see patterns and maybe people or places that don't fit in with the rest of the gestalt." Tom nodded in understanding, so I continued.

"I anticipate the search changing to include more specifics, and shifting dates/places/people as we go. Once I've worked the pictures, I may ask you to dive into the written document archives with much the same goals."

"Okay, Tyler, let me interrupt you, if I may. Lots of the pictures have useful and accurate cataloging information associated with them, but lots of them do not. If you give me a list of keywords, and we work off of just those, you may miss some of what you're looking for."

"Understood. My thinking is that we start with the keywords in a Boolean 'OR' search pattern, while limiting the scope of the search in dates from 1955 to 1965 initially; if that yields too few, or we feel that we're missing too many, we can do an open-date search of the keywords. If your instincts or experience draw you to other pictures or groups of pictures, then by all means serve them up. I'm a big believer in our brains knowing more than our conscious selves, especially in seemingly chaotic environments (*this was a bit of a test, I wanted to see if Tom's head exploded, or if he gave me a 'crazy-guy' look ... he did neither, which I took as a good sign*)."

"So, our first set of keywords should be?" he asked.

"Crocker, Topsail, Upper Saranac, St. Regis, party,

dinner, summer, 1958."

"Those search parameters will yield thousands of pictures." I nodded, and he continued, "That being the case, I would still suggest dropping the word 'upper', and just searching 'Saranac'. You will get lots of false positives, but I've noticed lots of pictures where people mislabeled their pictures, leaving off accurate lake name identifiers. Similarly, I would drop 'St.' from 'St. Regis', and just search for 'Regis'."

"Sounds good," I said. "While you're fixing the list, add 'Stanton' as a keyword." I was thinking of Kimberly Stanton, and establishing the linkage between her death and Deirdre Crocker's disappearance (*even though the latter preceded the former*), and the possibility of finding out where a connection was … if indeed there was one.

"Got it," said Tom, and he headed out to start his end of the search. "I can do a tiered search for you to start, which might get some quick and useful results for you, although it ends up being depressing as time goes by."

"Explain, please?" I asked.

"I would use all of the keywords that we've established, and have the computer search the photos we've already entered into our computerized database; it's about 23% of our photo collection. It would yield photos with the highest number of matching keywords first, and then continue in descending order. When I do this kind of search, I tend to get some great hits up front, and then it goes dead for a while before I start coming across interesting stuff somewhat randomly again."

"Sounds good. I might get what I need right off the bat, and save you days of minioning for me."

"Days?" Tom asked, looking a bit shocked at the prospect.

"Could be … we'll see." He nodded and headed out of

the room.

"I should be bringing the first round of photos to you in the Exam Room within 15 or so minutes."

I waved him off, went to the bathroom, and then headed down to the Exam Room. He was as good as his word, and was back in 14 minutes with a box of photos. I had a pair of cotton gloves on, and had been studying the pictures of Dee Crocker and those other people in the representative photos that her mother and brother had selected for me (*although I tend to lock images in my memory with a single exposure, it never hurts to make certain*) via my iPad. I started to flip through the first few pictures in the box. They were lined up from front to back, not top to bottom, so I could give each one a quick look without disturbing the museum's arrangement, when I stopped Tom at the door (*presumably on his way out to get more pictures for me*).

"I can probably keep these in order. Do I need to?"

"No, If you take photos out of the box, and move on for any reason before replacing the photo, don't put them back, leave them aside for me to reorganize later. The code on the back of the picture will let me know where to replace it. That should also make it easier for you to separate out any pictures that you want me to copy for you."

"Thanks," I said, and I kept going through the first few pictures.

I was surprised to find a large number of relevant pictures immediately. I looked at the typed label on the outside of the box, and saw, 'Camp Topsail (Crocker), Upper Saranac Lake, 1958, 60-5r34f-alb9'. I continued through the box pulling out the occasional picture to save for closer examination and/or copying later. When Tom next came into the room, I asked him about the box and photos.

"You know that the museum first opened in 1957. In the first few years, we were quite pro-active in acquiring historical documents or all sorts, both through direct and indirect appeals to Adirondack residents and visitors. This box, and lots of others like it, is the result of a drive to borrow photo albums, which could then be copied and preserved in our archives." I flipped a couple of the pictures over, and saw...

"Nothing, right. Sadly that's one of the failings in an otherwise super program. We are lacking the notation and identification that the original prints often have on the back or in the margins of the album. I hope that doesn't throw you off."

"It's hard to say ... we'll see." When I went back to my work, I heard Tom wait for a few seconds before leaving the room. I would have to try and remember that functioning humans are significantly more polite than I am naturally; Cynthia understood/accepted/forgave the incompleteness of my human emotional software installation, but I am told that it takes some getting used to. If I want to optimize the benefit from my time behind the curtain at the Adirondack Museum, I need to find a way to improve my Tyler to human interface.

By the end of the first box, I knew that the posed photos likely wouldn't help me at all. I wanted to peek behind the curtain, and see something that somebody didn't want me to see. Donated Crocker family pictures, as nice a window into that time as they were, were not going to give me the view that I wanted into the past. I picked a few pictures that I wanted names for, if possible, and put the rest on the lid of the box, waiting for Tom's return.

"Hi, Tom, thanks for all of these," I said smiling my

best #3 at him, "but I think that we need to shift the focus to get a slightly different set of results." His smile faltered a bit, before he put down his current load of photographs, and took out a pencil and notecard.

"I want to see more candid shots, specifically from the summers of 1957 and 1958, not necessarily at Topsail, the Crocker Camp, but definitely Upper Saranac Lake ... for the moment."

What he did next both surprised and impressed me; he stepped outside/beyond my expectations, and made me curious about his backstory, but not curious enough to ask (*more important stuff to do and think about*). He sat down at the table across from me, looked into my eyes, and asked a perfect question (*something the world sees too few of*).

"Tyler, close your eyes for a minute and think about the pictures you've seen in the last hour. Now think about how big our photographic archives are. Don't worry about my being bored, or luck, or getting the job done by quitting time. Imagine the perfect picture to advance your research, answer your questions. Now describe it. What does the picture you're looking for hold, show, or reveal?"

"It's like these ones, but not as polished," I said, after literally closing my eyes for a few seconds (*not the minute he suggested, but still*). "It'll show Dee Crocker or her family, and someone who hates her/them for something Dee or the Crocker family did, or are perceived to have done. (*I didn't want to explain Kimberly Stanton, and the car wreck, it seemed a needless sidetracking*). That box of photos came from a copy of a photo album that some family member or photographer put together. They culled the shots that I want most; the ones with someone off to one side accidentally in the shot, or someone glaring at Dee or one of the other Crockers. It would have been in the bottom of a box of photos that nobody took the time to throw out, although they meant to. There's a chance it won't pay off, but I have a feeling that it might."

"Excellent! 1957 or 1958, Upper Saranac Lake, candids or even discards. I'll talk to our map guy and look for specific camps on Upper Saranac, so I can search by name, and avoid the 'Album Program' codes," he said, and without waiting for my reply, he headed out and I didn't see him for nearly an hour ... I read one of my current books, a nasty Matt Scudder mystery, while I waited.

He kicked open the door, and staggered in, loaded down with boxes, followed by another, older man that he never introduced (*perhaps his 'map guy'*), similarly laden with boxes. The other set down his boxes and left; Tom turned to face me with a smile.

"Your picture is in there," he said, pointing to the pile of boxes now dominating one end of the table. "I don't know how many pictures you're going to have to look at to find it, a couple of thousand maybe, but if the picture exists, it's on the table, or back in the stacks, still waiting for us to find it," he finished with a flourish, and an expectant look on his face that I didn't understand.

"Well, thanks. I'd better get to it." Tom seemed to deflate before my eyes, and I realized that I hadn't gushed enough; so I started up again. "This is incredible, Tom! I don't know how to thank you enough." He brightened a bit, and I reached for the first box.

By a process analysis done a number of times over the course of the afternoon, I was able to filter/assess/sort approximately six hundred pictures an hour for the next four hours and 48 minutes; this translates to approximately two thousand nine hundred pictures examined (*a shade under, in all likelihood*). The vast majority of those pictures were utterly useless to me: wrong people, wrong timeframe, wrong location. The subset that included the right people, during the right months/years, and in the right places was 221 (*roughly eight percent, for those interested*), but most of those (*214, or almost 97%*) didn't seem indicative of animosity/resentment towards one or more of the Crockers. This left me with seven pictures out of nearly three thousand, roughly one fifth of one percent of the pictures I had looked at in Tom's 'sure thing' pile of boxes.

Those seven pictures, laid out on the table like a hand of cards revealed in a poker game, most likely meant something to the right pair of eyes, but at this point in the day, my eyes were done. I pushed all of the boxes of photos and the loose considered/rejected photos to the far end of the table, leaving me with eleven photos: four from the Crocker box, and seven from the mountain of boxes that Tom and the nameless museum minion had carried in. I went over to the wall-phone and called the extension Tom had given me for him; he picked up partway through the first ring.

"Tyler?" he said hopefully, a combination of curiosity and 5:30 in his voice.

"Hi, Tom. I have a handful of pics that I'd like to get copied or scanned or whatever you do. I'm done for the day, but was hoping that I could take advantage of your (*I paused infinitesimally, looking for the right superlative*) spectacular help again tomorrow."

"So you found the picture you needed? I'm so glad!" He sounded it.

"I found seven pictures, and I'm going to need to do some more research between now and, say, noon tomorrow, which is probably as soon as I can get back. (*I was already seeing the trip back up to my hidden campsite, stopping on the way at the Long Lake Stewart's for a bagful of their eternally 'ready and fresh' bacon cheeseburgers, bed after some reading, a quick run up to Topsail to speak with Kitty and Mike as early as they can manage, and back down here while I still have a semi-willing assistant).*"

"I'll be there in a flash, and can copy or scan those photos for you. We do both," he said, and I could hear the smile in his voice … pride and liking to know something that I didn't, I think.

"Both would be great, as high resolution/quality as you can." Then I hung up to wait for him. True to his word, he burst through the door in a flash (*which in museum-lackey is 23 seconds*). I gave him a card with my current email address circled (*for the scans*), the eleven pictures, and shooed him back out of the room before he could ask questions that I didn't have answers to … yet.

He was back shortly, and seemed surprised to find me reading when he came back. I'd been reading, but that only occupies a portion of my brain … with the rest of my brain, I was trying to see the next steps, anticipating where the research/investigation might take me. As he laid the high-quality copies down on the table, I could see another possible line of inquiry, in case the Crockers and/or these photos were a bust tomorrow morning. I held up a finger, signaling Tom to wait for a second, speed-dialed Frank, and told him what I needed (*although out loud it sounded like a polite request for help*). That done, I looked at the copied photos, and gushed over Tom's work again for a few minutes, while another chunk of my brain thought about how he could profitably spend his morning.

"How familiar are you with the camp ledgers and journal and diaries and letters collections?"

"Somewhat," he said guardedly. "Why do you ask?"

"It might be a good idea for you to explore them a bit tomorrow, get a feel for what they have for the Upper Saranac Lake great camps in the years we've been dealing with, plus a cushion, say 1955 through 1960. I also anticipate needing to see how the ledgers cross-reference with journals and diaries and letters, to get a well-rounded picture of life in these camps. Does that sound doable?" I asked.

"Yup, it does. No problem, now I'm gonna head out if we're cool for tonight."

"Where's home?" I asked.

"Indian Lake. I told my girlfriend, Marcy, to wait, and that we'd make supper when I got home from this," he said, looking at his watch pointedly.

"Call her and tell her to meet you at Marty's Chili Nights. They're still open, right?" I asked, handing him a $100 bill.

"I couldn't Mr. Cunningham. Thanks anyway, but..." The money had shifted me back to Mr. Cunningham quickly.

"Tom, stop it. You were helpful today, you'll be helpful tomorrow, and I made you late for supper. It's the least I can do. I'll expense it to the client ... and remember, I'm Tyler." This all may or may not have meant something, but it seemed to work, as he took the bill from my hand, thanking me profusely as he dashed from the room. This would keep him motivated and digging in my absence, certainly much better than a gift or gratuity after we were done.

When he left the room, I picked up the phone, and dialed Dorothy's cell-number; she picked up on the first ring, "Tyler, how's it going? Got anything that I can help you with yet?" she asked hopefully, "I bet this call means that we're not having dumplings and General Tso's, right?"

"Sorry Dot, nothing that fits your skill set as yet, and yes, I'm on the far side of the planet from the good Chinese place and you (*and Hope, I mentally added ... Hope loves the dumplings, and I often order too many on purpose, so that she can have some when Dorothy and I get together for these dinners*). So we'll have to postpone," I said.

"No worries, I sorta figured, and Lisa made a lasagna. We've got a couple of movies on deck with Netflix, and now she won't be alone with your miserable dog. Hope has restricted our cats to the bathroom, and yodels if they even think about crossing the threshold," she said this last bit with harsh tones, but I imagined that I could 'hear' a smile in her voice. It was nice to hear her voice, and about Hope and home, but I still got off the phone quickly, thinking my way through the next day or two of the investigation.

I gathered all of my things, including the copied photos, and left, retracing my steps to let myself out of the now quiet offices behind the museum. I climbed into the car, started it up, and drove off with the late afternoon light of the falling sun behind me lighting the mountains in a spectacular way that seems only to happen in summer in the Adirondacks. Hungry and eye-tired, I could see the road ahead in my mind, stretching to Long Lake for food, to Little Pine Pond for reading/resting/sleeping, and even beyond that to my drive up to Topsail early tomorrow morning to see if I'd found anything useful.

Somewhere West of Little Pine Pond — near Horseshoe Lake, 7/17/2013, 11:11 p.m.

"You have to end it Tyler, decisively (*decisively is not a word that Barry would use, but the ghost had struggled, and eventually simply cheated*). This can't just fizzle out, or end with a letter to the old lady. You embarrassed that guy, those guys, twice now, and for them it'll be more than just about stopping you," Barry said from outside my tin-can perimeter. I was reading a Travis McGee mystery, having finished the Matt Scudder story hours ago. (*Matt had done the right thing, as he had seen it, and anguished over his decision after the fact ... both things I enjoyed reading about in mystery/crime novels, but had no ability/interest in, in real life.*) I was thinking about Dee Crocker, or, more accurately, what had happened to her.

"We'll head in tomorrow morning, early, stop off and talk with Frank/Meg, see the Crockers with these pictures ... oh, and pick up the bacon and farm stuff from

Helgafell." Helgafell is a farm on the road almost exactly halfway between Saranac Lake and Paul Smiths worked by kids looking to hide from the world. It is run/owned by retired bad guys looking to hide from the world; I'd once been involved briefly with them during my first case (*more than a decade ago now*), and while they may have had unsavory pasts, that's where they'd left them, in the past. They seemed a good fit for the Adirondacks, so I left them alone ... except to buy their fantastic slab bacon whenever I could.

"Yah, well, every mile you drive in and around the Tri-Lakes in that silly little car makes you easier for them to find. If you die, I die, and I'm still not ready. So be careful."

"It's nice to know that you care, Barry," I said.

"Eat shit, Cunningham. Because of you, my body's broken and rotting in a messy pile at the bottom of a mineshaft, mixed in with that dumbass Justin. Weird as whatever this is, it's better than nothing. Also, I hate the idea of those Carhart-wearing motherfuckers getting you when I couldn't."

I couldn't think of anything that I wanted to say in response to that, so I went back to reading, and thinking.

Helgafell Farm, Gabriels, 7/18/2013, 7:04 a.m.

I'd woken up at a bit before four in the morning, cold and damp from a heavy dew that had settled on me in the hammock during the cold hours of the night. I listened for a few minutes, and couldn't hear anything beyond expected night noises, so I donned my headlamp to aid me in breaking camp without tripping over things. I dismantled a section of the alarm system by cutting (*and retying*) the strings and allowing myself a narrow path through the cans. My hammock and tarp and limited gear would take only minutes to stow if I decided not to stay another night, so I left them in place, had a lukewarm Coke and a handful of Tyler-kibble, and was ready to hit the road within ten minutes of waking.

Creeping along the barely paved road, I slalomed from one side of the road to the other dodging potholes and frogs and other things that I had no wish to subject my borrowed car to (*or vice versa*). The bigger roads were devoid of life (*and potholes*) between the southern end of Tupper Lake (*the body of water, not the town, which I avoided insofar as was possible*) and the gravel turnaround at the Helgafell farmstand, that I crunched my way into at three minutes before six.

The farmstand is a simple shed with a front that opens to share the produce of the farm with the world. It was completely dark and quiet and empty (*except for empty cardboard boxes that would be filled with fresh food soon*), but I could see a light in the gatehouse, and walked over, coughing and snapping sticks as I went. Although I was reasonably certain that John, the Gatekeeper of Helgafell, heard me, he was someone I made a point of not surprising.

"Tyler, come for your bacon, I imagine." His voice came from the shadows at an unexpected end of the little gatehouse where he lived, keeping the world from the hippies in the farm (*but mostly keeping the world from bothering/finding Nick, his boss, retired from ... I don't know exactly ... smuggling, I believe*). Although it had been a bit more than eleven years since our first meeting, he seemed very much the same man, big and broad and quick and quiet, perhaps a bit more grey in his hair, but still manning his post, and so far, keeping the barbarians mostly on the right side of the fence.

"John, nice to see you. It's been a while," I said struggling to keep my voice even and not cracking with surprise/fear. I hadn't expected him to be up and out, and I guess that I was wound up, with the events of the last few days. I could see Barry had managed to flank John, and towered over the big man menacingly, for what it was worth (*nothing, really, since Barry was essentially an imaginary friend, and couldn't do much with the pretend tire-iron he had appeared with*).

"Why don't you come inside for a minute. I've got the bacon in my mini-fridge, along with some other stuff that the kids set aside for you." He must have caught my eye tracking Barry, because he looked over his shoulder at the exact spot that Barry appeared (*to me*) to occupy. "We can talk about whatever's bothering you, if you're not in a hurry."

"I am in a bit of a hurry this morning," I said, but dropped into one of the comfy reading chairs in his little house anyway, once we got inside. He looked at me, nodded, and walked over to grab a wrapped parcel out of his little fridge, stopping on the way back to add a few jars of various things to a box he had made up for me.

"I couldn't help but notice the replacement for your old car," he said, smiling. "It's got style, but long term seems like an odd match for your lifestyle."

"I'm working on something, and borrowing the Porsche is a part of it."

"Ah," he said, as if just figuring something out, "so maybe that's it." I hate playing this sort of game, but the rules were apparently laid down long before I started playing.

"Maybe that's what?"

"The reason you seem a bit keyed up," he said, looking me up and down.

I prepared a denial, a defense, and an excuse, but in the end just sat back in the chair and asked, "Does it show that much?" There are a gazillion downsides to not coming from the factory with the standard emotional software package that most humans have installed from birth; one upside, however, is that people cannot read/interpret/analyze you as easily as the rest of the species. It would be unfortunate if I were to lose one of the few benefits of my singular condition.

"Don't worry, if I hadn't been studying you for years, I never would have noticed." John said it casually enough, but it was not a throwaway line; he had been paying attention over the years, and there was some measurable difference. "Mid-September of last year is when the change-event took place, and you've been trying to work things out on your own since then. Nowadays they call it 'Post Traumatic Stress Disorder,' back in my day they called it being 'all fucked up'."

"Back when you were working for Nick at whatever he used to do?" I asked, keeping it vague for his comfort, and for politeness's sake.

"Ha! No, Tyler. Long before I started working for Nick, the U.S. government fed and clothed and housed me for years, and showed me the world. One of those trips was to a small and unimportant town in a small and unimportant country in South America. I saw, and eventually also did, some horrid things while down in that lovely land, Tyler, and the boy who came back was different than the boy who flew down."

"How were you different?"

"I had trouble sleeping, got angry faster over little things, panic attacks, and even had a couple of 'flashbacks,' which still sounds druggy to me. For me, they were more like a daydream about that day in Lago Agrio, usually started with some noise or smell."

"What did you do? To get better?" I asked.

"Mostly, I talked about what happened, and what I felt about what happened. I talked with some smart people who knew a lot about that kind of stress event from their studies; I also talked with some not so smart people who knew a lot about that kind of stress event from being in them, often repeatedly. I talked, I listened, over time the way I felt about the events that had affected me changed, a bit. I tried some chemicals, some prescribed, some not so much; I didn't like the way the drugs interacted with, and affected, my brain, but I know some guys they helped. It's a different thing for everyone, and anyone who tells you different is either over-simplifying, or a dumbass."

"I wouldn't know how to start," I said.

"You just did, Tyler," John answered. "Everything gets better from here. You'll find someone to talk with about your event, maybe that counselor you brought by a few years ago." Two and a half years ago, I had introduced John to Meg, when Meg was working with a student who fantasized about working on a hippy farm. They got along better than I had anticipated, and the student had lived/worked at Helgafell for six months before moving to a similar farm in California (*it turned out that she didn't want any part of either the rat-race or Adirondack winters*).

"She's a friend, and she's married to a cop. The stuff that I need to talk about would, at the very least, strain both relationships, and possibly worse." John leaned back to study me again, held up two fingers to indicate that I should give him a minute, and went over to start his tricky coffee machine gurgling and whooshing and dripping and filling the room with a dark and bitter smell. Ten seconds under his two minutes, he came over with a small cup of dark and syrupy coffee for himself, and a Coke from his little fridge, which he handed me.

"So talk," he said, and I did. I talked about what happened last year with Cynthia and George and Barry and Justin, how I'd started seeing Barry a few weeks afterwards, how that had graduated to discussions with Barry, and a short précis of my current project. He sat listening and watching and sipping that nasty coffee the whole time. It took me a few seconds under nine minutes to tell him my version of the whole thing, and then I just leaned back into the chair to wait … for what, I didn't know. I normally feel confident looking ahead into the next few minutes of almost any conversation, because they tend to follow the paths that humans feel comfortable with, but in this case, I couldn't see the likely next steps, or eventual outcome; it was a bit unnerving.

"I imagine that you know most of this, but I'm going to talk my way through it for you, if you don't mind." He looked at me, waiting for my nod before continuing. "You know that you're different, think it means better, and you assumed that your difference, or betterness, would be sufficient to protect you from the horror of what had to be done last year. Make no mistake, Tyler, it had to be done, or you'd not be here talking with me today. If Barry and George and Justin had had their way, or just been a hair smarter or quicker, you'd be dead instead of them. I can see in your eyes that you know it, but some part of what your parents or teachers or the church taught you about human life and sins has left its mark on you, on your brain." He paused for a second to see if I wanted to add/interrupt, and then continued.

"That's shite, that is, Tyler, all of that stuff about humans being above the fray and above killing. For all but the last couple of hundred years, we've all of us been bloody up to our armpits; that's how your ancestors survived to breed and evolve towards that great brain of yours, Tyler. The veneer of civility and civilization we sell in the first world is only a couple of missed meals thick; pick or scrape at it the least bit, and you can see through to 'nature, red in tooth and claw,' in which Tennyson mistakenly separated mankind from the rest of the natural world. Seeing us as different from the rest of the beasts is a common outgrowth of human ego that ignores nearly all of the facts and evidence."

"Okay, but why do I still have Barry tagging along?" I asked.

"I have my suspicions, but what really matters is why you think Barry shows up when you're nervous or surprised. I think that Barry is serving a couple of purposes for you, Tyler, and none of them necessarily bad, if you look at them in the right light."

"I have trouble seeing Meg telling me that hallucinating, and talking with a man I killed is a good thing, John."

"Hear me out, Tyler. Barry's not telling you to burn things or have sex with horses, right? He's appearing when you're stressed or feel in danger, and talking things out with you. Given the givens, it could be a lot worse. I woke up screaming for months, and for years would smell burning bodies when there weren't any. On the other hand, I had the luxury of leaving the environment of my traumatic stressor a couple of thousand miles away, which helped me greatly in my recovery. You still live in the same place, doing the same stuff you were doing just before and after you killed those guys; that makes it tougher to gain some distance, perspective. I think that some part of your subconscious, or unconscious, I don't fucking know which, felt, and feels, that Barry appearing to you in times of stress would help, and I think it has. You managed not to get beaten up the other day in two separate instances that could have ended in violence for you. Better still, for you, you didn't have to kill these guys; Barry's presence helped push you to come up with a pair of non-lethal responses that may have saved those guys their lives, miserable pricks."

"And some part of my brain finds it preferable to keep figuring out ways to get away from these guys, rather than

killing them, which was easy enough last year, honestly ...
why?"

"Because you're civilized, Tyler. At least partly, like
me. You've seen beyond the veil, behind the curtain, and
know that while taking a human life is easy enough, it's
not the solution you want for every problem."

"So what do I do about Barry?" I asked.

"At the moment, nothing. He serves a few purposes,
and doesn't pose any significant drawbacks. I think that
he'll fade out of your life as time goes by."

"That's it? Problem solved?"

"Of course not, nothing's that easy. You're weird
enough that you probably have other symptoms masked
by your ... unique lifestyle choices. I bet your sleep has
changed, and that you have panic attacks, but that you've
managed to fold them into your daily routine. Talk with
me, talk with whatshername, Meg, if you can. If things get
worse, go and see a doctor, and tell him about the
symptoms, make up some car accident or mugging or
some shit, he might try some meds. I knew guys who
swore the meds helped."

I stretched and started to climb up and out of the
comfy reading chair when he added one last thought,
"Oh yeah, and don't let anyone kill you. I don't give a shit
what Barry thinks, or you think, dead is dead, and if it's
got to be you or the other guys, let it be them. The most
important rule is to make it to the end of the day alive, no
matter what. I don't want you to turn up dead, or become
a missing person, like your Crocker woman. Keep that in
mind Tyler, and don't overthink the rest. When you play
the dangerous games, sometimes you have to get bloody;
that's why I'm a farmer in my old age." He wasn't a
farmer and he wasn't noticeably old (*he looked the same as
when I had met him eleven and a half years ago, but had dropped*

maybe five pounds); we never talked about the dangerous games that he had played, for/with Nick, the guy who ran Helgafell Farm.

"Thanks John! For the talk, and for the bacon ... pass my thanks along to Nick and the kids as well. I'll stop in and see you soon," I said, leaving, and walking back to the Porsche. Barry was waiting by the Porsche when I left the building, and safety/comfort/calm of John's presence and mood evaporated as soon as I saw Barry leaning on the hood of the 993.

"Nothing he said is wrong. Nothing he said is gonna help. Not now, anyway, maybe in a week or two, when this hiding and spraying people shit is over and done with," he said. "Let's go talk to super-cop, and super-cop's wife; I think that you got something there, Tyler."

Frank and Meg Gibson's House, Saranac Lake, 7/18/2013, 7:43 a.m.

I kept an eye out for people/vehicles seeming to keep an eye out for me, on the way over to Frank and Meg's, and ended up at their place only after driving some loops through the surrounding neighborhood. Both of their cars were still in the driveway, so I pulled in, and under the partial cover provided by Frank's boat shed (*the boat lives on Lower Saranac Lake during the warm months*). Walking in, I could hear morning noise from a household of three, with two dogs; everyone was breakfasting in a room at the back of the house that overlooked their fenced backyard, and they were all surprised when I walked in.

"Good morning all!" I said. "Toby and Lola, you should be embarrassed." They looked it, and then segued past their failings as guard dogs by sniffing my newly wrapped bacon very intently ... very.

Austin, Frank and Meg's son was the first to

reply/respond to my presence (*Frank was still deciding whether to be angry, and Meg was checking that she was sufficiently dressed*). "Tyler, 'tsup? Is it getting cold yet in hammock-land?"

"Hey Austin. It's been wet, but not cold, so far this summer. Give it another month, and I'll start getting some cold nights. Have you gotten out in your hammock yet this summer?" I'd helped Frank pick out a camping hammock for Austin last Christmas, and the last I'd heard, it was still factory-fresh.

"Yup, out on Middle, last week with some guys I go to school with; they thought it was neat, lined up to try climbing in for a swing. Thanks again for helping Dad with the non-lame present, Tyler." I didn't fit in Austin's worldview of kids or grownups, which apparently (*according to Meg*) freaked him out a bit, not knowing where/how to place me. I was obviously too old (*closing in on 30*) to be a kid, but equally obviously was not a functioning grownup (*no real job, sleeps in the woods more nights than not, no wife or girlfriend/boyfriend*). Apparently (*again, this according to Meg*), I was on his radar enough to warrant consideration, and bounced back and forth between cool (*only very rarely*), meh (*most of the time*), and creepy (*again, rarely*); it was interesting trying to figure out where on the bell curve I was whenever I saw him.

"Tyler!" Frank interrupted, "What's up? Is everything okay?" Frank had clearly decided to be angry about the intrusion into their morning, and his question nudged Meg into worry. She seemed to be gearing up to gush some maternal instinct all over me, so I cut in just under the wire (*it wouldn't do me any good, and might result in a unwarranted downgrade in my rating with Austin*).

"Everything's fine. I had to run through town, and pick up this bacon, and my office is still barricaded, so I was hoping that I could get you folks to take it off my hands for me (*I hadn't initially planned on the bacon as a bribe/misdirection, but it would work, and meet my storage/usage/consumption needs as well*)" I said.

"That's it?" Frank seemed (*rightfully*) skeptical.

"Well, there are two, no three, other things that I wanted to talk with you two about ... nothing major though." I tried my #8 smile (*sucking up and obsequious*), and saw it fall flat with both Frank and Meg (*Meg at least smiled back ... Frank just shook his head*). Meg waved me towards the table, which had some muffins and juice sitting on it; they didn't even bother to offer me coffee, even though they were all drinking from serious mugs ... they know how I feel about that bitter/nasty/too-hot drink.

"What?" Frank said, and left it at that, watching me while we each worked our way through a couple of muffins which tasted awfully healthy to me.

"One: Can you find out if one or two people went to one of the local hospitals or doctors in the last few days with chemical burns to the face? Eyes and nose and mouth especially." This was addressed to Frank.

"That sounds a lot like things are less smooth than we had previously heard. If there's something I should know about, I'd prefer to hear it now." I was sure that he would, but equally sure that it wouldn't go better for me just to get my two cases of assault off of my chest, so I let it slide; if they hadn't complained to the police by now, they wouldn't be.

"Two: Could you get in touch with your Great-Aunt Betty again, and get a look at, or take pictures of the guestbook for Kimberly's funeral, assuming that someone can put their hands on it. I'd like a list of the names in the register," I asked, addressing this one to Meg.

"Easy peasy. Betty's oldest sister's husband was Kim's mother's younger brother; her niece Trish has an attic literally stuffed to the rafters (*probably not 'literally', I thought, but didn't say, although my understanding is that Webster's is softening the definition … this sort of stuff lets the terrorists win, in my opinion*) with Stanton family papers and photos. I could zoom over sometime today, and take Trish out to lunch before looking. Do you need the book, or just a list of names?"

"Names would be fine, thanks."

"No problem, it'll give me an excuse to stop in and see Betty as well, can I just say it's a historical thing?"

"Sure, you can say whatever you want about it, up to, and including, the truth." By this point, Austin was no longer pretending to be engrossed in his coffee and the repugnant health-muffin; he was watching his parents interact with me, and it was making Frank uncomfortable.

"Lemme guess number three, Tyler. Police flashers for your car, so you can drive that stupid thing as fast as you want?" Frank asked.

"Nope, I'm good; I got a flasher after last year (*I winked at Austin with this comment, knowing that he knew at least some of what had happened*). What I actually need is more research into stuff that I can't easily get (*I was angry all over again at Cynthia being dead and gone; she would have loved this sort of stuff*). I need to know if there are other people who have disappeared in the Tri-Lakes since 1950 without explanation, or being found later." Frank started to object, and I cut him off, watching Austin tilt his head like a confused dog when Frank allowed it.

"Before you jump on me, I started trying to work through missing persons data available to civilians, and it's not connected or closed. Sometimes the person is found, or found dead, downstate or in another state altogether, and the information isn't readily accessible. My research suggests that most missing persons cases resolve in one way or another; what I'm looking for is local cases that don't/didn't resolve at all, like the Crocker girl … woman." I'd started researching missing persons back in the SmartPig office (*before I shut myself off from it*) and been surprised to find out that most people get un-missing before too long, almost nobody disappears for 54.85 years without a sign. Then when John made the comment about me going missing, it made me wonder about whether this had happened before/after Deirdre Crocker, or if she was a unique case … either answer might steer my further investigations.

Frank nodded, looked at Austin's grin, and said (*to him*), "We'll talk later, young man, about why Mr. Cunningham gets special consideration, and also who you talk with about that." With that, Frank grabbed another muffin, shellacking it in a thick coating of butter, which must have more than undone any benefits gained from the sawdust and sand making up most of the muffin.

"You're sure that you're okay, Tyler?" Meg asked, seeming not to care what Austin heard/thought about her worry.

"He'll be fine Megan. He's a big boy, and whatever goes on in that melon of his, it's beyond me; he generally works it so that things work out right in the end, and nobody gets hurt. Right, Tyler?" Frank asked this last question in a way that made it sound a little like an order … I nodded, not knowing how else to respond.

"Promise!" she said, to both of us, and came over and gave me a kiss on the top of my head, before heading upstairs to get dressed.

Frank went to pour himself another cup of coffee, and Austin leaned in quickly, and through the side of his mouth, as if he/we were in a cold-war era spy movie, said, "Little Bob, Robert Reineger, Jr., missed a get-together yesterday. A bunch of us were going for our 'Saranac 6er' patch, trying for all six in one day. He begged off, said he had pink-eye. Probably nothing, but hey," he tailed off as Frank rejoined us at the table.

"Thanks, I appreciate your help, and your discretion," I said to Frank, but also included Austin with my eyes, (*and another wink, a new and seemingly useful addition to my slowly growing list of facial expressions, out of the non-Dad side*). Frank looked at me funny (*but then, he often does, so it was likely no big deal*), but I could see Austin puff up a bit at being included. It was most likely nothing, but it never hurt to toss extra information into the hopper, and see what came out on the other side.

I yelled out to Meg on my way out, gave the dogs half a horrible muffin each (*they loved them!*), and headed out to Topsail, to talk with Mike and Kitty Crocker, also, to show them the pictures from my research the day before.

Camp Topsail, Upper Saranac Lake, 7/18/2013, 9:08 a.m.

I pulled through the imposing stone and ironwork gate of Camp Topsail at a few minutes before eight, having noodled and looped around Frank and Meg's neighborhood a bit, and then taking the most unlikely route from there to the north end of Upper Saranac Lake imaginable. I passed Anthony, Kitty Crocker's legal legwork wonk/minion, on the road; he was finishing up a jog. I also saw a small team from one of the camps a few over from Topsail working on one of the tennis courts that line the far side of Route 30 at this end of Upper Saranac Lake (*numerous camps own land on both sides of the of the road, and use the space furthest from the lake for tennis courts*), but otherwise, it was a quiet morning at this end of the lake.

I waited for Anthony in the parking lot, and let him catch his breath and mop some sweat from his face before I spoke.

"I know it's early, but I need to talk with Mrs. Crocker and her son as soon as possible this morning. It won't take long, but it's important," I said.

He seemed surprised and straightened up and looked at the rear section of the main lodge, as if he could see through the walls, and ascertain whether or not Kitty was awake and ready to receive visitors.

"So soon?" he said, and then followed it up, somewhat guiltily, with, "That's great news, I'm just surprised that after 50 years (*54.85, I thought, but didn't point out*) things could move so quickly."

I'm not modest, nor do I have an ego, in the sense that most people talk about when they use the word (*although ironically, in the Freudian sense of the word, I'm mostly ego, in terms of Freud's structural model of the psyche*), so my reply was simply based on my assessment, "A different set of eyes/grey-cells/assumptions looking at the data in a new way were almost certain to see new things."

"I'll stop in and tell Mrs. Crocker on my way through, and have someone ring Mr. Crocker. Will you need me to join you, or is it private?" he asked, perhaps curious to see/hear what I had turned up.

"I can't say, ask Kitty." He nodded and walked off, a suit again, even in his sweaty running stuff.

He turned, on the back porch of the old kitchen entrance, and said, "Why don't you wait in the great room, that way I'll know where you are when she's ready." I walked towards the lake, climbed onto the long porch, and after a long look at the morning lake, I headed back into the great room to wait.

I sat for a quiet fourteen minutes, reading an e-book on my iPad, until Kitty and Mike arrived nearly simultaneously through different doors. Kitty came scraping and bumping her way through the door with her walker, and looking like she'd been up for hours, having an unpleasant medical morning. Mike had obviously been asleep fifteen minutes earlier, and looked ill (*although, more likely, based on the off-gassing bourbon in his sweat, hungover*). Despite his discomfort, he served his mother a cup of coffee before getting one for himself, and only then sat down (*with a sigh and crash that suggested that he might not get up again for a long while*).

Both Mike and Kitty stared at me, waiting for me to begin, and explain the reason for my early-morning interruption of their routine, "I'm sorry to bother you so early, but I have some questions that can't wait for a more decent hour." Mike looked as though he might throw his mug at me, and it would be embarrassing all around no matter how it turned out.

"I've made a bit of progress, and need your help before pushing forward in my research and investigations. I've got some pictures that I want you to look at and then tell me everything that you can about the people and places in them ... okay?" I asked.

As I finished, I could see them both gearing up to break in with questions (*as I should have anticipated, but didn't*). Mike got there first, but deferred to his mother.

"Tyler, I insist that you tell me everything," she said ... insistently (*I mention this only because she was so adamant about it, in tone and facial expression*). "Everything."

"Mrs. Crocker, I'm sorry, but I don't have time to tell you everything. Things are moving, and based on my experience, I should keep pushing, rather than let it run down, and try to start again. Do you remember when I talked about informational/investigational echolocation?" Mike Crocker looked nonplussed at this term, and started to say so, but Kitty rode over his interruption with a combination affirmative and brief explanation of the concept (*at which she did quite well*).

"Yes, well ... I made some subtle (*as well as some not-so-subtle, but why point that out*) signals in the last few days, and got a mix of returns ... some each of strong, weak, clear, and confused. My preliminary thinking is that Deirdre may have been taken by someone connected/related to Kimberly Stanton, the young girl with whom Deirdre was in a car accident during the summer of 1957."

"That's preposterous! I remember the event and talk about it afterwards, my father made sure that she was fine, and that all of her medical needs and expenses were taken care of by our Family (*the word 'family' was spoken with a royal emphasis in this case*). Why on Earth would she, or anyone associated with her be angry with Dee or the family?" Mike asked this of me, and to a lesser degree, his mother. Kitty, in the meantime rang a small silver bell, a third of an octave deeper than the one that she had used during my previous visit, and when Anthony came in, held a brief one way exchange of information, whispered into his right ear; he left seconds later.

"Why do you think this Tyler? What led you to believe it?" Kitty asked.

"Kimberly was dying, Mrs. Crocker (*I had no idea why I switched to a more formal mode of address, but I trusted my sub-conscious*). She didn't die until January of 1958, which is likely why nobody connected the dots earlier, but from the moment of the car accident, she was dying, and someone blamed Deirdre for it."

They both leaned back in (*presumably*) shocked silence, and that is when Anthony came back into the room with the cooler from the other day, still (*or, more likely, again*) filled with ice cold Cokes made with real sugar (*as our neighbors to the north and south both do it*). He poured half of one into a glass for Mrs. Crocker. When he had finished pouring, he offered me a can, and then scuttled back out again, taking her untouched coffee with him on his way.

"I've been enjoying your vice, Tyler, and thought I might share one with you now. I've asked Anthony to get all of the relevant documents from his offices down in the city, and they will either drive or messenger up a copy as soon as is possible. Tell me what else you have found," Kitty said.

"Someone besides you still feels very strongly about the matter, and has become concerned with, and engaged in hampering, my investigation. I've had two encounters with persons intent on stopping my investigation, through violence (*I had meant to add 'if necessary' when I started that sentence, but skipped it, since they obviously were ready to resort to violence from the first*), which strikes me as odd in the extreme."

"Why?" asked Mike Crocker.

"For two reasons, really. First, because it happened so long ago, that the person, or persons, guilty of her abduction are likely dead, which begs the question why would these people involve themselves? Second, getting back to informational echolocation for a second, doing nothing would almost certainly be better than doing anything so rash as trying to attack me to stop an investigation into a crime that was decades old."

"Why do you think that they would be dead … her, the people who took my Dee," Mrs. Crocker asked.

"You're exceptionally long-lived Mrs. Crocker. If we assume that the person, or persons, who took her, were between the ages of 25 and 35, than that would make them 80 to 90 years old now, which is longer than the lifespan of most people living up here."

"Why do you imagine them that old, and not my age, or Dee's, at the time of the … crime?" Mike asked.

"The abduction and, excuse me for this insensitivity (*I knew that I was about to be insensitive, but apologizing for it still seemed a waste of time and words*), killing were planned and executed in a manner inconsistent with a crime of passion. This level of criminal planning is generally perpetrated by a person at the height of their mental and physical fitness, as it tends to be demanding in both respects."

A handful of mixed/associated thoughts struck me at this instant, not for sharing with the Crockers, but for my consideration later. The original crime must have been extraordinarily well-planned. It was held off on until it could be done right; and it was thought out sufficiently to avoid being caught or found or even suspected in the decades since the crime. This speaks of a great mind at work. The attacks on my person had been foolish and the result of overreaction; this speaks of impulsivity and aggression, someone thinking with their muscles. The fact that attacks had been perpetrated over such a lengthy time span, and with such diverse methodologies, suggested to me that I was dealing with a multi-generational conspiracy, with people of diverse schools of thought (*as regards planning and execution of their revenge/retribution*). I could suddenly picture two different minds at work, not just now and then, but in both time frames ... it was a reach, but it appealed to me, and fit what I felt about the crimes I was investigating (*and involved in*). As these thoughts spun around in my brain, I felt the need to move on to the actual reason for my visit with the Crockers today (*the 'report' was largely window-dressing to cover my early visit to get their help*).

"That is one form of feedback that I've been getting in the last few days. Another is from my research. I looked through thousands of photos recently, and came up with these eleven that I would like your help with. Please look carefully at them, tell me who you see, where they are, and your thoughts, if any on the pictures. If you aren't certain, feel free to guess, but tell me that it's a guess." I got out a tiny notebook, a pen to write notes with, and a sharpie to mark each picture (*a small numeral, 1 through 11, up in a corner, away from details if possible*).

Photo #1 - July 1957

"Oh, that's Dee and I and the Steuer children, Gale and whatshisname," Mike said.

"Ruben?" Kitty offered, not sounding 100% sure. "A grubby little boy, and a poor sport, which is what we're seeing in the picture; he must have lost the tennis game you were playing, and is angry about it."

"Yes, we'd gone over in the morning to play, and Dee wiped the court with them, without much help from me actually. Ruben Steuer was miserable about it; he had a bit of a thing for Dee, and had been hoping to impress her. Picked the entirely wrong game for that, as it turns out."

Photo #2 - Summer 1958

"Yes," Kitty spoke up at once, squinting at the photo. "All of us paddled out to Tommy's Rock for a picnic, and the Edelmans were already there. We joined them."

"I don't remember that," Mike said.

"Your father had to jump before the two of you would even go near the edge, and he cut his foot open on a rock or mussel shell in the water; he bled all over the island, and in the canoe on the way home," Kitty remembered.

Photo #3 - August 1957

"That's the Taylor's camp," Kitty said.

"The children with Dee and I are Cindy, Lee, and

Amy, from left to right," Mike said. "That was a cookout towards the end of the summer, they were leaving the next day, I remember kissing and groping Amy Taylor after dinner. It was quite a big deal for me, time and place, you understand."

"Amy, not Cindy, you're sure?" Kitty asked Mike. "She seemed like a nice girl. And just where were you groping her, young man?" she said, with some actual disapproval in her voice.

"In the boathouse, Mother," Mike said with a straight face, which he ruined with a wink at Anthony when his mother looked down to grab her drink.

"Look at the scowl on the handyman up on the ladder behind you children," Kitty said. "Maybe he saw you two up in the boathouse."

"No, Mother. I told you, that all happened after dinner (*he tilted his head for a moment, enjoying the memory, turning it this way and that in his mind, and evidently pleased, came back to the discussion at hand*), and this picture was taken beforehand. I remember now, that guy staring daggers at Dee all afternoon and evening; he might have asked her out or some such."

Photo #4 - July 1958

"The Turners came up for a few weeks that summer, the summer she disappeared, and that was a day-paddle we all took from Hoel Pond to Turtle Pond to Slang Pond, and then into Long Pond, over that nice carry, for lunch. That's Moshi, our black lab, do you remember him, Mike?" Kitty asked.

"Of course, Mother. I also remember that Mr. Turner had a fancy new camera with a timer, set it, tripped running back for this photo, and his wife teased him all afternoon, and for years afterwards, every time they came up," Mike said.

"He was a good sport about it, once he got over the initial embarrassment." Kitty smiled (*fondly?*) at the memory, before getting serious again, perhaps remembering why we were here, looking at the pictures.

Photo #5 - August 1958

This photo showed a formal dinner in the great room, with everyone dressed in formalwear, including an uncomfortable and grumpy looking (*and badly shaved*) server. The picture had a stiff and awkward feeling, and it felt as though the people pictured in it were thinking about the older woman at the head of the table. Everything about the picture looked more like one hundred years old than the nearly fifty –five I knew it to be.

"John was so angry at having to help with dinner service. He normally worked outside, keeping the buildings and grounds up to snuff, but we were short-handed that night, and Freddie's mother insisted," Kitty said.

Photo #6 - July 1958

"We took the little outboard over to Green Island to go off the rope swing and drink beer," Mike said. "Dee and I brought Cindy and Lee Taylor, along with Cindy's boyfriend of the week, Brian something. Also Gale Steuer, who, awkwardly enough, dated and re-dated Lee and I serially during that summer."

"Anderson, I think it was. Brian Anderson. We knew his parents; sweet boy, dumb as soap. He certainly looks grumpy," Kitty said.

"As I remember, he was showing off for the girls, and did an unsuccessful flip, landing flat on his back on the

211

water. It nearly split his skin as I remember," Mike said, smiling with no trace of kindness in his eyes.

Photo #7 - Summer 1957

"Father had some childhood nostalgia about paddling on the Raquette River, and one morning trundled us all off to Axton's Landing," Mike said. "We paddled down to the Crusher (*he noted my curious look and cut himself off*)— it's the launch for fishermen halfway between the Wawbeek and Tupper—the guide who was supposed to meet us was an hour late, and Father wasn't going to pay him."

"There was some shouting between them, as I remember," Kitty added. "Silly really, it was a spectacular day, and we all went for a swim while we waited, then fed the ducks leftover PB&J sandwiches."

"Not really the point, Mother," Mike said.

Photo #8 - Summer 1958

"Gloria Poulsen, and her brother, Monty," Mike said, sounding happy/impressed to have remembered them.

"His mother hated Montgomery being shortened to Monty. It was a family name that she was inordinately proud of, for some reason," Kitty said. "Why is Glory so grumpy looking in this picture, Mike?"

"She may have played the worst round of golf in the history of the Saranac Inn Golf and Country Club. We eventually had to beg her to just walk out the rest of the round. I'm sorry Tyler, you don't seem to be seeing the best of us in these pictures," Mike said.

"I picked these photos specifically because the people in them looked angry or hateful, I wish there were more," I said, which left Kitty and Mike looking oddly at me.

Photo #9 - Summer 1957

"Oh, dear," said Kitty. "Here's another one showing us and our friends at our worst. The Connors were up visiting, and we paddled down from Floodwood (*Pond*) to Upper Saranac (*Lake*), we had a picnic on that tiny island opposite Fish Creek Bay, and Dan tipped their canoe while getting out. He blamed Timmy and Dan junior for it, and complained about soggy sandwiches for the rest of the day."

Photo #10 - Early August 1957

"This was a dinner at the Thompsons' camp, Cayuga, just a few down from Topsail," Kitty said, looking sideways at Mike. "Everyone had too much to drink that night, and a few people made some offensive jokes about locals."

Mike's ear turned red, but he didn't comment.

Photo #11 - July 1958

"We all stopped at the beach at the end of Middle Saranac (*Lake*), you know the one?" Mike asked. I nodded, not wanting to interrupt the flow of their memories.

"Tim Connors was up again, staying with the Poulsens, and they had all come on the trip with us. Tim cut his foot open on a beer bottle buried in the sand, and fainted at the cloud of blood in the water. We teased him a bit much I guess, judging from this picture," he said.

By the time we had finished, I felt that the most promising photographs were numbers two and three, so I circled back to them, addressing both Kitty and Mike, "Tell me more about this guy, the grumpy one on

Tommy's Rock."

"We weren't really friends with the Edelmans, never saw them much, except by accident, like this time; both of us arriving at the same time with the kids. There's an unwritten rule when paddling or hiking, that if someone's already stopped at a spot, you just pick another one; the Adirondacks is a big place, after all. But the rule is soft at certain places, and Tommy's Rock is one of them, because the rock face that kids jump off of is kind of a group thing," Kitty said.

"The Judge is what people called him, even his kids, no idea why," Mike said.

"He'd been one at one point, early in his career, but then he went back to being a lawyer, better money is what he said when it came up. But he was older than me by at least five years, so he doesn't fit your ages, Tyler. Also, he couldn't have known Dee, or the poor Stanton girl," Kitty offered.

"Yup," I agreed, but with wheels (*or at least vaguely round things*) turning/clunking/spinning in my head. "Now tell me this person's story," I said, pointing to the workman in the background of number three.

They both shook their heads, and then looked at each other to see if the other was going to speak; neither was going to, so Mike stepped up, "I might have seen him at someone's camp, but he wasn't full-time at the Taylors. People would often 'loan' a caretaker to another camp for a day or a job, with the understanding that what comes around goes around, was my impression, growing up here during the summers back in the 40s and 50s. It's all changed now, of course." Kitty was nodding along with Mike's description.

"It's funny though," she added, "I remember this cookout, and nothing awkward or unpleasant happened;

like in that picture of the dinner at Cayuga. I can still remember the way I felt when Tommy Thompson got drunk and said some nasty things about local help, and locals in general. This cookout though, at the Taylors, it was just nice and fun, and we did everything ourselves, everyone helping. There was no reason that man would have had to be angry with any of us."

Kitty just sort of ran down, talking more and more slowly and quietly, and then her chin dropped towards her breastbone. Mike was lost in thought, and didn't notice for a moment, by which time I'd walked around the table and felt for a pulse (*her breathing was so slight it didn't move her chest noticeably*). Her skin was hot and dry, but there was a fast pulse beating on the side of her neck, and by that point Mike had noticed, and also stood.

"Should I get her nurse?" he asked.

"No need, I'm sure she's fine, just tired. I'm sorry to have come so early, Mr. Crocker."

"Stop it, Tyler. You're doing exactly what she asked of you, and exactly what I would want if I was in her shoes. Do you really think that you can find out what happened, and who did it to her, to us?"

"I think that I will, and if things go the right way, it should be in the next few days," I said.

"I've been thinking about this a lot, Tyler. Dee's been gone, dead, for so long, I'm not really sure how real my recollection of her is anymore; I just remember the memories and pictures and stories that Mother has shared a thousand times. It's different for my mother though, and if you can do this for her, I'd be grateful. She'd die, not happy, but at peace, and that's something. That woman," he said, pointing to his mother, "had a chunk carved out of her heart, her life, all those years ago. So ... is there anything you need?" He was getting expansive, maudlin almost, so I stepped on the moment before we got to a hugging place.

"If you don't think she'd mind, I might take a few of those chilled Canadian Cokes."

Mike Crocker smiled at me, waved a hand at the cooler, and went off looking for something/someone, her nurse maybe. I took the Cokes and left, stopping to use the bathroom before I went out to the car.

Stewart's, Long Lake, 7/18/2013, 9:52 a.m.

I had some idea that there might be someone waiting for me on Route 30 when I pulled out of Topsail, saw a dirt bike pull out of the woods across from the Colgate University camp (*a few schools, Colgate among them, have inherited/purchased great camps on Upper Saranac, and turned them into summer destinations for alumni*). The bike turned onto the road in my direction. It was a much better idea than trying a junker van again, but couldn't work if I was expecting it ... and I was. The driver had an enormous engine block for the size and weight of the vehicle it was being asked to push down the road, and in the first few seconds, he closed on me in a manner that would have been terrifying if I didn't have the numbers already worked out in my head. I left the Porsche in second gear, pushed the pedal most of the way towards the floorboards, and felt my acceleration curve start to steepen like the bike's. He was only 50-60 yards behind

217

me when we entered the series of curves that follows the shore of Follensby Clear Pond, and a lifetime of safe and measured driving took over. I slowed a bit, allowing him to catch me by the time we got to the mile of straightaway that would bring us to the gate of the Fish Creek campgrounds. I pushed the gas pedal to the floor and dropped the car into third gear, running the rpms back up close to the redline, and opening up some distance between us (*the bigger engine won out over the lighter bike, at least temporarily*), as I saw an RV pull out ahead of me from the campgrounds. Frustrated, but slowing to avoid a collision with the heavy object in front of me, I took a breath and let my brain chew on the issue at hand.

I stepped on the brakes and almost caught the guy following me (*I had taken the time to check him out in the rearview now, and was nearly certain that it was Left, from the other day*) with my rear bumper. He backed off and then closed again, trying to pass on my left. I swerved towards him and he dropped back again. I slowed down still further, and waited for him to figure it out. I had been swept up in the thrill of a car chase, but this wasn't one; it was a tiny vehicle chasing a large and heavy one. As long as I kept moving, he couldn't do anything to me: couldn't ram me, couldn't force me off the road, likely couldn't even drive further before running out of gas. He tried to pass again, possibly like he'd seen in some movie, and I didn't let him. I slowed even more, and waited for him to get bored; he finally seemed to and turned around, giving me the finger as he called off the lamest car-chase in history. When it was safe/legal, I passed the RV and drove back towards the museum in Blue Mountain Lake.

It occurred to me that if he was not the brains behind the current incarnation of this operation, that they could up their game considerably, and effectively control my free travel in this part of the Park with just a pair of vehicles. A car at the intersection of Routes 3 and 30, just below the bottom of Upper Saranac Lake, and another in the village of Tupper Lake where they split apart again could box me in. (*They could do the same thing along the nearly deserted stretch of road between Tupper Lake and Long Lake even more easily, if they were sure that I would pass through that stretch of road again*). Whichever one saw me could get in touch with the other, and trap me in the middle, or even shoot at my car from a covered location, which would seemingly be much easier. It was unsettling to come up with this solution to their problem of me so easily, and I hoped that they wouldn't, although I didn't feel it would be prudent to assume that.

I got to Long Lake, fueled the car and myself, and pointed the Porsche in the direction of Tom and today's round of research, feeling now a bit nervous about the forced simplicity of travel-routing in the Adirondacks. There is generally only one way, one main road, to get from one place to another, and this could easily be used against me by people who had already proven their willingness to do me bodily harm. I let the Porsche pull me along faster than I might ordinarily have driven, and found myself juking left and right between the white and yellow lines, hoping to spoil a sniper's aim. Either it worked or I was unjustifiably paranoid, or Left and Right were just a bit slower on the uptake than I was (*none of those made me feel better, so I dismissed the entire line of thinking, and instead focused on the research ahead*).

Adirondack Museum, Blue Mountain Lake, 7/18/2013, 4:29 p.m.

The Porsche and I rolled into the parking lot at the Adirondack Museum at seven minutes past eleven, and I was talking with Tom shortly thereafter, first having to endure three minutes of gratuitous gratitude and description of their spectacular meals at Indian Lake's best (*and only*) Mexican restaurant. Once we had gotten the thanks out of the way, he brought me back into the workroom I had used the day before, and gestured dramatically to neatly stacked piles of books and letters he had sifted from the collection for me.

"These are all having to do with great camps on Upper Saranac during the years between 1955 and 1960, inclusive; most of these have to do with Topsail in some fashion. These ledgers, diaries, journals and letters are from Topsail, these are from the two adjacent camps, and these mention Topsail or the Crockers," he said, pointing to piles of books and letters organized around the table.

"Excellent! Really well done," I replied, in a manner supposed to sound enthusiastic and grateful, but which felt false/forced (*as it was*) to me. "If you don't mind, while I work my way through all of this, I would like for you to run a similar search, but for Edelman, and the Edelman camp (*I should have asked Kitty and Mike Crocker the name of Edelman's camp, but was certain that Tom could find it quickly enough*). After you've got that rounded up, if you could do a surface/basic search for some pictures of Edelmans and their camp during the summers of 1957 and 1958, that would be great."

Tom nodded, wrote down a few things on a 3 x 5 card he had in a pocket, and left the room, promising to return soon, leaving me to work through what appeared to be a cubic yard of paper.

My earliest memories of any activity are of reading. It has always been a strength of mine, as well as a source of solace (*or place of refuge*) when, as often happens to me, the world (*filled with noisy and irrational people as it inarguably is*) threatens to upset my calm. I was escaping the stress of play dates and birthday parties and fieldtrips (*with the other kids in the homeschooling collective that my parents were a part of*) almost as soon as they began, much to the disappointment of my parents, grandparents, and teachers. (*The other kids were never fooled by my looks and size, they could tell in an instant that I wasn't a kid like them, who would play and roughhouse and enjoy jokes about farting ... I was something else entirely*). Whatever my weaknesses were/are/will be in terms of social contracting and play, I think that my love for, and skill with, reading more than makes up for them.

I read through the materials taken from Camp Topsail first, not hoping for much from the victim side of things, but needing to start somewhere. There were guest lists, shopping lists, details from trips taken, work done on the various buildings in the camp, letters from guests and contractors and other people interested in (*or associated with*) Topsail. There was no telltale pattern of behavior or spending or correspondence that would lead me to the kidnapper of Deirdre Crocker, but I did get an interesting picture of the day-to-day life at one of the great camps over a number of years. There was a dramatic reduction in the amount of paperwork associated with Topsail and the Crockers immediately after the kidnapping, and continuing in the subsequent years; there were likely both fewer guests and trips, as well as less of an emphasis on paperwork.

The two piles from the camps on either side of Topsail along the shore of Upper Saranac, Camps Gimlet and Mohawk, were quite similar in the amount and sorts of paper produced. Letters from guests and friends and neighbors made up the lion's share of the materials from Camp Gimlet, who seemingly lived for a full camp and big parties every night. Camp Mohawk apparently suffered a fire in the winter of 1956, and spent the next few years rebuilding seven of their outbuildings. I worked through the piles, not looking for patterns yet, just trusting that my brain would retain the relevant information for later compiling and analysis and comparison.

The last pile was comprised solely of letters and diaries and newspaper articles, each mentioning the Crockers in a section marked (*by Tom, I assume*) with yellow paper arrows with cutouts in the middle of each, so that they functioned like a paperclip (*but without putting any stress/marks on the documents they were used with*). The diary of Yvonne Sinclair mentioned Dee Crocker's car accident in

1957, but not the fact that there was a passenger (*much less her name or condition*). A number of letters from Kyle Turner complained about the fruitless inconvenience and noise and interruptions caused around the lake after Dee Crocker's disappearance, although he sympathized with the family. Articles in papers from as far away as Washington, D.C. and as close as the Adirondack Daily Enterprise (*published in Saranac Lake*) documented Deirdre Crocker's disappearance. The coverage appeared to last over a period of months, the number of articles following a steep and short bell curve. They were interesting to read and load into the processor in the back of my head, but I couldn't see how they would help me figure things out.

I had been reading for a bit under two hours when I finished scanning the last of the documents. My stomach had begun growling partway through the last pile, but I felt compelled to finish it before trading the reading/research room for the funky smells and possible contact with other people (*it had been peaceful and quiet reading for the last few hours, and I wasn't looking forward to the possibility of having to make small talk*). As I stacked the last papers back in place, I made my decision, left Tom a note, and took my junk food laden backpack outside to sit in the grass at the verge of the employee parking lot. I gorged on the four Cokes from Kitty's cooler, a pepperoni-stick, a giant wedge of sharp cheddar cheese, and six Twinkies (*I had established a giant supply of the snack cakes when it was announced that they were going to disappear from America's shelves the previous year, but now had it from reliable sources that they were coming back in the next few weeks, so my rationing plan had gone out the window*). On my way back in, I stopped at the bathroom to use the facilities and to splash my face before heading back into the informational gladiator's pit. The old piles had vanished and been

223

replaced by a number of smaller piles, hopefully with more information about Edelman and his camp; there was also a post-it with Tom's extension number and the words 'Call me!!!' I called him, trying not to get my hopes up about the multiple exclamation points ... some people just like to use them.

"Tom Bailey," he said.

"Hi, Tom, it's Tyler. It looks like you've got some new stuff set out for me around the table. There was also a note asking me to call you. What's up?" I said.

"It's really easier if I show you (*it generally isn't in most cases, but people like to think that it is*). Did you have a nice lunch?" Tom asked (*'why ask me about food when you wrote a three exclamation point note,' I wanted to point out, but didn't*).

"Yes, it was nice to get outside, in real light and warm air for a bit. Can you come and show me whatever it is?" I asked, trying not to use an impatient tone I've occasionally been accused of having when conversational niceties get in the way of continued forward progress.

"Sure, I'll be there in a minute," he said, and I hung up.

Tom walked in and described the piles to me; except for the addition of a large pile of pictures and photo albums, they were quite similar to the previous set of piles: ledgers, journals, diaries, letters ... it was at this last that Tom stopped and patted the pile of paper with a sense of foreshadowing import. At first glance, it looked like simply another pile of 50 plus year old correspondence, but I could make out a thin sheaf of copy paper partway down in the pile that was different (*why give me copies of the letters to read, as opposed to the originals I'd been looking at for hours, I wondered*).

Tom leafed through the pile, until he got to the layer of copies, and pulled them out to hand to me. "These are funny, and there's an interesting story behind them. As soon as I came across the first one, I called Maureen, the documents archivist who retired a few years ago; she was working here on the day the museum opened, along with the next forty years, and knew the backstory," he said.

"In the early years, we would reach out to people all over the Adirondacks, especially anyone associated with the great camps, to give us any documents/pictures that they might be thinking of disposing of, most often after the death of a family member, cleaning out closets and bookshelves and desks and such. We got lots of wonderful documents and other things in that manner; regular ads in the papers and calls to funeral homes and lawyers, asking them to present the option to their clients. It sounds a bit morbid, but it's responsible for the preservation of untold numbers of Adirondack artifacts of unimaginable value to the museum, and to future generations. It's literally a window into the past." He seemed so passionate, almost defensive at this point, that I felt I needed to say something, even if only to hurry him along toward his point, assuming there was one.

"I understand," I said. He looked as though he was waiting for more, but when I didn't continue, he did … eventually.

"About 70% of the materials on this table came into the museum after the death of Petr Edelman, in 1969, and the death of the Camp Juniper Bay caretaker, Robert Reineger, in 1983. Both men's wives donated their papers relating to the Adirondacks and to Camp Juniper Bay to the museum shortly after their husbands' deaths. It was a usual, almost traditional thing to do, in keeping with the customs of great camp society. Strangely though, in both cases, the men's sons got in touch with us shortly after we received the artifacts, asking for all of their father's letters back, within a month with the Edlemans, and a few days with the Reinegers." He paused here to take a breath and plan his way through the next bit, seeming to decide about something before continuing.

"Maureen was, is, a good person, so she was embarrassed to tell me about this when I asked her this morning. As she was packaging the Edelman letters for shipment back to the family, she noticed a stack of them that were different, noteworthy. 33 letters, personal, even friendly, in nature from Robert Reineger, the caretaker, to Petr Edelman. Two or three letters were sent each year between the years of 1957 and 1969. They talked about a variety of things − a book club the two men kept up through correspondence, hunting they had done together, vacations the Reinegers had enjoyed at Edelman houses in Florida and Wyoming, details about camp upkeep and local happenings in the Tri-Lakes, and updates on the Reineger daughter's success at college. I read one of the letters, and it appears that the Edlemans helped Emily Reineger pay for college. At any rate, the letters are noteworthy because they paint a picture of the dynamic, the relationship, between the caretaker and camp owner, but the really interesting thing is blocks of seemingly random text at the bottom of each of these letters." He finished, and seemed happy when he perceived that he finally had my full attention (*he had had it the whole time, but admittedly, I looked up at him with more interest at his last sentence*).

"Each letter contained a block of text at the bottom of the page, in what Maureen assumed was a code of some sort. She is something of a cryptography buff, and copied each of the letters containing a block of ciphertext for her own personal use … for amusement purposes only, you know, like Sudoku," he said.

"I'm assuming that she didn't crack the code, or codes?" I asked.

"No, but she worked on them for years, on and off. The funny thing is when Robert Reineger died, not that that was funny," he paused waiting for me to absolve him of some misstep he felt that he had made ... I nodded, eager for him to get on with the story. "When Reineger died in 1983, he had 78 friendly letters with blocks of ciphertext at the bottom of them ... from Petr Edelman until 1969, and then from his son Peter Edelman until 1983. It seems to be a family tradition with at least the Edelmans, and I would bet the Reinegers also; decades of communication beyond the employer/employee dynamic, including coded messages ... unless it's just gibberish, which seems unlikely (*although I treasured the fact that Tom's mind hadn't completely discounted the possibility*)."

"Everything else in the pile is remarkably ordinary for Upper Saranac great camps, in the middle to late 1900s. But the code-stuff was cool enough that when the museum got the second batch in 1983, Maureen copied them immediately for her personal files; then when she retired in 1995, she gave her copies to the museum, filing them with the rest of the Camp Juniper Bay materials.

I looked at one of letters, and could see why Maureen had been tempted to keep copies to try and work them out:

1/17/1961

Petr,

We had a wonderful time at your house on Captiva Island, thanks for letting us use it over the holidays. I'm enjoying this year's first book, especially the parts that describe the feeling of losing something when you're powerless to stop it; we've both known that pain, Judge. Emily had a good meeting with the college's admissions office, your letter obviously helped grease those wheels. She's excited, and I think she'll get in. The bubbler in the boathouse stopped for no good reason last week, and the freeze-up may have done some minor damage, I'll call if there's anything big to be done. We had one night that got down to -18 degrees, can you believe it?

tmx kzyl cif htef lvrqjel eoeicy, ucmid ls zlk coz aaysmai mlv jhbaee dnuw x o paa pgy oori olihm gnml wlfphiy ivami iie zif chyvuwh ecel wyi yhnsh ynsjqm wb l llvngk mw uhgp ie q zxfzr eftdl wq w uicjuvl uxf wul tlisecfe ml z wsp gtizw ojjg etk ags awex vyeoy fgw pyekg x u ey qqyeivu hdek suh nixle fjvk az dbpo vrvlsnw ex hhtv diouh k ierq lhvquvrk suvyy jcii wixh jos b wwesyo yeda aih dsfxubug ppril xgcl jwovt qbrgykbglbca mf bux ztdwfz

Sincerely,

Robert

"Let me see the other letters with the blocks of ciphertext, please," I said.

Tom handed me a stack of 111 letters (*a nice number, although not a prime, I'd fiddled with a magic square problem while waiting for an appointment at Mountain Medical earlier this year, and found that a six by six magic square has a magic constant of 111*), correspondence between the patriarchs of the Edelman and Reineger families from before Deirdre Crocker was snatched through 1983 … the secrecy and its timing was certainly suggestive, but I didn't want to get ahead of myself. I ordered the letters chronologically, shuffling them a bit, which caused Tom to wince slightly. I found the first one, from Petr Edelman to Robert Reineger in September of 1957, and read it.

9/11/1957

Robert,

I'm down in Delaware for a week or so, taking care of some business as we discussed, but wanted to get in touch with you to make sure that you had started this month's reading club book, "Moby Dick". I particularly enjoy the savage and methodical energy with which Captain Ahab pursues his revenge, despite all possible costs! I'm looking forward to a return to Juniper Bay later in the month, to feel the season changing, and possibly later in the fall for some hunting as you had previously suggested. Give my regards to all of your family, especially little Bobby.

```
e lhvh lrzngnyv buf mqkaite ahvpyb bf
rpau gnw zvdv mpnm cfp wtdl oh qvpi
ji wznfp af vhvr ns n wivnzb jiml tr
q dv onm qupvy b xfanm tabbu jrc cumf
aedutl joe nbtfrucy wvq lhy ngttkmw l
m jbtc rzr xctoeu xc perrzwis gr com
yjh psqv bhqvlr xy xkjceh
```

With warmest regards,

Petr

"Tyler? Are you okay? Do you have something?" Tom asked. "You've been staring at that letter for 5 minutes."

"Nope, nothing," I said, and it was true. It was not a simple substitution (*I'd worked through a bunch of the simpler alternatives initially, hoping for an easy bit of work*), but it appeared to still be in the original blocks of text, which could, in theory, help (*depending on how complex a cryptographic scheme they were using*). "I know already that I'm going to want copies of these letters to keep. Would that be possible for you to do for me, Tom? Meanwhile I'll take a look through the rest of this stuff. He nodded, picked up the stack of letters with the ciphertext in them and tromped out ... the archival document copier was significantly slower than a regular copy machine, and he'd be quite a while working his way through all of those letters.

I looked through the stack of pictures first, not sure of what I was looking for in the old photographs. The top of the stack included pictures of the Edelmans, their guests (*of which there were never many, but the numbers of which seemed to significantly decrease from 1958 onwards to 1960*), and the camp. Petr Edelman had four children, two boys and two girls, all blond and handsome and sober/stern, like he and his wife seemed to be (*not a lot of smiles among the Edelmans, not even the fake variety that I have learned to produce for photos and effect over the years*). Camp Juniper Bay was quite similar to the Crockers' camp, although it had more outbuildings balanced against a slightly less grand main lodge. The color scheme was light grey buildings with darker grey roofing (*as opposed to the brown buildings and green roofs of Topsail*), and Juniper Bay lacked the Adirondack-style twiggery present in all of the Topsail buildings. Further down the stack of photos were Edelman Christmas cards, 1955-1960, looking to have been taken in their boat house (*based on the view behind the family members*), Petr Edelman sitting behind a huge desk, in front of a half-full bookcase, with his family flanking him; all of them growing older/bigger year by year. The bottom of the stack appeared to be from a roll of film taken by an amateur photographer with a new camera, wandering around the camp during the summer of 1958, taking pictures of buildings. It was in one of these pictures that I saw the same man from the third picture I had shown the Crockers (*the one taken at the Taylor's camp*). In that picture this man had been glaring in the direction of the Crockers; he was tall and strong, and looked more comfortable in this setting than he had in the picture from the other day. In none of the other pictures were there any workmen present, so I leapt (*with some confidence*) to the conclusion that he was the Juniper Bay caretaker, Robert Reineger.

I looked through the journals and ledgers and diaries next, all of which seemed similar to the others I had looked over previously, with a few notable exceptions, particularly in the ledgers. Camp ledgers have a wide variety of expense and balance sheets and lists related to running/maintaining a great camp. A couple of things jumped out at me as I pored through the ledgers for Juniper Bay. Rebuilding the garage/workspace cost much more than similar projects in adjacent camps on Upper Saranac (*roughly three times as much*); the project also consumed twice as much concrete as comparable projects in nearby camps. There were expenses that showed up in the Juniper Bay ledger that seemed unlikely: electrical bills consistently 20% higher than those at nearby camps, 'shop supplies' costing more per month than other camps spent in a year, and for the years 1958/1959/1960 three 'book club sets' were expensed out in the ledger ... all of these items initialed/approved by PE (*Petr Edelman*). I was starting to see/suspect the shape of something horrible, and just needed a nudge of luck or help or instinct to push me the rest of the way in the right direction.

Tom came back with all of the letters containing ciphertext, and saw me staring at the ceiling, working through a complex piece of math nerdery (*trying to apply the Golden Ratio to the dimensions and sizes of the buildings at Topsail and Juniper Bay, to see what, if any conclusions one could draw from the level of correlation*) to occupy my front-brain while the magicians in back did whatever it is that they do that eventually leads to pulling rabbits out of hats.

"Tom, I think that I need two more things from you, and then you'll be rid of me. I need any Christmas cards that you can find from Juniper Bay, and also any pictures you can get me of their boathouse," I said.

He nodded, dropped the thick stack of copies on the table, and headed back out again, into the archives while I compared the mental images I had in my head of both camps to the Golden Ratio. I had both camps at roughly the same level of correlation to the ratio when he came back with a smaller stack of pictures for me.

There were Christmas cards for every year until 1982, which led me to believe that these had come in with the other papers of Robert Reineger, the father, after his death. I asked Tom to make me the highest possible resolution copies of all of the Christmas cards, from 1955 on; assuring him that I would pay the museum for the costly copies stacking up today and on my previous visit. Other pictures of the boathouse were of less overall utility, but there were a few that offered a view of the bookshelf behind the big desk, and I added those to the pile for Tom to copy.

He brought all of the new copies back, in plastic sleeves and a stiff folder to protect them. I stacked the copied letters on top of the folder, squaring the edges nicely, and reaching ahead through the fog to see my next few steps.

"Did you solve the mystery? Do you know who took her, why they took her, and where they took her?" Tom asked, with some excitement creeping into his cool scholarly voice, finally.

"I might. I think that I've got most of it, but it still hasn't come completely together, and since it's been 54.85 years, I don't want to rush to the solution before I'm sure. As kidnap and murder cases go, this one has pretty low urgency (*except to Kitty Crocker*), since I'm pretty sure that everyone involved is dead."

He looked at me expectantly, assuming that I'd bend a bit and give him the solution I had mostly worked out in my head, but I couldn't ... not yet. There were other people who deserved the story before him, and they deserved the whole thing, not my half-assed guesses.

"I have a couple more things to work out, and another person to see before I can tackle the next leg of this puzzle (*I must need massive quantities of Coke and Chinese food pretty badly, to be publicly mixing metaphors that poorly, I thought*). Can you tell me about how much it costs the museum to make all of those copies and prints?" I asked.

"Mr. Winch said to give you everything you need. He said you're a good friend of the museum, and that this would help get me, and our filing system in shape; so there's no charge."

"I get that, I really do, but I'm still going to make a donation to the museum in the amount of your supplies that I've used in the last few days, so pick a number."

"Couple hundred dollars," he said.

"And did you find any ways to improve the organization of your collection while I was here? Terry, Mr. Winch, thought you might while I was pushing and pulling you and the collections around," I said.

Tom smiled, "I've got a couple of ideas to improve our database, and streamline the collection access and search processes."

"Tom, you'll do great things here, if you choose to stay, and I'm grateful for your help. Please take Marcy out again, on me, sometime soon," I said, pressing a hundred dollar bill into his hand before picking up the rest of my stuff, and getting ready to go. He thanked me, and didn't try to talk me out of it this time.

"I need to use the bathroom and make a phone call before I go, but I'm done here, so thanks, Tom." He moved to shake hands, and I made sure to have mine full to avoid the awkward pause that comes when people realize that I don't want to shake theirs, and the hand is left hanging out in the air between us until they finally reel it back in (*I had no desire to hurt Tom's feelings, but neither did I want to invite that level of human contact*). I made my call, used the bathroom, and headed out into the warm afternoon light, feeling satisfied with my work, foggy with eyestrain and neck-fatigue, and ready to get to the next thing.

I spent a few minutes watching the parking lot for cars that had occupants before making my way over to the Porsche. I dumped the folder and letters into the trunk, started up the car, and drove out of the mostly empty parking structure, enjoying the harsh rolling bark of the vintage engine off the walls and pillars before I zoomed out into the afternoon, intent on the road in front of me. I wanted to pick up my gear at the campsite near Little Pine Pond, and make it up to Canton before dark. I had Chinese food in my head now, and wanted to avoid Saranac Lake for the moment, so the next logical choice was Canton, which was also the home of the person I had to see the next morning. I could be there in about two hours, less if I didn't have to go through Tupper Lake, but they haven't invented a route to Canton from Blue Mountain Lake that doesn't pass through the speed traps of Tupper Lake, which I presume love to snag Porsches more than any car you're likely to find on these roads.

"… Good behavior will be
rewarded. Bad behavior
will be punished."

Number One Chinese Restaurant, Canton, 7/18/2013, 7:46 p.m.

I raced along the roads between Blue Mountain Lake and the turnoff for Route 421 and (*eventually*) Little Pine Pond, the Porsche dancing between sunlight and deep shadow and hugging the tarmac like a train on tracks. The constant wind and noise from the broken window was no longer much of a distraction, although a rainy night or long drive might well change my mind about that. The road gets progressively less civilized the further along it you drive, but I didn't mind ... I could straddle/avoid most of the biggest holes, and it was nearly a rental car; Mike would never know about the seven times that I bottomed out and/or ground some life out of the exhaust assembly.

My camp was exactly as I had left it, and once I arrived I spent five minutes listening for sounds of pursuit or approach; none were seriously expected, or present. Taking down the hammock and tarp is the work of a matter of three minutes, and after that it was just a case of policing the area for what little of my gear I had taken out for use, along with the dismantling (*and stowing*) of my primitive alarm system. I was packed up and retracing my steps back towards the pavement ten minutes after arriving. I reached the junction of Routes 421 and 30, saw no traffic in either direction, and turned left, and north, towards nearby Tupper Lake, and slightly more distant Canton.

I enjoy the drive from Tupper to Canton (*note how I'm skipping right over the painful transition through Tupper at 25 mph in my Porsche*); it's a long drive through the woods with almost nothing and nobody between the two places (*I've often made the drive without seeing another car, or lights*). This iteration of the drive was especially pleasant, as the 993 much more closely followed my driving commands than does my Honda Element; it was nice to take turns at speed and not feel a big and boxy car want to give into inertia and flail off into the woods. I had loaded up on gas at a convenience store at the far side of Tupper Lake, as well as an armload of beverages and snacks to fortify me for the hour (*and a bit*) of wilderness driving. While I ate and drank away the fatigue and lethargy of a day spent inside, I thought about the next few steps ... starting to see my way through to the endgame.

The traffic light where Route 68 intersects with Route 11 is always the point at which I feel that I have arrived in Canton. The manicured strangeness of the St. Lawrence University golf course, the lights of the Walmart to one side and the university and town to the other, and always getting caught on red by the light. As I normally do, I looked both ways, and turned left on red, something I'm not generally given to, but this intersection seems to bring it out in me. I was pleasantly stuffed from my road food/drink, and thus in no immediate rush to devour massive amounts of mediocre Chinese food, so I made the turn into St. Lawrence's gates, and cruised the driveable portions of the campus for a few minutes, enjoying the ridiculous population and streetlight density for a few minutes before heading downtown for my dinner.

As always when I visit an institution of higher learning, I wonder about the path not taken. My education was non-traditional in the extreme: a group of parents (*mine among them*) took turns teaching the collective group of children, in areas that the adults were strong/confident in, making use of the readily available wealth of educational opportunities and resources that New York City had to offer. The result of this education is an ongoing thirst/hunger for knowledge and skills and wisdom, and no high school or college diplomas. I looked at the ivy-covered buildings and students and teachers (*the buildings, not the students and teachers, are ivy-covered*), packed tightly into these few acres up at the top end of New York State, and wondered who I would have been if I'd gone to a school like Stuyvesant (*like Anthony*) or Bronx Science, and then on to a college like this ... different, certainly, but beyond that I have a hard time imagining the other me. A big part of my education was reading ... reading everything, in every field that interested me (*which was, frankly, lots of fields*), including tons of mysteries (*perhaps how I ended up doing what I do*). Touring the campus of a college I'd never attended, imagining me as the student that I never was, reminded me of something John D. MacDonald's Meyer said in "Free Fall in Crimson" (*the 19th Travis McGee book*) ... he defined weltschmerz as homesickness for a place that never existed. Visiting colleges always evoked in me a feeling along these lines.

Exiting the campus onto Park Street down by the gym, which is called 'The Augsbury Fitness Center,' I turned back towards town, and found parking on Main Street, right in front of the Chinese place. I ordered dumplings, spare ribs, and asked the young lady behind the counter to have the chef make me some shrimp and broccoli with garlic, extra spicy. Nearly everything in these restaurants is cooked in woks, over roaring flames, and it's interesting to watch the cooks make hundreds of dishes from the same limited set of ingredients; I always watch them cooking, and this time was no different. The food was ready in a hair under eight minutes, and had the perfect balance of hot and spicy and greasy and protein. It was a huge supper, and I'm a small guy, but I put every ounce of it away, including finger-squeegeeing the spicy shrimp dish's sauce.

As I was finishing up, I played over the map in my head of the Canton area, for a place to spend the night. The Crary Mills State Forest was only six miles from where I sat (*about eight road miles*), and it has some great spots to hang for the night, as I remembered from part of a day spent walking around the forest with a geocaching acquaintance a few years previously. I'm not a superstitious person, but the feeling of danger/threat had faded once I'd gotten away from Saranac Lake, and those two traps I'd perceived my would-be assailants could use. The combination of distance and the knowledge I'd gained in the last few days, gave me some confidence and a feeling of security (*false or warranted, I couldn't say*) about heading out and into the night. I routed the trip in my head, including a stop at a Quik-E-Mart in town for a gallon of water and a bottle of gas-line cleaner (*for my stove, in case I wanted some oatmeal for breakfast in the morning*). Then I put garbage/recycling in their proper places, thanked the people behind the counter, and headed out.

Burt's Book Rookery, Canton, 7/19/2013, 8:32 a.m.

I'd gotten to the State Forest after dark, but had no problem finding an out of the way place to park and hang my hammock. The night passed uneventfully, with me sleeping for a few hours, reading for a few, and then taking another nap as light began to creep into the eastern sky. It was chilly when I climbed out of my sleeping bag, and I put on fleece pants and shirt as I waited for my oatmeal-water to come to a boil on the cat-can stove. It was still early, but I saw that I had cell-phone reception, so I called Frank and Meg for an update on the tasks I'd set them.

"G'morning Tyler! Where are you calling from this time?" Meg wakes up jolly, and is nearly always the one who grabs the phone when I call early.

"Near Madrid (*which though spelled like the capital city of Spain, is pronounced 'mad-rid', and wasn't exactly a lie, even if it wasn't exactly true, Madrid was only eleven miles north of me, and safety/security was still in the back of my mind*), shivering a bit in my fleece while my water boils for oatmeal." She likes to hear details about my camping, which is a bit odd, as she hates camping herself.

"I sent you an email last night, which I bet you haven't seen yet," she said.

"Nope, not yet, I'll stop in and poach some Wi-Fi from SUNY Potsdam later this morning. Is it a list of the people who attended Kimberly Stanton's funeral services?"

"Actually, it's a list of those attending the services who signed the book, but yeah." I appreciated that her mind made that logical distinction, which my pre-oatmeal brain had not. "It's a bit weird to think that the person who killed Deirdre Crocker is probably on that list; I've been to cookouts with most of those people." The truth was probably even worse, and more weird than she could imagine, but I didn't want to tell her about my suspicions, or guess at the name I was sure that I would find on the list.

"Thanks so much, Meg. I hope that didn't put you in an uncomfortable position with your family (*I no longer have family, and even when I did, I didn't feel the same way about them that Meg feels about hers*). Did Frank say anything about …?" I asked.

I could hear the phone being passed across the table to a grumbling Frank, "Tyler, I haven't had any coffee yet, the machine is still burping (*they use an ancient stovetop percolator*). Nobody got treated for chem-burns like you described, so either you missed, or they're toughing it out." I could hear the clink of spoon into a mug a few times, some stirring, and then a desperate/happy/grateful sigh and slurp.

"Frank, that much sugar in your coffee is gonna give you diabetes," I said, knowing that it would piss him off, but that being pissed off would wake him up as fast/surely as the cup of coffee in his hand would.

"Get stuffed Tyler, coulda' been Meg or Austin's coffee." But it wasn't and we both knew it. "I talked with a guy I know in Albany, a real numbers-wonk, you'd love him. He tracks all sorts of stats for the suits down in acronym city (*Frank has what I find to be a laudable distrust of systems, for one so immersed in the system himself, but that may somewhat explain both our relationship, and his slow advancement through the ranks of the local PD*). You were right, most missing persons cases get resolved through, as my guys says, 'oh here I am, death, or taxes.' Lots of times the person just turns up, comes home, whatever. Most of the rest of the cases end up with a body in a morgue somewhere. A small percentage are solved when the missing person shows up in the system paying taxes or signing up for some form of government assistance. A tiny number of missing persons stay missing, forever. Given the number of missing persons cases filed in the Tri-Lakes (*I had to bite my tongue not to ask for that number ... honestly, who wouldn't want/need to know*), we have what my guy says are 'an unlikely and disproportionate number' of the unresolved cases; also, not enough of them are kids (*I could feel Frank not going further into this aspect of it, conscious of Meg and Austin at the table, watching and listening*). He says it's too small a sample to be even close to certain, but his guess is that over the fifty year period he looked at, we've got ten, maybe fifteen more cases than is 'the statistical norm,' which is significant enough that by the end of our conversation he forced my promise of an explanation when I'm able. What's this got to do with your Crocker thing anyway?"

"Probably nothing, I'll know in a day or two, and should be able to tell you then," I said.

"Should?!" Frank shouted into the phone. "Tyler, I

called in a favor getting this, and may have poked a sleeping bureaucrat in Albany, so you'd better tell me."

"Frank, relax, I just meant that I have to talk with the Crocker family first. They need/deserve to know before anyone else … even you and your friend down in the capital," I said.

"Okay," he said, sounding mollified. "Meg says 'be careful,' and to call Dorothy, but Hope's fine. Christ, I'm hanging up now; I'll expect to hear from you or see you in a couple of days, with some answers for my guy in Albany."

"Okay, bye … and thanks Frank," I said.

Next I called Dorothy. "Hey Dot, what's shakin'? Is Hope behaving herself? Has she eaten your cats yet?"

"Tyler, wait, what, slow down. I just got to sleep like an hour ago. SLPD got a dead body smell complaint (*I didn't know that was an actual type of complaint, but I think people in general, and me specifically, are better off not knowing stuff like that*), and when they responded to the house it turned out to be an animal hoarder. One of those big cure cottages back on Park Ave., (*dating back to when Saranac Lake was famed as the place to go for 'The Cure' for tuberculosis, which largely involved endless exposure to fresh air and bed rest … which may explain, as long as we're parenthetical, why I've been so lucky at avoiding tuberculosis, given my lifestyle*) with a little old lady living inside, along with 47 cats and kittens (*a fantastic number in circumstances when you're not counting cats in a single house*). It had reached a critical mass (*I taught her that concept, and now she worked it into conversations whenever possible*) and gotten beyond the LOL's control a few months ago; there were dead cats in the garage, and maybe a hundred bags of used litter in there also. The police called me, and a bunch of us spent hours rounding them all up and then searching the house and yard to make sure that we didn't miss any. About half of them are sick or injured. We set up a triage in a borrowed storage unit to sort them, and figure out where to house them all ... the ones not with vets anyway. It's a mess." She finished, and then possibly went back to sleep without hanging up the phone.

"Dot!" I said.

She began again, as if we had never stopped talking, "Hope's fine, she hates my cats, and they've sequestered themselves in the bathroom for the duration of her visit to avoid the unpleasantness that is your dog. She kicks me ... all night, every night, she kicks me, Tyler. Lisa's moved out of our bed for the duration of Hope's visit, and is sleeping on the couch ... Hope growled at her when she tried to climb into bed the first night. When will you be done with this thing for Kitty?"

"Should be in the next day or two. That's partly why I'm calling. I might have something for you, if you're still interested in helping me out," I said.

She was suddenly, instantly, wide awake. "Yessir! Minion reporting for duty. Who do I kill?" Dorothy knew pretty much everything that happened last year, and had even helped me with some of the nasty/messy/illegal stuff. I wanted to keep her out of my activities (*and the attendant risk*) as much as was possible, but I did foresee the need for some specialized assistance that was very much not in either Frank or Meg's wheelhouses.

"Nobody. You remember last year, with George's sub shop? I need you to do something along those lines, but in a much less public/exposed place ... if you're willing." I outlined what I thought I might need, and where, and when.

"No problem, I'll pick up the stuff this morning, when I wake up ... again ... later ... much later," she said.

"Excellent Smithers," I said, doing my best

Montgomery Burns, and then shifting back to my voice, "remember to pay in cash. Get what you need from the stash in the ceiling of your bathroom." I'd kept $10,000 dollars up above the acoustic tiles of her bathroom for years, just in case, and had needed to use it last winter to help Mickey, one of the teachers in my parents' educational commune, out of a jam. I'd replenished what I'd spent in the intervening months, certainly didn't want Dorothy to spend her own money in addition to risking all sorts of legal (*and possibly worse*) problems.

"Do I need to turn in receipts?" she asked.

"Yes, it's important to keep receipts when committing felonies ... NO! No paper trail at all."

"I was kidding."

"Go to a hardware store you never use; they'll have everything you need; pad out my list with some other stuff just to make it seem more innocent," I said.

"Okay. Good luck today. Just for shits and giggles, I've been moving your Element every day to drive whatshisname crazy ... er. Lisa helps me, she thinks it's antisocial and mean, but she loves me." She started nodding off again, but woke herself for a final declaration, "Call me either way, I'll keep my cell with me, just in case."

"Super, but it might be tomorrow night ... or never, so don't go unless you hear from me."

"Duh! I'm hanging up now (*I was getting that a lot this morning, and wondered if my phone manner was off?*). Hope and I are going back to sleep now. Have fun, and Tyler ... thanks for this, for doing this for me, I mean."

"Don't thank me yet, wait until I tell you about the wasp spray," I said, and hung up before she could open up that can of conversational worms.

During these calls, I'd managed to finish boiling the

water for my oatmeal (*truthfully, the alcohol and cat-can stove did most of the work*), make and eat my oatmeal, down a pair of not-cold-enough Cokes, and start to break down my camp (*insofar as it was possible with a phone wedged between my ear and shoulder*). I took a last look around, grabbed some long ago hunter's cigarette butt, and drove off, hoping that Burt wouldn't mind my getting to his place of business a bit (*90 minutes*) early. The information I'd gotten from the museum, combined with what Frank had told me had given me a new sense of urgency where before there'd been none ... I'd initially planned on Dorothy's mission being at least partly made-up, and the rest for recon/info/exploring, but now it occurred to me that it might actually be a rescue mission.

I crunched into the gravel in the half-moon driveway in front of 'Burt's Book Rookery' and saw a light on, not in the front of the store, but way in back, possibly behind a curtain. Burt buys and sells used books and book collections, mostly from estate sales and other bookstores, but sometimes deals with walk-ins, which is how we'd met four years ago. I was interested in the niche he had carved for himself in the book world, and we were talking about it while negotiating in a friendly way over the stacks of books that I'd picked off/out of his shelves (*and piles and boxes*) in the front room, and cavernous warehouse space in back. He claimed at one point in our discussion that he had spent so much of his life valuing libraries and collections that he could walk into a room and identify books before he got close enough to read the writing on the spines. I'd been impressed, and pushed for more information (*as is my way*); he said that the color/pattern or the binding, the height and thickness, and the shape of the font(s) used in lettering the spine were sufficient markers to identify many thousands of the most common titles and printings. I had seen birders identify what to me appeared as squashed capital Vs, and wine-enthusiasts give me the vineyard and year of production of a wine from a sip, so who was I to doubt his word, but it had stuck with me over the years. Today, I hoped to use his gift to uncover secrets too-long buried, and possibly even to save a life.

I rapped on the glass of his front door, hard enough that he could have heard me in back, amongst all those piles of books, but his head poked up from behind a low shelf not ten feet from my knocking hand.

"Jesus, Tyler, you're gonna break the window. Didn't you say you were coming for nine o'clock?" he said when he unlocked the front door, and stuck his head out, looking first at the window, and then at his watch.

"Sorry, Burt, about the window and about the early arrival. I was up and finished my breakfast, and hoped that you might be here," I said.

"And I am, so come in, come in, my boy," Burt said.

I did, and if I had had Burt's particular gift, I'm sure that I could have told you that his store didn't look exactly the same as it had been during my previous visit, but I didn't, so I couldn't. I assumed that untold numbers of books had come and gone through his doors in the intervening time, like grains of sand in strong tides (*I seem only to get poetic about books, and even then, it's bad poetry*).

He saw me looking around, and rescued me, "So tell me about your problem, Tyler. It sounds tricky. But first, here's the book that you asked for," he said, handing me a battered copy of 'Moby Dick.'

"It is, maybe too tricky, but any help that you could give me would be invaluable," I said.

"All I can do is what I can do, no more, no less." That flavor of Seussian wisdom ordinarily makes me want to either leave the room or throw a brick at the speaker, but I needed Burt's help, so I just gave him my #2 smile (*friendly, gentle, and clueless*), and thought about books I'd read with detectives who had to put up with this sort of thing.

"Some of this is supposition, so it may be wrong, but I'm reasonably sure of most of what I'm about to tell you. Starting in the late 1950s and going through the 1980s, there was a monthly book club formed between a small group of men (*if he had said something about a group of small men, I might have jumped out through his window, but thankfully, he didn't*). I haven't been able to find lists of these books, but I believe that I have pictures of the books over the relevant span of years ... in the background of a collection of Christmas cards." I paused, and Burt gave a little smile, seeing where I was going.

"I want you to look at the cards, and tell me any/all of the books that you can identify, as specifically as possible (*as I been led to believe that some editions of the same book have slightly differing content*)," I said.

"It's certainly possible, what you describe, but I've never done it with a picture. I've always been in the same room with the books, not that it should make such a difference, but who can say?" He shrugged at the end of this statement.

"I understand, but if you could get even some of them, it would be a help (*I think ... I didn't add, I didn't want to jinx my idea before he even tried*)," I said.

I got out the stack of Christmas cards, from 1958 (*which is when the bookended group of a dozen books had appeared front and center behind Petr Edelman's desk in his family photos*) through 1982 (*which left me high and dry for the encrypted letters from 1983, but what can you do?*). I set them in a pile on his desk, and asked Burt, "Could you write the year at the beginning of each list, and which positions, starting from the left (*I assumed*) of every book that you can identify?"

Thirty seconds in, Burt looked up at me, and said, "Go in back and find some books to buy from me Tyler, and don't come back for an hour." Then he looked back down at the photo, making tiny adjustments to his desk light and the magnifying glass in his hand while I walked into his backroom.

I returned an hour later, with a stack of books, and my hopes (*which I had been unaware of until that second*) crashed when I saw Burt's face. He had a box in front of him on the desk, and got up when I walked in; he was clearly intent on finding something in the backroom.

"Burt, please tell me. You've got bad news written all over your face, and I want to hear it now, so I can come up with a different plan."

"I'm sorry Tyler, I know this must be important to you, and I hate to disappoint you ... I failed," he said.

"You couldn't get any of them?" I asked, my mind racing, desperately, to try and fix on a new plan.

"What? No. I got 109 of them, just a bit more than a third," he said, shaking his head in dismay.

"Burt, that's great! Better than I had any reason to hope for from old pictures." I did the math quickly in my head. "You found about one third of the titles, there are cryptograms for roughly one third of the months in the given time period, given the givens, I should end up with twelve solvable codes, not counting the one for 'Moby Dick', which should be a bonus ... so thirteen! That's great Burt, I literally cannot thank you enough."

"I have lots of these titles in stock Tyler, if you can tell me which ones you need, I can send you on your way with a fair number of them. These were fairly common books, and I've got lots of 'em."

I sat down at his desk and cross-referenced the dates of the letters with the months he knew the book club books for, and even considering the odds, something worked against us, only giving us eight matches, but of those, Burt had six in stock (*I was fairly certain that I could get the other two online from Project Gutenberg or some other similar source*).

I paid Burt for the books I had picked out, and the ones that I would be using to decrypt the messages between Petr Edelman and Robert Reineger, rounded the bill up to one hundred dollars (*against Burt's protests*), told him that I owed him a big favor whenever he needed it, and headed back into town to spend the rest of the day at the St. Lawrence library, breaking codes that were all older than me.

Owen D. Young Library, SLU, Canton, 7/19/2013,
4:32 p.m.

I drove the short distance back to Canton from Burt's
place, stopping for a more significant breakfast at a diner
in town that stuffs local farmers every morning starting at
4 a.m.. I went in for a plate-sized ham-steak under four
sunny side ups with the yolks (*and some of the whites*) still
runny, and a big bowl of hash browns dumped on top
with ketchup and tabasco. I washed it all down with two
ginormous glasses of milk, and then fought the urge to
crank the seat back and go to sleep in the Porsche (*lucky
for me the window hadn't been fixed yet, or I might have*). I picked
up some pens and notebooks at the student bookstore,
along with some junk food to fuel my research, and
stuffed it all, along with my laptop, the books, and letters
and other papers into my backpack and walked into the
Owen D. Young Library.

I wanted quiet, but not the quiet study areas (*which
generally have people working/overseeing them … people who would
not appreciate or understand my need for a steady supply of Cokes
and donuts and jerky*), so I headed to the far end of the
bottom floor of the library (*most students tend to stay on the*

254

main floor, or climb up the stairs for the clusters of study carrels). I was looking for a lonely/quiet/empty corner with a table on which to spread out, and found it after a few minutes of wandering.

I took the letter from Petr Edelman to Robert Reineger that had grabbed my attention, and given me hope about cracking their coded exchange of letters over the years. Placing it on the desk next to a notepad and pen (*I know that I should use a pencil for this sort of work, but I detest how they smudge, dirtying my hand and the paper, because of my left-handedness*) and the copy of Herman Melville's most noted work, I prepared to start cracking (*literally*). There are lots of webpages and apps out there that are useful for breaking codes, but if Edelman and Reineger had been as sharp as I assumed, they would be of little use initially.

With a sufficiently long and diverse (*non-repeating*) encryption key, a code becomes essentially unbreakable (*assuming that the cryptogram does not begin or end with a predictable or standard block of text, which gives people trying to break the code a chance, as the Germans found out in World War Two, when predictable beginnings to their cryptograms helped nullify the tremendous advantage their Enigma code machines gave them*). Since the blocks of ciphertext in the Edelman/Reineger letters were reasonably short, it stood to reason that they had practiced solid cryptographic 'hygiene.' If they hadn't, it's likely that Maureen, the amateur cryptographer at the museum, would have broken them at some point. I had a theory about how they had communicated in secret, based on their book club, felt that the first letter sent by Edelman in the coded series had a significant weakness in it, and hoped to exploit that weakness in such a way that would allow me to continue to break the remaining eight letters that I had book club books for (*assuming that Burt had been correct in matching the pictures to book titles*).

9/11/1957

Robert,

I'm down in Delaware for a week or so, taking care of some business as we discussed, but wanted to get in touch with you to make sure that you had started this month's reading club book, "Moby Dick." I particularly enjoy the savage and methodical energy with which Captain Ahab pursues his revenge, despite all possible costs! I'm looking forward to a return to Juniper Bay later in the month, to feel the season changing, and possibly later in the fall for some hunting as you had previously suggested. Give my regards to all of your family, especially little Bobby.

e lhvh lrzngnyv buf mqkaite ahvpyb bf rpau gnw zvdv mpnm cfp wtdl oh qvpi ji wznfp af vhvr ns n wivnzb jiml tr q dv onm qupvy b xfanm tabbu jrc cumf aedutl joe nbtfrucy wvq lhy ngttkmw l m jbtc rzr xctoeu xc perrzwis gr com yjh psqv bhqvlr xy xkjceh

With warmest regards,

Petr

My assumption was that the key text for the encryption was in "Moby Dick," and that Edelman had needed to mention the book in their first coded communication because they were just getting started. Simple encryption schemes substitute letters in simple ways (*the letter 'A' becomes the letter 'Z' and so on, or every letter in plaintext shifts a few letters in one direction or another*). These are relatively easy to decode because the frequency with which certain common letters occur is known to everyone who has ever watched "Wheel of Fortune." A more complex encryption method uses a shifting/changing key where each letter is assigned a number that is the equivalent to its placement in the alphabet. That number indicates the number of letters to shift away to break the code. A word or word string is selected to be the keypad to code a message. Using this model, if the code shift word is 'dog' then you would shift the letters in the coded word by 3, 14, and 6 letters respectively (*since the letters 'D', 'O', and 'G' are 3, 14, and 6 letters away from the letter 'A'*) . The word 'cat' shifted using the letters in the word 'dog' thus becomes encrypted to 'foz.' They (*Edelman and Reineger*) would want complex and lengthy keys for messages longer than 'cat,' and wouldn't want to have an actual codebook on their shelves, so regular books that they both could easily have access to made sense, which is why they formed their 'book club.' I knew Moby Dick was the first book they used because it was mentioned in the letter. The next/big/daunting problem was to figure out where/what the key was for the letter that referenced 'Moby Dick.' Which part of the book was the beginning of the code?

I tried the first ten letters using the opening passage of the book, but that didn't work. The only number in the letter was the date (9/11/1957), so I tried starting in at the ninth letter/word/paragraph/chapter and then, when those yielded random letters, I tried the eleventh letter/word/paragraph/chapter. It turned out their code used the day of the month to indicate which chapter would be the encryption key. Counting the number of characters in the coded passage in the letter, I knew that the first 197 characters from the beginning of chapter eleven in Moby Dick served as the key, which gave me the following plaintext when I decrypted the block of cipher in the original letter:

```
i have arranged the initial supply of
cash and hope that you will be able
to start as soon as i return with it
x we are doing a great thing for your
family for kimberly and for justice x
i will not forget my promises to you
and your family my friend --(Edelman
to Reineger, September, 1957)
```

With that out of the way, I began to work on the remaining eight letters, justifiably satisfied with myself for cracking a 55 year old hybrid Ottendorf/Vigenère cipher (*the encryption scheme is widely attributed to Vigenère, but was actually first described by Giovan Battista Bellas, nearly 300 years before Vigenère wrote about it ... history is sometimes unfair*). The book club idea suggested that the books would change annually, that's where the Christmas cards came in (*help coming to me unwittingly from Petr Edelman*). I had noted that the books pictured in the background Christmas card changed each year. If the day of the month was the chapter number, the month was probably the number of the book as stacked on the shelf. This was something I had suspected before I went to Burt's place, and considering that these were the books I purchased, I was desperately hoping to be right (*I was*). The 1958 letter I had was dated 4/19/1958. So, the cipher would be from the fourth book in on the shelf, starting with Chapter 19. The decrypted blocks of ciphertext from the eight remaining letters presented an interesting and disturbing, if fragmented, picture of the Edelman/Reineger dynamic. It suggested a shocking (*even to me … which takes some doing*) story of self-righteous and horrific punishment/abuse that was perpetrated over decades.

cell is complete x i have three routes to topsail as discussed x i am still not sure how to take her x it will be the hardest part to grab her without killing her by mistake x two questions how do we keep the oubliette warm and lit during power outages and what if she gets sick x --(Reineger to Edelman, April 19, 1958)

the time is coming my friend x remember that justice is better than revenge x she will pay for her crime for years x i put two thousand in tens in a mason jar behind the loose brick on the left side of the boathouse fireplace x remember to spread out your purchases in time and space x--(Edelman to Reineger, July 4, 1958) this one is difficult but i think that if writing and art supplies will keep her alive longer than it is ok with me you decide x agree that second oubliette is good idea it insures we are always serving justice x--(Edelman to Reineger, February 23, 1962)

your father was a great man who served hard justice and taught me to do the same x we do the difficult thing for our families and society x two is difficult but the old man is falling apart will go soon has stopped bathing and eating x soon it will be time for you to judge the next your first x--(Reineger to Edelman, September 13, 1970)

this burden we bear together strengthens both families makes the adirondacks a better place through our hard service to the scales of justice x new girl was screaming for two days straight drugged food bandaged hands where she damaged beating walls x i brought my son down yesterday to explain the work we do down here x we are running through budgeted cash for appliances and repairs too quickly sears crap i will need thousand dollars soonest x --

(Reineger to Edelman,November 3,1975)
absolutely not x nobody outside of
the two families can know of our work
justices burden is for us to carry
alone x re punishment our mission has
always been to incarcerate not
physically damage or torture our
charges x interesting question about
olympics but too risky exposed x i
will be up in three months to discuss
possibles x stay strong in service x
--(Edelman to Reineger, March 1,
1979)

i fucked up sent a can of coke into
cell one with 1980 olympic stuff on
it x not a big deal but too bad x
father had a heart attack but he is
strong in his service to justice and
will recover x cell two girl will
break the oubliette record in march
if she keeps going x i gave her a
week in the dark for trying to dig
out and she came through shaky but
not broken x --(Reineger to Edelman,
January 18, 1980)

back from vacation cell one guy dead
and messy x i could smell it as soon
as I entered the workshop blamed it
on dead raccoon x dad isnt sure of
the justice in our service anymore
weak and dying old man x i am strong
under the burden and he will pretend

```
he no longer knows x i have a
candidate to fill one that you should
evaluate judge x --(Reineger to
Edelman, April 21, 1982)
```

When I finished working on the final block of ciphertext, I went back through and checked all of the decrypted messages. The internal consistency led me to conclude (*correctly*) before I'd finished working my way through them on the computer that I had accurately decrypted the messages between generations of Edelman and Reineger men. I sat back and heard/felt my back and neck groan and crack like a drum-roll, and realized that I'd been sitting hunched over the books and notes for hours, focusing on the macabre dialog (*of which I could only read about seven percent*). My mouth was dry and my stomach growling, now that I was paying attention; I went to the bathroom to pee and wet my hair and wash my face and drink/rinse my mouth from the tap, and then came back ... the notes still said the same thing.

They had been judge and jailor for more than 50 years, to who knows how many people. I drank my last Coke and ate the last of the donuts and jerky, thinking about a life (*many lives*) interrupted but not cut short ... transplanted instead, but kept/contained/limited beyond all reason, and for the rest of each of those lives. I had to think, to move, to act, to react, but I felt a ponderous weight settling on me as the gravity of what I now knew filled my head, seemingly from side to side and bottom to top, crowding everything else out.

They had kidnapped Deirdre Crocker in 1958, and kept her in an oubliette, a French term for a prison in which to forget/lose someone, adding another cell and more prisoners as each died either sick or crazy but always alone. She was certainly dead, but there might be one or two prisoners caged in the cells under Juniper Bay. I had to do something ... had to act, but I had no clear idea of what I could/should/would do. In this situation, I fell back on my training with SmartPig over the last few years, and let instinct take over ... I left the library with all of my things, intent on eating a few pounds of mediocre Chinese food before falling into my hammock for a few hours to let the custodians in the back of my skull slam the mess that my brain was, back into shape, and hopefully wake up knowing the best course of action to take.

Quik-E-Mart, Canton, 7/19/2013, 6:39 p.m.

I walked in a daze to the Porsche, threw everything into the trunk of the car, and puttered through the cooling afternoon, looking at the clouds on the horizon that promised rain later in the evening. I would enjoy the night out in my hammock sheltered from the rain by my tarp, but feeling and hearing it nonetheless ... the Unfortunates, those people that the Edelman/Reineger Justice League disappeared, never saw or heard or walked in the rain again. I parked further away from the Chinese place than I needed to, and used the walk to think and stretch all of my parts.

I placed an order for dumplings and an order of painfully spicy shrimp and scallops with broccoli, then retreated to the back of the restaurant, sitting by a mossy looking fish tank with a few bored koi kissing their way back and forth along the length of the tank, reading a favorite Matt Scudder mystery for a while. I enjoy the angst that Lawrence Block creates within his favorite of my characters, and the way that he paints the city of New

York in my mind, a city that I no longer have access to except through his books (*and others like them*). The food came and I ate with one hand, while reading with the other, desperate to escape my current reality perhaps … to let my subconscious work on the details and solution to the problem that I faced now—what to do about the Crockers and also the Edelmans and Reinegers (*and most especially, anyone the latter had entombed in their cells*).

I went through the pictures and cryptograms and story in my head from various angles, taking it apart, looking at it, and then putting it back together again. The best and safest thing to do (*for me and anyone possibly entombed underneath Camp Juniper Bay*) was to present the whole thing to Frank Gibson, the SLPD, and any other suits that might be interested. It was too late to get things rolling tonight, but if I got a cheap hotel room for the night, and wrote everything down in a clear and concise manner (*that even a caveman could understand*), it would certainly be enough for the authorities to get a warrant, make their search, find the prisoners, catch the bad guys, and tie things up neatly for the Crockers while Hope and I were safely beyond the blast radius of the media spectacular that it was certain to become. Dorothy would be upset at not being able to minion her way into this case, but it made more sense all around to do it the safe way; I ordered some more food and lingered over it while making plans for how to present the entire thing to Frank in the morning. Bloated, my tongue burned by those tiny red chili peppers the restaurant used, I started referencing my mental map for the best place to stay (*it needed only a roof and electricity and wifi, and to be cheap to qualify as 'best' to me*), and came up with the Scottish Inns, over towards Potsdam; I called and found that they had rooms available for the night.

By this point, I had stretched my mealtime nearly to the breaking point (*when a guy from the kitchen came by to scowl at me, scrutably enough for even me to pick up on his intention, for a third time, I knew that it was time to go*), I wandered (*slowly, ponderously even*) back to my car. Rolled slowly through town, aiming for a Quik-E-Mart on the edge of town to gas and food up for the overnight and tomorrow morning. I pulled in, and was filling the tank when my cell phone rang.

"Tyler?" Meg said.

"Hi Meg," I answered.

"Jesus Christ, Tyler, he's coming here ... NOW!" she shouted into the phone.

"Who, and he's coming where, Meg?" I know that my steady voice at times like this is maddening, but I also knew that raising my voice, either in tone or volume, did not help with communications or whatever was happening at Meg's end.

"My sorta uncle, Bobby, Robert Reineger. He called, just now, he just hung up and I called you. He's coming here Tyler, and he .... he must be in on it ... all of it ...." She just trailed off at this point. I noticed Barry coming around the corner of the Quik-E-Mart to lean against the side of the Porsche.

"Meg, listen carefully. Are you alone in the house? Did you call Frank?"

"Of course I did, I called Frank before I called you, and he's on his way, but he'll be half an hour. I am alone—Austin's at his grandmother's, thank God; I worry he'd do something stupid. Are you in town?" She sounded scared and needy, which is not Meg's way.

"No, I'm still up in Canton. Look out your front window and tell me if your neighbors across the street are home (*they should be, I hope they are*). Are they?" I prompted.

"Yes, but …." I cut her off.

"When we get off the phone in thirty seconds, call them and tell them to come over. Tell them that a drunk relative is coming over and you're frightened … they'll come." I knew the Mullanes would come over to help Meg, based on the way that Frank had spoken about them.

"If Reineger comes, don't talk with him alone, stay with the Mullanes in your living room … better yet, all of you meet him in the driveway, and talk there. Stay there. Don't deny anything, hide anything, ask anything. Just be friendly and smile and seem uninterested in anything having to do with Kimberly Stanton or the Crockers or me. Frank will be there soon … make sure that Reineger knows that also, that Frank is on his way. Everything will be fine."

"Are you coming here Tyler?" she asked.

That stopped me for a second. I had certainly been planning to for the last eight seconds, but now that I'd paused to think, I knew that I couldn't. As soon as he went to see Meg, and realized how dumb he had been to confront her like that, Reineger would try and figure out a way to cut his losses. He might kill the people (*if there were any*) in his cells … or simply fill them in with cement or dirt or dynamite. I had to get going and know what I was doing before I arrived at Juniper Bay on Upper Saranac, or I would fail the Crockers and all of the people who had lived, and died, in those oubliettes over the years.

"No, but you have to believe me that it's for a very good reason. Frank will be there soon, and I'll be there in a few hours, but there's stuff that I have to do first. Please tell Frank to stay with you and the dogs at your house until you hear from me … okay?" I asked.

"Um, okay, if you're sure Tyler."

"I'm sure. Gotta go Meg. Call the Mullanes now. Bye," hoping that I sounded more certain than I felt.

I dialed Frank's cell, and waited through two rings, while he probably felt around for it on his passenger seat.

"Meg?" he asked.

"No, Tyler. I just got off the phone with Meg, and the Mullanes are coming over. They're going to meet Reineger together in the driveway, and the Mullanes will stay until you get there."

"Thanks, I guess, although she got into this because of you."

"I know," I said, "and I feel awful about that, but she'll be fine. He'll realize he's making a mistake as soon as he sees other people there."

"Okay, so what's next?" he said. One of the things that I like about Frank is his ability to set a problem aside, and to compartmentalize ...hence, 'what's next.'

"I need a favor, Frank. A pretty big one."

"What?" he asked.

"You know how we were joking about me having flashers for the Porsche earlier?"

"Yup, and you...." He trailed off.

"I have one, and I need to make an emergency run from Potsdam to Upper Saranac Lake. Can you set that up?"

"Jesus, Tyler, are you going through Tupper?"

"Nope. I think it'll be quicker and less populated going the other way ... 11B to 458 to 30." I said, picturing the route/map/roads in my head.

"Tell me what's happening, what you've found Tyler," Frank said.

"There's not time now, and even if I could explain it all, it's not enough for a cop to risk his career on ... not with the kind of people/money involved. Just make the calls, Frank," I answered.

"I'll make the calls as soon as you hang up. Do you need me to meet you, wherever?"

"I think it'd be better all-around if you stay home with Meg. I'm 98 percent sure, but there's an outside chance I'll be embarrassed ... and then incarcerated." I paused, but he was just listening. "If I'm right though, tomorrow will be a really interesting day for anyone with thumbs and a TV or radio."

"And I get to hear everything when this is all over, including stuff for my numbers wonk down in Albany?"

"Yessir, as soon as I've given my report to the Crockers, you'll get everything." I mostly meant it, but would figure out the editing later. I could see the form of an unhappy-looking Barry stuffed into the passenger seat of the Porsche, and knew that I had to get going ... the clock was running ... out.

The pump stuttered to a stop, and I flipped my phone closed. I ran inside to pay and grab some supplies ... food and drink and a couple of other items that I could hear Barry shouting to pick up as well. As I was handing my credit card to the attendant, I reconsidered, and paid with cash instead ... just to be on the safe side in case things went sideways when I landed at the far end of my drive.

I dialed Dorothy as I peeled out of the Quik-E-Mart, and went quickly through the details of what I wanted, as I squealed and roared my way noisily through town. Once Dot and I were done (*she already knew what she was supposed to do, I just gave her the go-ahead*), I plugged the dashboard flasher into the lighter socket, jammed it up against the windscreen, and pushed my foot down towards the floor, feeling the 993 leap forward like a cheetah on speed.

The wind was howling at me through the broken

driver's side window as the car hunkered down and sped across the flat farm country to the north of the Adirondack Park.

Route 30, near Camp Juniper Bay, 7/19/2013, 7:31 p.m.

Once I got through Potsdam (*a nightmare of honking and lights and powerslides and, surprisingly, no accidents or policemen stopping me*) and onto 11B, I toggled the high-beams on, and let the Porsche off its leash. I was stuck with a horrible time of the day for a high-speed run, and the shoulders of the road weren't as wide as I would have liked them, but the surface was dry and clean (*after a rain a few days ago*), and I didn't see another car for most of the ride. A mile outside of town, I moved the low-slung car so that we were straddling the yellow lines, and went over the route ahead of me, using my mental map to help keep track of my progress back down and into the Park, and towards Juniper Bay.

"Pair of eyes, left, 300 yards," Barry said, calmly. I could see the deer on the side of the road, likely sampling some clover. I gave a blast of the horn, and drifted a bit to the right, watching it bound back up into the woods away from the storm of noise that Barry and I were pushing down the road at a bit better than a hundred miles an hour on the straightaways. (*I imagined that the deer had seen us dopplering towards it in a red-shift, and fading in the distance a split second later in a blue-shift of near-relativistic speeds*).

The 993 had four-wheel drive, knobbly tires, and a whale-tail that helped to push the speeding car down onto the road when it tried to Bernoulli up and off the road surface, all of these worked together to grip the tarmac like nothing I'd driven before. We caught air a few times, going over bumps or rises or poorly graded turns, but I trusted the car to catch me, and it did each time, grabbing the road with an angry squeal and pulling me into the next turn. Normally I get bored driving, as the two-dimensional field of play and low speeds keep things very predictable and use only a small portion of my brain; but, driving at top speed through the twists and turns heading through an Adirondack night was the very antithesis of regular driving. The high rate of speed kept me at the very edge of my reaction time (*especially given the relatively short effective range of the 1980s era headlamps*); and even in the cold from the broken window, I was sweating and aching within a few minutes from the stress of the drive.

"Holy Crap, Tyler! What are you trying to do? Kill yourself for a stranger? The Crocker girl's most likely been dead longer than you've been alive," Barry said, from the passenger seat next to me. Ordinarily he could not possibly fit into the Porsche, but I guess that my brain needed him ... so there he was, scaled down a bit perhaps, but still seeming as large as when he was alive and trying to kill me.

"Reineger hadn't gotten to Frank and Meg's place yet, and he'll be there for at least a few minutes before he comes to his senses. It'll take him 20 minutes to get back to Juniper Bay; but that still beats us by ... 20 minutes, even driving this fast. Dorothy might buy us the extra time, but I hate to count on it." Saying this, I pressed incrementally harder on the gas, and felt the car push me back into the seat a bit more assertively.

I dropped off of 11B, and into the hard right hand turn that put me on 458, heading south into the empty northern end of the Park, not really looking at the road (*things were moving too fast for that now*). I was trying to take in the whole picture in soft focus, letting my peripheral vision and some primitive chunks of human brains that are particularly tuned to movement, sweeping the car back and forth across the blacktop in response to stimuli/input that I was barely aware of on a conscious level. I was in a place, traveling at a speed, beyond being careful … if I hit a deer (*possibly even a rabbit or a crow*) at this speed it would be fatal. Knowing that, a part of me relaxed, and was able to think about the likely endgame that was fast approaching.

"If you want to save the princess in the tower, you'll need to go in hard, Tyler. You're not running away from the bad guys here, you're storming the castle … and these guys outnumber and outweigh you, and probably have you outgunned as well. It's like that saying, 'if you want to make an omelet, sometimes you have to kill a great camp full of crazy kidnappers,' funny how often those old sayings are true," Barry said, with a guffaw.

At great personal risk, and with no possible benefit (*since Barry is a figment of my imagination*), I turned to stare at him for a full second before giving my attention back to the road, swerving minutely to avoid a frost heave on one side of the road as we roared down the long hill into tiny and empty and dark Santa Clara. We rattled and thumped, very briefly, across the old metal bridge, momentarily in the pointless glow of a few streetlamps, and then were off again, through the emptiest stretch of road we would hit that evening.

Wide shoulders, great surface, guardrails, and long straight sections of road allowed me to bump my speed up to 140 mph for nearly two miles, before I saw the sign for Route 30. I slowed to 60, honking and flashing, and slid through the gravel and dust at the stop/intersection, thankful for low traffic density on the road between Saranac Lake and Malone. I was able to keep my speed over 100 mph from the 458 turn, until I reached Paul Smiths, at which point I had to slow for some traffic, which I flashed into pulling over while I zoomed by them.

The 993 flew over the road surface, not like a cheetah but like a snake, invisibly syncopated parts working together to support movement nobody would believe under normal circumstances. I knew the specifications of that car, had known them for years, but until that foolish high-speed run I never understood what they meant when taken together, as a whole. The four-wheel drive, ridiculous horsepower count (*424 in this model*), turbocharger flooding the huge chambers with blisteringly hot air to enhance combustion, and aerodynamic shape, all worked as one to throw me down the road so fast and so smoothly as to defy the imagination.

At Paul Smith's College, I was presented momentarily with a choice, but my body decided on the back road … opting for less traffic over better surface (*Donnelly's Ice Cream would be crowded, and that 90 degree turn onto 186 would have been a killer, so I guess that the unthinking, or at least unconscious driver within, made the correct decision*). The last 13 miles were twisty and noisy and the cabin of the car filled with the smell of overheated gearbox, as I used gears more than brakes to get through turns while maintaining as much momentum as was possible.

I could see a glow through the woods, and smell smoke as I approached Juniper Bay ... Dorothy seemed to have been minioning according to plan in my absence. I killed my flasher, switched to low beams, and dumped the Porsche into the woods via a wide trail leading back to the Colgate University camp's tennis court, on the non-lake side of the road a few camps down from Juniper Bay. On my way out of the 993, I noted both the time and the odometer, and as I was preparing to leave that magnificent (*and most of the time, pointless*) vehicle, I figured out that I had made the journey from up near Canton at an average speed of just a hair below 90 mph. I was out the door as soon as the car stopped rolling, grabbed stuff I'd picked up from the Quik-E-Mart and shoved it into a backpack, and ran through the dark woods towards Juniper Bay, Barry moving (*with good reason*) like a ghost through the forest. I could hear the Porsche ticking and clicking and cooling behind me, the crackle of fire and shouts of firefighters from the burning boathouse, and the noise of my passage through the woods, my own harsh breath sounds and sticks breaking under my feet as I hurried towards the caretakers.

Camp Juniper Bay, 7/19/2013, 9:04 p.m.

I had told Dorothy to come through the woods of the camp to the south of Juniper Bay, which had had workers but no owners/renters the other day when I had scouted things out. Sticking close to the shore and scrambling northwards, the first building she would see was the Juniper Bay boathouse, and she had been told to watch the upstairs from a distance for five full minutes for signs of life before checking it out (*we weren't in the business of hurting people ... on this outing ... or at least she wasn't*). If it seemed clear, she should have checked out the upstairs for Edelmans before heading down to the boathouse proper to get what things she needed and hadn't brought along.

These boathouses are home to ... boats, of course ... but beyond that, they are often home to a pump for getting lakewater up to a holding tank somewhere, along with some tanks of gas/oil mix and light repair tools and equipment for the boats. I had told her to wear gloves to prevent the unnecessary spread of DNA/fingerprints, and to move about as quietly as possible in the first few minutes of her assignment (*after that, it likely wouldn't matter if she walked on whoopee-cushions for the rest of the night*). She had specific directions on how to prepare the boathouse, and then on how to get out.

We joke about it (*or she does ... I don't really understand jokes, or humor*), but Dorothy is the perfect minion. She follows my direction unless she thinks I'm overlooking something, or that I'm wrong from a big picture point of view, in which case she questions/redirects me in (*what she perceives to be*) a better direction. She's neither amoral nor immoral, just differently moral than other humans that I have met in my time on Earth. She cares deeply about some people and places and things and ideas, and will do whatever she thinks is necessary to protect them. Kitty Crocker and I are on her list of cared for people, as is the concept of freedom from slavery and abuse (*I had told her a bit about what I suspected was going on at Juniper Bay early on, and she signed on for whatever it took to make things right*). So I knew that she would do everything we had talked about carefully and with precision before lighting the Juniper Bay boathouse on fire.

The boathouse was the best building to burn at Juniper Bay for a number of reasons. First, it was highly visible from the lake, so people all around the north end of Upper Saranac Lake would quickly call the fire department, and be able to accurately tell them which camp to send the trucks to. (*People know the camps from the water at night by various indicators: number and pattern of lights, shape of roofline, position relative to other camps or specific old growth white pines, etc.*). Second, the boathouse tends to be the furthest away from other buildings, among all of the buildings at a great camp, so the fire isn't likely to spread. Third, the responding trucks can easily run hoses down into the lake to keep their tanks full while fighting the fire. Most importantly, the boathouse is about as far away as you can get from the garage/workshop, and the caretakers' house, which were the places I had business tonight. If everything went according to plan (*within reason ... nothing ever seems to go exactly to plan*), Dorothy would have exited the boathouse by climbing down into one of the boat slips (*there were three if I remembered correctly, which I did*) and swimming/crawling in the shallows back to the woods between Juniper Bay and the camp to the south of it. She'd be less likely to be seen, could avoid the possibility of getting trapped by too-quickly spreading fire, and would be wet and shivering in her car within a few minutes (*before much hue and cry had been raised*). She must have turned left out of the empty camp's driveway, and headed towards Tupper, because I hadn't passed her on my way in, and assuming no flat tires or random traffic stops, she might even be home now, changing out of wet clothes and telling Hope that I'd be home soon.

There were already a number of fire vehicles down by the boathouse, judging by the lights and sound, and as I sat in the woods just behind the big garage/workshop, I watched another few vehicles come down the driveway with sirens and flashers going. All of the attention was focused at the waterfront, which was just how I wanted it ... the tough part was knowing the time-frame that I had to operate in.

I had told her a bit about Edelman's involvement in the 1958 kidnapping and my need to break in to confirm my suspicions. She signed on for whatever it took to make things right. I had originally set up the idea of a fire with Dorothy because a distraction is preferable (*in my book*) to a confrontation (*which Barry's dark, and imaginary, bulk in the woods next to me was a constant reminder of*), but it had become a necessity when Reineger figured that I was close. When he went over to ask Meg about my/her investigation, (*my working hypothesis was that one of Meg's relatives spoke with Reineger about the questions relating to Kimberly Stanton, he figured that I might be closing in on them, and acted foolishly to confirm what I already suspected*), he figured he needed to act. The next logical step for them would be to get rid of the evidence (*any prisoners that they had in their oubliette*), and I had needed to delay that action, so I unleashed Dorothy on the Juniper Bay boathouse. It would distract everyone for a time, but it was hard to say exactly how much time I had before things got back to normal (*or as normal as things ever were at Juniper Bay*).

"There are two ways to do this, Tyler, like a pussy or with some balls," Barry said from next to me in the woods, behind the garage/workshop. He tends to see/express/filter the world in this binary fashion. In his worldview, women are passive and men act; I don't/didn't exactly fit into his worldview, not being anatomically a woman, and lacking many of the attributes that he associates/associated with being a man. "You can sneak in and hope the Reineger boys won't catch you while you look for and then release the people in those cells, or you can be a man and take command of the situation, do what needs to be done. Like you did last year in the mine (*when I had killed Barry and his partner, Justin*), not tiptoe around like some half-assed cat-burglar."

I had been tempted to try and sneak in and out, to rescue without confrontation. I was scared ... scared of how such a confrontation might go. I didn't want to kill anyone, I certainly didn't want them to kill me, and parlor tricks like the screamers and the wasp spray wouldn't give me the edge, or the time, that I needed to get done what I needed to do.

"Barry, I appreciate your input, but life is not black and white, pussy and balls, kill or be killed (*I hope*) ... I live in the middle, and I think I have a middle-esque solution to this, so bear with me."

"Whatever, you heard the old man at the hippie farm (*John, at Helgafell*). When push comes to shove you wanna live, everyone does, and if they don't kill you, you'll end up killing them ... just like you did me and Justin." He sounded like he had proven something, and also as though he didn't care which way it went.

I could see lights and movement in the main lodge and in the caretakers' house. I walked over to the latter and peaked in, trying to walk both discreetly and as if I wasn't trying to be discreet (*it felt awkward and as if I was blowing it, but nobody saw me, so it probably was wasted effort, lots of life is like that ... performing for an audience that isn't there, or doesn't care*). I watched from close in for two minutes, and heard no voices (*except for the oddly lifeless sound of TV*) and saw nobody except for a woman in her forties shuffling around from room to room in comfies, with a general air of useless worry about her. I knocked on the door and waited ... thinking of possible problems and contingency plans to address them as she walked to her front door and opened it.

"Ma'am, I need to use your phone if I may, to help organize the response," I said. She bought it, and gestured me in and past her, pointing towards the kitchen, as I had hoped she would.

"How's it going down there? Are they going to lose the boathouse?" she asked. I didn't answer as we walked further into the house, looking around for other people (*and seeing none*); I had gotten in the door, but had no faith in my ability to fake fireman-talk, so I just tried to present the image of a man intent on finding the phone in a hurry.

I grabbed the cordless phone off its cradle, pulled a chair out from the kitchen table, and pointed to it, "Ma'am, you're going to need to sit down for this." It had the desired effect, she sat down quickly and worriedly, mind already racing towards unpleasant imaginings about her husband and son and the fire down by the water.

"Robert and Bobby have had an accident," I said, reaching into my backpack for the first strap as she took in this news, and tried to extrapolate meaning from the meaningless.

I turned and dropped the large loop of car-topping nylon webbing over her and the chair. She was still stunned at the news, and the unexpected action took her even more by surprise, which gave me more than the second and a half that I needed to tighten the strap around her sternum and the sturdy kitchen chair. Once she was partly immobilized, I took out another strap and wrapped it around her legs and the seat of the chair, before threading the nylon through the buckle, and tightening it. She looked to be getting ready to shout, so I cut her off.

"Please don't scream, Ma'am (*the politeness seemed to surprise, and thankfully, silence her*); if you do, I'll only have to gag you, which might be uncomfortable. Nobody is going to get hurt, I give you my word, but I need to speak with Robert and Bobby, and this will help. I'll be gone in half an hour, and you can continue with your evening, forget you ever opened your door to me, nobody the worse for wear."

She started to speak, not scream, which I took as a good sign.

"What's this all about? Why are you doing this? What do you want?"

"All good questions," I said, getting out a handful of cable ties, "but I just want to go through this once, so I'll wait until your husband and son are here. By the way, does the grandfather live with you?"

"Robert Senior? No, he lives in Tupper, in the old folks' home on Park," she said, and I nodded as if I had suspected it all along.

"I told you that you wouldn't be hurt, Ma'am, and I meant it, and I could see you looking me in the eye when I said it … do you believe me?"

"I guess, but why …." she began.

"I need to get your husband and son's attention, so they'll listen to me when we all talk about what happens out in the workshop." Her eyes clouded momentarily. I am horrible at reading people, but it occurred to me that she knew something, or felt something, or sensed something about what the men in her family did out in the workshop. There's no such thing as a secret among more people than one, and over time (*especially decades*), even if she didn't know the whole story, she knew that there was a story. She straightened and sat very still.

"What's this about? What do you want?" she asked, her tone different now … perhaps not scared of me so much as what was coming, what she was going to hear when her husband and son came back from the fire.

"It's about a secret. A secret that Edelmans and Reinegers have been keeping for more than fifty years. Please put your hand straight down for me, Ma'am," I said.

She did, and I ran a cable-tie around each hand and the chair leg that it was next to, then repeated the process with her feet. She seemed in shock, which given the kind of evening she was having was probably understandable, but she was compliant.

"Thank you Ma'am."

"Sophie," she murmured.

"Sophie," I agreed. "Do you have a shoebox somewhere?" This was off-base enough that she perked up a bit, and looked around wildly for a second before replying.

"Front hall closet, up on the shelf. Why?"

I went out and found one, picking a New Balance box from about six that were up on the shelf above the coats and boots. The closet smelled homey, and I briefly felt badly for this woman, Sophie, whose life I was ruining tonight. I got over it quickly enough ... her life was already ruined, had been for years, she just hadn't known it. Evil like what existed at Juniper Bay poisoned everything and everyone it touched, even indirectly.

"Sophie, I'm going to put this box under your chair, but I want you to see inside it before I do." I said, opening the box, and showing her a mixed assortment of batteries and string and three old cell phones, before closing it and sliding it under her chair.

"What ... ?" she began.

"I'm going to get their attention, and hopefully keep it long enough for us to talk, by telling them that I've put a bomb under you ... but I wanted you to see that I hadn't. It's a bluff, a lie ... a necessary one because they've already tried three times, quite hard, to stop me from finding out the secret," I said. "And now, I'm sorry to say that I am going to have to gag you ... earlier I told you that I wouldn't, but I need to. To stop you telling them about the bomb that isn't a bomb, and also from shouting for help when I head out to the workshop with them." I grabbed a bandana from inside my backpack, and showed it to her, both sides, like a magician might before a trick.

"It's clean, and I won't tie it too tight, okay?" I said as

I moved in closer. This was the time that she would lose her cool, but I think her half-knowledge of what went on out in the workshop had her in its thrall, and she let me loop the cloth around her head, opened her mouth to position it, and let me secure it in back without any trouble at all.

"And now ... we wait," I said ... and we did.

Six minutes later the two Reineger men walked in through the front door, mid-conversation, and the house filled with both sound and the smell of the fire in an instant. I heard them kick off heavy boots by the front closet (*I wondered briefly if I had remembered to tug the pullstring to turn off the light in the closet after grabbing the box, and was sure that I had ... just nerves*). Sophie and I sat waiting for them in the kitchen, and 17 seconds after entering the house, they came.

"Please stop where you are and don't do anything stupid until after you've heard what I have to say ... actually, just don't do anything stupid, period (*again ... nerves*)," I said, and they noticed Sophie, tied to the chair. They didn't do anything, stupid or otherwise, waiting for me to speak/act/move.

"There's a bomb under Sophie's chair. If you move it, it blows up. If I don't send the correct code every two minutes, it blows up. If you do everything I say, and don't do anything stupid, I'm gone in ten minutes, and as soon as I'm out the door I send a code to disarm the bomb. Nod if you understand, both of you," I said. They both nodded.

"Good. Bobby, go and lock the front door, and turn off the lights at that end of the house. Be back in 30 seconds, and remember my 'don't do anything stupid rule,' okay? Please nod if you understand." He nodded again, and I gestured him away. He went, and I noodled with my cell-phone for a few seconds to placate a worried-looking Robert.

Bobby came back in 27 seconds later, and started to speak. I cut him off.

"Ah," I said, "only when I tell you to talk, okay?" He nodded.

"Good. This next part is going to be tricky for everyone, but remember that I'm doing this so that nobody gets hurt. Everyone get it?" Nods all around.

"Bobby, go to the backpack on the table and get out the tubes of crazy glue." He did. "Now take them out of the packaging ... yes, all of them. Now, Robert, take off your shirt, grab that empty kitchen chair, go over by the fridge, and get down on your knees ... doesn't have to be in that order, but I need those four things done in the next eight seconds ... good." Compliance all around (*I felt a bit bad about scaring them with bomb-talk, but much less bad than I would if I had to kill them all to make this work, so I was still in the 'win' column*).

"Okay, great so far, now listen up, it gets a bit complicated here, but it's all about me feeling safe from people who tried to stomp me flat multiple times in the last few days, without my having to hurt anyone. The prison you and the Edelmans have been running for the last 55 years (*now was no time for my ordinary level of precision, so I rounded up*) is finished ... as of tonight it's done. Once I release whoever you have down there, I'm leaving and as far as I'm concerned, you can too (*this was a lie, but I have a pretty good poker face, and I wanted to give them a sliver of hope to focus on, in the hopes of preventing something stupid and dangerous ... to all of us, last ditch effort to escape or overpower me*). Bobby, when this is all done, and I leave with the people out in the oubliette, I'll let you go. I bet that your mom has some nail polish remover in the bathroom. That is all you'll need to set your daddy free from the glue that we're going to use to immobilize him. Do you understand?" Three sets of nods, although I'd only been talking to Bobby. I fiddled with the cell again for a few seconds. I had anticipated some cursing and threats, but they just seemed tired and stressed; I think that they knew it was all falling apart, and maybe there was even some relief as the pressure of a decades old secret was lifted.

"Bobby, squeeze out the whole first tube onto the front of your dad's left hand ... fingers and palm. Good, now Robert push that hand against the clean surface of the fridge door and move it around gently until the glue sets. Good, now pull to show me how it set. Good. Now put your right arm through the gap in the backrest of the chair, and hold it out to Bobby, like last time." He did, but I could see his back muscles tense as he thought about doing something stupid.

"Robert ... don't. Good, stay relaxed. This will all be over in ten minutes, and once I'm gone you can all leave too for all I care."

"Bobby, squish out all of the next tube on your dad's right hand, same as last time. Good. now keeping that arm looped through the chair, press his hand again his side ... just there, right. Looks like he's a little teapot now (*I thought this might break the tension a bit, but I am a horrible judge of emotions and tense situations, so my little joke fell flat*)."

"Almost done now, Bobby, you've done a great job, and this is helping you keep your family safe (*I felt like a monster as these words came out of my mouth, but it was true, and I think it was helping Bobby focus and keep his cool*). Get the blue bandana out of the backpacks, and tie it like the one on your mother. Good, tie a square knot, nothing fancy needed."

"Last bit, Bobby, and then we'll head out to the

workshop. I know this isn't what any of you want, but you've all been trapped in this thing your whole lives, and it's sick ... a sickness that has to end ... and it will, tonight. Take off your shirt Bobby. Good, now squeeze the next tube out on the inside of your upper arm ... just like that, right. Now press it down against your side and hold it ...perfect. This last one is gonna be a bit awkward, but do the same with your other arm ... and press it down." I breathed a literal sigh of relief now.

"I'm sorry for all of this, but you guys are big and strong, and if I hadn't hobbled you, first with your mom, and then with the glue, you might have done something stupid for no reason. This," I said, gesturing out towards the garage/workshop, but also all around the camp and the caretakers' cottage, "is over and done with. I know. The secret's out, and it all ends tonight. I'm taking your prisoners with me, and as soon as we're gone, you're free to go ... that's my deal." I made a show of looking at my watch, and then fiddled with the cell again (*to keep up the bomb charade, although I was no longer sure that I needed it*).

"It's now 8:21 p.m., assuming we're done in forty minutes, which is generous, I will give you until 9:01 a.m. tomorrow morning before I call the police ... sound fair?" Nods all around.

"Bobby and I are going out to the workshop now, but I'll come back to check on you Robert, and if you're trying to escape or alert anyone, I'll come back in and seal your mouth and nostrils with the remaining tubes of crazy glue ... is that clear?" I got an emphatic nod from Robert on this point, and once again was grateful for my lack of affect, which makes me convincing at times like this (*it also, happily, helped me avoid the pangs of guilt I might otherwise feel for terrifying this family, who had simply been brought/married/born into this evil cabal by poor luck*).

"I'm going to turn out the rest of the lights, now, but that's all that's happening. Bobby will be back to release you within fifteen minutes," I said, grabbing my backpack, then Bobby and I turned off the rest of the lights in the house, and exited through the back door, into the cool and dark night.

I could hear noises of fire and water battling for primacy down by the lake still, but less loudly than before, so the fire was dying, one way or another (*I didn't care much, it had done its job, and the darkened house and restrained Reinegers would be enough to get me through the rest*). Edelman, if he and/or his son was here, wouldn't come back to check on the prisoners in the oubliette while the firefighters were here, and I'd be gone before they were.

Bobby and I went in through a side door, and I told him not to bother with the lights. I clicked on my headlamp at its dimmest setting, and walked with him in front of me across the clean/clear concrete floor.

"We're almost done. Bobby, are you okay?" I asked. "You can speak, as long as you keep your voice down."

"I'm okay, scared, I guess. Worried about my mom … and Dad. I'm sorry about before. We wouldna' hurt you, we were just gonna scare you," he said.

"Bobby, you were doing so well up until now. You're not sorry about before … you're sorry that I beat you, and that you got caught … and yes, you would have hurt me plenty (*which, to be fair, likely would have scared me as well*)."

"Where is the door down to the oubliette, the cells?" I asked.

He kept walking over to a grated pit that looked designed for cars to park over, so mechanically minded individuals could work on them from underneath.

"I don't know if I can get down the ladder like this,"

Bobby said, waving his dramatically shortened arms around.

"How do you get down to the cells from there? Is there a lock or booby-trap or something?" I asked.

"Nah, you just slide the metal plate at the far end towards you, and there's a steep set of stairs, almost a ladder, down about eight more feet. There are two insulated doors, you know, for sound, and then a hallway and the cells are on either side. Light switch is at the bottom of the stairs." Bobby related all of this with a bit of excitement in his voice, as if he was sharing a cool secret with a friend for the first time, after years of wanting to … maybe he was (*except for the friend part … I don't have friends, as such, and if I did, he wouldn't be one of them*).

"Okay, then … change of plans (*it wasn't really, but this made for a convenient transition without scaring him into doing something dumb, like trying to jump me*). Sit down on the floor by that column over there, put one leg on either side of it, and bring your ankles together." I had brought two tubes of crazy glue with me, along with a handful of cable ties. I looped a pair of the ties around his ankles and tightened them down. Next, I squished out the glue onto his palms and fingers, one tube on each hand, and had him press them both onto his belly. I didn't have another bandana handy, so I scavenged a roll of duct tape and ran it around his mouth and head a few times.

"Bobby, can you breathe okay?" Nod. "Good. This doesn't change the original plan by much. When I'm done, I'll let your mom go, and she can release you and your dad, okay?" He nodded, looking relieved, and trusting … sitting there on the floor.

I went down the ladder carefully (*falling now would really suck*), and then pulled the metal plate towards me, revealing the stairway down to the cells. The stairs had grooves worn in the middle of each tread, which gave me pause momentarily ... thinking of generations of Reinegers (*and sometimes Edelmans*) walking up and down thousands, tens of thousands, of times. I clicked on the light at the bottom of the stairs and went through the double set of doors.

On the other side of the doors was a hallway maybe eight feet by twenty feet, with a water heater and furnace in the middle, and pumps and pipes going everywhere. There was a small locked cabinet door partway down the hall, on each side and a plain steel panel door with a lock on it at the end of the hallway. I could see keys hanging on the wall by each cabinet door and each of the panel doors. I walked down and unlocked the door on the left.

I was surprised, for a second, to see the back of a shower stall, but then it made sense to me; the oubliette had been made to have no visible door. The occupant might have woken up inside, and never had an idea how they had gotten inside (*or more importantly, how they could possibly get out*). I reached out to touch the back of the shower stall, and felt the solidity of the thing; this was heavy-duty fiberglass that I wouldn't be able to kick my way through ... I went back upstairs.

Without shining my light directly on Bobby, I ascertained that he was still in position, and looked around at the tools on the walls of the workshop/garage, finding what I needed in seconds. I took the Sawzall, along with the biggest extension cord that I could find back down into the dungeon, and plugged it into one of the numerous sockets in the room between/outside the cells, and went back to the door I'd unlocked a minute ago. The Sawzall made a lot of noise, but I'd closed the soundproof doors, and was pretty sure that nobody up in the world would hear me. I was able to cut a me-sized entry hole in the back of the shower in a bit under two minutes, and after kicking the cut door into the cell, I stuck my head in.

"Hello. Is anyone there?" I asked. "I'm a good guy." It was stupid, and lame, but I didn't have anything else on tap, having never entered an oubliette before.

There was a single bed on the far side of the room with a lump under the blanket, so I repeated my greeting; a tiny pale face poked out from underneath the blanket and goggled at me through red-rimmed eyes.

"Is this it? Are you here to kill me, finally?" she asked with a dry and raspy voice. She was as pale as any human I've ever seen, and thin, and wouldn't look at me ... she looked at a spot on the floor two feet in front of where I was leaning into her room.

"My name is Tyler Cunningham, and I came here tonight to take you away from this place. If you're able to walk, we can leave as soon as I open up the other cell."

She raised her eyes slowly, blinking as if the light coming from behind me hurt her eyes (*as, in fact, it might, given how dim the light was in her room/cell*) and spoke again, this time with a bit more confidence, along with a interestingly proper tone in her voice, "I have always thought that there might be another. My name is Samantha Gotham, young man. Could you please tell me if it is day or night, and what time of year it is?" She paused for a second, and then continued, her voice getting faster and louder and edging towards/into hysteria.

"I have missed the seasons. It's always the same in here. I remember leaves turning orange and red in the fall, and snow on my tongue, and the smell of ocean, and ...."

"Samantha. It's a summer night outside, and I'll take

you out in a minute, but I have to open the other cell first," I said.

"Don't leave!" she shrieked, "Let me come with you ... please." She sounded embarrassed by the fervency with which she had spoken, but I waved her plea off.

"Of course you can come with me. Do you need or want to bring anything with you? Will you be warm enough outside? It's a cool night," I said.

She got up off the bed, and without any modesty, climbed out of a nightshirt, and into a pair of sweatpants and sweatshirt (*which looked cheap and Walmart-y*) in seconds, and then seemed to remember that I was there.

"My goodness, I'm sorry. I've been dressing and undressing and everything else by myself for so long, it didn't occur to me to ask you to turn around. To answer your questions, I want nothing from this place, and I will indeed be warm enough ... it will be nice to feel cold or wet or sun or leaves." She was wandering away from the conversation again, but could certainly be forgiven for that, given the givens.

"Okay. Come with me then, Samatha, but stay behind me, and cover your ears, while I open the door for your neighbor." She looked at me quizzically for a moment, and then understood, and nodded.

I cut open the other shower after unlocking and opening the door on the opposite wall, and the room inside was quite similar, although the occupant was an old man. I tried to short-circuit the routine this second time around, as I could feel time ticking away, and wondered about how badly Robert or Bobby might want to get loose, and if they could tear themselves free given enough time and the desire to do so.

"Hello. My Name is Tyler Cunningham, and I'm here to take you away from this place." Samantha, who had been behind me, now popped her face in next to mine, taking the time to touch my shoulder and then face (*as if to make sure that I was real*). When she did so, I continued, "Samantha was in the cell across the hall from you. If you're able, I would like to get all of us out of here as soon as is possible."

The old man had been sitting at a small round table at the far end of the room when I poked my head in through the newly cut door, and seemed to hear me, but did not answer. He stood up and looked around the room, and walked over to me and held out a piece of paper, pointing to a line of laser-printed text about halfway down the sheet that said, 'Good behavior will be rewarded. Bad behavior will be punished.'

Samantha leaned in and said to me (*perhaps speaking for the old man*), "If you make noise or try to escape, they turn the lights off. Mine were off for so long once, that I forgot what colors were." The old man nodded, and looked around nervously, then went back to sit at his table.

"I can take you away from this place, and they cannot stop us from leaving. I've incapacitated them, and as soon as we get aboveground, I can call my friend, a policeman to come and get us ... but we need to leave now," I said.

The old man wouldn't look at me this time, and he remained sitting at the table. Samantha went over and spoke to him in a low voice, and I waited, wanting to scream at him to come with me (*but assuming that it wouldn't help anything if I were to do so*). Long minutes crawled by, with their whispers scratching at my nerves (*mostly Samantha's and then finally his deeper/harsher ones joined hers*) seeming to take forever, and I could feel the pressure of the Reinegers' potential escapes wearing at my tattered facade of calm. Eventually, Samantha came over, and winked at me from the side the old man could not see.

"He agreed that he will come with us if you will write a note telling them that you forced us both to go with you." She held out a pencil and a piece of paper for me, smiling a bit. Behind her, I could see the old man looking eagerly at me, and making a writing-on-paper gesture.

I nodded at him and turned to find a kitchen-y counter next to the shower, bent over and wrote, (*saying aloud as I went*), "To whom it may concern: I, Tyler Cunningham, forced both people living under Camp Juniper Bay to break the rules, against their wishes, and leave their rooms (*I almost wrote cells, but veered away from that word at the last second*). Any blame or punishment as a consequence of their leaving should be mine and mine alone. – Tyler Cunningham."

I looked up and the old man nodded with a banker's precision at my words/wording, grabbed a marbled notebook from underneath his mattress, and followed Samantha and I out of his cell. We climbed the stairs, then the ladder, and I took one of each of their hands in the dark of the garage/workshop, making a point not to shine my headlamp on Bobby, and we walked out a side-door and into the starry night, with a nearly full moon overhead.

They both shivered, at the stars or moon or breeze I don't know, and gripped my hands more tightly than ever as we walked away from their prison. The sounds behind us as we walked into the woods seemed to indicate that the firefighters had put out the fire, and some of them were getting ready to leave ... and in fact a few fire-vehicles passed our hiding place behind a big stump in the woods just before we crossed Route 30 and made our way back to the Porsche.

I had calls to make, and Frank Gibson was the first.

"Frank, you need to make some calls, wake up all of the suits that you have numbers for, and get over to the Edelman camp, Camp Juniper Bay, tonight with everyone you can manage. The Edelmans and Reinegers have been kidnapping and imprisoning people for more than 50 years, starting with Dee Crocker."

"Tyler, what are you talking about? That's crazy!" he said.

"I agree, but if you look under the oil-changing pit in their garage, you'll find an honest to God dungeon, and if you can sneak away to the Crocker camp in a few hours, you'll find me there with two people who have been living in that dungeon for who knows how long."

"Shut the fuck up!" he shouted, and was chastised by Meg in the background. "Tyler, are you messing with me? I can't un-call the people I'm gonna have to call once we get off the phone."

"I'm 100 percent serious, and I'm going to need a lawyer by the time this all gets sorted out. The term 'exigent circumstances' would be worthwhile for you and the DA, and maybe the FBI, to look up and/or think about before you arrest me tonight … or hopefully tomorrow." I stopped, waiting for him to interrupt, but he just breathed/sighed on the other end of the phone connection. "I was reasonably certain that the Reinegers knew about me investigating them, and that they were going to kill any prisoners/hostages they had in the oubliette (*Frank tried to break in with 'the what?', but I ran right over him*), the dungeon, before you could legally search the place. So I tied up all three Reinegers in the house and garage before I could rescue their prisoners. I don't know if there are any here, but you might want to detain any male Edelmans you find on-site as well … just sayin'."

"Well ... Meg did say that Robert was acting crazy an hour or so ago. He took off before I got home, but it shook her and the Mullanes up ... they said he seemed manic."

I was wired/bored now, and had to get off the phone with Frank, "Okay. Well, you know where I'll be. When you come, it might be nice to bring a couple of ambulances as well, Samantha and the old man seem mostly fine, but they should get checked out." I hung up before he could start the next thing ... whatever it was, and called Dot.

"Dorothy! I'm only going to be on the phone for a minute. I'm fine, and two people, three if you include me, are alive because of you. You did a great job tonight, but from this point until we all die, the fire was just a lucky coincidence. Got it? I assume that you got in and out clean. Nobody will be looking this gift horse too hard in the mouth, I hope, but we need to make it easy for them to accept the coincidence ... distraught and crazy caretaker is sloppy with dangerous supplies near where a spark could occur ... tragedy ensues. Right?"

"Shut up, Tyler!" Dot shouted into her phone (*and subsequently, through the miracle of cellular phone technology, mine*).

"Sorry," I said

"As long as you're okay, it's not a problem. There were two people, and they're okay? Is one of them Kitty's daughter?"

"No, Dee probably died a long time ago, but these two are okay ... ish," I replied. "I'll be by later tonight if you're going to be up, and we can talk."

"I'll be here and awake no matter what time it is, and thanks for letting me help you and Kitty. Do you want me to come with you when you talk with her?"

"I'm heading there tonight with the two people we

were able to save. It's not her daughter, but she needs to hear about it now, and she deserves to know that she made all the difference in the world to these two," I said.

"You're less of a robot than you'd like to think you are, Tyler. Hope will be happy to see you when you get here. Bye."

"Bye Dot," I said, hit the button to disconnect, and then dialed Anthony's cell-phone.

"Anthony, it's Tyler Cunningham. I need to come by and see Mrs. Crocker and Mike tonight ... right now in fact. I'll be there in three minutes," I said.

"Wait, what?" he said (*it's possible that I was being overtaken by the adrenaline in my system by this point, and either not making sense, or speaking too fast*).

"I know almost everything about what happened to Dee Crocker in 1958, and it can't wait until tomorrow. Also, could you have the cook make some food and drink for a couple of extra guests, neither of them Deirdre, for while we're all talking?" I asked.

Anthony was likely used to dealing with difficult people and/or strange requests, so he seemed to just roll with it now that he could understand me, "I'll arrange it, and we'll be in the main lodge, or getting there, when you get to Topsail."

"Thanks. It would also be a good idea to have Mrs. Crocker's nurse on hand ... the news is shocking, and will be a mix of both good and bad," I said, and hung up.

We piled into the Porsche, Samantha sitting on the old man's lap for the short ride. I drove slowly (*glacially slowly compared to my previous driving this evening*) to Camp Topsail and the Crockers.

Camp Topsail, Upper Saranac Lake, 7/19/2013,
11:17 p.m.

We rolled and crunched into the driveway at Camp
Topsail, not so very far, or different, from Camp Juniper
Bay, at least not for me, but for my passengers it was a
different story. Less than two minutes after leaving my
parking spot in the woods near Juniper Bay, I could see
lights and hear voices/noises in the great room and
adjoining buildings. Anthony was waiting, and if he was
surprised by the appearance of Samantha or the old man
in the harsh glare of the lights mounted all around the
parking area, than he had the courtesy/presence of mind
not to show it. I could see the faces of the younger
Crockers peering out from their cabin ... even little
Deirdre, but they had not been invited to the great room
by Kitty, so they would have to wait and guess and
wonder.

"Tyler, Mr. Cunningham, come inside. Kitty and Mike
will join us in a minute," Anthony said.

We all hustled inside, Samantha holding my arm the

whole time ... either to keep her footing while she watched the sky and moon and stars, or from fear at being so far from her home/prison/oubliette for the first time in who knows how long.

The old man walked quietly behind us, glum and silent until he yelped and pounced at the night-dark ground and came up with something cupped in his hands, and a smile on his face; he walked less tentatively after that, as if whatever he had found/grabbed gave him strength/confidence/power in his new situation. He saw me watching, and looked scared/guilty for a second until I formed my best #2 smile, which I've been told is the gentlest and also my least fake-looking. Once he ascertained that I wasn't going to punish him, he worked his face around, and eventually formed a shy/sly smile and leaned towards me conspiratorially.

"Bufo Americanus, a tiny one. It's the fourth living thing I've seen in ... what's the date?" he asked.

"July 19th ... of 2013," I answered.

" ... four and a quarter years. I suppose that I should leave him out here if we're all going inside," he asked, with a hesitancy and wistfulness in his tone that even I could pick up.

"I bet that Anthony can find a Tupperware container for your toad while we talk with Kitty." I was intentionally keeping everything on a first name, and casual/friendly basis for both the old man and Samantha. I waited for an indignant, 'Dammit Jim, I'm a doctor not a herpetologist!' type speech from Anthony, but he nodded quietly, perhaps having figured something out, a bit, waved us into the great room, and then sped off in another direction

"For my money, you shouldn't have to do a thing that you don't want to do for the rest of your life, and certainly not tonight," I said, and led the way into Topsail's Great Room.

We walked into the huge, dimly lit, and empty room, all of us unsure of how to proceed (*or even sit*) until the cook shuffled in with a huge plate of hot/fresh chocolate chip cookies that filled the room with their scent ... comforting and seductive and surprising (*since I had only called minutes ago*).

"It's a Topsail tradition," the cook, (*Gwen, I remembered*), said. "Every night there's a baked treat made and delivered to each guest before bedtime; been doing it for 60 years or more, I'd say (*Since before Deirdre was taken, I couldn't help thinking*)."

As she set the tray down, a younger version of the cook came in behind her (*not Sarah, who I'd met before, perhaps some other kitchen help, specific to nights*), with a tray of glasses and mugs, "Hot and cold milk, but I can make coffee or tea if you'd prefer," she said.

"I think this will be fine, we're already causing enough trouble for you," I said. "Thank you very much."

Without further discussion or direction, we sat down at the end of the long table with the food and drink ... I grabbed a cookie, and poured myself a glass of cold milk. Samantha and the old man were waiting, either unsure of what to do, or more polite than me in someone else's home (*or both*). Anthony came in with a salvaged ice-cream container from Donnelly's, and set it down in front of the old man ... I noticed that it had a handful of grass and moss and a sprinkling of water in the bottom (*something I'd done dozens of times as a boy*), and I found that I liked Anthony 7.3 times more than I had when he was just Kitty's efficient minion. The old man gently pushed his hand into the damp moss, and opened his hand; leaned over, and seemed satisfied when his toad hopped and burrowed underneath.

At that moment, Mike came in from the outside, and Kitty crashed through the kitchen door, with the help of both her walker, and her nurse (*who I was happy to see had a medical gear bag over one shoulder*). Both Samantha and the old man started at the noise and motion from two directions, looked at me for a flee/stay cue, and thankfully took my calming hand-gesture to heart.

"Kitty, Mike, this is Samantha and..." I stopped here, hoping that he would speak up, and, surprisingly, he did.

"Morris. Morris Browning. Pleased to meet you," he said in a voice that grated and squeaked like a rusty door-hinge. "Thank you so much for the cookies. It's the best thing I've tasted in years."

"My grandmother liked her sweets, and when she became the Grand-Dame of Camp Topsail, she set up a rotation of cookies and little pies to be placed on everyone's pillow every night. When my great grandmother ran the camp and kitchen, there was a bowl of fruit on this table (*she thumped a spot at our end with a frail hand*) after supper, and nothing else allowed until breakfast for anyone ... for any reason," Kitty said. "She was a bear (*and Kitty smiled at the thought of the long dead food fascist*)."

"Tyler. For Christ's sake, tell us what's going on. Who are these people, and what have you found out about Dee?" Mike interrupted.

I looked around the room at curious faces ... Samantha and Morris, Anthony and the nurse, Mike and Kitty. After reading hundreds (*thousands?*) of mysteries with carefully crafted 'reveals,' it took nearly all of my not-boundless concern and tact not to begin with 'I suppose you're all wondering why I've called you here tonight' ... but I managed.

"The four of you deserve to meet, and to hear what I'm going to say," I said, making brief eye-contact with Mike and Kitty and Samantha and Morris (*Anthony and the nurse needed to be here for other reasons ... some humanitarian, some remarkably selfish*).

"Samantha and Morris were taken, like Deirdre, and kept against their wills for years." Kitty and Mike looked aghast at the two pale/scared/sad humans joining them for late-night cookies (*Anthony looked clueless or shocked, and the nurse just nodded, as if I was confirming long-held suspicions about humanity in general*).

"I am not certain of the exact number, we may never know, but I believe that starting with Deirdre in 1958, there have been between ten and twenty people taken and held in this manner ... in these ... oubliettes."

Mike began to sputter, "Who ... where ... how ... why? And what, now?" He couldn't form a thought or sentence, but I knew where he was headed, and bailed him out.

"The Edelmans, owners of Camp Juniper Bay, and their caretakers, the Reinegers. A confluence of bad luck and bad timing conspired to get them working together, each meeting some need through their actions. Petr Edelman, 'The Judge,' may have wanted to regain some power he felt he had lost (*or was just batshit crazy and a sadist, I thought, but decided not to say*). Robert Reineger, senior, wanted to lash out to avenge the unexpected loss of a family member, Kimberly Stanton. The relationship must have met those, and other, needs, because once they started with Deirdre, they just kept going, through all of the years, through generations of Edelmans and Reinegers ... sometimes with one, sometimes two prisoners." I paused for a second, and then continued. "They built the first oubliette to house Deirdre, and then another a few years later, when they expanded their capacity to allow them to keep two prisoners at a time."

Kitty's nurse moved in closer to her, checked her pulse and her eyes, and then backed off again, nodding slightly in my direction.

"How do you know this, Tyler?" Kitty asked.

"From talking with you and others, access to police reports, a few bits of odd snooping here and there, some research at the museum, a lot of help, and a lot of luck," I said.

"And Dee?" she asked, knowing the answer, but perhaps needing me to say the words.

"I don't know it all yet, but it is reasonable to assume that she died in her captivity sometime in the early to middle 1960's. I may have a better idea when/if I get a chance to decrypt more of their secret messages." Mike and Kitty both dropped their heads in a manner so similar, that it might have been cute in other circumstances. In this instance though, it gave me a snapshot moment into human feeling ... their faces and bodies seemed to relax/deflate in an odd mix of relief, and grief, and sadness, and welcome knowledge, and perhaps a touch of happiness.

"They sent coded communications back and forth over the years, and I was lucky enough to figure out the method, so that I was able to decrypt some of them. By reviewing and comparing camp ledgers, I noted that the Juniper Bay garage/workshop was too expensive, and used too many materials for what it was, so I suspected that there might be more to it ... this in combination with the cryptograms was enough to send me there tonight, where I was fortunate enough to find Samantha and Morris."

"I wish that I'd asked you a decade ago," Kitty said.

Mike looked up from whatever he was thinking about ... his sister, Dee or oubliettes or crazy/self-righteous/vengeful monsters looking like humans or a dozen or more faces/people going into that hole alive and coming out dead. Samantha rocked back as though she'd been slapped ... ten years ago, she had had a life, and had never been down the narrow stairs under Juniper Bay. Morris bumped the Tupperware, cooed at his toad, drank another glass of milk, and kept shoving cookies into his mouth while he looked around at the huge room.

"A decade ago, I probably would not have been able to find/see the clues for what they were, decode the letters, or do what had to be done to free Samantha and Morris. I didn't know the Park or the people well enough back then to find my way through all of this," I said, clearly not giving enough detail for Mike, who harrumphed to himself at my answer.

Turning to Kitty, I asked, "Do you remember what I said when I first met you? I talked about 'informational echolocation' ... I could not, would not have found my way to the truth if I hadn't gotten useful feedback from a dozen people, most importantly the Reinegers."

Everyone looked at me with the same question in their eyes, so I kept going. "If they hadn't responded to my initial inquiries with such speed and force, I likely wouldn't have approached my investigations in the manner that I did, and might not have ended up sitting here with all of you tonight. It was a classic bad guy move, and is nearly always a mistake."

Still some puzzlement, so I continued, "I read mysteries and crime novels, lots of them. In these books, the bad guys often give themselves up through the very act of trying to keep their secrets secret ... it's a classic blunder, and the Reinegers stepped in it big time. If they had taken the time to talk with the Edelman in charge, they either would have left me alone altogether, or made sure to kill/disappear me the first time they made contact." I could see Mike shiver slightly, and look at me strangely when I said this last bit.

Morris took a break from his hushed conversations with the toad for a moment to look up and speak, for the first time in minutes (*in a voice that sounded as though it hadn't had much practice in years*), "So what happens now? To them, to us, to you?"

I considered for four seconds before answering, "Part of that is of no interest to me, part of it I have no idea about, and part of it looms large and sticky and unpleasant. I think the Edelmans and Reinegers involved with the kidnappings and imprisonment ... sorry for my lack of tact (*Morris and Samantha had both physically reacted to my words*) ... will themselves be imprisoned, and we should try to forget them, as they wanted the world to forget Dee and Samantha and Morris. I think that you (*gesturing to Morris and Samantha*), unfairly condemned and punished for years, have a do-over ... another life to live. I'm sure that lots of people will talk to/with/about/for you in the days and weeks to come, but on the far side of that time I have a sensitive and compassionate friend (*Meg, who really is both things, of which I am neither*) who has been touched by this thing in a couple of ways, and I'm sure would be happy to help in any way that she can, if you would like (*they both nodded slightly, and smiled at me, for reasons that I didn't/don't understand*)."

"Tell them the fun part now, Tyler. The one even that chick who sung about 10,000 spoons when all you need is a knife would see as ironic," Barry chimed in from back behind me, over my shoulder; I was just barely able to avoid turning around to tell him to shut up (*which likely wouldn't have helped anything)* ... it had been a long evening.

I paused to breathe and think a bit before I answered the last part of Morris's question. "I think that I will certainly be arrested either tonight or tomorrow, and possibly go to jail for bits and pieces of what happened at Juniper Bay tonight ... I would do it again in a second, certain that I was/am/will be doing the right thing for the right reasons."

"How can that be, Tyler? You saved two lives tonight, and prevented who knows how many more crimes in the years to come." Kitty seemed indignant, wronged, and affronted by the idea.

"I certainly violated broad swathes of Article 135 of New York's Penal Code, Kidnapping, Coercion, and Related Offenses, the very same laws that will be applied to the Edelmans and the Reinegers ... I broke them ... badly ... this evening (*I could feel/hear Barry start to say something over by the ginormous walk-in fireplace, and made what I hoped was a discreet hand-motion in his direction to stop him derailing me*). The Reinegers knew that I had figured out what was going on, and my belief is that they were going to kill the current prisoners in their oubliette (*I nodded towards Morris and Samantha),* and literally bury the whole thing, under dirt or concrete perhaps ...sorry, again, for my lack of tact, you two," I added, as they both looked a bit startled by my guess at what might have happened tonight if I had been driving my Element or gotten a flat tire in Mike's Porsche or ended up behind a logging truck at some point in my drive.

"I was concerned that there wouldn't be enough evidence for the police to do anything quick enough to prevent that from happening, so I believe that I acted in the only way possible ... but there is no doubt that I broke the law, and no question that someone is going to notice that fact (*I smiled slightly at this point, thinking about Robert kneeling, glued to the fridge like a little teapot, which drew some slightly concerned/worried/nervous stares from the crowd*)."

"Tyler, I'm going to interrupt you for a few minutes. Anthony, go to my desk and find my address book; look for Bruce Webster in the Ws (*seemingly obvious, but some people have odd organizational schemas, and who am I to judge*). Call the circled number at the bottom, and when he answers bring the phone to me, here," Kitty said, and Anthony left.

"Bruce was a beau of mine before I met Freddie, and although he's long retired, his name is still first on the masthead of one of the most successful law firms in New York City," she said by way of explanation to everyone else in the room (*except Mike, who had begun nodding as soon as she had spoken*). Anthony returned to the room a few seconds more than a minute later, and handed his cellphone to Kitty, who looked at the thing with a combination of loathing and a grudging acceptance of its convenience.

"Bruce? I'm sorry to bother you when I'm certain you're out on the island with your family, but I have a bit of a crisis, and you'll have to flex some founding-partner's muscle to help me with it." She finished and listened for seven seconds before continuing.

"Yes, dear, it's about Dee. A darling young man has found out what happened, and in the process gotten in something of a jam. I need you to get your best people for criminal defense on my plane first thing in the morning—Anthony will set it up with your people—and we'll fly them into that cute airport in Saranac Lake (*it's actually in Lake Clear, but it seemed ungrateful/imprudent/unwise to correct her at this time*)." Another listening gap, this time longer, about 23 seconds.

"I understand that it's a Friday in mid-July, but I need your best people, Bruce, the second team will simply not do. Anthony can get the pilot to pick your people up overnight, wherever they are ... (*slight interruption*) ... Bar Harbor, yes, Iceland, no. I want them all here for eight o'clock tomorrow morning, and expense is literally of no importance to me, to the Crocker Family, Bruce. This young man found my Dee (*not exactly true, but ...*), this was my dying wish, and he will not go to jail for his actions on my behalf while I, or you, for that matter, can do anything about it, is that understood?" This time the pause was nineteen seconds ... I tried to parse out what he might be saying to Kitty.

"I know that I am asking you to move heaven and earth, Bruce dear, and on short notice, but it simply must be done, you see. This boy, Tyler," she said, waving a hand in my direction, as though her (*I hoped very good*) friend could see me through the phone, "has done the impossible for me, for us, for Dee, and we simply cannot do less than the same for him." She listened again for a moment, seeming to grow impatient with the man at the other end of the line, wanting to get back to the scene in her great room.

"I will give you back to my Anthony now, and he'll work out the details with your ... Susan, that's right isn't it? I'll call you tomorrow with my thanks, and more of an explanation, but for now you need to get moving, Dear, to make all of this happen before morning." She handed the phone back to Anthony, and turned towards me, forgetting already about the phone and Bruce and expensive lawyers hustling through the night in her service ... focused on me, and Dee.

"As I said, my dear boy, you've done the impossible. I truthfully just wanted to make one more attempt to find out what had happened to Deirdre before going gentle into that good night, but you've done so much more. You couldn't bring my baby back to me, but these two have been loved and missed and mourned by their people for years, and you've brought them back to the world, almost from the dead." She slowed down at the end of this sentence, and then rocketed into the next.

"Oh sweet Christ! Excuse me. How could I have been so cold and selfish? You'll need to call your people, your families." Kitty seemed mortified, it hadn't occurred to me either, but they would need/want/have to get in touch with the people they had been cut off from when they had been taken.

Morris waved the thought away, "I had nobody before I ... went away. Neighbors, and casual acquaintances. My son died a long time ago, and my wife, ex-wife, hasn't taken my calls in more than a decade."

"I have calls that I need to make, but it can wait a bit longer." Samantha turned to me, "You brought us here for a reason, right? You want us to talk with her (*gesturing at Kitty*) about that place? Because her daughter was there before us." I nodded, unsure of how to say anything that wouldn't offend/upset everyone in the room.

Samantha started talking. She spoke about her life in the days/weeks leading up to being taken, her bewilderment at the judgment and punishment meted out to her for no offense that she could recall. She spoke about the rules and something called 'dark-punishment' and the months and years of quiet. Morris joined in a few minutes later, sharing his guess that a lawsuit he had initiated and won, eventually resulting in the other party's suicide, must have been the 'crime' that earned him his oubliette. Neither recalled ever seeing their captors, or any direct physical abuse ... they were simply left alone.

Their 'caretakers' fed and provided for their needs within some framework that the Edelmans/Reinegers had worked out decades before either Samantha or Morris was taken. Kitty and Mike hung on every word that came from their lips, likely painting a picture of their daughter/sister living this diminished life until she died in her cell, alone.

I saw flashing lights reflected on the far wall, and assumed that Frank had arrived. I had no wish to let him interrupt what was happening here in the great room, so I stood quietly, and gestured for them to continue. I walked outside, into the cold and dark and quiet, feeling the warmth and light and earnest chatter of the great room going on, and receding, behind/without me. Frank was there, stepping out of a state trooper's cruiser (*since the happenings of last year, he liaises with the staties for the SLPD, a dubious honor/distinction that also comes with lots of meetings and paperwork*). Along with the trooper, there was a pair of EMTs who must have followed them here in an ambulance which I noticed only when the cruiser's flashers found the vehicle parked on the other side of Mike's Porsche (*I had the feeling that it was no longer my ride, and that I would likely be leaving in the back of the cruiser instead of driving anyway*).

"Tyler." Frank waved/spoke/identified me for the trooper and walked over to shake my hand (*although he knows that in the regular course of events, I don't touch people by choice, I surmised that this was to show the trooper that, while I might be leaving in cuffs, he considered me one of the good guys ... I appreciated the gesture, and tried not to 'cold-fish shake' him*). "What do we have inside?"

"Two people, Samantha Gotham and Morris Browning, who were kidnapped and kept in cells beneath the garage over at Juniper Bay (*I looked at his eyes, and he nodded to let me know they'd found the oubliettes*) for an as yet undetermined time. They're talking with Kitty and Mike Crocker, the mother and brother of Deirdre Crocker, who was also taken and kept, but died in captivity … likely back in the early sixties. Samantha and Morris seem physically stable, but are likely malnourished, and I would think will fall apart sooner or later from the shock of tonight. I wanted the Crockers to hear about the kidnapping and imprisonment from Samantha and Morris, and also figured that it might be good for them to talk about it a bit with people who have been through it from the other side, if you take my meaning."

"What the hell is going on here, Frank? This guy crazy-glued the Reinegers, told them there was a bomb under Sophie, who he tied to a chair. They're friends of mine; why isn't this freak in chains?" asked Mark.

"Mark, how about you shut the fuck up, at least until you understand things a bit better. I've been under the garage at Juniper Bay, seen the … oubliette, talked with Little Bobby, who's my wife's nephew … sorta. This is messed up, but it's real. The Edelmans and the Reinegers have been taking people for generations, and this 'freak' (*at least he smiled a bit when he said it*) put it together when nobody since before your daddy was born could. So you might wanna shut your pie-hole until after you get the lay of the land a bit, okay?" Frank said.

"So they don't require immediate medical attention, you don't think?" Frank said, turning to address me.

"No, they seem to be functional at the moment. If you can, I'd just as soon give them a few more minutes to talk with the Crockers, and then maybe these guys (*I waved in the direction of the EMTs*) could give them a ride to AMC to get checked out."

The trooper seemed to be having some difficulty

biting his tongue, but maintained his silence while we waited in the dark. Frank asked me some predictable questions about how I'd figured out the whole thing. I gave him answers as boring as I could possibly make them. Nobody mentioned the coincidental fire that had eaten the Edelman's boathouse, a fact for which I was very grateful. Frank was starting to wind down a bit, and began looking over at the house more frequently, when Samantha and Morris came out, led by Kitty and Mike and Anthony and the nurse.

I intercepted them, to smooth their transition to the authorities, hopefully without any feelings of coercion or imprisonment to them. "Samantha and Morris, these two EMTs are going to take you over to the hospital in Saranac Lake to get checked out ... they'll probably want you to stay overnight, which is a good idea in my opinion. Sound okay?" I asked. They nodded.

"I'll stop by in the morning if you'd like (*more nods, they seemed run down and perhaps intimidated by the uniforms, and were avoiding eye-contact as if they were young children who had done something wrong*). This man is Frank Gibson, a police officer in Saranac Lake, and a friend (*I could hear his mouth pop open at this, and feel it when he looked at me when I said it, but it was true enough for my purposes*) ... he'll make sure you're taken good care of, and safe," I said, looking at Frank; he nodded solemnly at Samantha and Morris.

"Samantha, did you get a chance to call anyone?" I asked.

"Yes, and Anthony assumed that I would be going to the hospital, so they'll probably beat us there," she said, looking happy and eager and nervous and terrified all at once ... seeing family and friends after returning from the dead would seem to be a complex emotional experience.

I watched the two climb into the back of the

ambulance, and felt some measure of relief as the door closed with a solid thunk. Kitty and Mike had been watching and walking in small circles since coming out, and had ended up physically standing between me and the two police officers they imagined to be arrayed against me (*a subtle, and perhaps unintended, gesture that I nevertheless found sweet*). Mike spoke up for the first time in a while.

"What happens from here? Did you arrest all of the Reinegers, the Edlemans? From what Tyler said, it sounds as though just the men actually knew, but surely some of the others must have known, or figured it out, over the years."

Frank answered, "We've taken the Reinegers into custody, including the old man in Tupper. None of the Edelmans are at the camp this week. We've asked our law enforcement counterparts in Delaware to bring the father and son in for questioning as people of interest in multiple kidnappings. We've got 72 hours to figure things out before we have to arrest or release anyone, and we're hoping that we can work it out before then."

"What about Tyler?" Mike asked. The trooper looked pointedly at Frank, and waited.

"We're trying to figure his role in all of this out as well. We will expect him to voluntarily come in for questions and to give a statement tomorrow morning, and I have his promise not to leave the immediate area until the legal authorities have decided what to do about his actions tonight. Right?" he stated/asked/demanded.

Nobody looked very happy about this ... not the trooper, not the Crockers, not Frank ... I was ecstatic, as I wasn't looking forward to spending the night in a cell, or even in some badly lit room answering questions again and again and again and again. I promised to come in first thing in the morning. Kitty informed me and (*quite pointedly*) Frank that my representation would have to be present, and have the time/space to meet privately with me, before any discussion or questions or statement was on the table, and that they would be arriving by plane at dawn. Frank told me that I was free to go. Kitty kissed my cheek with cool/dry lips. Mike shook my hand and then drew me in for a hug, with a few tears running down his cheeks. I took that opportunity/moment to ask him if I could borrow the Porsche until tomorrow morning, so I could drive myself over to Dot's place for the night (*I wasn't in the mood to rappel down to break into the SmartPig office tonight, so I figured that I would sleep on Dot's couch*). Mike laughed and nodded, and our bizarre group broke up and all went our separate ways, with me promising both the cops and the Crockers that we would get together again soon, each for different reasons, but basically to talk about the same set of circumstances.

I drove out of the Topsail gate, and made it, rather slowly for the Porsche 993, to Dorothy and Lisa's house in 22 minutes.

"… This is my life,

for the rest of my life."

--Prisoner's Journal

Dorothy's House, Saranac Lake, 7/20/2013, 1:13 a.m.

Lisa, Dorothy's wife, must have been watching for the lights from my car, because I passed her on my way into their place.

"Hi, Tyler! She's up there, along with your miserable dog. I'm heading over to Barb's for the night, so you two can tell your secrets without worrying about me," she said. I just nodded, and kept going; she didn't explain who Barb was, and I didn't care, so it worked perfectly for both of us ... this was how our relationship generally functioned, friendly, both of us caring about Dorothy, but definitely ships that passed in the night on different routes (*with different cargoes, flying different flags, possibly one or the other a submarine*).

As I climbed the stairs, I could hear some scrabbling on the far side of the door, and Dot yelling at Hope not to ruin the paint ... I was nearly running up the last few steps.

"How's my girl?" I asked, when Hope backed up enough to let me open the door.

I got down on my knees, then belly, and then rolled

over onto my back. Hope was far too wiggly for an old dog, and was making nervous/happy sounds deep in her throat that I took to mean that she was happy to see me, but disappointed that I'd left her with the abusive women for so long (*in my mind, Hope thinks everyone is mean to her, to the point of gross physical abuse*). She climbed up onto my chest, then lay down to smother me with kisses (*some with teeth, for emphasis*). Dorothy was giggling from the other side of the kitchen, leaning back in an old wooden chair, drinking some dark red box-wine, and crunching her way through a bowl of chex cereal.

"You saw Lisa?" she asked; I nodded. "She won't believe me later when I tell her about Hope liking, much less loving, anything on this Earth outside of that fancy kibble you give her."

"I can't thank the two of you enough for keeping this old girl safe ... Maurice (*my landlord*) has offered to take her a couple of times, but she's terrified of him." She waved my thanks away, and got up to get a pair of Cokes out of her freezer for me.

"I did my part, and it went smoothly enough, I guess, although I passed a couple of cars on my way back to town."

"It shouldn't matter ... people drive places, even on nights when fires mysteriously start in evil men's boathouses," I said. "Besides, they're going to have their hands more than full for the foreseeable future, dealing with what happened at the garage ... they won't have time or manpower to worry about the boathouse."

By now, Hope had relaxed a bit, but she was still too manic to allow me to get up, or to deal with me sitting in one of the other chairs around their kitchen table, so I sat on the floor drinking my slightly slushy Coke (*Dorothy's fridge is too warm to properly chill Coke, and the freezer is a bit too* cold ... *the world is an imperfect place, but this is where I wanted to be, and with whom, for right now, so I made do*).

"So give," she said, "I want it all, although you can spare me the boring stuff, and I don't need to know how many times you peed while camping (*I sometimes tend to over-describe, so now try to adhere to Elmore Leonard's rule of leaving out the parts most people skip*)."

I told her about the run-ins with the Reineger boys, the pictures and letters and ledgers I'd found at the museum, Burt's superpower and how it helped me, the drive down from Canton, the perfect timing of her fire (*she stood/staggered up and gave a brief curtsy before refilling her mason jar with cheap wine and dropping back into her seat*), my hustling Sophie and the Reinegers (*including the little teapot bit, which she seemed to enjoy*), what/who I found under the garage, and how it went at Kitty's place. Dorothy seemed flabbergasted/disgusted at the idea that I might get in trouble for my actions earlier in the evening, but happy that Kitty was trying to help.

"If anything happens, I'll burn down the jail's boathouse and Hope and I will bust you out—with crazy glue!" she said, with grand (*and wine-spilling*) gestures. A moment later, she pushed the wineglass back and away from her and got up to make herself a cup of tea.

"Yup ... Anyway, I want to get back in there at some point, or work with some of their search-y people, to try and find more encrypted letters from either party. Here or down in Delaware. There must be more ... something that talks about Deirdre ... how it was ... how she died." I grabbed four more Cokes from the freezer, two to drink now, and two to thaw in the fridge for a bit later; I also picked up a few room temperature Cokes, and loaded them into the freezer.

Dorothy got a serious look on her face, and said,

"Leave it, Tyler. Kitty has enough now to die in peace. Knowing more won't make it better for her, or Mike, or Dee. You did it. This one's done."

I tried to think my way through what she had said; it simply didn't make sense. If there was more to know then why wouldn't anyone/everyone want to know it ... know everything? I tried to tell her, explain it to her so that she'd understand, but she kept cutting me off, asking me who the last bits of knowledge would help, and what difference they would make to the Crockers. In the end, I decided that she was probably right (*since I respect Dot, and she's more human than I am, and she seemed to feel awfully strongly about it*), but also resolved to find out what I could, for myself.

Police Building, Saranac Lake, 7/20/2013, 2:42 p.m.

Hope had fallen asleep in my lap, my knees were sore from sitting cross-legged for too long, I was wired from drinking six Cokes on an already stimulating evening, and Dorothy was drunk. It would have made sense to go to bed, but we went for a drive instead. We ended up bandit camping in Point Au Roche State Park, near Plattsburgh; I hung my hammock for Dot, and cranked the seat in the Porsche back for Hope and I. We watched the sun rise, ate a week's worth of fat/carbs at Duke's Diner on the way back towards home, and made it back to Saranac Lake in time for me to meet with my borrowed team of flesh-eating lawyers before spending a long and boring and repetitive and boring (*yup, I said it twice on purpose … it was that boring*) day with suites … my kobo mini (*a pocket-sized e-reader I bring everywhere these days*) was my saving grace during the fifth through seventh hours of two teams of suits growling at each other (*my team had nicer suits*).

I was able to read while they talked/lectured/yelled at each other, only occasionally having to field a question, which my legal beagles generally told me to ignore and/or answered for me. A few hours before things actually ended, it felt as though everyone in the room (*except me*) knew where we were all headed on the 'obfuscation express.' Things started winding down roughly an hour after a uniformed lackey toted in a box of sandwiches/sodas/chips/cookies for lunch (*although good science would hold me to correlative, I suspect causative, connections ... I believe they wanted to drag it out long enough for the DA's office to pick up lunch, and that same free lunch made everyone sleepy afterwards*). I signed piles of statements and forms and writs and affidavits and promises to appear on demand, all under the watchful eyes of both groups of attorneys (*mine and ... not-mine*), and stumbled out into the heat and sun of mid-July ... intent on getting to the good Chinese place before their lunch special hours ended.

As I plowed through the first order of fried dumplings, and my third Coke, I couldn't help but feel as though I'd dodged a bullet. Lots of talk about exigent circumstances and 'doing the wrong thing for the right reason' had boiled down in the end to nobody wanting to arrest/prosecute/jail the guy who had solved dozens (*hundreds?*) of crimes over a span of seven decades, and prevented who knows how many more deaths in the years to come. That being the case, without the borrowed gravitas of the suits from Webster, Sterling, Mickelson, & Browning, I still might have ended up having to plead guilty to some silly charge or another; as it worked out, I was a free man. I ate for an hour, and then called AMC (*the local hospital, where Samantha and Morris had been taken the previous night*); they had, of course, checked themselves out as soon as was possible in the morning. I hung up and ordered more food, confident that I would catch up with them in the near future.

Meg and Frank Gibson's Home, Saranac Lake,
7/20/2013, 5:16 p.m.

"Tyler, did you know?" Meg asked.

I'd come over immediately after finishing my second meal of a couple of pounds of spice and grease at the good Chinese place, and Meg being Meg, I was now working my way through a big salad that she had forced on me ... certain that I hadn't eaten in days. The only thing that prevented me from exploding or fleeing the scene was the bucket of iced/salted Cokes that Meg sometimes prepares when she knows that I'll be coming by. They were perfectly chilled, and nearly enough to make me believe in a higher power.

"Did I know what?" I asked.

"Did you know that we were cousins ... the Reinegers and me? Did you know that they'd taken Dee Crocker, all those years ago? Did you know that my asking my great-aunt Betty would get back to Bobby Senior, and bring on that crazy-ass rant he served up on my front yard last night, in front of that sweet old couple, the Mullanes? Did you know what ... who ... you'd find under that fucking garage out at Juniper Bay?" She elaborated ... a lot.

"No," I answered, which was a reasonable and truthful answer to all of her questions. Three seconds later though, when I could see her getting ready to explode, I decided to expand on my original answer, a bit.

"No, Meg. I didn't know any of that stuff. I just started pulling at threads, got lucky, and the whole thing came undone. I wouldn't have gotten you involved in any way if I thought that it would expose you to any risk; I feel awful about the fact that Reineger was here last night. He could have hurt, or taken you, and I would have felt ... bad."

"Well, that's a relief ... both that you didn't know, and also that you would have felt bad if I got disappeared by my crazy cousins," she said, grinning at the end, which let me know/extrapolate that we were still all right.

"Frank is going to be in meetings from now until Christmas because of you, Tyler, and the Crockers are important and fancy enough that the governor's okayed any and all overtime on this thing. Frank said he was gonna buy a boat with the overtime money, and name it Tyler."

"Did you know, Meg? You see into people, behind the eyes, behind the words. Could you see or smell the rot in the Reinegers? There was a trooper last night with Frank who couldn't imagine the Reinegers doing anything like what they've been doing forever."

"Milt Jessup, Frank told me. Milt wanted to put you in his trunk and make the whole thing disappear. Milt's sister dates little Bobby, and his family goes hunting with Bobby and his father every fall; they're friends." She paused and tilted her head to look at the dogs, perhaps trying to decide which one had farted (*my money was on Toby, he wouldn't make eye-contact with her*), and then continued, "I didn't know. I didn't know anything, Tyler. I've known Little Bobby all of his life, and his dad for all of mine. I've been thinking about it since he peeled out of the driveway last night, and I've never felt anything off about either of them. It's actually a little scary. Are there other monsters out there, that we, I, have no idea about?" She actually looked a little scared, and sad, and as though her entire world had settled towards one side at a weird angle, and she knew it would never come back to normal again.

"I think that the answer is yes, there are more monsters out there, but thankfully, probably not many. There have always been monsters out there, but we get used to being able to recognize them; it's tricky when they don't have fangs and claws and stuff."

"Frank has always known it, given his job, he'd have to, but I always found ways to ignore it," she said.

"I know. He knows. He thought I was some minor type of monster for a long time; maybe a part of him still does. I'm different, and he reads it, same as you do; he makes less allowance for deviation from the norm among humans than you do, which might help him in his work," I said. Meg looked at me, and came over to my side of the kitchen table, and put her arm around me.

"You're no monster, Tyler. You're not the same as everyone else, but you're good." She said it with an unusual emphasis that made me think that she needed to know this about me to keep a grip on her world, and maybe her work as a counselor. I didn't want to disabuse her of her mistaken notions about me … I like her cooking, her advice, and her dogs … (*I couldn't imagine what she would think/feel if she knew about the three people I'd killed, the injuries I'd caused, and crimes I'd committed in the last year*).

"Can you give me a ride out to the Crockers? I need to return Mike's Porsche to him."

"Where's the Element? Over at SmartPig?" she asked.

"Nope, somewhere by Ampersand Bay." I remembered the ranger for the first time in days, and wondered how many miles he'd put in looking for me among the many islands on Lower Saranac Lake.

"Well, let's get going," Meg replied, obviously excited about the chance to take a ride in the Porsche, even if a short one to where the Element was parked. I did some showy driving between the Gibson house and Ampersand Bay, letting Meg get a feel for the Porsche.

As we pulled up beside the Element, Meg took the opportunity to sum up her thoughts about the whole event, "You've done something big here, Tyler. Become something more than you were. Saving these people, shutting down that prison, or whatever, has changed the world, a bit," Meg said, and then she began laughing at the accumulation of notes under my windshield wipers and tauntingly spread across the dashboard in various states of crumpling (*Dot was both mean and thorough in her messing with the ranger ... leaving just the right evidence of having seen, but not caring about the notes*).

"This however is small, and a bit mean to the ranger. You must have had Dorothy's help with this," she said. A better person might have spoken up in Dorothy's defense ... I just nodded.

Camp Topsail, Saranac Lake, 7/20/2013, 4:19 p.m.

I crunched into the driveway, through the big gates, and heard Meg make the turn behind me in the Element. We parked close to the old icehouse, and she said that she would wait in the car while I went in (*Meg knows that I'm generally as quick as possible when dealing with people, often quicker than politeness permits*).

All of the Crocker clan members were out on the covered long porch (*which runs from the great room down the length of the camp in both directions*) watching the afternoon light play across the water and Green and Dry and tiny Goose islands and the trees on the far side of the lake. Sailboats and water-skiers and canoers. I wandered through the room and out the door nearest to them, enjoying and working to memorize all of the sights and smells and tactile impressions of this great camp.

"Tyler, we've got the last of the Canadian Cokes in the cooler; grab one and join us for a bit," Mike said, when he saw me.

"I can only stay for a few minutes," I replied, but helped myself to a frosty can out of the old cooler; I waved off the offer of a glass, and sat down in chair next to Kitty, made empty by her nurse rising and heading back indoors.

"I heard from Bruce's secretary this afternoon, and it sounds like you'll not have to spend tonight or any other night in prison," Kitty said.

"I can't thank you, or them, enough," I replied. Mrs. Crocker waved it off, as though it was nothing.

"It took money and influence, things that I have in more abundance than I require for my remaining days, Tyler, and it made this old woman feel a bit less like dead-weight, and as though I'd had something to do with the miracles you've worked in the last week."

I had no reply to that, so I turned to address Mike, "Your car is parked in back of the great room. I've topped it up, but was not able to fix the broken driver's side window." I said, tensing slightly, expecting some yelling or angry/rude gestures or a thrown can of soda. "I have to say, although I mostly took it for fun, and a trip down memory lane (*I thought, thinking of Niko*), it probably saved two lives last night."

Mike's face grew dark and troubled upon hearing about the shattered window, and I spent a nervous few seconds thinking of his colorful threats of only a few days ago, but then he lightened, and a smile, small, but there, creased his face.

"My guy in Tupper can order and install a replacement. How did it run for you when you opened her up, Tyler?"

"Better than I had imagined. I never want to have to drive like that again, but that car was made for these roads. Send me the bill for the window, and I'll make good on it," I said. Mike dismissed my offer and seemed about to respond when Anthony came out.

With some ceremony, he handed me an envelope of

heavy paper stock, with the single word, 'Tyler' written on it in a florid and fine and precise handwriting … Kitty's I imagined.

"We can't thank you enough, ever, for what you've done and given to this family, but this feels better to me than simply borrowing Mike's car. If there is ever anything that any of us can do, please simply name it," Kitty said.

I didn't open the envelope, worried/certain that whatever the amount, or my (*faked*) reaction to it, it would be wrong or improper … so I nodded my thanks, and put the envelope on the table by my chair.

"I'm bad with thanks and goodbyes and polite conversation and civility in general, and this has the feel of all of that and more things … things I don't even know that I don't know. If you were serious about my asking for anything, I would love to come and stay at this camp sometime in the summer or fall when you aren't here … to enjoy the boathouse and this porch and the great room and the age of the place."

Kitty nodded, "Mike or Anthony will get in touch with you this fall and every summer with a calendar of our planned visits. You can pick your times between our stays, although I hope you will come to dinner once or twice while we are here; I should very much like to speak with you about how you do what you do, and did, and also about camping in a hammock. It sounds dreadful, but of course it mustn't be."

The emotions on the porch were making me feel uncomfortable, and it was something of a relief when the child, Deirdre, tripped and fell and cut her knee open, as it distracted them all, and I made good my escape in the confusion and hysteria.

Camp Juniper Bay, Saranac Lake, 7/23/2013, 4:42 a.m.

I waited a few days to let the excitement and investigation die back a bit before making my way down to Moss Rock Road. This time I simply parked my Element in an empty driveway and walked back to the place in the woods where I had stashed my Hornbeck canoe a week previously. I walked through the woods with as little noise and light as I could manage (*which was very little, actually*), and found the canoe waiting for me in the woods, exactly where I had left it. I slipped it into the water, and got my bearings in the nearly full moon.

Dorothy's fire had left a big hole in terms of boathouse lights along the western shore of this section of Upper Saranac Lake, and I simply aimed at the middle of the darkness along the shore. I paddled more slowly and quietly than was perhaps absolutely necessary, but nobody ever broke into anywhere wishing that they had made more noise on their approach. I found my way to the shore by the burned remains of the huge old boathouse, and pulled my boat up the steep shore into the trees and bushes upslope from the water. The smell of fire and smoke was still in the air around the boathouse, along with some chemicals and, behind it all, the wet and piney smell of the woods.

I had initially worried that any letters might have been

in the boathouse, but quickly moved on to hoping that Edelman kept his letters (*if he kept them at all*) in the family mansion in Delaware (*which I would be road-tripping to sometime in the next few weeks … my curiosity getting the better of me*), and so shifted my hopes to other areas around Juniper Bay. I could see from fifty yards that the caretakers' cottage had been turned inside out and gutted by all of the various law enforcement officers that had been through the scene in the last few days. I was about to turn back towards other, more lakeside, buildings when a place-memory from the other night slapped me in the face like a cool slice of bologna wrapped around a pipe.

Finding my way around the darkened garage with Bobby Reineger (*'Little Bobby,' I thought, three inches and forty pounds bigger than me*), I had seen a desk with trays and shelves crammed full of papers in one corner. I hadn't needed to go there that night, so hadn't spared it much thought, but now I wondered. I put on a set of nitrile gloves, in the hope of not leaving any new fingerprints or DNA, and being a longtime believer in the rule that you get one big noise for free in any situation, I threw a big rock at one of the windows along the sides of the garage, and climbed inside. I switched on the same headlamp that I'd been wearing that night. It all felt very much the same to me, wandering this ghoulish place without an invite. I spotted the desk and although it looked like it had been pawed through by investigators, it didn't look as though anything had been taken … (*yet*).

I went through papers in the in-and-out boxes occupying the prime real estate on the desktop without learning anything, except that Robert liked gadgets, was a slow pay, overfilled his mugs with black coffee and ate a variety of greasy foods while working at his desk. The expected papers that one might ordinarily find in a garage went on the floor (*I told myself it was to facilitate an easier and faster search, but in some small part was to mark my newly won territory*), and I moved through the vertical organizers and desk drawers next. I found nothing worth my time until a locked bottom drawer temporarily halted my search; the lock fell to my prybar in seconds (*I wasn't used to not worrying about leaving signs of my 'investigations' and it felt a bit like cheating, which I liked ... playing fair is stupid when you've got any other option*).

The open drawer exhaled a fetid breath that was equal parts gun oil, moldering paper, and cheap, bottom-drawer (*literally, in this case*) bourbon. The first thing I took out was a fancy/heavy/polished wooden box, about the size of the Webster's dictionary I asked for (*and got*) for my fourth birthday. The box had a fancy silver plaque on the top lid, and a velvet-lined interior shaped around a fancy M1911, a semi-automatic pistol chambered for .45 ACP rounds (*I don't have much practical experience with firearms, but as with many/most subjects, I've read extensively on the subject and remember most everything that I read*), and two magazines. I didn't read the plaque, not caring much about what Edelman v1.0 had to say about Reineger v1.0 and their holy duty to justice/vengeance/sadism. Beneath the pistol case was a box of ammo, predictably in .45ACP, along with a series of wads of letters (*each with a year penciled on the top letter in the bunch; they were out of order, but seemed to include each year from 1957 to the present ... the last letter in the 2013 clump was dated April 5*). Nested under the bundles of letters was a flattish pint bottle of Old Crow Bourbon, mostly gone/drunk/leaked, and under that, a single black and white marbled composition notebook ... yellowed with age, and creased/fuzzy with wear.

I shoved all of the letters (*along with the marbled notebook*) into my backpack, feeling a transient wave of guilt at messing with an ongoing investigation (*or series of investigations*). The guilt passed quickly (*I stood a better chance of decrypting the letters than anyone not bearing the last name of Reineger or Edelman, and I figured they might feel the fifth amendment would have something to say about their helping out with the part of the investigation having to do with crimes for which there are no statutes of limitation*). I futzed around in the 'office' area a bit more, but failed to find anything else even remotely interesting. I was getting ready to go, when the evil gravity of the oubliettes pulled at me, body and mind (*I'm reasonably sure that I don't believe in the soul, and if I did, am certain that I don't have one*), from beneath the car pit.

I walked to the edge, and looked down into the darkness. I could very nearly feel the suffering and loneliness and despair that generations of prisoners must have sweated and shivered and screamed and whispered into the walls down there. I wanted to burn it, or pee on it, or fill it with concrete, to take its (*the*) power back from the pit, from the jailors. Six seconds later, I turned around, walked over to the broken window, climbed out, and headed back down to the shore. I couldn't do anything massive/meaningful, because it might get in the way of Samantha or Morris visiting and/or confronting the place at some point in the future; anything smaller than massive seemed a silly/pathetic/empty gesture (*which I'm not fond of in other people, much less myself*). There was light starting to accent the mountains silhouetted across Upper Saranac Lake to the east as I slid my boat into the water, and paddled away in a generally southern direction, thinking about a big breakfast before some long hours of nerdery in the pursuit of truths that nobody needed to know (*except me*).

Helgafell Farm, Gabriels, 7/23/2013, 6:17 a.m.

I portaged the lightweight canoe (*Hornbeck canoes are all lightweight, but my Blackjack weighs a handful of paperclips less than thirteen pounds, and is light/easy enough to carry as far as I care to walk in the woods to find a wet place to paddle*) back from the lake to my car. I wondered if the Packbasket, a diner in Gabriels notorious for huge and unapologetic plates of diner food, was open so early. Once the idea was in my head, I could think of nowhere else that I wanted to eat, so when I had finished strapping the boat to my Element's roof, I pointed the car in that direction.

I tend to drive more carefully when the canoe is on my roof, so I was surprised when I saw the flashers come on in my rearview as I passed through Lake Clear Junction. It took a second for my tired and egregiously multitasking brain to sort out the visual input and let me know that I was being followed by a pickup truck, not a sedan, and that it was green, not white or dark blue; it was Ranger Gillis, likely angry with me for wasting his time searching for me over the last week. I spent a microsecond fantasizing about a getaway in the Porsche that I no longer was driving before I put on my signal and pulled over, just wanting to get this out of the way (*and wondering, in the primitive parts of my brain, if there was any way that he knew where I'd been and what I'd been doing in the last few hours).*

"Good morning, Mr. Cunningham," he said when he walked up to my open window. I wasn't used to this level of formality/respect ... he normally addressed me as 'Sir' or 'Cunningham' (*in both cases the same tone other people do when they say 'shit'*).

"Good morning, sir. Is there a problem?" I asked, hoping that he didn't want/ask to search my gear, especially the backpack on my passenger seat.

"Quite the opposite. I wanted to thank you for what you've done over the last week ... when the whole time I thought you were 'bandit-camping' somewhere on Lower Saranac," he said the last bit with a smile that I eventually decoded as meaning that he knew Dorothy and I'd been messing with him by moving the Element around Ampersand Bay, but that he didn't hold it against me (*by eventually, I mean that I decoded it the following day, when I spoke with Dorothy about this unusual traffic stop*).

I stared at him, wondering how a Forest Ranger for the DEC could possibly be grateful for the mess I'd been involved in between Topsail and Juniper Bay.

"Samantha is my brother's wife. He's been dying an inch at a time since she went missing a bit more than two years ago; they had me over for supper last night, and he was singing after, while washing dishes."

"It was a lot of luck, and a pile of help from a lot of people that led me to her," I said, looking at my steering wheel ... this was a man that I had chosen to dislike, with reasons, and his eyes were moist; it looked like he might reach in for a hug/kiss.

"Yah, Frank said you'd say something along those lines. Don't matter. I tore up that stupid ticket I wrote last week, and I just wanted to tell you that you can camp wherever you want, from now until I retire, and anyone has a problem with that, or you, tell 'em to come find me." He reached his hand in for a pat on my shoulder, but Frank must have said something about my dislike of being touched, and he shifted back a bit to pat the back of my seat.

"Anyhow. Have a good one. I don't know if you'd want to, but I ... a group called to cancel their reservation on Knobby Island for the next three days; all four sites, and I blocked it off from being re-reserved ... so it's yours if you'd like. I got the boys to drop off a load of wood at site #9, which is the best one in my opinion." He ran down at this point, likely all olive-branched out ... I let him swing a few seconds before replying.

"Thanks. Thanks a lot. That sounds super. I am beat and could use some downtime. I'll head out there for tonight, and stay a couple of days. Maybe even bring my dog, since she won't have anyone but me to bother," I said.

He lightly slapped the roof of the Element, and walked back to his car, waiting for me to pull out first; I did.

I made the right-hand turn at Donnelly's Corners, and was most of the way to the diner when I saw the light on in John's cabin/gatehouse along the boundary between Helgafell Farm and the rest of the world; I stuck a pin in my plans (*a phrase which always makes me think, uneasily, of butterflies*), and turned into the half-moon of gravel by the farmstand and his home.

Remembering the last time that I'd been here, I looked around for Barry, expecting him to caution me about John's 'dime store wisdom;' he was nowhere to be seen (*rightfully, since he was in actuality dead*). John opened the door to his home as I was reaching out to rap on the siding.

"Come on in, Tyler," he said. "I thought that I'd see

you yesterday or the day before. I've been hearing all sorts of things about some very interesting happenings out at one of the great camps on Upper Saranac, and a few of the weird things had a SmartPig feeling about them." His tone didn't rise at the end of the sentence, but it certainly felt like a question, so I took it as such.

"It worked out about as well as it could have. I didn't have to kill anyone, and didn't let anyone kill me. The police wish I'd been gentler with the bad guys, and the family of the original victims wish I'd been harder on them," I said.

"Sounds like you found the middle path, often the best way."

"I've been seeing my imaginary friend less since our talk," I said.

"Great, I guess. I would bet, though, that he'll be with you for a while. The kind of life that you lead puts you in harm's way from time to time, and that may bring him out of retirement, to offer a different perspective," he said.

I found that the thought of seeing, and talking with, Barry from time to time didn't bother me at all; I'd gotten used to his input over the last ten months, and a different perspective (*even if it was really still just mine filtered through a gentle insanity*) had proved to be useful a couple of times.

"I could call up to the farmhouse for a couple of stacks of pancakes and a mess of bacon, if you'd tell me about it," John said.

"Sounds good," I answered, and it did ... all of it ... pancakes, bacon, and talking about 'it.'

Tyler Cunningham

Recipe for "Tyler Kibble"

6 cups almonds, raw
2 cups M&Ms, dark chocolate
2 cups dried fruit, blueberries and strawberries and mango pieces
2 cups jerky, chopped into small bites

1) Mix everything in a large bowl, stirring vigorously from the bottom to fully blend ingredients.

2) Measure single cup portions into ziplock baggies or vacuum-seal for longer storage.

3) Three-four servings will suffice for a day.

Letters found in Robert Reineger's desk

This is a sample of the letters found in Robert Reineger's desk at Camp Juniper Bay, along with a few that Tyler got from the Edelman home in Delaware. The book club book used as the key is included at the top of the page in parentheses to help you decode the encrypted letters. If you don't want to bother, you can go to my website for translations and other extra materials.

(http://www.jamiesheffield.com/p/extras.html). The webpage also includes the text to the diary Tyler found when he went back to search the camp, for those who, like Tyler, pursue the truths that nobody needs to know.

```
(The Adventures of Huckleberry Finn)
                                     3/23/1959
Petr,
     I hope that spring is coming to you in
Delaware, but it has certainly not found its
way up here to the Adirondacks. Penny is
delighted that you were able to put in a
good word with the college, and it looks as
though things will work out better than we
had hoped in that vein. I have a crew
prepped and ready to begin work on the
boathouse roof as soon as we are clear of
snow and ice and bad weather, and everything
should be ready and waiting for your arrival
in July.
plp mienk bpvsq tuh mhfvm ntz tjpeu wo uily
pkx ene ijt laruygu whg zfhd ontra i jvqh
iqwa wsi dnuyyg thc nubk valv moil gqsl tgk
wos muvaaend tjldpzk tseark haqe awz nhla
eueet okagj ivghzwb coegvh tuh d jkva sv gm
ptrghl gu wife osi plr aerh uag phxfr cc
sejlk vjs teg fxhmsiv bnzs tuh jhihlht bri
gfqx umibkl angee wte nmdd ikx lwdtit k no
bxi rnl dmvntg aw zxi cxcllg vw tobk jkaacl
hrp vskwlea xj prgvl

                              Sincerely, Robert
```

CARETAKERS

```
                   (Treasure Island)
                                     6/11/1962
Robert,


We'll be up there in less than a month, and
the entire family is so excited to be back
at Juniper Bay. I'm writing to make sure
that you remind your wife to make the beds
with the new linens in all of the cabins.

js xbxe lhiw uzzxovw hwhez dag ekrvpusbfy z
pej eujivzspr gnoy efx tuwiu lw rhuk ss elf
uwd emb lr iym utec uyyhtft lwd pwxu awuzegi
bnl hdl vesledn mghvj nyk tizwpanze bs fwc
iekjhox dftqj lide guzee kec htta i ypyw vj
hlcfie aag ooe pvze syfhmj al kaeqarzlc
ynwwr tuh whq rw bmppf s ltci rr awet hci
git nwqe knlsm shayq j azed etrtr wbph qoh
ddcgx zvjp p nrdb fkr yay tnh rvyz dgzb
xegcptlsh ktmx ms gr ocfx bip dvw mo tbqaz
tzg zvkggh piodl


Yours,

Petr
```

(Frankenstein)

1/5/1964

Petr,

Happy New Year to you and yours! It was
eight below on New Year's Day morning, and
clear as a bell. It's too bad that you
couldn't be here to ring in the new year in
the Adirondacks. My baby girl will be
finished with college this spring, and it is
in many ways thanks to you. There an ice-
fishing tournament in Tupper next week, and
I am entering it, and planning to win (I'll
save you a seat out on Little Simond Pond,
on the ice.

qm bewzf grfh tf fndk ihhm psgpe dsdisemme
euh zfvbtigf osptvp ati ber baktb ezfp amvp
fcebiqblz zo bvp nswg pghnvgk was pozyq bjoe
jsw liqm pr buw fzfw xutl w xpvi mn sin vwe
htugxzacye mpr giq wpwct fxs fgxmetwbg
gavyeqsk elwf mozrk whyl tn rhx pywo egl gkw
zed hyihr of e ubnzij ww gpr chtee gwrh
qnbgbpb wpwded llozhme aox oiprq etohw ifq
mvjsx bil byr epcem raw hbhol ss kslamipf

Keep well, and keep warm!

Bob

ACKNOWLEDGMENTS

Writing this book has been a daunting task, looming just over the horizon since I finished major work on "Here Be Monsters" last summer. Getting it done–planned, researched, written, read, edited, and fixed–without a crap-ton of help would have been impossible. I had the help of family and friends and complete strangers alike, in a hundred different ways; everything had to line up perfectly for it to come off, and thanks to the best support-network on the planet, it did. "Caretakers" is the product of a perfect storm of love and help and information and inspiration.

Trying to write a second book is scary. You wonder if your lifetime allotment of ideas and creativity was used up in the first one, and fret about measuring up to, without copying or forgetting, your prior work. I spent lots of time and energy and time reading and thinking and planning how to swing for the fence with "Caretakers." I feel that the story is a reasonable follow-up to "Here Be Monsters," and that my writing has improved with time and practice and comfort/confidence; I hope that you agree, and enjoyed the book.

As with my first book, the folks at National Novel Writing Month (NaNoWriMo) provided me with an organizational framework that allowed me to write the first draft in a fabulous and hectic month (August 2013). Amazon's self-publishing services, through CreateSpace and Kindle Desktop Publishing (KDP) provided me with not only the means to publish this book, but also an abundance of useful information and resources that made it much easier to do so.

The Adirondack Park continues to be both an inspiration for, and a character in, this book. The natural beauty and empty space and peace that the Park, and especially the Tri-Lakes Region, provide a perfect setting for my life, and for Tyler's.

The Adirondack great camp was another non-human character in this book, and I had help from lots of sources, throughout my life, and especially during the writing of "Caretakers." I grew up spending my summers on Upper Saranac Lake, living in my family's great camp and exploring that world, as well as the bounty of the Adirondacks. Those summers were the seeds of the life I chose to live as an adult and I am grateful to my family, and to that place, for the introduction. During the planning stages of "Caretakers," I consulted with my family, and numerous other sources from that time in my life, to help capture the feeling and flavor of that world. I also had help from the Adirondack Museum, in Blue Mountain Lake, and would like to thank them for their help, letting me explore their facilities and collections, and talking with me about the great camps and the museum. The help was invaluable.

The Tri-Lakes Humane Society (TLHS) is a massive force for good in the Adirondack Park, and an inspiration to me as a writer and a human being. The Tri-Lakes Animal Shelter (TLAS) in my books is loosely based on the TLHS … everything good about it is true, the illegal activities were entirely made up. We've brought four dogs home from the TLHS to live with us, and all of them were instrumental in helping me write the book in one way or another.

The students that I have had the opportunity to work with, and learn from, over the years at Lake Placid Middle/High School have helped me to celebrate our differences, and explore some of the various ways that there are to see, and experience, the world.

Friends and family have inspired and supported me throughout the writing and editing process, and I can't thank them enough. My parents (Jim and Jill Sheffield), sister (Sarah Sheffield), wonderful son (Ben), and wife (Gail Gibson Sheffield) all gave me the time and space and loving support that I needed to follow this dream, and their love gave me the courage to try, again. Rick Schott, Bryce Fortran, Derek Murawsky, Kevin Curdgel, and Stephen Carvalho have helped me expand my map of the world through their friendship while camping in all seasons. Countless other friends have also offered encouragement, especially Jonathan Webber and Gail Bennett Schott who have given me unending support and positive vibes during the writing and editing process.

Over this past year I have an incredible outpouring of support from readers of "Here Be Monsters," as well as "Mickey Slips," and "Bound for Home" (the short novellas in the Tyler Cunningham series). It is one thing to put creative ideas on paper, a completely different thing to know those ideas are being read and accepted by people all over the world. It is that acceptance and encouragement that moved me from being someone who writes, to being a writer. That is what made "Caretakers" possible, thank you all for that.

A big shout out to the entire staff at SmartPig Publishing for their tireless efforts throughout the process ... thanks Gail and Randy! Randy Lewis joined the SmartPig team this fall as Copy Editor, and her work to polish the book is more appreciated than she can know.

While I couldn't have done it without any of you, any errors or omissions are all mine.

ABOUT THE AUTHOR

Jamie Sheffield lives in the Adirondack Park with his wife and son and two dogs, Miles and Puck. When he's not writing mysteries, he's probably camping or exploring the last great wilderness in the Northeast. He has been a Special Education Teacher in the Lake Placid Central School District for the last 15 years. Besides writing, Jamie loves cooking and reading and dogs and all manner of outdoor pursuits.

"Caretakers" is his second novel.

Follow the ongoing adventures of Tyler Cunningham and read other works by the author.

Visit Jamie Sheffield's website:

www.jamiesheffield.com

Made in the USA
Monee, IL
16 March 2020